BY KEITH ROSSON

Fever House
Folk Songs for Trauma Surgeons
Road Seven
Smoke City
The Mercy of the Tide

FEVER HOUSE

RANDOM HOUSE
NEW YORK

FEVER HOUSE

a novel

KEITH ROSSON

Copyright © 2023 by Keith Rosson LLC
Excerpt from *The Devil by Name* by Keith Rosson copyright © 2023 by Keith Rosson

Published in the United States by Random House, an imprint and division of Penguin Random House LLC, New York.

RANDOM HOUSE and the HOUSE colophon are registered trademarks of Penguin Random House LLC.

Library of Congress Cataloging-in-Publication Data
Names: Rosson, Keith (Novelist), author.
Title: Fever house: a novel / Keith Rosson.
Description: First edition. | New York: Random House, [2023]
Identifiers: LCCN 2022053820 (print) | LCCN 2022053821 (ebook) |
ISBN 9780593595756 (Hardback) | ISBN 9780593595763 (Ebook)
Classification: LCC PS3618.O853544 F48 2023 (print) | LCC PS3618.O853544
(ebook) | DDC 813/.01—dcundefined
LC record available at https://lccn.loc.gov/2022053820
LC ebook record available at https://lccn.loc.gov/2022053821

This book contains an excerpt from the forthcoming book *The Devil by Name* by Keith Rosson. This excerpt has been set for this edition only and may not reflect the final content of the forthcoming edition.

Printed in Canada on acid-free paper

randomhousebooks.com

2 4 6 8 9 7 5 3 1

First Edition

To the librarians and booksellers out there,
and how you've given me a million lives

FEVER HOUSE

1

THE HAND

HUTCH HOLTZ

Tim Reed sits in the driver's seat of his ancient and rust-punched Datsun hatchback, balancing a screwdriver on the tip of his finger. Hutch and Tim are killing time, waiting for some poor guy to come home so they can terrify him and, if necessary, perform grievous harm to the fragile architecture of the man's body. It's the usual deal: reluctance to pay a debt owed. When this happens, when their boss encounters someone offering resistance, there are phone calls. Verbal requests. Polite reminders. A process old as time. And finally, after all that, Tim and Hutch come by. It's just work. The screwdriver handle, pitted red plastic, wavers only slightly as they sit in the gloom, Tim's features lit pale green by the ghostly glow of the dashboard. The rain's coming down so hard it sounds like someone's flinging pennies onto the roof.

Hutch runs an arm across the fogged window but there's nothing out there to see. Sweet and gentle homes locked in slumber. Windows glowing, cars snug in their driveways. A nice neighborhood. It still surprises him sometimes, the vastness of people they get sent to talk to. All different sorts. Often, they're the furthest things from hard men. Just regular folks. Regular people with their big ideas vanished, people suddenly stuck behind one too many bad moves.

Hutch finally tells Tim to put the screwdriver away.

"Why?"

"Because it's gonna look fucked up if a cop drives by and glasses us, is why."

They had a thing go south last week, *marginally* south, Hutch and Tim and a lazy-eyed meth addict named Dolph, and Hutch's knuckles are still scabbed-up from it. Tim's cheek laddered with scratches from Dolph's dirty fingernails. That sort of thing rarely happens, but they already look sketchy as hell.

"Just do it," Hutch says.

Tim sighs and drops the screwdriver to the floorboard.

They wait. The rain tapers off a little. Tim smokes, cracks the window. They've parked across the street from the guy's house. Hutch gets a little nervous every time headlights roll across the windshield. Tim's car—its rear passenger window a milky cataract of plastic and duct tape, the seats so shredded it looks like a family of four has died of a knife attack inside—doesn't fit the street. The guy most certainly has enough money to upgrade to something nicer. Something that doesn't look like shit, at least. Feels like a big screw-you to the world, this car. They're both felons, and Tim, he knows, has a .38 tucked behind a panel in the driver's-side door. Guy's still on parole too. They're both a wrong look away from going back to prison.

They wait. Listen to Tim's tapes. When Peach Serrano sends you to retrieve a debt, you retrieve it.

"What my concern is," Tim says after a while, lighting another smoke off the previous one, "is which king died and made you, like, second in command. That's my question."

"You're being serious with this?"

Tim shrugs, pushes a lock of dark hair behind his ear. "Have they, like, sewn a tapestry with your face on it, my lord? Your fucking countenance or whatever? You sitting on your throne, looking all majestic?"

"Look around you," Hutch says. "Now look at us. Look at your car."

"I don't get what that has to do with me dicking around with a screwdriver—"

"Because," Hutch says, actually getting kind of mad now, "the last thing we need is some cop driving by this piece-of-shit ride of yours, thinking you're in here playing with a knife or something. 'Oh, no, it's *actually* just a screwdriver, officer. We're just two fucking leg-breakers hanging out in the dark, sir. Felons, with an unregistered piece. No problem at all, sir, how are you?'"

Tim sniffs. "This still doesn't explain why it is that *you—*"

They're saved when a car pulls into the driveway of the house. Tim nods, immediately all business, and Hutch starts the stopwatch feature on his watch. They step out quickly—Tim long since having smashed out the dome light—and walk fast and quiet across the street.

"Excuse me," Hutch says. The guy's leaning over, getting groceries out of the backseat, in a hurry to get out of the rain. He's just some guy. White, doughy. Khakis and a North Face jacket. Where do they come from, these people? How does a guy like this get in deep with Peach? He looks as dangerous as a painting in a motel room. The fear walks large across his face.

It makes sense: It's raining, dark. There's two guys standing in his driveway. One of them a huge smokestack of a man with half his head dented in. The other one grinning with yellow smoker's teeth and a scuffed leather jacket and a—is that a *screwdriver* he's holding in his hand? It is. Hutch swears under his breath.

"Get your ass inside," Tim hisses. He presses the tip of the screwdriver against the man's belly.

No kids, they'd been told. No family.

Just this guy and his debt.

They sit him down in his living room. He weeps on his couch, holding a pillow in his lap.

They don't touch him.

He pays in full, has the cash right there in the house.

"That was under five," Hutch says when they get back in Tim's car. He's feeling good.

"The hell it was."

Hutch shows him his watch. It's still going. He presses *stop*. Four minutes and thirteen seconds have passed from the time they got out of the car to the time they got back in it.

"A bet's a bet," says Hutch.

Tim mutters and hikes his hips up, fishes out his wallet from his back pocket. Passes Hutch a twenty.

They stop for burritos and eat them in the car. Tim texts his wife to say he'll be out late and they toss their garbage and head across town to the next job. It's a Friday night and traffic sucks. Hutch is tired. Dolph's scabs itch. When they make it to the second address on the piece of paper Peach has given them—no way they do any of this using GPS or over text or anything—they see that the apartment building is a two-story L-shaped affair with a parking lot maybe half full of cars, most of them only slightly less ruinous than Tim's. Far from downtown, this is the land of check-cashing kiosks, grated windows, open-air dope deals. Chinese food places next to tire repair joints with misspelled words on the marquees. There's a pair of dumpsters against the far wall of the building, tagged and overflowing with trash.

Tim reaches into the door panel and puts the revolver in his pocket.

"You sure you want to bring that?"

He snuffs his cigarette in the ashtray, and says through a mouthful of smoke, "Sure I'm sure. I don't like apartments, man. You get jammed-up in an apartment, you're fucked. I feel like we've had this conversation before."

Hutch looks at the building. It's started raining again. He believes in intuition, has survived on it at times, and something in him agrees. Something's off. This one will give them trouble somehow. "What's this guy's name again?"

Tim fishes the piece of paper out of a cassette case in the console and squints at Peach's terrible handwriting. They'll burn the paper at the end of the night. It's a system that has worked with few logistical hang-ups for twelve years, ever since he and Tim started working for Peach Serrano.

"Wesley."

"Wesley?"

"That's what it says. Dude is in *deep* too. Shit."

He passes Hutch the paper.

Hutch squints in the weak streetlight. "Does that say twelve thousand?"

"It does," Tim says. He lights another smoke.

That bad feeling. Just right there, right in front. "I'm gonna get the bat," Hutch says, and Tim pops the trunk. A guy twelve thousand in the hole is willing to do a lot of things. Twelve's absolutely worth trying to pop a couple guys that come to the door. He roots through the trash and bungee cords and empty bottles of motor oil in Tim's trunk until he finds the little wooden fish bat, all scarred and dark with oil. Tim steps out, gets the pizza box from the backseat. Puts the baseball hat on. Eighty-second is a few blocks over, a white-noise machine cut through by the occasional throb of bass from a passing car.

"Ten minutes on this one?"

"I don't want to play this time."

Hutch is surprised. Tim sees the look on his face.

"I don't feel good about this one, dude." He's got the revolver there against his leg. "Alright?"

Hutch says, "We could just tell Peach we tried and no one was home."

"He'll just make us wait, man. Hang out in the parking lot all night. You know how he is." Tim's right. Peach demands results. If no one's home, he'll just make them spend the night in the car, watching the place.

They step quietly up the cement stairs to the second floor. The guy has a corner apartment and the blinds over the window are drawn shut. Little shards of light shine between the slats. Hutch walks with the bat against his leg. They've done this a lot over the years, and it still floods his mouth with spit each time. Adrenaline, fear. The potential for ruination is always there—his or someone else's. You have to love it a little bit to do it, and a part of Hutch does.

He steps past the window, presses himself against the wall on the other side of the door. You have to be careful. Apartments are tough places to press up on someone. Easier to break someone's arm in the street, even. Apartments, especially on the second floor, the cops get called and you're stuck in a room.

Tim holds the pizza box in front of him, hits the doorbell. They share a look: In and out. No fucking around. Hutch presses hard against the wall, out of sight. They can hear the dim chime of the doorbell inside the apartment. The brim of the baseball cap throws Tim's face in shadow.

"What," someone says through the door. A woman's voice.

"Mianci's Pizza," Tim says.

"We didn't order a pizza."

"Crap," Tim says. He names an address, asks if he has the right place.

"That's down the street." Tim gives an awkward little wave; the woman must be peering at him through the blinds.

"Crap," he says again. "Well, I'm screwed. We have a 'deliver in thirty minutes or the driver pays for it' deal going on, so I'm out twenty-five bucks now."

Silence from behind the door.

Tim sighs. "Listen, I'll give you this thing for ten. I might as well make a little of my money back, right?"

The silence goes on long enough that Hutch is weighing the possibility of just cracking down the door when the woman finally says, "What kind is it?"

"Large pepperoni and olive."

More silence.

"Ten bucks?"

"Yeah. I just gotta make some of my money back, you know? You'd be doing me a favor."

The door starts to open and Hutch feels that old surge—*we're moving*—and he slaps at it, pushes the door open with his palm and strides in like doom itself. The woman shrieks once, briefly, and they're inside. Tim already has his wheel gun against a guy's forehead, walking him backward to the couch. Hutch walks the woman up to the opposite wall, holds a hand out to keep her there. He smells ammonia-burn, enough to make his eyes water: the reek of cat piss and the ghost of spent meth. He asks her if there's anyone else in the apartment.

"No," the woman says.

"Don't lie to us," says Tim.

"I'm not."

But there's *something* here, isn't there? Some pulse. An itch in the dark meat of the skull. Tim was right, something feels off. Like standing next to something hot, but you could only feel it in your brain. He does a walk-through of the place. It's a one-bedroom apartment. The bathroom's its own unique horror show, with grand washes of pink and gray mold along the shower walls. Garbage spills from a can onto the floor in the kitchen. Old foam meat wrappers on the counters filled with congealed blood, the natter of flies. A bedroom with clothes mounded on the floor and a galaxy of stains on the sheetless mattress.

Back in the living room, he steps up to the woman as her eyes jitter wildly around the room. Thin, sore-spotted cheeks, bad stick and poke tattoos on her arms amid yellow bruises. She's skeletal in a tank top and a pair of sweatpants. She's thirty or sixty. Hutch asks her what her name is.

"Don't tell him shit," the guy on the couch says. Tim pushes the barrel of the gun against his cheek until the guy's got his head pressed against the wall.

"I'll scream," she says. "The neighbors hate us. They'll call the cops again."

"It'll be the last thing you ever do," Tim says over his shoulder.

"Listen," Hutch says. "You can do that. You can. Or you can just go for a walk. You know? Just go cop somewhere, I don't give a shit. Give us ten minutes with Wesley here and we're good."

"Don't do it, Shawna," Wesley says, and Tim rakes the gunsight across his forehead. Wesley squeals, claps his hands to his head.

Shawna licks her flaking lips. Hutch steps back. Holds an arm out toward the front door. Shawna scratches at a sore in the crook of her elbow and says, "Are you gonna kill him?"

"God, no."

"You promise?"

"Jesus Christ," Wesley says.

"He's in deep with a friend of ours," Hutch says. "We need to talk to him, is all."

Her eyes bounce between them.

"I don't wanna go," she says.

"You don't owe this guy a thing," says Hutch.

"That's not why," she says.

"Shut the fuck up about it, Shawna," Wesley says, loud.

"Lady," Tim says, "you better go before we change our minds."

Shawna nods and runs her wrist under her nose once, then picks up a denim jacket off the floor. She crouches down in the doorway next to the litter box and puts her shoes on, her eyes bright and hunted the whole time. She walks over to the coffee table, and with shaking hands, her hair hanging over her face, she grabs a pack of Camels and a lighter. She stuffs them in the pockets of her coat.

"Those are my cigarettes," Wesley says.

"You speak to her one more time," Tim says, "and you're gonna be able to roll your teeth on that coffee table like dice, man. I swear to God."

Shawna rifles through the trash on the coffee table, her eyes locked on Wesley. She picks up a box cutter, the handle wrapped in black electrical tape, then grabs a plastic baggie cinched with a rubber band, puts that in her coat too. It's maybe a teener of meth. Tim laughs outright.

"You're dead," Wesley says wearily.

"Shouldn't have hit me, motherfucker," Shawna says. Hutch opens the door for her like a valet. They can hear her footfalls reverberate through the wall as she runs down the steps. Hutch locks the door behind her.

"She's gonna call the cops," Wesley says, touching his forehead. "Y'all are fucked."

Tim laughs. "She's going down the street to do your dope, is what she's doing."

"Cut the shit," says Hutch, crouching so he's eye level with Wesley. "You owe Peach Serrano a lot of money."

Wesley leans back against the couch, spreading his arms wide. Rail-thin, pit stains in his shirt, a beard coming in patchy. Wesley's maybe twenty-five and looks like heated-up dogshit. His forehead's beaded with blood. "Peach Serrano?" He grins, and Hutch sees that his gums are bleeding too. "Peach Serrano can lick my withered balls."

He considers hitting Wesley as hard as he can. Just pushing the table aside, slamming him right there in the chest with his fist. Could he stop Wesley's heart? He doubts it, but he bets he could crack the man's sternum. The desire is right there, bellowing and insistent.

Tim says, "You owe Peach twelve grand, dude. He's given you two extensions with low-as-shit interest and you're still fucking him. Be reasonable. You gotta call the guy back when he calls you."

"Oh, what," Wesley says, and grins. "What're you gonna do? Knock my teeth out?" He reaches into his mouth with a pair of dirty fingers. Latching onto a yellow incisor, he starts working it, rocking it back and forth. He pulls the tooth out of his mouth. There is a soft pop that Hutch actually hears, and watery blood spills down the man's lip. He tosses the tooth on the coffee table. It bounces off, falls to the carpet.

"Be my fucking guest," Wesley says.

Tim stands in front of him, delighted. He grins over at Hutch. "This guy's alright," he says, and then he bends down and breaks Wesley's nose with the butt of the .38.

"Bathroom is *gnarly*," Tim calls out.

Wesley's face is a pulped mess. He's slumped over on the couch. Blood everywhere. Tim has done his work with vigor; it was rare that someone doesn't buckle when faced with the two of them. And the thing with the tooth—that was wild. Hutch can see why Tim's gone a little extra on the guy. A leg of the coffee table has gotten busted in the process, trash avalanching onto the carpet. They've bound Wesley's hands in front of him with electrical tape. Hutch glances nervously at his phone. They've been there sixteen minutes. Way too long.

Tim stands in the doorway of the bathroom, wiping his hands on his shirt. His knuckles are pitted with Wesley's teeth marks, still welling blood. "He's dumb as shit."

"He thinks he's untouchable."

"You think you're a fucking made guy," Tim calls from the doorway in a terrible Italian mob-guy accent, puffing his chest out. Wesley snuffles blood onto the couch cushions. "You think you got your button, man? You little dope-fiend asshole. You're a shot-caller?"

"I'm invincible," Wesley says, grinning through the blood.

Just lean in and crack his chest. One punch. Just do it. Some dark animism inside Hutch wants to go to town on him.

Tim walks over to Wesley, stands there with his hands on his hips. "We smoke him," he says, "or we take him to Peach."

Wesley's eyes fly open.

"Oh, *that* woke you up, huh?"

Hutch grabs Wesley's arm, hoists him up. "We're taking a ride, son."

"I ain't leaving," says Wesley.

"The fuck you're not," says Tim, who takes hold of his other arm. "Let's get him to the warehouse." To Wesley, he says, "You got about ten minutes until an ex-cop is popping your eye out with an ice-cream scoop or something truly terrible like that, dude. Digging around under your fingernails with a nail file like he's looking for treasure. You really want that?"

"I can't leave my shit," Wesley says, and the veneer slips. He sounds hurt, finally. Scared. Want is carved and writhing in every word. "I can't, man. Please."

"What shit is that, Wes?"

He lifts his head toward the kitchen. The three of them head in there. Behind bags of ice and a half-pint of generic vanilla ice cream, there's a tied-off bread bag. Tim lifts it, wincing; even without opening it, Hutch can tell that the bad feeling is coming from this, from whatever's in there. It drifts from the bag like radiation. Emanates from it, and Hutch feels halved—in such close proximity, some part of him wants to puke and mewl, while another part wants to just start biting at Wesley's face, the skin of his neck. Just savage him.

Absolutely no part of him wants to get away from whatever's in there.

Tim spins the bag open—it's a Wonder Bread bag, white with little colored polka dots all over it—and peers inside. He stares at it for a while.

"What is it," says Hutch. Wesley's like a wax statue beside him. Glassy and slack-jawed.

Tim exhales, looks up at him. When he does, it's a look that Hutch, in all their years together—both as lifelong friends and as men who openly hurt other people for money—has rarely seen. It's a kind of fearful wonderment. "It's a hand," he says.

"What?"

"It's a hand."

"Like a real one?"

"Like some dude's hand, yeah." He spins the bread bag shut and Hutch can see the weight at the bottom. "A chopped-off fucking hand."

They all live in that moment for a while. The desire to bite and punch, just fall into the red darkness of the thing, is so strong in there, in that small room. Finally, Hutch comes to, like he's pulling himself from a dream. "You got the rest of a body in here somewhere, Wes? Under the floor or something?"

Wesley sighs like someone drifting off to sleep.

Hutch looks at Tim. Twelve years working together. Friends since they were juvenile dipshits in Rutherford. His closest friend, without a doubt, especially when you considered the number of deadly secrets they share. The pair of them have done difficult, sometimes awful things to people in the pursuit of money, in feasance to an objectively bad man. If Wesley doesn't come home alive from Peach's warehouse tonight, the cops will eventually search this apartment. Shawna can describe the two of them. Neither he nor Tim are much of a challenge in a lineup. But no matter what, if the cops search the apartment and find a severed hand in a bread bag, it's even more of a problem. A problem for them is a problem for Peach, and it's easy to figure out how that ends. He still wants to rend Wesley in half, luxuriate in the man's guts, and part of him—to his dismay and wonder, it's a not insignificant part—wants to do the same to Tim.

"Let's take it," he says. "Just put it in the car." Tim nods, and the look of relief on his face is obvious.

They both want it around.

Wesley sags like a punch-drunk boxer all the way to the hatchback. Tim makes sure to clang his head against the Datsun's doorframe as he puts him in the backseat.

They put the bread bag and the pizza box in the trunk, under a spare.

Hutch breaks protocol and texts Peach: *It's complicated.*

Don Sr. calls him back a minute later. A rarity. Nine out of ten times, Hutch and Tim get a debt paid, either in full or in part. Just by showing up. The other 10 percent, the debtor gets worked over, like Dolph had, the severity dependent on a number of things: where Hutch and Tim have cornered the guy, the amount of money owed, and, absolutely, the guy's attitude. Once the damage is inflicted, the debtor's given a date when they'll return. It is a simple enough equation, and it almost always works. Unrepentant men like Wesley are not unheard of, but rare. When it does happen, they go to the warehouse and have a palaver with Don Sr.

Hutch is sitting next to Wesley in the backseat. His thinking is still off. It's muted, now that the hand's in the trunk, but it's still there, like the hum of an appliance in the back of his brain. Dark and warm, full of whispers and weird recriminations. Blood. Paranoia.

Over the phone, Don greenlights taking Wesley to the warehouse. They know enough not to get too specific over the line.

"He had a friend there," Hutch says, "but she left."

"You let her leave? That ain't smart."

"Yeah, well."

"Yeah, well," Don parrots. "Is it a complication or not? Will this bite us in the ass?"

Hutch looks out the window, the smeared neon of Eighty-second. "No. We can tell you in person."

Don had been a cop for thirty years before going to work for his son-in-law, and waiting is hard for him. "I'll be here," he says, and hangs up.

Hutch finally can't stand it anymore. The noise is just too much, the snarl of it. The bloody clamor in his brain. He reaches over, grabs Wesley's skinny thigh and squeezes as hard as he can, which is pretty hard. Wesley screams and bucks and Hutch feels good for a second. Up front, Tim laughs his hoarse laugh and lights a cigarette.

"Was that your girlfriend in there?" Hutch says after Wesley calms down. "Shawna."

"You're gonna fucking die," Wesley sobs. "You're gonna die so bad."

"Pay attention," Tim says in the rearview, snapping his finger. "She said you hit her. You like to hit women, Wes? You into that?"

Nothing.

"How'd you get ahold of a chopped-off hand, dude?" Hutch leans in close, smells piss and body odor, that acrid meth-sweat. He resists the urge to bite Wesley's ear clean off his skull. "You're running out of running room," he says. In the trunk, the hand throbs, mutters, sings.

"You feel that, right, Hutch?" says Tim in the front.

"Oh, I feel it."

"I just want to fucking *hurt* something, dude." Tim takes a jubilant drag off his smoke and laughs again. "It feels awesome."

OPERATION: HEAVY LIGHT

S/NF/CL-INTEL A-13/22—SECRET TRANSCRIPT—EXCERPT

DATE: XX/XX/XXXX

Q: Michael, hi. It's David. How are you feeling today?

A: . . .

Q: Michael.

A: . . .

Q: Michael? Can you hear me? Hey. There you are, my friend.

A: Ah.

Q: Oh, Michael. Damn.

A: Ah.

Q: Yeah, you're not doing great, Michael. Not great at all. I'm sorry. But you're still being of service, aren't you, Michael? You're still helping us.

A: Hello, David.

Q: Can you hear me?

A: I can hear you.

Q: Michael, we need your help.

A: Yes.

Q: Do you think you can help us today?

A: I think so.

Q: I don't want to hurt you, or make you feel bad. I want you to get your rest.

A: Okay.

Q: Do you believe me? Do you believe that I don't want to hurt you?

A: Yes, David. I believe you.

Q: Okay, Michael. That's good. But we need your help. Someone took the remnant. Please find it for me—find the hand for me—and you can rest. Okay? Can you do that for me? Someone took it. Can you tell me where it is?

A: I'm very tired, David.

Q: Oh, I know you are. I know. But we need you, Michael. Please try.

A: I will.

Q: I don't want to hurt you.

HUTCH HOLTZ

Don Sr. is sweeping the warehouse floor with a push broom when they drive in. A heavyset older man in a short-sleeved dress shirt and a pair of chinos, Don has a thin patina of ink-black hair on his dome and wears a heavy gray mustache. Rings glitter on each hand. He pushes the broom around a metal folding chair in the middle of the floor. Tim pulls inside and parks the Datsun near the back wall; Don hits the switch that brings the warehouse door back down. Then there's just the silence of the ticking engine, Hutch's blood roaring in his ears. He pulls Wesley out, not particularly gently, and leans him against the car.

"Just hold on to him for a second," Don says. He pushes the dirt he's gathered into a dustpan and dumps that into a steel garbage can at the far end of the room. Shelving on both walls runs all the way to the ceiling, shelves filled with various wrapped boxes and pallets. At the back wall is an industrial sink covered in decades of grime and paint spatters. Beside the sink is a door leading to an office, its darkened windows looking out onto the warehouse floor.

"Where's Peach?" says Tim.

Don waves his hand dismissively. "Don't worry about Peach."

He walks into the office, where he loosens his tie and drops it onto the desk. When he comes out, he's carrying a white plastic bucket that he fills at the sink. He walks over to where Wesley is standing.

"So who we got here?"

"This is Wesley," says Tim. "He's into Peach for twelve, and gave us endless amounts of backtalk."

Don sizes him up. "Well, it looks like you fucked him up pretty good." He steps forward and looks in Wesley's eyes. "Twelve thousand dollars is a lot of money, son. What do you have to say for yourself?"

"Fuck you," Wesley says, his eyes half lidded.

Don sighs and walks over to the folding chair. He empties the bucket over it. The water splashes off the seat, darkens the cement beneath, spreads and runs into a drain set in the floor. Don sets the bucket down and watches the water drain, his hands on his hips. "Like to get a pressure washer in here someday, is what I'd like to do."

He turns and gestures at the chair. Hutch walks Wesley over. Wesley sits, his lips moving in some private incantation. His hands are still bound in tape. The throb in Hutch's skull is quieter; he can at least think now.

Don, with some effort, his shirt straining at his gut, crouches down before Wesley on one knee. "Son," he says, "I want to ask you this, and I mean it with all the sincerity I got. How far do you want this to go? It's only money."

Wesley stares at some distant point above Don's head long enough that Don gets bored. He stands up and tucks his shirt back in. Runs a hand over his skull, sighs. The knee of one pant leg's wet now.

He turns to the two of them and says, "So what's the complication?" and Wesley springs up, almost preternaturally fast. His hands still lashed together, he is already biting Don's face as the two of them fall to the cement. Don writhes beneath him, screaming, as

Wesley bites and bites. His screams are bright and terrible things in the cavernous room.

Tim grabs Wesley by the hair and pulls him back. "Hold him," he spits. "Hutch, goddamnit."

Hutch grabs Wesley by the throat, throws him to the floor. The man's eyes are wide and glazed, hardly there. He's still snarling, Don's blood on his mouth. Hutch has heard about bath salts and all that; remembers the baggie that Shawna took. Don is shrieking, his legs spasming as he covers his face with his hands. Wesley thrums like a wire, already starting to stand up.

Tim walks over and presses the .38 against Wesley's forehead. He pulls the trigger. A small gout of brain matter exits the skull, falls to the wet cement. The dead man's expression hardly changes as he drops.

"*The fuck,*" Don is screaming, "*the fuck.*" He touches his hand to his cheek; it comes away red and he lets out a little shriek of disbelief. Pushing himself onto his knees is a slow and unlovely process—Don is getting up there in years—and by the time he's standing up, he's panting. Blood pinks the collar of his shirt; his neck is threaded with it. Hutch stands there like a dipshit, stilled by the sudden flurry of violence.

Don takes Tim's .38 and walks over to Wesley, bending at the waist. He shoots Wesley's head five more times. Fire curls from the barrel. Wesley's head is caved into a red mash with glints of bone peeking out. Becomes a head by suggestion alone.

Don kicks the body, his teeth glinting amid the red mask of his face. His rings glitter in the light. He begins stomping on what is left of Wesley's head and Hutch turns and vomits. Hutch Holtz has killed two men and hurt countless others in his twelve years of fealty to Peach Serrano, and he has never, ever seen anything like this.

He and Tim walk around the side of the warehouse and stand under the eave, watching raindrops jitter on the blacktop a foot in front of them. Hutch bums one of Tim's cigarettes. Tim's hand shakes when he passes it over. They don't even look at each other.

After a while, Don comes around the corner and barks at them to come inside. His face is a mishmash of bandages, most of which have blood still blooming beneath them. They follow him in.

"How you feeling, Don," Tim says with bright, false cheer. It's clear he's terrified.

"Get the fuck in here, dummy," spits Don.

He has managed to roll Wesley in a clear tarp. The body is lying next to Tim's car. Blood and brains still in smears on the cement floor.

"You," Don says, pointing to Hutch, "tape him up so he doesn't fall out of that thing." He throws Hutch a roll of duct tape and then lifts his chin toward Tim. "You, wash all that shit into the drain there. Chop-chop, gentlemen."

"Don," Hutch says. Realizing the severed hand is still doing its work, still nattering and cajoling in his mind.

Don turns. "Is this a time for conversation? Am I not being clear here?"

Hutch pulls off a hank of tape.

They put on some painter coveralls and latex gloves. It's a thing where you get dressed and your whole life sits with you while you do it. Your past, your future. How every decision you ever made brought you there, next to a dead man, in coveralls and gloves. They lay Wesley's wrapped body in the bed of a Ford pickup that Peach keeps behind the warehouse and hardly ever uses. Any DNA they've left behind has already bound them to the man. It is what it is. The woman, Shawna, is a loose end that will have to be addressed too. Shit went south, is all. They lay a tarp over the body, weigh it down with machine parts.

Tim drives. He finds a utility road the railroad crews use, one that laces the Willamette River, the city in the distance glittering like a handful of jewels. The truck's shocks are a joke. Tim's face is haunted and drawn in the dashboard light, and Hutch figures he looks about the same.

"How long we known each other?" Tim says.

"I don't know. It was at Rutherford. You had that Discman that you'd snuck in, and a burned CD with . . . *And Justice for All* on it."

Tim smiles. It's a terrible sight, that smile, because it's so forlorn. Like Tim's already on his way toward accepting what's happened, and whatever will happen next. "It wasn't . . . *And Justice for All*, it was Megadeth. Some Megadeth album."

"Dude, it was Metallica. We listened to 'One' so many goddamned times."

Tim laughs. "Nah, I totally remember Megadeth."

Hutch runs his sweating hands down the legs of his coveralls. "Either way."

"Either way," Tim says. "We been friends a long time. Just kids. Crazy to think. We went from sharing headphones in Rutherford when I was what? Thirteen years old? Scared shitless. So tiny. How many times you been to my house, you think? Best man at my wedding. Got groceries for us when me and Jessica were just leveled with the flu that time. All that, to *this*? Us in this truck?" He hoists a thumb over his shoulder. "That dipshit in the bed back there? That's crazy to me. You know?"

"I know it," Hutch says.

The hand is in the trunk of Tim's car, back at the warehouse, and now that there's distance, it's a profound relief to be rid of it. Like his life is slowly coming back to him.

"That chick saw us," Tim says. "Shawna."

"Yeah."

"We were the last people to be seen with him, man."

"It doesn't matter."

"Oh, it matters. You fucking kidding me? It matters."

"What I mean is, I'm not killing anyone else," Hutch says. "No one else dies."

It's a while before Tim says anything. He pushes in the Ford's cigarette lighter and waits for it to pop back out. When it does, he sounds a little sad when he says, "Thing is, I don't know if you're the one who gets to decide that."

They pull off the utility road and bounce through some weeds until they coast right to the riverbank beneath a wash of scree and little fist-sized trees. They lift Wesley's body from the bed and drag it down the embankment. Wading in thigh-deep, the water is cold and black, the bottom a gelatinous muck that threatens to pull their boots off. They push Wesley down under the surface. The plastic tarp is milky and thankfully obscures the red ruin of his face. The body sinks, and then begins to rise again.

"Air's getting in the tarp," Tim says.

They watch as Wesley's body floats there, half-submerged.

Tim pushes his way back onto the bank, looking like a ghost in his painter coveralls. "Nothing to be done about it," he calls out. "Let's go."

Hutch heads back to the bank, then stops, stands there knee-deep in the water. He hears the lapping of the current against the shore. The highway's din like pressing a shell to his ear.

Tim flashes the headlights. When Hutch gets back in the cab, he finds Tim with his phone on the dashboard. Speakerphone. It's Peach.

It's a big thing, Peach talking to them on the phone. It means things are truly fucked.

"You both there?" he says.

"Yeah," says Hutch.

"I want both of you to take a trip, you hear me? This is a mess. Go to LA, San Diego, whatever. Look at chicks on the boardwalk, buy a T-shirt, order room service, I don't care. Just get out of town and stay low. Jesus Christ."

"You sure?"

There's a beat, and then Peach's voice comes in sharp. "When have I not been sure?"

"Okay," Hutch says. "Sorry."

"Get cleaned up and catch a flight. Head back to the casino and the greeter will give you some chips." This is code—*Head back to the warehouse and Don will give you some walk-away money.*

Tim casts a glance at Hutch and says, "There's a bit of a problem."

Peach laughs bitterly. "More than we have now? What's that?"

"I'm not sure we should say it over the phone."

"The fuck you bring it up for then?"

"Boss," Hutch says, wiping his mouth, "there was a hand. The client had a hand in his freezer." Silence. "Like a chopped-off hand, I mean."

Another beat. "Yeah, that's probably not something to bring up over the phone."

"We're just saying." Hutch opens his mouth to explain, but how do you explain that fever? That ache to bite and rend?

"It made us feel real weird," says Tim.

"Jesus Christ," Peach mutters again, more to himself than them. "Go back to the greeter. He'll get you squared away."

They're mostly silent on the ride back to the warehouse. Hutch can't stop thinking about how he'd gripped Wesley's thigh like he'd wanted his fingers to punch through muscle, down into the bone. It had been a curious heat, both terrible and luxurious. He's done E a few times, and this was a little like that, but run instead through a kaleidoscopic filter of bloodlust and violence.

"I wanted to kill him," Tim says. His eyes are hooded and unreadable in the darkness. He sounds conversational, but Hutch has known him long enough to know that there are always machinations going on beneath Tim's surface. He never slows. "Even before he jumped on Don. I wanted to fuck him up."

"Yeah," says Hutch. They are off the utility road and pass under a sodium light; Hutch's hands look fish-white in his lap, the hands of a corpse. "Felt like I had a fever."

"Yeah!" says Tim, adjusting on his seat. "Felt like my brain was all fogged up."

"It was the hand," says Hutch.

"Oh, it was *totally* the hand," says Tim. It's a thing that sits between them—this statement of impossibility that is still somehow true.

Hutch keeps seeing Wesley's brains fall in a clump onto the floor, that single dark spatter. Don leaning over the body and dumping rounds into the skull. Blowing smoke from the corner of his mouth, Tim says, "My grandma was a witch, I ever tell you that?"

"Yeah? This the one with the big toenails? The one that tried to whip you with your grandpa's belt when she caught you pulling it that one time?"

Tim winces. "No, man, this is the other one. This is my mom's mom." They are nearing the warehouse, and Tim slows. "One time when my brother and me were playing guns with some other kids in the woods outside my house—I was maybe nine, ten—she was visiting. She only visited us two or three times my whole life. Anyway, we were playing guns and I got this kid but he kept saying I didn't get him. It got heated, right, and he wound up getting in my face. I'm not the biggest dude now, but back then I was even tinier. Like way small. He was about to punch me when my grandma came out on our back porch. There were five or six of us playing, and she just comes out and looks at this kid. Kyle Brautigan, his name was. Huge kid. Ate his boogers, made other kids eat them. Just a dick. Terrible human. He's got my shirt in his fist and his other hand cocked back like this. He's just gonna drop me, I know it, and then my grandma comes out and mutters something and waves her hand in kind of a shooing motion, like this."

Tim pulls into the parking lot of the warehouse and begins inching the truck around back. "He tells her to fuck off—this ten-year-old, to a grownup, right? To some old lady he doesn't know—and my mom comes out and gives him hell. He starts walking off, back to his house. We had a long driveway and we could see him walking, kicking rocks and stuff. Not one minute after my grandma came out, he's halfway down our driveway and he puts his hands on his knees and leans over and just pukes his brains out. His mom calls my mom later, wondering what we fed him; Kyle's got a hundred-and-two-degree fever for the next week. Sweats out like twenty pounds. Never fucked with me again. Never even looked at me."

"Where's this going?"

"I'll tell you where it's going, man. There's some dark shit at work here. I don't know what it is. But if Don comes after us when we step inside, I'm dropping him. I'm not waiting for anyone to do any magic on me. I'm just, like, moving forth. Straight ahead."

"That's a true story? About your grandma?"

Tim snuffs out his cigarette. "On my life," he says.

They step out, and Hutch points at the ashtray.

"What?" says Tim.

"DNA on those butts," he says.

Tim snorts, but he fishes them all out. "Oh please. We're dropping DNA like it's confetti, Hutch. Be lucky we don't get lethal injections for this."

"You seem pretty calm about it."

"I'm not calm. I'm just ready."

They open up the back door, and through the office window they can see the entire warehouse floor.

Tim's car is gone.

So's Don.

OPERATION: HEAVY LIGHT

S/NF/CL-INTEL A-13/22—SECRET

DATE: XX/XX/XXXX

MEMORANDUM FOR THE DEPUTY SECRETARY OF DEFENSE

SUBJECT: Containment and chain of custody notice for Subject EXT/NH/014 ("Saint Michael")

(S/NF/CL-INTEL) Under a Memorandum of Agreement dated XX/XX/XXXX between U.S. Army Intelligence, Homeland Command (HCOM) and Defense Intelligence Security (DISC), ARC AGENCY has appropriated custody of Subject EXT/NH/014, to be included as an intelligence-gathering asset in the OPERATION: HEAVY LIGHT program, headed by Program Director David Lundy. Subject EXT/NH/014 will be utilized for his remote viewing and psychoenergetic capabilities, with the intention of assisting in the location, collation and seizing of HEAVY LIGHT mission objectives. Subject was previously in custody of HCOM for psychoenergetic intelligence-gathering purposes, but given the time-

sensitive nature of HEAVY LIGHT's Mission Objectives, the Subject has been transferred indefinitely to ARC AGENCY's custody. This is within accordance of Army Intelligence, HCOM and DISC directives, and approval from all agencies has been granted. *(See enclosures 1 and 2.)*

(S/NF/CL-INTEL) Given his involvement with HCOM's previous psychoenergetic IG programs—including but not limited to OPERATIONS MOON SPOON and LOW TIDE—Subject EXT/NH/014 has shown to be a valuable asset in U.S. intelligence-gathering. His remote viewing capabilities have a higher rate of accuracy than many of his peers (see enclosure 3 for a list of previous predictions and their relative accuracy) and the Subject has shown a willingness to engage in intelligence-gathering if sufficiently prompted. Necessary prompts can be found in previous U.S. Army Intelligence and HCOM memorandums, as listed in the enclosed index.

(S/NF/CL-INTEL) Given the unusual political makeup of Subject EXT/NH/014 as a non-citizen of any acknowledged nation, U.S. Army Intelligence, HCOM and DISC have approved the use of noted physical and psychological prompts until Subject EXT/NH/014 is deemed no longer able to provide accurate intelligence (see previous memorandums for accuracy guidelines) or is rendered physically incapable of doing such. According to previous U.S. Army Intelligence memorandums, ARC AGENCY should expect no geopolitical consequence should Subject become physically incapable of intelligence gathering, though all means should be taken to avoid such an event, given Subject's nature as a valuable IG asset.

(S/NF/CL-INTEL) U.S. Army Intelligence, HCOM and DISC have all approved Subject EXT/NH/014's disengagement from other agencies, so that OPERATION: HEAVY LIGHT becomes Subject's sole focus until such time as Mission Objectives are met. ARC AGENCY has sole custody and responsibility of Subject until otherwise noted.

HUTCH HOLTZ

They're pretty much done cleaning when Peach double-honks out in front of the warehouse and pulls his Mercedes coupe onto the floor. It looks like nothing ever happened in here. Even the water's mostly dried. Surely there's evidence to be found—the drain in the floor probably has a decent amount of Wesley's blood and hair in it, his brains, but without a CSI team in there, it looks innocuous and pedestrian. Boring.

Peach slams the door of the Mercedes. His face is ghastly and pockmarked under the light. The man comes up to his chin but has no problem sticking his finger right in Hutch's face.

"The *fuck* are you doing calling me twice? You want to meet up, have Don arrange it." He turns and storms over to Tim, who squints but doesn't move, knowing that to flinch under one of Peach's rages would be to invite something even worse. Still, Hutch thinks of what Tim said, and understands it's two against one. Turns out, all it takes is one bad night for their loyalty to wither. "I told you to go back to the greeter and keep your mouth shut. You two should be gone already."

"Yeah, except Don's in the wind, boss," Hutch says.

Peach spins around, glares at him. "What do you mean he's in the wind?"

"We came back here from dumping the body, and he was gone."

Tim toes the cement with his boot. "Took my car and my wheel gun."

"Who, Don did?" Peach looks confused.

"Yeah."

"Took your car?"

"Yeah."

"Where's his car?"

"His Lincoln? It's in the back, by the truck."

"The hell. Did you call him?"

"Yeah," Hutch says. "He ain't picking up, though."

Peach looks between them. "The fuck is he taking your car for? Is he dumping it?"

Unhappily, Hutch says, "Well, there's the hand."

Peach licks his lips, his eyes bouncing between the two of them. Hutch has seen him shoot someone before, years back. Shot the guy in the stomach and then the balls, and the guy died a couple days later. The way Peach is looking at them right now is the same way he'd looked at that guy.

"You keep talking about this hand. What about it?"

Peach is silent on the way back to his house. He's got some reggaeton playing in the Mercedes, so loud Hutch can feel his ribs vibrate. He and Tim are sitting in the backseat; their evidence-slathered coveralls and rubber gloves are in plastic bags in the trunk. Peach has informed them that he'll dispose of the coveralls himself, and Hutch understands that this likely means that he'll hold on to them indefinitely, and plant them in such a way as to take the heat off himself, should the need ever arise to feed Hutch and Tim to the cops. Peach is far from stupid, and of all the moving pieces here, Hutch and Tim are the most expendable.

More he thinks about it, seems likely that they are, in fact, a liability.

If it's not a mansion, Peach's place comes close enough. Hutch lives in a one-bedroom apartment with walls so thin he can hear the neighbor's asthmatic cough at night, the laugh tracks on his sitcoms. Meanwhile, Peach's driveway is one of those half-circle affairs. Man's got pillars. He's kept Hutch and Tim on the payroll—under the table—for all these years, and it's just enough that Hutch can get by with the occasional shift checking IDs at Harriet's or the Devil's Dime, as long as he never gets sick. He's had to occasionally take out advances from Peach—the thing in Gresham was one, when he couldn't work for months—and he hates the weight of indebtedness that hangs over him when it happens. But it has never occurred to him until now to be resentful of Peach. Never crossed his mind that he and Tim might be getting short-stringed for the amount of work they've done for the man. The terror they've inflicted on his behalf. Busting fingers, taking punches, threatening lives, collecting debts. And the end result? A one-bedroom apartment with water stains on the ceiling. Face looking like a badly cut jack-o'-lantern.

Peach glides the Mercedes to a stop. Cement lions brace the door. Stained glass, door knocker shaped like a dragon, everything gaudy and imposing. Peach kills the engine and Hutch and Tim sit there in the back like chastised children.

"We're gonna go inside," Peach says, "and I'm gonna have a drink. And you all are gonna tell me *exactly* what has gone down since you rolled into that dope fiend's place. Step by step."

Ten minutes later, Peach stands before them like some disgruntled playboy, mixing a cocktail under chandelier light. He listens to them prattle on about the killing of Wesley Kramer. How they dumped the body in some brackish and desolate part of the Willamette at Don's behest. He's a master at silence, Peach is, knowing they'll fill in the holes themselves, anxious to not disappoint him. Stepping all over their own dicks. Hutch knows it and he still rattles it all out. If the room is bugged, they're well and truly fucked. Between any recording and the coveralls, the DNA in the warehouse drain, Hutch could feasibly have the next fifty years of his life planned out, bunking with some toothless white-supremacist shitbag in a supermax somewhere.

"Now what the fuck," Peach says, "are you talking about with this hand? What fucking hand?"

"It was in his fridge," says Hutch.

"Just bad magic," says Tim. "Just this thing you could feel."

"It was like it had an aura," says Hutch, who had once, with all the strength he could summon, hit a man in the knee with the claw end of a Craftsman hammer because Peach had told him to. Him, talking about auras.

"It was like it was cursed, man," says Tim.

Peach looks at both of them, swirls the ice in his glass. "You're going to have to try harder than that. Because right now I just think you're high."

"We're not fucking with you, Peach."

Peach's eyes settle on Tim. "You smoked him?"

Tim inhales, lifts his chin. "I did. He had the drop on Don. Biting him and shit. Bit his face a whole bunch."

"And then what happened?"

"And then Don got up and emptied the rest of the wheel into his head."

Peach sips his drink. "And you're saying this hand made you feel all fucked up."

"Like bloodthirsty," Hutch offers.

"Crazy violent," Tim says.

"A hand with a curse on it," Peach says. "Like a witch's curse."

"I mean, it was like a voice in my head, and nails down a chalkboard, and like I had a fever," says Tim, and that's exactly it, isn't it? That's what it was like.

"But like you *wanted* it to mess with you too," says Hutch. "Like it felt good."

"Okay," says Peach, looking out the window. "Okay."

Five minutes later they're sent out. Their directions are clear. *Do this thing for me, and then go visit sunny California until I tell you otherwise.* He's handed them both a generous stipend for room and board, some money to give to Tim's wife so she's not worried and talkative, and Hutch feels some relief; Peach wouldn't go through the trouble of bankrolling them if he was going to put them in a ditch.

Out on the sidewalk, Hutch takes out his phone, starts calling a ride. The night is rich with the scent of rain. The street gleams.

"We're gonna get nailed for this," he says, looking down at his phone.

"No shit."

"So what do we do?"

"I mean, we do what Peach tells us to do."

"You said you were gonna drop him half an hour ago."

"That was before he gave me a pocketful of money and told me to hang out in LA for a week."

"Shit," says Hutch, thinking again of the way Wesley Kramer's corpse had half sunk to the bottom of the river muck in his tarp. He marvels at how used to this life he's gotten, how even now it's taking on the cadence of a thing that just happened, a thing to get used to. "You don't feel anything?"

"What do you mean?"

"I mean when you killed Wesley. You don't feel nothing about it?"

Tim shrugs, spits on the ground. "My thinking was he was dead the second we dragged him into my car. How you think Don would have done him? An inch at a time, is how. This way, the guy didn't get all his shit chopped off first. I did him a favor."

"You did him a favor."

Tim's eyes are flint in the dark. Hutch sighs, runs a hand down his face. He wants, he realizes, to go home. Forget about all of it. Sleep.

"Why the fuck did Don take my car?" says Tim, but it's not worth answering, because they both know. Wesley's vacancy, standing there in the warehouse like he was on another planet. Whatever Don's doing, it's got something to do with that, the way the hand works you. Wherever he is, Don ain't in charge.

"My question," Hutch says, "is whose hand is it?"

Headlights wash across them, and he squints against the glare, then dares for just a moment to shut his eyes.

JOHN BONNER

8560.

TUFF LUV. Or possibly *RUFF LEZ,* Michael's not sure. *A tooth.*

The leads Michael gives them, as ever, are cemented in strangeness and inanities. Information spied through a veil of smoke, which they must then discern working patterns from. Like deciphering meaning from tea leaves, a cupful of flung bones.

There are reasons for this, according to the rumor wheel that is the ARC Agency. People love to talk, man. Michael cuts himself, they say, and spills the blood on a paper, and on the paper, words are formed. He pulls out an incisor and scratches clues upon his alabaster skin; the tooth grows back and blood weeps from the skin, telling an answer. They cut his wings and the cartilage twists itself into images. Or he coughs, sick as he's become, and stardust bursts from his lungs, shaping itself into runes and glyphs.

Bonner knows that Michael's real, an asset in their agency's custody, but whatever mystery surrounds him, he's sure, is exaggerated. Has to be.

It had been Bonner's suggestion, upon receiving the clues, that *8560* was actually part of an address, and it's Weils who sees the tag—TUFF LUV—on the dumpster at the side of the building. They have spent entire days trying to discern Michael's visions before, and the fact that it happens here so easily, so quickly, makes him wonder if their fortune is finally changing. They're due for a break.

They pull up across the street from the apartment complex. It is an L-shaped building with maybe two dozen units across two floors. The distant throb of Eighty-second ghosts through Bonner's open window. Almost every unit has its blinds drawn. The rain's stopped, the comforting scent of wet asphalt drifting through the SUV.

"So what apartment is it?" Bonner asks, not because he actually thinks she'll answer him, but because asking questions annoys Weils. Bonner was transferred to ARC four months ago, and Lundy must have told the other agents what happened to him, how it was that Bonner wound up there, as his pariah status appears to be fully formed. Weils is particularly combative. After four months, Bonner's given up trying to appease her, and has found that annoying her is both easy to do and something that feels akin to an obligation. *Fuck 'em all* is where Bonner sits in the equation, emotionally speaking. ARC is a black op agency, cleared for wetwork—sanctioned assassinations—and is ferociously tight-knit, with a small enough footprint that every agent gets noticed by Lundy, the director. Bonner should be thrilled—it's a job that career intelligence folks would gleefully knife each other for. And the fact that it's clandestine, insular: he should be sending roses and champagne to the handler that greenlighted his transfer. He knows it.

But Bonner's got the mark on him, and between Lundy and the dozen or so other field agents working Heavy Light, it seems he's a liability. Not for what he's done—Bonner doesn't know a single cop or law enforcement agent who's thrilled about the public's revived thirst for supposed racial justice or "police oversight," and most cops would high-five him for what he did and how he did it, if they knew—but because people clearly called in favors to get him there.

He can see it from Weils's viewpoint—an elite, highly classified gig, and he's just been given a seat at the table. But Bonner knows different. They put him in ARC to keep him quiet. It's a time-out, and no one's happy about it.

He asks her again about the apartment and Weils ignores him. Her treatment of him is pretty simple: She ferries in condescension, irritation, or silence. He wonders, legitimately, if Lundy has ever actually used the word "babysitting" with Weils when discussing him. It seems possible.

It's inane work, driving around and door-knocking based on intel that is flat-out unbelievable at times, or so cryptic that they don't know how the hell to decipher it. Months now chasing this supposed talisman. A severed hand, and always a day too late finding it. Sometimes a handful of hours. Attempting to regain ownership of this strange and supposedly deadly object. An object that, four months ago, he never could have imagined even existing. Lundy's flat, measured debriefing of the hand upon Bonner's arrival to ARC had inspired him to quietly reach out to his handler and request a transfer. But his handler had just scoffed—you don't transfer out of ARC without Lundy's blessing. You especially don't request a transfer when it's the only thing keeping your head above water. He imagines the handler probably talked to Lundy after that, told him to rein Bonner in, because Lundy's been a cold motherfucker to him since. Bad moves tiered upon bad moves.

"Do you believe what they say, Weils? About the hand?"

She doesn't answer for long enough that he thinks she'll ignore him again. But then she says, "What do they say about the hand, Bonner?"

He looks at her. Weils's face is limned in darkness. A wash of streetlight across her dark slacks, the pale white of her hands, her wrists.

"That it belongs to the devil. I mean, that's what Lundy implied during debriefing, right? Even if he didn't come right out and say it."

Weils cracks a smile, looks out the window as if to hide it from him. He has no idea how long she's been with the agency, but Lundy clearly trusts her. She asks Bonner if he believes in the devil.

"I think it's one of those situations," he says, drumming his thumbs on the steering wheel, "where it doesn't matter. If the devil believes in me, it's all over."

And then Weils opens her door and she's striding across the street, calling out to someone, raising her hand. Bonner gets out after her. There in the shadow near the dumpster, near TUFF LUV, she's already got a woman up against the wall. When he gets closer, he hears the woman say, "I ain't doing nothing, damn. The fuck you want?"

Weils, he sees, is good-copping it; she pulls out her wallet and makes a show there next to the dumpster, beneath the streetlight that casts long shadows on the wall, of counting out money.

"We're looking for someone that lives in these apartments," she says. "Someone specific. You know people here?"

"I don't know nobody."

"What's your name?" Bonner says.

She glances at him as if seeing him for the first time, making a face like she's eaten something sour. "My name is *fuck you, cop.*"

Bonner laughs. "Nice."

"Look, we want to do our thing and get out of here," Weils says. "We're not here to give you a problem."

The woman leans back, bends a leg and kicks her foot up against the wall. A denim jacket. Beneath that, she's wearing a tank top that was probably white at one point. Sweatpants. *Strung out* does not begin to describe her. "I don't talk to cops. Ever."

"We're not cops," Bonner says. She laughs, rolls the back of her head against the brick wall.

"We're looking for someone in there," Weils says, grabbing her wrist and folding the money into her palm. "He's got something that belongs to us."

The woman's eyes close. "You're not cops. Dealing dope, then. Right?" Her money-hand dips into her pocket and then comes out empty again. "You got some dope for me?"

"We're looking for someone with a hand," Weils says. "It makes you feel bad when you're near it. But good too."

Bonner imagines the look a normal person would give, hearing a sentence like that. Just the brash, unabashed *weirdness* of it.

He'll say this about Weils—she's fast. The woman, before Weils is even done talking, is trying to pivot away, to run, but Weils is on her. She's got the woman in an elbow lock, her other arm jammed up against the woman's neck. Side of her face pressed flat against the wall. Bonner looks around.

"I'll scream," she says.

"No one cares," Weils says. "And you'll get a broken wrist in the deal. Where's the hand?"

Weils adjusts her hold. The woman hisses like a cat, her eyes squeezed tight.

"You're crazy."

"Bullshit. You've seen it."

"Not me."

"I wanted to do this one way," Weils says, "and you've decided not to. So now we do it like this instead. *Where is the hand?*"

"It's Wes's."

"What?"

"It's Wes's hand."

"What does that mean?"

"It's Wesley's hand," she says, enunciating, like they're stupid. "He bought it from someone."

"Of course he did," Weils says. "Where's Wesley?"

"Some guys took him."

"Some guys took him?"

"Yeah."

"What apartment's he in?"

"Fifty bucks."

Weils doesn't let go of the woman's wrist, but she doesn't hesitate. "Fine."

"Apartment twenty-four. Second floor. I don't know if it's locked. I got my keys. In my coat."

Weils nods at Bonner, who fishes through the pockets of her jacket. Plucks out a small bag of gray-ass dope, mostly gone. Half a pack of cigarettes. A lighter. A box cutter done up in tape, the two of them sharing a look when he pulls it out. The bills Weils just gave her. A bottle-opener key ring with three keys on it.

Weils lets go and the woman turns and sags against the wall. She eyes Bonner. "You better not be taking my bag, motherfuck."

Bonner drops her shit into her cupped palms. Weils counts out another fifty, hands it to her. "Who took Wesley?"

Some vestige of outrage creeps into her voice. "They come in with a gun, put a gun in Wes's face. Hit him with it. Said he owed some-one money."

"How many guys?" The money disappears into the woman's jacket again.

"Two. One's a little rat-faced shit, long hair. The other one was huge, look like his head got blown up and put back together."

"How'd you get out?"

She cuts her eyes away. "They let me go."

Weils stands there with her hands on her hips. A car drives by slow, bass drifting from the windows. "That was nice of them."

"I mean, I hung out. Got smoothed out a little and waited. I do love him. Wesley, I mean. We fight a lot, but me and him—I love him." Her eyes bounce to the pavement, then back up to Weils, as if daring her to refute such a thing. "They put him into a car."

"Did they take the hand?"

"I don't know."

"We're going upstairs," Weils says. "Show me where it is."

The apartment's unlocked. Cat piss and the chemical stink of meth do battle in the close rooms. Living room's all torn up, the cof-fee table busted. A cat wails under the bed, and the woman goes to comfort it until Weils lays a staying hand on her arm. She pulls her sidearm and Bonner reluctantly does the same. It's an easy enough place to search, and Bonner feels none of that maddening tug Weils and Lundy claim he would feel if the hand were near.

They're brought to the kitchen, where flies circle over the dish-strewn horror that is the sink. "We kept it in the freezer." Bonner opens it and roots through. Plastic sacks of frozen, ice-blown things, empty ice cube trays, a bag of rice so old it's wreathed in frost and rooted to the freezer floor.

"It's not there," the woman says. "That's where we kept it, in the back, when we weren't using it."

Bonner and Weils turn to her. "Using it?" Bonner asks.

The woman puts a filthy thumbnail between her teeth. Casts her eyes to the floor again. "We'd pray to it sometimes. Held it. Did stuff. It made you feel good."

Weils hands her another fifty. Where did the two of them get the hand in the first place? Who was it that Wesley owed money to? Can you describe the men's car.

As they're leaving, Bonner steps on something hard amid the spill of garbage on the living room floor. He bends down and picks it up. A bloody tooth. He drops it, revulsion rippling along his scalp.

"Do I even need to say it?"

This from Bonner, on the highway back to Camelot.

"What?"

"They were banging, right? They'd take out the hand and do a sé-ance or something, and then bang. 'We did stuff.' Jesus."

Nothing from Weils.

Such is their palaver. Bonner drives, Weils thumbs away at her phone, checking in with various agents, with Lundy, who knows. Bonner is the gopher that ferries her around.

The name itself—Camelot—is moored in irony. ARC is housed in a busted-ass barracks and single hangar that's tucked away in a busted-ass corner of what's mostly a busted-ass Air National Guard base outside of town. Low profile, a small intelligence footprint.

Bonner shows his badge and they're ushered through the gate without a word. Base personnel know little about ARC, given their classified status, but they do know that infringing on an agent's movements can land you a discharge and prison sentence. Bonner and Weils are among, in total, a few dozen ghosts stationed there. They're left alone.

He drives the SUV into the hangar, the hangar door sliding shut behind them. He doesn't even have a foot on the cement floor before Lundy comes storming out of the doorway of the adjoining office. Sweat rings beneath his white shirt. Red-faced. Lundy's done intelligence-gathering work for what, thirty years? Most of it black, silently funded? Even after all that, he remains merciless in his ambition. The man doesn't stop.

"Michael came through with more," is all he says, shutting Bonner's door for him as he pushes him back inside the SUV.

Weils leans over, stares at him. "Already?"

"He's on a roll, baby." He hands Weils a printout, a single piece of paper, through Bonner's open window. Bonner sees what looks like a USB stick dangling from a cord around his neck. Lundy sees him looking and absently tucks it back into his shirt.

"What is this?" Weils says. "Is this a license plate number?"

"It is," Lundy says. "And a rough idea of the make and model, *and* a general vicinity."

"Holy shit."

He grins and says, "It's a fucking home run, Weils. Dude's giving it up. Dude's *working*."

Bonner starts the ignition. Weils and Lundy share a look, and it's as happy as Bonner has seen her in four months.

"We're close," Lundy says. He grips Bonner's door sill and fixes them with those deathly blue eyes of his. "Don't fuck this up."

HUTCH HOLTZ

Their driver drops them off around the corner from Don Sr.'s house. Rain falls in spats and a chill blows up Hutch's coat sleeves. He's got killing on his mind, the relentless image of Wesley's bullet-shattered face, and it's a terrible thing to walk around with. A bad weight that sets in your bones.

They hoof it around the block, and Tim lets out a snort of rage when he sees his car parked in Don's driveway. "That motherfucker." The car's parked at an angle, a front tire on the lawn, like he pulled up in a hurry. They keep walking, not wanting to draw attention. They make it around the corner and stop again.

Don's neighborhood reads as "quaint residential": family homes, well-kept yards, probably lots of Christmas lights up when it's that time of year. People pay attention to two men like them in a neighborhood like this, skulking around in the dark. It's not quite as bad as Tim's playing with screwdrivers and shit, but every moment they're out here makes the likelihood of being remembered by a neighbor more obvious.

Peach's new instructions, since Don had done his little disappearing act: *Find him and talk to him. Ask him what the fuck he's doing. And bring me the hand. I love my father-in-law, but he's hotheaded.*

They both know there's not a chance they'll ever ask Don "what the fuck he's doing." Even without a mysterious severed hand involved, talking to Don Sr. like that is a fantastic way to get pistol-whipped, find your important bits stuffed in a garbage can somewhere.

Either way, I want *that thing, you hear me? Whether he gives it to you or you take it.* The two of them had shared a look and Peach had rolled his eyes, put out his hands. *Don't fucking kill him for God's sake, that ain't what I'm saying. But just let him know,* I'm *the one runs this show. He can call me, or he can hand it over to you. But I want it.*

And that's the thing about Peach Serrano. Peach and his collecting—once he wants something, that's it. He's been like that as long as Hutch has known him. Sending Nick Coffin to the ends of the earth to gather all these obscure objects for him; Peach's need for the *ownership* of a thing is like its own fever.

"So we storm in?" Tim says now, fiddling with the zippers on his leather jacket.

"Well, or we knock."

"Knocking's a good way to get scattergunned through the front door. Popped through an upstairs window or something. Especially if he's all spun out."

"Fair point."

"Can we just agree," says Tim, "that this is some fucked-up shit? Peach sending us up against Don? His own father-in-law? It's his wife's old man."

"He's always had that bug. That collecting bug. If something's one-of-a-kind, he's got to have it."

"Yeah, but it's our ass right now."

"I hear you. No one's killing anyone. I already told you that."

Tim nods, sucks at his cheek. "I'm thinking we do the thing where I knock on the front and you go in the back."

This surprises Hutch: Tim can be vicious, and he can be clever, and he can be funny. But being brave—taking the risk, knocking on the door, making a target of himself—is generally not in his wheel-house. It takes Hutch back a bit.

"You sure?"

Tim grins. "Smaller target." He bobs and weaves, his fists coiled in front of his face. "I can stick and move. You're just a fucking mono-lith or whatever, standing there."

"Monolith, huh?"

"See, I read," Tim says. "You don't think I read."

"Okay," Hutch says. "We just talk to him."

"I mean, one of us going through the back of his house kind of implies that we don't trust him, but whatever."

"*Do* you trust him?"

Tim snorts. "Fuck no." He glances at Hutch and there's a tender-ness there, an acknowledgment that again surprises him. "I shot that dude. Wesley. And that's not going away. I own that. I've done it before. It's a thing that sits with you."

"I know it," Hutch says.

"I know you do. Guy's floating in the fucking Willamette right now, and that's ours. That's something that belongs to you and me."

"Yeah."

"But what Don did after? Just round after round into the dude's head? I might trust him a little if that hand wasn't around."

"Maybe," Hutch says.

"Yeah. Maybe. But right now, no, not a bit."

Hutch cuts down the driveway and threads like smoke past Tim's car. At the end of the driveway is a fence that laces one side of the house, and he opens the gate as quietly as he can, stepping into a small, well-kept yard. There's a flagstone patio, and Hutch treads along silently, ready to kick the door in should he hear gunshots or screams.

It's a sliding door with vertical shades, offering zero information about what's beyond the glass. But it's unlocked, and he moves it along its tracks as delicately as he can, trying to quell the panic threatening to grow wings inside him. Don, even back when he was a cop, was a killer. Hutch's two killings (three, now, even if he didn't pull the trigger) rattle inside him like stones, but Don's on a different level. Hutch knows the man's responsible for a lot more bodies in the Willamette than just the one tonight. There's a disconnect with him that Hutch will never match, a willingness, and he'd be a fool to think otherwise.

He steps into Don's bedroom. The bedroom door opens up to the hallway, the hall light casting a weak pall into the room. There's Don's unmade bed, clothes mounded on the floor. The drone and tinny laughter of the TV down the hallway. Hutch walks over to Don's nightstand, where he sees Don's phone and a loaded pistol—a Glock, not Tim's revolver. He spends precious seconds sliding the clip out, wincing at the noise. It's loaded, all seventeen rounds. He reinserts the clip, jacks the slide, thumbs the safety off. Feels somehow more terrified for the fact he has a gun. On the floor beside the nightstand is a black bag, worn, flaking leather with a clasp on top. Like an old-timey doctor's bag, Hutch thinks. It's open, and when Hutch peers in, he sees stacks upon stacks of banded cash. Cold sweat floods his scalp, his forehead. The fuck is happening here? He picks up the bag.

The throb and mutter of the hand suddenly reaches out to him.

Tim pounds on the front door and Hutch, there in the dim light, nearly starts firing in panic. His heart lurches. There's no response anywhere in the house as far as Hutch can tell—no creak of furniture, nothing scraping across the floor. Is Don in the bathroom? Is he at the other end of the hallway with a shotgun, ready for Hutch to step out?

Somewhere nearby, the hand reaches out again and feathers his brain with rage and blood. Hutch bares his teeth, creeps forward.

Another flurry of knocks at the front door and Hutch steps through the hallway, pistol raised. Nothing. He turns and pivots into the living room.

There's Don. On the couch.

The television bathes the room in a flickering, wavering light. To his left is a doorway with a swatch of tiled floor: the kitchen. To his right is a wall-mounted flatscreen, the couch beneath the front win-dow. A recliner that's reduced to a dark shape in the gloom. The stink is what he notices next—the bright, coppery fug of blood—and the way the hand's mutter sharpens into a snarl the closer he gets to Don. TV light pools in the dead man's eyes.

Hutch lets out a shaky, trembling breath, and hisses in fear and anger when Tim bangs on the front door again, only feet away from him. He storms over and unlocks the door—without gloves on, shit—and Tim comes in, his eyes bouncing around the room.

The first thing Hutch says is "Don't touch a thing." He wipes the doorknob and the deadbolt with the sleeve of his coat.

"Holy shit," Tim says, staring down at Don.

Shirtless and fish-pale, Don leans back against the couch, like a man exhausted after a long day at work. His mouth is slack, a ridge of small yellow teeth visible beneath his mustache. Some of his ban-dages have come off, and the bite marks on his face are garish and black in the poor light. Tim steps back, turns on a lamp. It makes everything look so much worse.

A straight razor lies in Don's free hand, which rests gently on the couch cushion. His other hand—his right, like the gray, mottled hand that lies on the coffee table and sings out its deathly, one-note hymn—rests in his lap, hanging from his wrist by a few grisly strings of flesh. Gore paints Don's belly, his pants. The cushions glisten wetly with blood, catching the sheen of lamplight.

He'd been trying, Hutch understands, to saw off his own hand.

To replace it.

"We got to get the fuck out of here," Hutch says in a ragged whis-per. He shows Tim the bag and Tim hardly even looks in it. He peers around the room, licking his lips, his eyes white in the dark.

"Take the hand," he whispers.

"I'm not touching the hand, Tim. Fuck that."

Tim pivots and gags, just once, and then stumbles into the kitchen. A light goes on in there. Hutch can hear him rooting around in the cupboards. He stares at Don's body until Tim comes back with a plastic bread bag. It crinkles and hisses in his fist as he shakes it out.

"I can hear it," Tim says. He inches closer to the hand on the coffee table, as if it might suddenly try to escape.

"Me too."

"I've seen some shit, man, but this is . . . I don't know what this is."

"Just grab it. If you have to grab it, just do it and let's go. Ah, God."

Tim inches forth and leans over, his hair cloaking his face—and in any horror movie, here is where Don would rise up and bring the straight razor down on Tim's own reaching hand. But nothing happens. He's dead as anything. On the television, a man solemnly discusses his erectile dysfunction and Tim uses the TV remote to push the hand off the edge of the coffee table and into the bread bag, the odor of Don's blood and shit right there, cloying and warm. The hand falls into the bag and Tim spins the top of it shut. He tosses it in Hutch's newly acquired doctor bag, and this is when Tim begins gagging in earnest, turning and dry-heaving with his hands on his knees. The television cuts to another commercial, for antacids this time, a woman in white wincing in discomfort before holding up a pale yellow pill and smiling in relief.

They stumble out to the driveway, Hutch with the bag in one hand and the pistol in the other, and it's only when they're outside that they realize they need Tim's car keys.

"I'll do it," Hutch says, shoving Don's Glock into his coat. He sets the bag at the rear of the car.

Tim leans with his arms on the roof, his eyes closed. "Maybe they're in his pockets."

Hutch walks back into the house. Nothing has changed, of course. A sitcom is on, an old one in which an anthropomorphized lasagna lives with a family, offers sage advice, tries to convince a widowed neighbor to have sex. A resoundingly odd, short-lived series Hutch remembers from his teenage years. Don remains gore-slicked, couch-bound. Hutch takes in a breath, steels himself to begin fishing through Don's pants, when he sees a key ring on the coffee table. He picks it up and rattles the keys, wonders if it's Tim's or Don's and how the fuck he might figure out such a thing, when he sees Don's eyes move toward the sound.

Hutch backpedals, trips over the edge of the coffee table, lands hard on his ass. It is unmistakable—Don is looking at him. His eyes absolutely *alive* above his bite-scored cheeks. Hutch stands, his breath tight and harsh, his throat constricting. He runs.

Outside, he throws the keys to Tim, who catches them with one hand and fishes through them. He sees the look on Hutch's face as Hutch picks up the doctor bag and stands at the trunk.

"What happened?"

"Open the trunk."

"What happened, Hutch?" Tim opens the driver's door, pops the trunk.

Hutch tosses the bag in the back, runs to the passenger side, gets in.

Tim stares at him as Hutch buckles in, locks his door.

"Go, go. Seriously, man."

Tim reverses out of Don's driveway. "What's the problem?"

"He opened his eyes."

"Bullshit," Tim says.

"He did. He looked right at me. When I jingled the keys."

Tim wipes his lips, eases out onto the street. "Do we call the cops?"

"Fuck no," says Hutch.

"But he's still alive."

"He's not alive, Tim."

Tim opens his mouth to say something.

"He's not alive," Hutch says. "Believe me."

JOHN BONNER

PE 478.
    Rusted five doors.
Northern city, near the train hub.

Back out, and the rain has started up again. Wavering sea of red taillights ahead of them.

Bonner hits his blinker, merges. "What does 'five doors' mean?"

"If that's a license plate, maybe like a hatchback," Weils says.

"An Outback or something."

"A rusty Subaru."

"And what's the train hub? The transit center? The Rose Quarter?"

"Maybe."

"If they were at the Rose Quarter, Weils, they could be anywhere now. Could have crossed over the river, be eating hot wings in fucking Tualatin for all we know."

"We go with what we have. Just drive."

"I'm serious, though. Trying to find a Subaru in *Portland*? Give me a break."

He can't let it go. They've threaded their way west, down Broadway now, heading toward the river. "*Two* agents on this, Weils? If the hand is so important? This feels like an errand to me. I'm not getting a sense that this is critical."

"There are other agents on this."

"Yeah, how many? Two other teams? Three? Heavy Light has, what, *ten* field agents in total?"

"Do you ever stop talking, man?" She leans forward. "Pull over there. Get in the left lane. There."

They slow behind a Subaru with a KEEP PORTLAND WEIRD sticker on the back, but the license plate isn't even close.

"I'm telling you, we need cops out here. You get traffic cops on this? We'd have these guys in ten minutes."

"We both know that isn't an option." She pushes her hands against the windshield and stretches. "Just keep looking."

"It's night, it's been raining. We're looking for a single vehicle in a city of over two million people. This is a milk run, Weils. Lundy's screwing around."

"Yeah, well," she says, turning her face away. "You probably should be on a milk run, shouldn't you?"

For a moment there's only the sound of the wipers ticking away. Then Bonner says quietly, "What's that supposed to mean?"

"It means you're here because you had to duck out, right?"

He snorts, sits with that for a second. "Do you know what I did to get here, Weils?"

"I know someone called in a favor for you."

Bonner flashes back—shadow-quick, eyeblink-fast—to Pernicio, struggling beneath him, the protest, the acrid snarl of CS gas in the air, the way flash-bangs rattle inside your ribs like God's fist reaching in there and squeezing. "You think you're the only agent that's ever been in the field, huh?"

It's Weils's turn to be silent, but Bonner can't let it go.

"If I needed to duck out, why the hell am I spending my time driving around this shithole, knocking on doors, getting in people's faces? Why's that?"

Her smile's acid, pure dark. She's caught him. "Because this isn't Brooklyn, is why."

She's got the gist of it, if not the particulars. "Whatever," Bonner says. But it's a second too late; she's got to him, and they both know it.

"You're a long way from home, Bonner."

"Fuck off. Sincerely. From my heart to yours."

"Must be nice to have someone able to make some calls on your behalf."

What's the point in responding? Weils doesn't know anything about it, about what happened. He's sure that Weils has never done UC work, never gone deep anywhere. Her with her fucking wrist-locks, passing cash around. She doesn't know a thing. It's not like Bonner's grateful to his uncle. ARC's just the chair he'd been told to sit in for the time being.

A blip on Weils's cell phone then, the underside of her face lighting up. "Michael's got another hit."

"You serious?"

"Sky. Pizza."

Bonner glances at her. This infighting of theirs evaporates in a second—they're right there, at the edge of the thing. "I'm drawing a blank."

"Pie in the Sky, could be. The one with the neon pizza slice on top of their building."

"Shit," Bonner says, smacking the steering wheel, almost wanting to laugh—sometimes the way Michael works caught you like a fist to the chin. *Sky. Pizza.* "That's, what? Thirty blocks from here?"

"West Burnside," Weils says. "Go. It's five minutes if you haul ass."

"How do you want to do this?" Bonner says.

It's not a Subaru at all, it turns out, but a black Datsun hatchback, probably forty years old if it's a day, with weeping patches of rust climbing down the doors. Plastic over one window. The parking lot is almost full. Weils has walked inside and ordered something and walked back out, casing the men in the car. When she steps back in, she informs Bonner she's been made.

"Who made you?"

"The big one, in the passenger seat. He knows."

It's their guys. The driver, she says, has a ponytail and a leather jacket. The other one's huge, accordioned-up in the passenger seat. Matches the woman's descriptions she gave outside the apartment. The front of their SUV is facing the rear of the Datsun, a passageway for traffic between them.

Bonner suggests they just ram the car and then go in and pull the men out. "They're armed," he says. "We know that much. I don't want to play with these guys."

"We can't damage the remnant."

Other teams, Weils says, looking at her phone, are forthcoming, should be there in minutes.

"You're sure the remnant's actually in there?"

"I'm not sure of anything," Weils says. "But this is where Michael led us. And they're clearly our guys." She looks down at her watch. "I got you breadsticks."

"What?"

"I got you breadsticks. Order should be ready in five minutes. I can go in, grab it, come back out and ask them something at the driver's-side window. Distract them, then you flank them." A family walks into the restaurant, the boy and girl racing ahead through the rain to get to the front door. They walk right past the hatchback.

"There's people all around here, Weils. We can't do a kill box in a parking lot, man."

Weils glances at her phone. "Okay. Shit. Davis and Porter are three minutes away. Hang tight." She tosses her phone on the dashboard and leans forward, pulling her sidearm from the holster at the small of her back.

"Do you feel anything?" Bonner asks. "I don't feel anything. How close do you have to be?"

"I don't know," Weils says. "Never dealt with it out in the world. But if they move, we move."

"Right, but what—"

The Datsun's passenger door opens and the big man steps out. Dude has to be six-four at least, and something terrible has happened to his face. Cragged red scars draw across his forehead, and beneath that—he looks right at Bonner, *right* at him, this bridge drawn between them—are these absolutely cold and assessing blue eyes.

"He's made us," Bonner says.

The man walks to the trunk, lifts it. He pulls out a bag and steps away from the car.

"Shit," Weils says, just as the man turns to them and fires a pistol.

They duck beneath the windshield. Bonner hears the deep, febrile thunks and twangs of rounds bouncing off the SUV. It's been outfitted to withstand such things, supposedly, but he trusts that about as much as he trusts anything else involving the agency. A round hits the pavement and clangs off the vehicle's underside.

Weils kicks open her door and falls out, returning fire. Bonner glances up, sees blued stars on the windshield. Nothing gone through the glass. He sits up. The trunk of the Datsun is open. Big guy's gone. He sees Weils roving between cars. People scream, run. The Datsun suddenly backs up, tires screaming on the wet pavement, taillights flaring, and the driver reverses the twenty feet between them in a boil of smoke, smashing into the front of the SUV. Bonner's face bounces off the steering wheel. More rounds popcorn throughout the parking lot. The hatchback pulls forward with a groan, metal snarling as the rear bumper pulls free, and then the driver's ripping out onto Burnside where he broadsides a sedan and stalls out. Bonner sees someone, incredibly, standing on the sidewalk, filming the entire event.

Weils runs low between two cars, fifteen feet away from the driver's side of the hatchback, then ten. She pumps rounds, five or six, into the door and the hatchback reverses and then veers off to the right, where it clips the rear of a pickup and comes to a halt again.

Bonner finally steps out of the SUV. His Glock 19, it's like holding a rubber fish in his hand. Feels alien, both useless and terrifying. He's never drawn his sidearm live before. Even during the thing with Pernicio, the protests. All these years, this is the first time. There are more people filming through the windows of Pie in the Sky.

Bonner trots low over to the Datsun. The driver's window is blown out; the man's chin dips to his chest. His hands are in his lap and filling with blood. It pours from his throat, which has been ripped open from one of Weils's rounds. A shattered cheekbone gives his entire jaw a crooked set. Blood everywhere, eyes gone pure blank with death.

Wheeling around in the street, he can't see the passenger. The guy's gone. Blood roars in Bonner's ears. Screams continue to zip up and down the street like fireworks. Weils is gone too. He realizes she might have taken a round, might be hidden by a car somewhere.

A shot rings out right next to him. He actually *sees* the round go into the hood of the Datsun. Bonner ducks and turns and, Christ, there's a man standing between the door and chassis of his own SUV, a pizza box sitting squarely on the vehicle's roof. Maybe, what, forty feet away? Aiming down at him.

"Get the fuck down," Bonner screams at the man, his voice cracking. He motions with his free hand—*down, get down*—but the guy's going to do it, he's going to shoot him, right fucking there on Burnside with the rain lashing down on all of them, a supposedly good guy with a gun just wrecking everything, and then there's another gunshot from somewhere and the guy sags against his ride, blood spattering against his window. Bonner looks over and there's Weils in a shooter's stance at the end of the block. In the dark? The rain? Not a chance in a million Bonner could have made that shot.

Bonner spins around wildly, rain in his eyes. Chaos, people running, people leaning on their horns. Lights gleaming off everything. Cars pushing against other cars, trying to escape. The ululating howls of emergency vehicles growing closer. Two dead bodies, including some random citizen jumping in the middle of it and catching a round in the mouth for his troubles. Christ.

And the big one, he of the dented head, the scarecrow face, he's taken off with the hand somewhere. Got away.

In spite of everything Michael's given them, the remnant's gone again.

HUTCH HOLTZ

"We want certain assurances, is all," Hutch says.

"What is this?" says Peach, and to his credit, he almost sounds hurt. They're sitting in the parking lot of a pizza place, he and Tim, and the hand, as ever, rattles incessantly in the backs of their minds. Neon from the front window of the restaurant paints the hood of the Datsun like a joyous smear of blood. Hutch sits in the passenger seat with his phone on one knee. It's on speaker, and he and Tim are afraid to even look at each other, like looking at each other will jinx it all. Make it definitive, what's happened to Don. Twelve years in, and they've never done this before. Never called Peach Serrano to negotiate terms. Before today, Hutch couldn't have even imagined a scenario where it'd be necessary.

Then again, Peach's muscle—and his father-in-law—just died while trying to saw his own hand off, and that takes a bit of Peach's fearsomeness away.

"What do you mean, assurances?"

Hutch says, "Things went south, is what we're saying. It's not in

your best interest to get specific over the phone, boss. Believe me."
Even in his periphery, he can see Tim lick his lips, nodding.

"Things are truly fucked, is what we're saying," offers Tim.

"Things are fucked," Peach repeats, "but you don't want to get specific. Is that right?"

"Yeah."

"You're not giving me a lot to work with here."

Hutch exhales. "It's a unique situation. We can fill you in, but I think meeting in public's a way better move. Nothing against you."

The seconds tick away. He can imagine Peach pacing the rug in his sitting room, some recorded MMA fight big and glowing behind him, dudes locked in combat with each other, grappling and busting teeth loose. Peach watches the stuff incessantly, calls it his meditation music.

"The fuck is this? Have I ever done you two wrong before? Did you go to Don's place or not?"

"Boss, you don't want us to talk about it over the phone."

Peach's voice climbs an octave. He isn't a man used to being told no. "Hey, Hutch, how tough you gonna be when I have Don take a pair of pliers to your orthodontia, huh? You feel me? You talk when I *tell* you to talk."

Tim licks his lips once more and says, in a slightly loud voice, like he's speaking to someone's grandfather, "I'm sorry, but that's not gonna be happening, boss."

Peach laughs. "Yeah? And why's that, dipshit?"

He finally looks at Hutch, and Hutch shrugs. They're in it now.

"Because Don's dead."

The seconds tick off, the car filled with that silence. In the trunk, the hand's blood-fog breathes, expands and contracts, fills the cragged parts of Hutch's brain and recedes.

Finally, Peach talks, and it's like something has cracked inside him. Like there's this whole new animal inside this guy they've known forever. The words come out blocky, distinct. Each one like its own stone tumbling to the ground. He says, "Who is? Don? Don's dead?"

Hutch nods at the phone and then realizes what he's doing. "Yeah, boss. He was dead when we rolled up."

"Dead fucking how?"

He and Tim look at each other again, because there's a lot of land mines stacked in that answer, isn't there? A woman walks past Tim's side of the car, dressed in a black jacket and tight black pants. A short bob of red hair. She opens the door to the pizza place and walks in, and something in Hutch's mind sends up a flare. Maybe it's the way she walks—it sings cop to him, military, something—or the assessing glance she gives the car, the way their eyes lock for a second. Maybe it's even the hand, who knows. But some lizard-whisper in his brain's all: *Cop. Bet your life that's a cop right there.*

"Dead fucking *how?*" Peach says again.

Hutch is pulled back to the phone. "Well, he took the hand, we were right about that. And uh, well." He trails off, looks to Tim for support. Tim shrugs, his eyes wide.

"And uh," Tim says, still in that loud voice, leaning over the phone, "like we said about the hand, it really makes you do crazy shit, and uh, he cut off his hand with a razor, Don did, like he sawed it off with a straight razor, boss, and, well, we're thinking he was going to try to, like, attach the hand to where his old one had been." Tim clears his throat. "If that makes sense."

Silence from Peach.

"Uh, long story short, he was like that when we got there, just dead as hell."

The woman comes out of the doorway and for just a moment their eyes lock again. It's all the recognition he needs. She's a cop, or a fed, or whatever—and she's zeroed in on them. Hutch watches her pass, watches her in the side-view mirror. She steps into a tricked-out SUV in the parking lot behind them.

Hutch is far from stupid. Particularly since Gresham and what happened there, he's stayed home, mostly, when he's not working, and he reads two or three books a week. Just part of calming the cyclone in him. Tough books sometimes too. So *apoplectic* is a word he knows, and while Hutch looks in his side-view mirror at the SUV parked behind them, he recognizes that Peach has become apoplectic.

"What in the fuck are you talking about? He sawed his own hand off? Don did? Bullshit."

"Boss—"

"*Bull fucking shit.* You two are making a play, aren't you?" His voice gets hot, fuzzed-out—he's screaming into the receiver. "You want to come for me? You want to edge me out? See what happens. You smoke a man's family, it's done double for you. I take everyone you ever cared about. They're gone. That's what's coming to you."

"See," Hutch says, "this is why we want to meet you in public, boss. We were worried you'd feel this way."

"What way is that? Like I'm gonna saw your legs off and make you walk to the hospital? Because that's what's gonna happen. I'm supposed to tell Cassandra that her old man sawed his own *hand* off? On purpose he did that? And then he died? That's the story you bring me?"

"Boss," Hutch says, "we got other problems."

Peach laughs. "Oh, I promise you don't have a bigger problem than me, Hutch. Not in this world."

"There's a couple of feds in an SUV behind us. Or cops." Tim looks over at him wildly. "I think they're gonna jump on us soon. I got this feeling. What do you want us to do?"

This appeasement, knowing when to do it, and how, has always been a strength of Hutch's. He's always been good like that. It strikes Peach, he can tell, as reasonable—their fealty is no longer in question, even if they are a couple of dumb, knuckle-dragging motherfuckers who claim that his father-in-law just pointlessly and gruesomely ended his own life.

"Feds?"

"Something like that. SUV in a parking spot a ways behind us."

"That could be anybody. They could be getting a pizza."

"One of them's armed."

"What, they showed you their piece?"

"It's just a feeling."

"You sure they're after you?"

"I mean, I'm not sure of anything. But given how the night's going, you know."

Peach chews on it for a while. Finally he says, "You got the hand with you?"

"Yeah." And a fuck-ton of money—my goodness, how strange that neither of them have mentioned that to Peach. It's Don's run-money, presumably. Hutch can picture it—blood-fogged, the hand singing its song in the dark meat of his brain, Don gets some big ideas. Figures he'll take his somehow newly attached hand and his savings, whatever he's got tucked away, and get out of town. Probably felt like God, figured he'd connect this hand to himself (but through what, Hutch thinks, magic? Osmosis?) and roll ferociously through the world like some kind of king.

"And you're *sure* Don's dead?"

Hutch is the one licking his lips now. Not a chance he's telling Peach what he saw. The hand makes it hard to think, everything sluggish and visceral, heated, but that—*Yeah, man, he was dead but then I seen his eyes track me, it was a trip*—is clearly too much.

"Yeah."

Peach doesn't speak for so long that Hutch wonders if the line's gone dead. Then he says, "Meet me at the bar. Twenty minutes."

Hutch knows which one. "Twenty minutes is pretty tight."

Peach snorts, exasperated. "How much time you need then?"

"Half an hour."

"Half an hour. With the hand. And no feds. And a fucking *reason*," Peach suddenly bellows, "that my father-in-law is dead, you hear me?"

He hangs up, and Tim cracks the window and lights a smoke

with shaking hands. His eyes bounce to the rearview. "Those really feds back there?"

"I don't know, dude. Maybe I'm getting paranoid. Maybe the hand's fucking with me. But I think so."

"I was feeling all dark earlier, like I wanted to hurt people. Now, I just feel scared as shit. Like I want to run."

"If Peach wants us at Mercy's in half an hour, we should figure out what we're doing."

Tim turns and looks at him, his face shrouded in smoke, and it is the same haunted quality Hutch saw when they first met, over twenty-five years ago in Rutherford Youth Correctional. That same mashup of sneering, cocksure rage and a simmering regret just beneath the surface. He pulls on his cigarette. "I'm sorry we ever walked into that dope fiend's house, man. Sorry we ever took that hand. I want to be rid of it."

And the hand is singing to him now, to Hutch. Hardcore. An aria full of hisses and sobs, his head full of this ancient, timeless cadence. No way this is just someone's hand. He sees images of stone smashed against flesh. Feels eons of static and guttural death-gasps. The lamentations of every mother who mourned a child, every lover who held their lost one in their arms, felt the blood cool as it spilled forth from the body. All gathered within him.

"You hear that?" he says, tilting his head, and Tim looks at him like he's not sure. Like maybe.

Like he's afraid to answer—because what if he doesn't? What if the hand has singled Hutch out?

Fine, Hutch thinks. Sing to me then. I'll do what you want.

"I'll take the hand," he says.

Tim exhales, nearly weeping with gratitude. "Thank you, man."

"Pop the trunk."

He does, and they both hear the heavy clunk of the trunk latch opening.

"Get to Mercy's," Hutch says. "I'll meet you there."

Without looking away from the rearview mirror, Tim opens the side panel and reaches in, gets his gun out. "I ain't got the same feeling as you. About the SUV."

"I don't know what to tell you, man."

"Is it the hand, telling you?"

"I think so."

Tim snorts. "Better check your source, then."

It starts raining again. The sound of it on the roof. Drops pinging on the hood.

"I love you," Hutch says, "but make up your mind. Go to Mercy's, or we make our move together on that SUV back there."

"If those are cops, Hutch, I'll be lucky to drive this thing out of the parking lot. What about the money?"

"If I'm taking the hand, I'm taking the money. I don't have time to do a split with you."

Tim looks at him, and *beseeching* is the word Hutch thinks of. How we all have the same scared kid nestled inside of us, the same small child we've always been just right there. Nesting dolls, all those pressed-down terrors. Hutch recognizes in Tim's eyes the boy he'd encountered in that Rutherford bunkhouse, Hutch holding off bigger, meaner kids until Tim could come into his own, until Tim grew snakelike and vicious in his own right. Became the man he is.

"I should call my wife," Tim says hoarsely, swiping a hand down his face.

"You can let them arrest you," Hutch offers, though he knows that won't ever happen. Not with what's in the drains at the warehouse, on the coveralls they wore. "If they're the arresting type."

"Yeah, right."

"Hell, you can flip on Peach, if it comes to that."

Tim wipes his nose with his wrist. Crying. Has Hutch ever seen him cry? Ever? He might've cried when he saw Hutch laid up in the ICU after the thing in Gresham, but that was about it. Maybe at Tim's wedding? So, yeah. Twice in his life, probably.

Tim says, "I wouldn't even make it to my arraignment if I flipped on Peach. We both know it." He fishes his cell phone out of his pocket, just sits there staring at it. "I was not planning on dying outside of a pizza place, man."

"We don't have much time," Hutch says again.

Tim nods, sniffs hard. He puts his phone back in his pocket, and slaps Hutch's shoulder with the back of his hand. "Get the fuck out," he says, half laughing, half crying.

Hutch kind of bops him on the knee with the barrel of Don's Glock. "I mean it, you're good in my book. If it happens somehow where the cops get me in front of a jury? If that happens? I shot that guy tonight. I did it all. It's on me. We've been through it together, man. After Rutherford? Gresham and those bikers? All of Peach's bullshit? Twenty-five years I've known you. I owe you, Tim. It's been a *ride,* man."

"Alright," Tim says, swiping at his eyes again. He exhales a shaky breath, settles his hands on the wheel. "I can't do the long goodbye, dude. Let's do this."

Hutch looks at the front door of the restaurant for a moment and then steps out, the pistol low at his side. Walks to the back of the car. There's the rusty groan of the trunk rising, and then Hutch grabs the bag and shuts the trunk and turns around.

He starts firing.

Tim closes his eyes for a second, then puts the Datsun in reverse and mashes his foot to the floor.

Hutch has never been shot before. He's been stabbed—twice—and struck with any number of things: fists, feet, rebar, a socket wrench, a fish bat, brass knuckles, whatever. Been hit by a car. The thing in Gresham happened when he was in a bar, waiting to talk to a guy for Peach, and while he was waiting he had a few drinks and then mouthed off to the wrong guys. *Those* guys made a phone call and ten minutes later a half dozen bikers, patched Crooked Wheel guys, big burly motherfuckers, had taken him outside into the parking lot. They'd knocked him around good and then dropped him to the pavement and stuck his head in the driver's-side door of a Ford passenger van, shutting it on him a few times. Brain swelling, orbital fractures, multiple skull fractures, shattered cheekbones. His teeth scattered on the running board. Doctors had spent a year piecing him together and after all of it he still looks like a kid's drawing of a person.

He remembered Peach asking if he wanted retribution. Insinuated that it could get political, bloody, a dick-swinging contest that might never end. But Peach had been willing to go to bat. Call in a chip and get some of those Crooked Wheel boys tied to a chair in a basement, get some work done on them. Put one or two of them in the Willamette in pieces. But he'd been right—it was the type of thing that would never end. Instead, Hutch had stopped drinking. Stayed home, stayed quiet. It had been his fault after all. You don't go into a bar like that and start shooting your mouth off. So he'd healed, slowly and poorly, and gotten sober, and read a lot, and continued again to break the arms that Peach told him to break, and that was that. He wasn't one of those guys that wanted the world on a plate. He wanted to do his shit and go to bed at night without a bunch of tweaked-out bikers calling him a faggot while they broke his head open in a van door.

Seemed a reasonable enough expectation.

But he should've known that that's not how life does it. Life runs the table and you just try to keep up.

So now here he is, having taken his very first bullet, hiding in the narrow mouth of an alley with piss in his pants and a high-pitched keening noise coming from his throat while he presses his fist to his gut, holds the doctor's bag with the hand singing its endless, twisted darkness straight into him.

He was blocks away from the chaos of the parking lot before he even realized he'd been hit. He remembered feeling like someone had jabbed him with an end of a bat, nudged him hard, and he'd bounced off the bumper of a car, but then he was running again.

Now he's leaning in a brick alleyway and there's a distant heat in his guts, this terrible sense of *spillage*.

Who knows what happened to Tim. Each of them on his own path now. He holds up a hand to his face and it's black with blood. He's afraid to explore the exit wound in his back. He's panicked, breathing fast. And still the hand murmurs and cajoles, offers up images, notions ringed in heat and suggestion: that he might storm through this back door here, whatever it is, and kill whoever he finds. That he might step out onto the street and find the first passerby and set upon them with his teeth. Even as blood pours out of him, he thinks of more blood.

Hutch punches his wound with a fist, not hard, but enough to send him retching between his knees. Hoping to clear his head.

Instead he thinks, or the hand thinks for him: *I could reach in there, into the hole, pull everything out. The loops of myself.*

And with the briefest clarity: *I got to get rid of this fucking thing.*

And then: *Call Nick Coffin. Pass it on to Peach like you're supposed to, but get rid of it. You ain't dying, probably, but it's not good. Let the kid handle it.*

Sirens begin knifing the air. He takes out his phone and promptly drops it to the pavement. Leaning down is an Odyssean journey that seems to takes years, and the phone comes up in his trembling hand with blood spotting the screen. He has Coffin's number in his contacts. He rises, leans against the wall, his legs these freezing pillars now, things without feeling that somehow still hold him upright.

Nick Coffin picks up.

"It's Hutch Holtz," he says.

"Hey," says Coffin, a little cautiously. "What's up."

"I got this thing for Peach I need to give you."

"Okay," Coffin says. "Did you want to come by my place?"

"I need you to come to me, Nick."

"Okay," Nick says. "You alright?"

The hand snarls and howls, makes Hutch want to hiss obscenities into the phone. "I'm good, dude, just a bit tripped up. I'm at a bus stop on Thirtieth and Belmont. I got to hand this thing off to you." The pun only registers after he's said it.

"Yeah, I can be there. You sure you're okay?"

"I'm alright," says Hutch, eyeing the street. "I'll see you." He hangs up, wills himself to push off from the wall. To walk on those freezing stilt-legs to the bench across the street and half a block down. Might as well be a mile. A hundred miles.

The bag with its treasure—hand, money, gun—clutched in one bloody fist, the night relentlessly unspooling before him, Hutch staggers on.

NICK COFFIN

Nick Coffin is all elbows and knees and combat boots that rise and fall, slap the wet pavement, a cadence to it. Nick Coffin, hauling ass to make it to a particular Belmont Street bus bench in front of a particular convenience store where an associate—a co-worker, though that feels resoundingly weird to say—has just called him, gasping, telling Nick to meet him there. To pick something up. Hutch Holtz is maybe fifteen years his senior, a monstrously large man with a head like a broken plate lazily glued back together. If Hutch Holtz has an aura, it's one suffused with a casual brutality that Nick has simultaneously envied and feared throughout their time working together.

One thing he knows: Hutch Holtz tells you to run, man, you *run*.

It's maybe a mile from Nick's apartment, and even with the rain coming down, he makes it quick. There, across the street from the dojo and the Thai place, there's the bus bench, encased in one of those plexiglass-and-steel affairs, protection against nature's punishments. And there's Hutch sitting inside. Right away Nick can tell that something's wrong. He slows to a walk and sits down on the bench next to him, where Hutch has his chin tucked down into his chest. He might even be asleep, but for the single eye that opens up, the foot that pushes the bag Nick's way.

"Take it to Peach," Hutch says. His voice is phlegmy and thick.

"And don't open it," says Nick.

"Right."

"You okay?"

Hutch just nods and closes that one eye.

The bag is black leather, something a doctor would carry on a house call, after traveling in his Studebaker and giving someone a heroin suppository or something. Nick pictures yellowed newspaper, a stethoscope inside. The air is distantly punctuated with sirens.

"Hey," he says, "I passed a shit-ton of police cars heading north on the way over here. That wouldn't have anything to do with this, would it?"

Hutch clears his throat. "Things got away from us."

"You and Tim?"

Again with the nod. "You should get going, Nick."

And it's only after Nick bends down and grabs the bag—you do what Hutch Holtz tells you to do, after all—that he sees the blood covering the man's hand, the hand pressed to the bunched fabric of his jacket.

Sirens in the distance. Nick feels the stirrings of a headache.

"Hutch," Nick says.

Hutch shakes his head.

"Let me call an ambulance."

Hutch lifts his chin and fixes those blue eyes on him. They are electric with intention. Diminished or not, gut-shot or not, here is a man that hurts people for money.

"Fucking *go*," Hutch says. "Please."

Nick stands.

Nick runs.

The blur of traffic, illumination of bar-light and streetlight refracting on puddles, on skeins of gutter water, rain-spotted wind-shields. The bag has some heft to it.

Dipping down a residential street, taking another turn here and here, then standing at a crosswalk waiting for a slow-ass Prius to pass by, he steps into a darkened parking lot and calls 911. Informs them of a wounded man at a bus bench. Gives the cross streets. When the dispatcher asks him to stay on the line, he hangs up. Puts his phone in his pocket and runs home.

He enters the lobby of the Regal Arms, a wide and expansive room, its luster long worn to the nub. Rain drips from his clothes. He opens the elevator gate and presses the button for the fourth floor, the cage lurching and rattling in its ascent. The elevator car is a miasma of odors: cigarette smoke, aftershave, something indefinable but explic-itly entwined with mold and age.

Nick's parents had bought the apartment in the Regal Arms when he was still a kid, after the first Blank Letters album had gone gold and something like that—a record on an indie label getting big—could still make a band enough money to live well. A four-bedroom affair in one of the oldest buildings in downtown: the Regal Arms, which has held on to its own allure the decades since by just the barest skin of its teeth. Propped up by a thin veneer of legacy and endlessly patient repairs by Mr. Contrallo, the septuagenarian main-tenance man, the building years ago placed on the city's historic reg-istry. This means little to anyone save for Contrallo, who's now legally constrained in the manner of which he can do certain repairs and upkeep, given the building's supposed historical importance. "It's no damn good, Nick," Mr. Contrallo has told him for years now, shak-ing his head. "Whole stinking place is just no damn good, I tell you. Falling apart around us."

But it's home nonetheless, and that means that panic is allowed at last to bloom. Hutch, holding his guts in like that. A knife? A bullet?

Stopping in front of his door, Nick peers down at the bag. It's worn with age, a cracked filigree to the leather. Older even than it had seemed at first. The throb behind his eyes grows, mutters.

He opens the bag. The clasp gives way with a satisfying click.

Inside the bag lie piles of banded cash and a severed hand, palm down, the knuckles dusted with hair.

Their front door opens into a short hallway where he and Katherine hang their coats, and this leads then into the large living room, with a carpeted walk-in closet directly to the right, the bathroom to the left. Beyond the living room lie the four bedrooms and the kitchen, all forking out like branches from a tree, hubs from some central wheel.

"That you, hon?" comes his mother's voice from her bedroom. His panic is still taking root in his body, and he quickly walks into his own room, passing his mother's open door. He wants to drop the bag. Throw it out the window. Put it in a dumpster. Wants mostly to step back in time. He shuts his bedroom door and shoves the bag instead into the dark expanse under his bed. Staring at his tangled sheets, he can't think. He's freezing up. A moment later he crouches down and pulls the bag out from beneath his bed and puts it in his closet instead. On the highest shelf, high enough that he has to stretch on his toes to get it there, behind the boxes of his father's archives, stacks of old correspondence and notebooks that Nick is forever telling himself he'll get to.

Is this Peach's money?

Did Peach order this man's hand be cut off?

Where, okay, where is the man who had this hand attached to his wrist at some point? Where's the rest of him?

Nick pivots, lurches, puts a fist to his mouth. Waits for the moment to pass.

He opens his bedroom door and there's his mother with her own fist raised, poised to knock.

Nick recoils, his hand flying to his chest. "Jesus Christ," he says.

"Sorry," says Katherine, looking a little hurt. Her hair is wet, wrapped in a towel.

"No, it's cool." He breathes. Bends over, exhales.

It's an assessing look she gives him, warm enough but measured. He knows he's coming off as weird. But his head suddenly throbs—once, sickly—and after all, there's a severed hand and an unknown amount of money in a bag in his closet.

"I just wanted to let you know," says Katherine, "I ordered pizza. There's plenty left."

"Cool, thanks," Nick says. "I have to run, though. You working tonight?"

"Yeah," she says. "Probably."

"Hit record or TV show?"

"Both, probably," she says, smirking.

"Cool. Let me know if you need me to grab anything while I'm out."

"Okay," she says. Theirs is no longer a relationship where she can demand things from him. It hasn't been that way for years. And that fact alone makes him feel a little guilty. The wretched land mines of love, when your parents begin to need you. And she does, she needs him more than most parents need their children, and he knows that she feels terrible it's that way. Katherine Moriarty has, in the years since her husband's death, stretched her arms around the width of these rooms and held on tight. This apartment is her life and her son is her lifeline and they both know it.

His mother, Katherine Moriarty, the rock icon, the aging troubadour, traveling the same thirty-block radius of her home for the past decade, fear rooting her forever to the same familiar ground.

"I love you," Nick says, managing a smile. "We'll dish when I get home." *Dish.* Their old word, their family lexicon.

Katherine smiles in return and Nick thinks for a moment of her throat slit, the way his hand would look gloved in her blood. His mouth suddenly floods with spit, a surge of nausea. Physical reactions to the horror he's just considered.

He gently shuts his door again and presses his head against the wood. He looks at his phone. It's from Peach. No message, just a call.

Nick calls him back, sits on his bed. The throb in his skull seems centered over his left eye, housed there in the bone. The image of his mother's throat slit is like something plucked from a nightmare and handed to him. Peach's phone rings and Nick, distractedly, thinks about ramming a screwdriver into that pained spot in his skull, imagines a skein of light pouring out, all sickness removed in a spill of trembling illumination. It's another strange thought, and were he not already terrified, that would do it for sure.

Peach picks up. "Nick? You're calling me?" This is unusual, and both he and Nick understand that.

"Hey," Nick says. "I need to talk to you."

Peach takes a moment. Assessing. "Okay. Is this worth talking about on the phone?"

"No. But I have something for you."

"You do."

"Yeah, someone passed it on to me."

"A friend of ours?"

"Yes."

"Good," says Peach. He sounds relieved. "You did good. Listen, we'll meet at our place, okay? Bring the thing. One hour."

"Okay."

"Let me ask you something," says Peach. "How are you feeling?"

"How am I feeling?" Nick laughs. "I'm freaked out, dude, if I'm being honest."

"Okay. But other than that."

"I don't know. My head hurts."

"You know what? Make it forty-five minutes. You've done good."

OPERATION: HEAVY LIGHT

S/NF/CL-INTEL A-7/03—SECRET TRANSCRIPT—EXCERPT

DATE: XX/XX/XXXX

Q: How much you get for it?

A: Sir, I—

Q: Christ, Seaver, don't "sir" me. We're so far past that. What'd you get for the hand? Who'd you sell it to? You get rich? Motherfucker, tell me you at least got rich.

A: Director Lundy, it's not . . . it wasn't like that.

Q: Yeah? Okay. Tell me what it was like.

A: . . .

Q: Seaver.

A: It wasn't . . . I didn't have a plan. I didn't sell it to anyone.

Q: What'd you do then? Because, to me, it looks like you just disabled every single safety protocol we ever set regarding the containment of a profoundly valuable and volatile asset, an asset owned by the government of the United States. A key asset, Seaver, to a clandestine, classified operation. And you walk out of Camelot with it like you're going out for a fucking cigarette. So go ahead and tell me what the plan was.

A: The hand got ahold of me, sir.

Q: . . .

A: It snared me, kind of.

Q: Jesus.

A: I'm being straight with you, sir. It got ahold of me, and I walked out with it, out of the base. I went down to . . . you know the Lucky Lounge?

Q: . . .

A: . . .

Q: Please tell me you're shitting me.

A: It was like I was in a dream. Like, I kept telling myself it was a bad idea, I knew it, that I was looking at a court martial—

Q: Oh, if you're lucky.

A: —and still, it was like I was moving through a fog. I can't explain it better than that. But it was exactly like the debrief, sir. Just like you told us could happen if we weren't careful. There's a reason we keep it in the box. I see that now.

Q: Motherfucker, don't appease me. Where'd you put it?

A: . . .

Q: Goddamnit, Seaver.

A: Should I lawyer up, sir?

Q: Lawyer up? You're serious?

A: I mean . . .

Q: If you lawyer up, it means I'll have to officially charge you. Given that this is an asset you just fucking *walked out of the base with,* you understand those charges will be dire, right? Why don't you just save us all some time and tell me where you left the hand, so I can figure out how to get this horror show wrapped up.

A: I left it on the toilet.

Q: What?

A: Uh, the toilet.

Q: You left the remnant on the back of the toilet. In the bathroom of the Lucky Lounge. There off Highway 99.

A: Yes, sir.

Q: This whole thing—the entire objective of this agency—is based on the idea of being *low risk*. Insular. Not a lot of intel trails. Off the books. This isn't Central Intelligence, it's not Langley. We do shit in the dark here. *That's* the gift. And then you fucking bring the remnant outside the wire? Jesus Christ. To a *bar*?

A: It got ahold of me.

Q: You keep saying that. You keep saying it. Should've kept it in the fucking box, Seaver. Now all we have is Michael—*dying* Michael, right?—and a handful of agents cleaning up *your* fucking mess.

A: . . .

Q: You have any idea of what you've done? Any clue the shitstorm that you've started?

A: I'm sorry, sir.

Q: Oh, man. Oh, I can't even tell you how little your sorry matters to me.

NICK COFFIN

Some items that Nick Coffin has procured for Peach Serrano:
A copy of the first pressing of the *Bullet 7"* by the Misfits, both vinyl and sleeve graded conservatively at Near Mint. Despite the fact that the record came out in '78, and was limited to only 1,000 copies, this one was actually pretty easy for Nick to line up. Not cheap, but easy. Just a matter of buying it off Discogs for $3,000, applying his 15 percent cut ("Be sure to add a little something for yourself" was Peach's usual gesture at playing a mafia don) and gingerly, in a padded cardboard mailer meant specifically for such things, sliding it across the table to Peach in their usual booth at Mercy's. Peach seems diametrically opposed to the punk type, but he is wealthy enough and willing enough to embrace his whims and peculiarities. He probably just heard about the band somewhere, and that was it. He is, above all, a collector of things, a man who must own and possess. While collectors are sometimes brutally niche about what they collect, sometimes they just want what they want. Randomness isn't something that Peach owns the market on, not by a long shot. A lot of the folks that use Nick are like this too.

A first edition of Charles Mackay's *Memoirs of Extraordinary Popular Delusions and the Madness of Crowds,* a three-volume set published in London in 1841. This one had taken some footwork; Peach could sometimes be noncommittal about the specifics of his wants. "The client," he'd said, "just wants an old-timey book about the mental state of witch hunts. You feel me? How it's a mental thing and not really, you know, about witches and shit. But old-timey, back when that was a kind of unusual idea or whatever."

"Old-timey?"

And Peach, perpetually unreadable, had just shrugged. Looked at him like *Come on.* "I'm not making the rules on this one, Nick. That's what the guy wants."

Sometimes Peach does this—does "the client" thing—even though they both know that Peach buys a thing for Peach because Peach wants it.

He'd fallen down some internet rabbit holes to line up copies of the Mackay books. Found a book dealer in Florida who became extremely animated at the prospect of selling the set when Nick called him. A price was discussed. Nick okayed it with Peach. The money was sent along with a significant amount of paperwork and a request for a certificate of authenticity. With Nick's cut and insurance and all the various fees, the three books had run over $13,000. Peach hadn't blinked. Yet this is the same guy who will send Hutch Holtz and Tim Reed after someone who owes him five hundred bucks.

A WWII Japanese *kyu-gunto* officer's blade. This hangs on Peach's wall in his den now, next to the flatscreen that constantly shows MMA fights. The last time Nick was over, Peach saw him looking at it and smiled.

"Looks good, right?"

"Yeah, man. Looks fancy up there."

"I walk around with that thing sometimes, when I'm thinking. Just getting my mind right. Freaks Don out, but whatever."

Nick at the time had found it hard to imagine Don Sr. being remotely freaked out by such a thing—by anything, really—but had wisely kept his mouth shut.

A Vietnam-era grenade. He'd just been told, "One of those grenades from 'Nam." That was all. He'd gone to Vicente Contrallo and asked where he might buy one.

"Does it need to have a charge in it?" Mr. Contrallo had asked. "If not, you can buy them at the military surplus stores. No problem." They'd been standing in the hallway, Mr. Contrallo working the vacuum cleaner up and down the carpet, and he'd turned it off and stared at Nick with an intensity that used to intimidate the hell out of him as a younger man. But that was just Mr. Contrallo—he looked at the world like he was ready to be disappointed in it. He'd been that way forever. But his question was a good one. He texted Peach with it, and got a simple Yes back.

"I guess it does, yeah."

"Well, son," said Mr. Contrallo, leaning a fist on the handle of the vacuum. "I can't really help you with that. Those grenades are, what? Fifty years old now. Thing might never detonate or they might blow up in your hand. I wouldn't mess with them, even if you find one."

"Alright, Mr. Contrallo, thanks much."

In the end, he had asked Hutch Holtz, who had talked to Tim Reed, who had helped Nick line someone up. Both men had required their own finder's fees, so his take on the grenade hadn't been much, but Peach had been happy, and Nick was only marginally embarrassed that two of Peach's other guys had done the bulk of the legwork for him.

The important thing is, he's a collector, Peach. First and foremost. And if he wants something, Nick helps him get it. He's got three, four other clients like Peach, though none who pay as well or as frequently. It's a job that gives Nick space to breathe, and allows him room to help Katherine out, keep an eye on her. At times he ruminates on the fact that maybe it is a small, inconsequential life he lives—helping questionably bad men procure things for their vanity, their sense of superiority, their need to own the world—but there are undoubtedly more difficult ways to spend his days.

Most recently, Peach had demanded recordings from numbers stations. "I want classified shit. None of that YouTube business. The real deal."

Nick had scratched his neck, uneasy. They were at Mercy's again, and someone was playing the Stones on the jukebox, loud. Peach didn't seem to mind, just drank his water and amaretto, looking at Nick like getting this stuff was the easiest thing in the world. Finally, Nick had asked, "Like, military numbers stations, Peach? Like spy shit?"

"Yeah," said Peach, grinning. "Just like that."

So he'd gone down another rabbit hole in an entirely different way. It had taken some searching and low-slung, veiled questions to people on various sub-lists and servers in order to find a guy who claimed to have what he needed. Again, there was the necessary financial permission-seeking from Peach, which he'd granted after Nick told him the guy's name and his eyes had brightened. "Oh, I know that guy! He's cool. Yeah, go for it, man."

Such was the small world of finders like Nick and buyers like Peach. So Nick, maybe three weeks before Hutch Holtz would give him a bag full of cash and a severed human hand, had boarded a plane, landed at JFK, then jumped on a shuttle. Navigating the subway, he'd run a few necessary errands until he'd found himself standing in front of a brownstone in Brooklyn, leaves shirring crisply at his feet. Everyone looked like a model to him, even the old men with their wool hats and bulbed noses, their hacking coughs. Nick found the name he was looking for on the callbox. It was not the name of the man he was supposed to see, but subterfuge was key to all this, wasn't it? Everyone loved their playacting. He took a moment, turned around, the Brooklyn sky like a caul, this tacit understanding that he was surrounded by millions of souls here, hundreds of millions of tons of brick and concrete and steelwork. His mother would have perished here, straight up, could not have managed a place like this, and it was a moment when he'd felt a little closer to her fears, her constrictions. A rare instance, that understanding, and he stood there with his finger poised over the callbox for a second, wanting to just stay there for a moment, live in that feeling. Then he turned and pressed the button.

Almost immediately, a static-heavy voice came over the intercom: "Yah?" Foreign accent. German, maybe?

"It's me," Nick said.

Then he was walking up a wooden flight of steps, the wood glossy at the edges, battered and colorless in the middle, a lifetime of shoes having done their work. The walls were popcorned and he traced his fingers along one as he clomped along. He wondered if Katherine was doing okay.

Rachmann's apartment door had been open, symphony music quietly drifting out, and he'd thought, Oh, here we go. This shall be a *presentation*, apparently. He was used to this sort of thing by now—he understood that Peach could have done all of this on his own if he truly wanted to dedicate the time and resources to it. It could be challenging, but not *that* hard. But the legwork and presentation, the endless fucking egos he came into contact with, they were all part of it.

A gentle knock on Rachmann's open door. Rachmann—the only name he was given, and most likely an invented one. Nick saw varnished wood floors, dark paneling that went up half the wall, a floor rug threaded with gold and crimson. The air smelled of incense. Prospect Park was across the street. The windows had hand-swoops cutting through the dirt. The place vibed safe house to him.

"Come in," Rachmann said, and Nick stepped through the doorway only a little afraid. What he was buying, after all, was not entirely legal. The data was not meant to be understood by laymen, and to seize it like this, like grasping a leaf as it floated along a digital wind, brought with it a certain risk.

Rachmann stepped out of a bedroom at the end of the hall. "You found me," he said, as if it was some kind of joke. The music was playing from speakers the size of Nick's fist, moored high on the walls. A coffee table, a wooden chair, a beaten couch the color of grass.

Rachmann sat down on the couch. He opened up a laptop on the coffee table. He was thin like Nick, with a dark shock of black hair. Roughly his age. He wore a black button-up with the sleeves rolled. Dark jeans. He motioned behind Nick with a wave of his hand. "Do you mind shutting the door?"

Nick closed the door and Rachmann gestured that he might sit on the couch as well. Now that he was here, it was hardly the skull-and-bones kind of subterfuge one might expect for the amount of money Nick—or Peach—was paying. It felt like a school play. Children pretending at spywork.

"How were your travels?" Rachmann asked, beginning to tap away at the laptop.

"Fine," Nick said.

"I'm not much for flying, personally." Not German, Nick decided. Austrian, maybe.

"No?" he said.

Rachmann shook his head. "I get a bit nervous. I mean, I can do it, I *do* do it, you know, but I feel like the plane has a certain arc. Like it rises and has this inevitable decline. A rock or a bullet or something, you know? I feel if we don't get back on the ground before the decline is done, well." He grinned, showing what was surely a childhood's worth of costly orthodontia. "Then it's all over."

Nick wasn't sure what to say, so he smiled, nodded.

"Anyway, you have the money?"

"I do." Nick was uncomfortable with traveling with that much cash, so Peach had wired it to him once he'd touched down. Nick took the stack of bills out of his jacket pocket and held it up.

"All there?"

"You can count it," Nick said, "but I'd like to get assurances first." It felt ridiculous, speaking like this, but if he made a mistake here and didn't discover it until he was back in Portland? Well, it was a long way back to Prospect Park.

"Sure," Rachmann said, "totally." He spun the laptop Nick's way and clicked the mouse, a program springing to life. The screen showed some kind of code—rows of colored columns, files—and a moment later came a musical burst of feedback, like a router booting up, and then the chilling, nearly robotic intonation of a woman speaking. "Omega Alpha Lima. Omega Alpha Lima. Alpha Six Four One Six. Alpha Six Four One Six. The bear is in the briars. We love her, we love her. The bear is in the briars."

He couldn't help it—he felt a thrill walk up his spine, the tingle of blood in his scalp. It felt like hearing a ghost. "This is a current station?"

Rachmann nodded. "This was broadcast"—he bent down and squinted at the monitor—"on Tuesday, from . . . Argentina, I think. Somewhere in the Gran Chaco region."

"Okay. Cool."

An expansive shrug. "But it's not like . . . Even this one," and here Rachmann clicked on another file and beneath the layers of static came the mechanical sound of a young child reading a five-digit code again and again, with a series of clicks buried beneath it. He stood up, brushed his hair back from his face. "Hear those beeps? Those clicking sounds?"

"Yeah."

"That's also code. The voice—and it's not actually a little girl, either. That's a Stasi Sprach machine that's just had its pitch adjusted to make it sound like a little kid—that isn't the real code. It's those clicks underneath, that's what's really being transmitted. And that's from last month." Rachmann scratched his nose. "Plus," he said, "they're able to bounce these signals. That one from Argentina? Might actually be down the street from here. They jump the signals. It's all about relaying minute bursts of untraceable information."

"But they're real?"

Rachmann looked a little offended. "I mean, yes, my friend, they're real. This is not my sister making these recordings in her bedroom."

"And these are the only copies?"

He looked out the window and then back at Nick. "I mean, they're the only copies *I* have. And it wasn't easy to gain access to this site. But can I guarantee these are the only copies in existence? No. These agencies—some of them legitimate, and others are . . ." Rachmann looked up at the ceiling. "Operationally black. You know?"

"Spies."

"Yes, okay. But funded secretly, I mean. Dark agencies. Not like the CIA, things in your Pentagon budget. 'We spend this much on pencils, this much on bullets, this much on encryption equipment.'"

"I understand."

Rachmann stuck a USB drive into the side of the laptop. "So, could I have made copies of these for myself? Yes. Have I? No."

"Okay."

"So you can watch me delete these files," Rachmann said, "but are they truly the only ones? No. Because these aren't intended for us, after all."

He typed briefly and pulled the thumb drive from the monitor, dropped it into Nick's palm. "I know that for people like you, you want the thing. Your clients want something tangible they can hold. And its rarity affords more value, yes?"

"That's what interests my client, yes."

Rachmann smiled. "I have an idea of who your client might be, and I agree with you. He is a motivated buyer. Meanwhile, these agencies will be able to tell that these files have been listened to, downloaded. I'll need to cover my tracks, as it were." He seemed pleased at the idea.

"Are you in danger?" Nick asked, meaning, of course, *Am I in danger?*

"No. Not like that."

And that had been it. Nick had watched him delete the files—or at least claim to. Rachmann counted through the money, Nick pocketed the thumb drive. They rose in that nearly empty room with the sound of traffic bleary and hushed through the dirty glass. They didn't shake hands.

"I'm operating under the assumption I don't need to threaten you or anything, right?"

Rachmann had smiled again, squinted one eye in confusion. "I'm sorry?"

Nick felt silly, but the idea of trying to find Rachmann again, particularly if Rachmann didn't want to be found and Peach was unhappy, seemed profoundly unappealing.

"It's a little tiresome, I guess, but if these aren't what you say they are, my client will be disappointed. And that, I promise you, is the last thing that you want."

Rachmann had put his hands in his pockets. "You don't have to worry about that," he said softly. Nick could tell he had offended the man.

"Okay. That's good."

They'd left it like that, and Nick had crashed in a hotel and flown back home the next day. And the day after that, he had met with Peach at Mercy's, given him the thumb drive, accepted his payment.

And now? Now he's headed to that very same bar with a worn leather bag in his hands and panic like a bird trying to flex its wings in his throat. It is hard to breathe, the elevator car clattering down to the lobby, Nick feeling the weight of his decisions threatening to undo him.

Everything's easy until it's not.

Mercy's is the same as ever. Glossed bar-top to the left, with the big expanse of the room—a pair of pool tables, a shitty jukebox, a shuffleboard as warped as the bridge of a prizefighter's nose—to the right. A line of booths. Burn-pitted tables here and there. Peach is in his usual booth, near the exit sign.

He nods when he sees Nick. Peach Serrano is a small, fit man in a wool coat and slacks, dressed too nicely for a place like Mercy's, save for the fact that no one gives a shit. They briefly embrace, Peach clapping his hand against Nick's back.

"Pissing out there," he says, watching Nick swipe rainwater from his hair.

"Yeah," Nick says. "It's been off and on."

"Thank you for reaching out, Nick." Peach sips his water. "This thing got away from me a bit."

"That's what Hutch said."

Peach nods. "You saw him?"

"At the drop-off." Nick cranes his neck to make sure they're alone. "He was gut-shot or something."

Peach takes a slow breath. "That's unfortunate."

Nick does not tell Peach that he called 911.

"Hand me the bag," Peach says.

Nick hands him the bag beneath the table.

"Did you look inside?"

He could lie, but it would be a lie large enough that his face would tell. Peach would see. "I did."

"And?"

"And what?" Nick asked.

"You said your head hurt. Does your head still feel bad?"

"Does what's in the bag have something to do with that?"

Peach shrugs. Meaning *You tell me*. Peach and his vacuousness. Making you earn every sentence, every gesture.

"Yeah, my head hurts. I don't feel good. I feel like the thing in the bag—and I'm not talking about the money—is poison."

Peach looks at him sharply. "There's money in here?"

"I thought you knew that."

Peach looks in the bag and spends a moment taking it in. He shuts it, and there are things at work in his face now, his eyes.

"I guess Hutch didn't tell you."

"It's not important," Peach says.

"I can see the value in the object, Peach. There's something about it. But I'm glad to pass it on too."

"Good," Peach says.

They step out onto the sidewalk. Trees skeletal and dripping, traffic. Moon glowing behind scudded clouds.

"Thank you again, Nick. I'll be in touch soon, and I'll compensate you for your work tonight. You helped me out."

"You think Hutch'll be okay?" And does Nick truly care? About Hutch Holtz? No, probably not, but he is a part of the gathering of men that surround Peach, men who cushion the harshness of his life, men who help afford him this air of invincibility.

If someone can hurt Hutch, someone can hurt Nick.

Peach smiles. He holds the bag in front of him, grips the handle with both hands. "Hutch has been through worse."

"Okay."

And then Peach frowns; he twists, staggers. Someone across the street coughs. Peach rights himself and touches his shirt, examines his fingertips. They come away black against the wash of neon light thrown from the windows. He looks up at Nick, confused.

A black circle appears on Peach's cheek. The size of a dime. Something wet happens behind his head, to his head. The window of Mercy's is suddenly starred, and spattered in clots of Peach's brains. Customers look up, confused, pint glasses halfway to their mouths. Someone screams inside the bar. It sounds ludicrous and strange.

"Urk," Peach says. His gaze has turned inward, pulled toward some dark interior. He falls against the window and then topples over onto the pavement.

Nick bends and picks up the bag—some grim insistence that he do so, some whisper in spite of himself—and he pivots, sprinting down the sidewalk as a flurry of bullets smack into the building, the window, the percussive quality of the gunshots getting louder and more ragged. It's a silencer, he thinks wildly, that's a silencer, and it's wearing out. He hears his own feet against the pavement, the fade of people's screams inside the bar.

The bag slaps against Nick's leg as he runs, and he's amazed at how light it is. He swears in the maddened whirl of his thoughts that he can feel the hand flopping around in there like a fish brought onto land, banging against his leg.

He runs.

Imagines too easily a bullet zipping through the dark, seeking the weak meat of his body, the sweet and fragile bowl of his skull, the brittle, standing tower of his spinal column.

He just runs.

JOHN BONNER

Weils offers him the shot.

Bonner knows it's a test—of fealty, of allegiance to the agency, of his ego. Probably, in Weils's mind, it's simply a test of what kind of man he is. He waves her off. Black ops is always a risk, but this is different. Saint Michael has given them one more clue—*Nicholas. Coffin.* Two clues, they thought, until Bonner suggested it might actually be a name. And it was. Saint Michael, doing the impossible, pulling an entire name from the ether. At great cost, according to Lundy, as his decay seems to be accelerating. They'd run the suggestion to Lundy—what if Nicholas Coffin is a name—and Lundy had run it through the databases at Camelot and come back with an address. An apartment building on the Westside, close-in.

"You'll never guess who he lives with," Lundy had said over Weils's speakerphone. "His mom's Katherine Moriarty."

Both Weils and Bonner had sat there.

Lundy, impatient: "You don't know who that is?"

"No."

"She's the singer in the Blank Letters."

Weils: "You mean the song?"

"Yeah, I mean the song, Weils."

"What the hell."

Bonner could tell Lundy was smiling over the phone. "I know, right? Wild-ass coincidence. Cosmic-level shit. Enough to believe someone's pulling strings on our behalf, baby."

Lundy had sent them everything the agency had on Nick Coffin over Weils's phone. It wasn't a lot. Father a suicide, mother living on residuals and smart investments. Coffin had never been arrested. His driver's license photo showed a thin, pale man, all neck and cheekbones. Mid-twenties, maybe.

"He's just a kid," Bonner said.

Weils, who had shot two men to death in front of a pizza restaurant not fifteen minutes earlier, said nothing.

Bonner wondered how Michael was getting all this information. The visions he had offered the agency previously had been sparing and infrequent. Lundy seemed to be pushing him hard now. Bonner turned the SUV around and headed for the Burnside Bridge, the dark thread of the Willamette beneath.

Coffin's apartment building was an old one, right off Burnside, one of the last bastions holding tight against downtown's influx of brushed-steel box condos and microbreweries. But before they even had a chance to get out of the vehicle, they saw Coffin step out of the apartment lobby with a black bag in his hands.

"That's the bag," Bonner said. He couldn't help himself, the excitement in his voice. "You want to take him?"

"Hold on," Weils said. "Just follow him."

"Weils."

"I want to see where he goes with it."

So Bonner had let Coffin get a block and a half ahead and then crept forward in the SUV. The guy's opsec was for shit, no scanning, nothing. But he was just some kid, after all. Weils took the phone off speaker, talked to Lundy. Then she hung up. "Okay, we're supposed to wait and see who he hands it off to."

Bonner had opened his mouth to protest and then decided against it. What would be the point? He was Lundy's dead weight—and his concerns would raise no flags. They followed Coffin to a bar called Mercy's, and Weils had him pull the SUV into a gravel lot across the street, a lot zoned for more condos and laced in chain link. Weils clambered into the back and took a case from the trunk. After the rifle was pieced together, the silencer fat as a soda bottle at the end, that's when she'd asked him if he wanted to take the shot.

"You're gonna drop whoever has that bag? Right here in the middle of town?"

"Drop him and whoever else comes out, yeah," said Weils. "Or you can."

This, after she'd executed the driver in the hatchback, the civilian in the street.

Bonner passes and Weils smirks, and her air of superiority diffuses through the SUV while they wait. Bonner, meanwhile, makes himself useful and quietly switches their plates with a spare set kept in the back.

Just as he finishes, Nick Coffin steps out of the bar with another man. Half a foot shorter, squat, dressed like he's on a dinner date. He's holding the bag with both hands, talking to Coffin. Weils is crouched in the backseat, using the windowsill as a rest.

It sounds like someone coughing in a library, that first shot.

There's no permission, there's no warning. She hits the well-dressed guy in the arm, and Bonner watches as he staggers, touching his shoulder in wonder and confusion, still holding the bag. Then another cough, and the man's head spills out the back of his skull and Coffin, as if he's been ready this entire time, grabs the bag from the ground and runs.

Weils, hard-ass and senior agent and all the rest, fires a volley of shots after him and, as far as Bonner can tell, misses every damn time.

We should've taken him on the street when we had the chance, he thinks, peeling out in a clatter of gravel, headlights tumbling and jouncing over the street. *Could've shot the guy in the legs and been done with it. Have the hand back in its dumb little box by now, finished with all this horseshit.*

And then he's gone, Coffin. Turns a corner and by the time Bonner rounds it in the SUV, he's vanished. Through a doorway, down the mouth of an alley. Leapt into a car, who knows. But he's gone.

"Fuck," Weils hisses under her breath. She gets on the phone to Lundy.

How many chances do we get, Bonner wonders. *The bodies have to stack up how high before we're done with this?*

Weils hangs up again. "Go to his house," she says.

"His apartment?"

"His house, Bonner, yes. His apartment." She climbs into the back and starts disassembling the rifle. "We'll wait for him there."

Bonner can't keep quiet. "That was some fucking tremendously reckless shit, Weils. I can't even—"

"Not another word," she says. "The last thing I need is a dressing-down from *you* about recklessness." She bends back to her work. "I don't want to hear it."

KATHERINE MORIARTY

It was never discussed, her taking Matthew's name. Some unspoken understanding between them—walking through the world with the name "Katherine Coffin" would've been too ridiculous. Or Kathy. Kat Coffin? Pure cringe-level idiocy. Maybe if the Blank Letters had done rockabilly. Her with a bouffant and a polka-dotted dress. Tattoo of a bat on her throat. As it was, she kept her name, but when pressed—and Matthew *had* pressed, to be certain, pressing had been ingrained into the very atoms of the man's personality—she'd let her son take his last name. It seemed a bad omen, in retrospect—her boy, taking on the name of a casket?—but Katherine was not one to lean toward omens. Intuition, yes. A scrappy sense of self-preservation, sure. But it wasn't like alarms had gone off—at least not in regards to that, his name. And Matthew had demanded, pleaded. *What if,* he'd said to her more than once, in all seriousness, *I die, Katherine? What then? The only son of an only son? I want someone to carry on my name. My blood.*

Back when the notion of his dying had seemed an abstraction. Some point in an argument to be proven.

But he had certainly died, hadn't he? Gruesomely and spectacularly.

Katherine is standing in the shower with her bottle of beer. It's a treat, an early evening nightcap before she hunkers down in her room and goes about writing her little songs, either ones she'll file away on a hard drive, or something for the next episode of *Bad Luck Gun,* the television show she writes scores for. She takes a sip, sets the bottle down on the lip of the tub, enjoying that brittle clack of glass against porcelain. She sighs, scrubs her face. When she was young, it was all unabashed rage, a dismantling of the walls, acidic contempt toward the powers that be. All of it done to a four-four beat, a chorus that made you want to ram your head through a wall. Now? Now she's old and tired and the world's a small and unyielding place. Getting old's the fucking pits, isn't it?

Stepping out of the shower, she wraps herself in her terrycloth robe, the one Matthew had bought for her. Was it the year before Nick was born? For a man like that, so inventive, it showed a profound lack of imagination. A robe. And he *could* be inventive, romantic, kind. Songs written for her, songs he never recorded, never played for anyone else. Airline tickets—when they could afford it—to some event she had randomly expressed interest in, some off-Broadway theater performance she'd heard of, or a band she'd wanted to see. *Let's get Glenda to watch the kid. I booked us a room at the Chelsea,* he'd say, sneering it, so aware of the deathly hipsterism of such a place and not caring. Embracing it, even. *We'll be back tomorrow night. Fuck it, Katherine, why not? You only live once.* He was not always like that, no, of course not, but who could honestly say they were? He was like that *sometimes,* though, pure like that. Kind. It was hard to remember that their life together had not all been misery and embattlement, that love had been at the core for a long time. Love had called the shots for years.

Anyway, here she is, wearing the tattered old thing. She's stitched its seams more than once over the years. She towels her hair dry, the steam slowly crawling off the mirror, her face growing more and more clear. Creams applied to her face, hands, elbows. "Unguents," she says to herself, and smiles for the first time that evening. Katherine is feeling better. She retrieves her beer bottle from the shower.

Into the living room. The windows are closed, the curtains drawn. She flips through her albums, puts on Randy Weston's *African Cookbook*—jubilant, buoyed jazz. She is feeling good. She *is* good, she decides.

In her room the bed is made, with the tasseled bedspread hanging in equal parts on all three sides. When your world is small like this, fastidiousness rules. Her bedside table has her book, her reading glasses, a coffee cup half-filled with water from the previous night. Her desk with her computer and a small Yamaha keyboard she uses to snag the melodies flitting through her head, easier to quickly grab them with that than the Les Paul Bulldog that leans in its stand next to a tiny Orange crate amp. The walls are decorated with framed posters, shows from Katherine's youth. Everything is cut-and-paste xerography, letter transfers, blown-out halftones. Her indie-rock days, her punk days, belting out songs of sex and irony and fury. This is how she lives now, this apartment her geography, the expanse of her world. A woman relentlessly cradling her younger self, a life clocked by the falling and rising sun, the striations of light as it bends throughout the rooms of the apartment. Then the endless nights. The tether of her phone to the larger world. The aortic sounds of the building's tenants as they move throughout their own lives. Her son's leaving and coming home and leaving again, the way he has returned to her since Matthew's death, even more beloved to her. Her history and her fear and her questions about Matthew, about what happened those last few strange and terrible days of his life, all binding her to these rooms like sutures. Like chains that root her to the ground. So many years of her life spent here, in these rooms.

She puts on a Bauhaus T-shirt and black jeans from her dresser, and the playful bass rollick of Weston's "Willie's Tune" meanders through the apartment. It is nighttime, but Katherine will be up for hours. She is sitting on her bed, putting on a pair of black Converse—

good luck shoes, *songwriting* shoes, baby—when there's a knock on the door and Katherine stops, frozen.

No one knocks. Nick just comes in with his key, and Mr. Contrallo has long ago learned to call first if there is an inspection or repair to be done.

She pads to the door—pausing when the break between songs takes place, as if the sounds of her Chucks on the carpet might inform the people outside of her whereabouts—and puts her eye to the peephole.

A man and a woman. She has a bob of red hair, a dark blouse and slacks. A look of drawn severity on her face. The man's in a suit, has the broad shoulders and bland handsomeness of a second-rate soap opera star. They minutely jostle and adjust themselves, waiting. The man frowns down at the carpet. The woman looks right at the peephole, right at Katherine.

The woman says, "Open the door, please." The man opens his coat and pulls out a badge, holds it before the peephole. The image is distorted. It could be anything. Something bought off the internet. They could be anyone. She realizes he's held up his badge because he can see her feet limned against the light of her living room, beneath the bottom of the door. They know she's standing there.

"We're detectives with the Portland Police Bureau," the woman says. "This will only take a second. We just have a few questions about one of your neighbors."

Worrying the collar of her shirt, her eye still to the peephole, Katherine says, "I'm sorry, I'm not decent."

"We can wait, ma'am. We don't want to inconvenience you."

She walks back to her bedroom and stands there in the open doorway, thinking. Perhaps they *are* police. Perhaps they *are* looking for a neighbor. It's not like Katherine is some bastion of—

The front door explodes with a crack. She screams, staggers against the bed.

"Watch her," the woman says, and begins making a quick circuit through the apartment. Katherine screams again—curdling, loud, something to bring the neighbors to their doors—and the man raises his pistol toward her through the bedroom doorway and calmly tells her to be quiet. His calmness is at direct, surreal odds with what is happening. Katherine crumples to the carpet and looks around for some kind of object to defend herself with. The man steps into her bedroom. He asks where Nicholas Coffin is, and it's like watching rocks tumble from someone's mouth, the way those words don't make any sense to her. That name. She can hear the woman knocking things over in the bathroom—there is the clatter of plastic bottles falling to the floor. Don't knock over my beer, she thinks randomly, and then it hits her like a blow—these people with their guns, they're looking for her son. Looking for Nick.

"What the hell is this?" someone says in the hall. "Katherine?" She half rises and there in the hallway is Mr. Contrallo. He is wearing a white T-shirt smeared with oil, and there's a tool belt on his hips. The front door hangs crooked on its upper hinges. The woman walks from the bathroom and fires twice. It's terrifying, how loud the gun is in the apartment. A bullet punches through the plaster and lath beside Mr. Contrallo's face. The second bullet hits his shoulder, spinning him as if he were the drunken father at a wedding, a man doing a dance move beyond his abilities. He falls to the floor. Katherine screams again.

The woman stalks into her room and grabs Katherine by the arm, hoisting her up. "Where the fuck is it?" she hisses.

"It's in the kitchen," Katherine sobs. "Behind the coffee pot." The woman shoves Katherine to the bed and heads that way and Katherine for a moment is left alone; the man is now standing over Mr. Contrallo in the hallway, pressing his hand to the old man's wound. Katherine runs out of her room, into the living room, out the front door and into the building's hallway. She hears the woman curse behind her, and the man rises to grasp at her as she passes, and Katherine is *on* him, snarling, her nails at his face, his eyes. His fist glances off her ribs and she goes breathless, staggers. Mr. Contrallo, there on the floor between them, he reaches up and grasps the man's wrist, and she's free, pivoting and launching herself down the hall.

"Don't do it," she hears the man say behind her. "Weils, goddamnit, you don't need to."

She turns the corner and hears Mr. Contrallo say, "No, please," and then there is the bright peal of another gunshot.

Katherine hits the stairwell door with both hands, hears thundering footsteps behind her, all the while his name in her mind, *Nicholas Coffin, Nicholas Coffin,* how strange it had sounded coming from that man's mouth.

NICK COFFIN

Matthew Coffin had leapt from the Hawthorne Bridge into the Willamette River when Nick was fifteen. Three months before that, Matthew had moved out, taken up residence in a loft apartment in the Pearl that some musician friend had let him crash in. He saw little of his father during those three months, and did not miss him terribly. The father he had loved so much—the man who had read books to him at night in the squeaky voice of one of Nick's stuffed animals, the man who had let Nick incessantly smack a hand drum while Matthew worked out a new song with his guitar and a notebook, and would casually inform his friends that he was in a band with his seven-year-old—that man had eventually, by the time he left, been carved into something different. Gone was the man who would almost shyly ask to hold Nick's hand as they walked down the street. Would randomly, as Nick got older, put a stack of CDs on his bed for him to check out when he got home from school. By Nick's fifteenth birthday, Matthew had started acting erratic and unpredictable, prone to rages, bouts of paranoia, and eventually Katherine had told him to pack his shit and go; they had been unhappy in their marriage for some time, Nick knew that much. He recognized, now, just how much the band had bound them together, and when the Blank Letters split, the marriage began to fray as well. Still cadaverously handsome, Matthew took to wearing sunglasses those last three months, day and night, even inside, even hanging out with Nick. He'd drift off in mid-sentence, would come out of these little nod-offs spasming and slapping at himself, like waking from a bad dream. Muttering to himself. He had become a different man. The only thing that made sense to a fifteen-year-old Nick was dope, and it felt like a knife in the heart, as if the man had had this one thing—a family, a son and a wife—and chose this other thing instead.

The loft his father spent his last months in was cavernous, dark. Dirty light falling on rough cement floors. A ceiling of high, exposed timbers. A toilet ringed in permanent water stains. The clatter and rattle of pipes through the walls whenever it was flushed. There had been no TV, just a little boom box on the floor with a scattering of cassettes and compact discs around it. His father had written feverishly in his notebooks on his bed while Nick had read his own book, somewhat frightened by Matthew's behavior. He'd only visited the loft a few times, and didn't even tell Katherine how unrelentingly strange it had been there, hearing the scribble of his father's pen in his notebooks, the whispering under his breath, his occasional giggle, knowing it would simply fuel her vindication. That she'd use it as another wedge against Matthew, when it made Nick more sad than anything else. Had he been a few years older, he might have been more suited to understand the depth of just how unwell Matthew had become.

He's certain Matthew Coffin had loved him. Nick has no doubt. For every memory of his father's rages, or his later erraticism and distancing, he remembers a man who laughed, taught him how to read, how to play "Blitzkrieg Bop" on the acoustic. Some biographies have attempted to paint his father as an unabashed narcissist—and Katherine would probably agree with that—but Nick has plenty of memories of his father's love, his involvement, the way he included his son, brought forth and nurtured Nick's better qualities. With shortcomings and flaws that glared brighter the closer you looked, he'd still been a dad. But the way those last six or nine months had unspooled in the apartment, and then the loft; *that* had felt different for sure. And it was, he thinks, the beginning of his mother's illness, her fear of the larger world. Not when Matthew died, but when he left—that, Nick believes, was when Katherine's world began to grow smaller and smaller.

Fans of the band have reached out to him, the son, over the years, as if he might serve as some kind of lifeline to Matthew, to the band as a whole. Might stir the ashes of history and sentimentality for them. But that type of thing, it's not for him. His allegiance now is to the living, to his mother. His mother needs enough help navigating the daily intricacies of her life; there's little room left to be constantly exhuming the corpse of his father's intentions.

It was the same reason why he's never gone through Matthew's archives, those boxes of paperwork in Nick's closet. Just . . . the resuscitation of it. Bringing all of that near his heart again? No thanks, man. Does he love his father still? Yes. Sometimes fiercely. The simple gesture of his father taking Nick's hand in his own rattles around inside him like some moaning, insistent ghost. Making his stuffed bear tell jokes in a terrible Brooklyn accent, his father smelling of cigarettes and coffee, the sound of the rain falling outside Nick's bedroom window. Memories bound like bent wire around his heart. But given the vast fields of pain his mother has trod through—and still does—regarding Matthew's death, the price of sentimentality is simply too high. *Yes*, Nick imagines himself saying, *my father could be incendiary*, some mic snapped to his shirt, staring at some middle distance away from the camera, a blown-up Blank Letters poster behind him.

Yes, at the end of his life, he grew distant and strange.
Yes, he could play the guitar like a goddamned monster.
Yes, he will be missed.
Yes, I loved him.

Nick feels his heart hammering in his throat. He backtracks, veers left or right down residential blocks, still waiting to be lifted off his feet by some sniper's bullet, dead even before he hears the shot. His throat is pinched with panic, only little squeaks of air getting through. All the while the hand with its brutal metronome of death and murder and anguish tattoos his brain.

Nick finally ducks behind a dumpster and drops to one knee. He unzips the bag and shoves handfuls of money into his pockets. He brushes against the hand, which feels both warm and gritty somehow, like fleshy sandpaper, or what he imagines a shark's skin feels like. Finally, the sensation—and the whirling, bloodied howl of his thoughts—is too much, and he shoves the bag, with the hand and a fair amount of money still inside, beneath the dumpster. He runs a hand down his cheek and his palm comes away pink; he is still spattered with Peach's blood. But even now, he's thinking, thinking. He hisses and pulls the bag back out, shoving the remaining money into his pockets, then pushes the bag beneath the dumpster once more.

Like a goodbye kiss, the hand whispers that he should consider ripping his own tongue out, plucking his eyes from his head.

It's only a few more blocks to his apartment. He walks, wipes the rest of Peach's blood from his face. A police car rips by, tearing the night apart. The feeling of *removal* is a luxurious thing, like slipping into cool water on a hot day. He walks some more, soon rounds the corner of Rawley Street, sees the red-and-blue trouble lights on two, three police cars parked in front of his building. He walks a block down, crosses, then heads to the rear parking lot of the building, which is so far unguarded. He tries the back door—sometimes Mr. Contrallo keeps it unlocked, if he has work to do in the back. This is one of those times. Nick enters the laundry room and then pushes the door open that leads up a short stairwell and into the lobby. Peering through the cracked door, he sees a pair of uniformed cops standing at the front entrance of the building. Dread feathering through him, he slips over to the stairwell door, lets it shut gently behind him.

Impossible to imagine this doesn't somehow relate to him. He'll get his mother and they'll flee. They will go somewhere safe and close by, somewhere in her ring, where Katherine is not bowed by panic, and then they'll figure out what to do next.

Spindly-legged Nick Coffin takes the stairs two, three at a time. He pushes through the landing door onto the fourth floor and turns the corner that leads to his apartment.

There's a cop standing there in his doorway. The radio on his chest lets out an indecipherable squawk.

Nick can see bullet holes in the wall opposite his door. Bloodstains. The hall floor is dotted with numbered markers.

The bottom of Nick's life falls out.

He stands at the far end of the hall, by the stairwell and elevator car. His hands have gone cold from fear, just like that. His scalp rippled in sweat.

He tries to keep his voice even and unaffected. "Hey, man, who got hurt?"

The cop turns to him and eyes him. "Sir, do you live in the building?"

"Yeah," Nick says, gesturing over his shoulder, "I live in 416. Who got hurt?"

The cop speaks into his radio for a moment and begins walking toward Nick. He takes out a notebook from his chest pocket and says, "There's been a shooting, sir. I need to ask you some questions."

"Is Mrs. Moriarty okay?"

The cop looks behind him for a moment and says, "Is that the woman that lives here? You know where we might find her?" and Nick turns and runs back down the stairs again.

Down the stairwell, four flights, through the laundry room again. Into the rain-swept night. Through the parking lot, onto the sidewalk, walking fast now but not *too* fast, he takes out his phone, his heart in his throat once again. He keeps his eyes glued to the screen as a pair of cops walk past him, slipping around him like water around a rock.

OPERATION: HEAVY LIGHT

S/NF/CL-INTEL A-66/92

DATE: XX/XX/XXXX

MEMORANDUM FOR THE DEPUTY SECRETARY OF DEFENSE

SUBJECT: Effective prompts for Subject EXT/NH/014's ("Saint Michael") successful intelligence gathering via remote viewing and psychoenergetics; also, Subject's relationship to HEAVY LIGHT OBJECTIVES

(S/NF/CL-INTEL) The Subject is prone to bouts of listlessness and lethargy. When in these bouts, his remote viewing capabilities are nominal. The Subject's language skills are impressive—documentation shows at least a rudimentary grasp of English, Russian, Arabic, French, Italian, German, Swahili and Amharic. Oftentimes the Subject can be convinced through polite but insistent and simple verbal requests.

(S/NF/CL-INTEL) There are other times, however, where agents must use additional prompts if verbal requests are unsuccessful. The Subject's physiognomy is unusual (see additional enclosures, as well as the 2019 co-sponsored U.S. Army Intelligence/HCOM report *Medical Anomalies and Non-Terrestrial Physicalities of Subject EXT/NH/014*), but he is not impervious to harm, despite early initial Intelligence reports. (See following statements.) The Subject is particularly susceptible to edged weaponry used against the sprouted tensile cartilage that grows from each shoulder blade. The Subject was allowed to grow his "wings" during his initial detainment with U.S. Army Intelligence (see enclosure 1), which resulted in a significant loss of life and damage to a containment center (see enclosure 2). Since that initial foray, Subject has been restricted to having said "wings" routinely severed, even when behavior is cooperative. Said severing is the most effective prompt, as Subject finds the cutting of the prehensile cartilage tremendously painful. Subject must be physically restrained during the event, and has begged staff not to do it at various points during his containment.

(S/NF/CL-INTEL) The Subject often speaks in oblique terms. Subject's answers to prompts can sometimes include riddles or cultural catchphrases he has picked up throughout his decades of detainment. His fluency of languages, as stated earlier, is significant, and his reading comprehension is at a young adult level in all noted languages. He is aware of spatial relations, and often recalls geographical landmarks when remote viewing for a particular object or location. He is unable—or unwilling—to understand time, and cannot read a clock.

(S/NF/CL-INTEL) U.S. Army Intelligence and HCOM personnel have long recognized the Subject's "mortality," i.e., the entropy the Subject seems to be experiencing while in containment. This process has accelerated in recent years. It is unclear if said entropy is due to the containment itself, the fact that his "wings" are regularly cut, or simply the Subject's non-terrestrial nature. It is also unknown if his acts of remote viewing exacerbate his condition. It has become clear that at some point the Subject will cease to reliably function, at which point he will be removed from the series of U.S. Army/HCOM/DISC operations (see enclosure 6).

(S/NF/CL-INTEL) As mentioned, the most successful prompts for the Subject are forceful but polite verbal requests. After periods of long silences or refusals, it's suggested that a reminder of "wing-cutting" is an option; the Subject will almost always continue his assignments after such a threat. After a "wing-cutting," the Subject is contrite and pained, eager to participate in sessions for a considerable amount of time.

(S/NF/CL-INTEL) The depth of the Subject's relationship with and understanding of HEAVY LIGHT OBJECTIVES remains unclear. The OBJECTIVES also appear to be non-terrestrial in nature, though it is unclear if they are of the same non-terrestrial form as the Subject. Subject has consistently denied this.

(S/NF/CL-INTEL) U.S. Army Intelligence/HCOM/DISC agents are well aware of the DoD's overarching desire to investigate the physiognomic nature of the Subject. There is a tacit understanding that Subject EXT/NH/014 is profoundly unique. OPERATION: HEAVY LIGHT, like all operations in which the Subject was previously a participant, requires the Subject's active participation, i.e., agencies have been thus far unable to discover a way to isolate and "make" the Subject utilize his unique psychoenergetic skills against his will. Attempts at isolating his abilities independent of the Subject have been unsuccessful. The Subject must be motivated to participate. It is also understood that other agencies within the Department of Defense are eager to explore the Subject's non-terrestrial physiology and psychoenergetic capabilities, and that such an investigation will take place after the Subject is deemed no longer capable of producing reliable intelligence by the Department's stated guidelines and an autopsy is performed.

(S/NF/CL-INTEL) It remains unknown how long the Subject will continue to be an active and useful asset to the HEAVY LIGHT program.

KATHERINE MORIARTY

S he didn't stop running until the panic stopped her, until the vastness of the streets slowed her to a walk, fire stitching her lungs.

She ran in a circle around the ring.

Katherine has a tight-knit area of safety around the apartment, "the ring" is what Nick calls it, a net of security that stretches from the I-405 overpass to the east and Twenty-eighth Avenue to the west. North and South are demarked by Taylor on one side and Lovejoy Street on the other; an area of a few square miles in circumference. It used to be smaller—anything past Twenty-first Avenue would send her spiraling in a panic. It has been this way since Matthew Coffin's death over a decade before. She has worked at it, at expanding the confines of her world, slowly and patiently. Katherine is blisteringly aware of how damn melodramatic it sounds, and also how understanding it doesn't count for shit when it comes to dispelling the fear itself. Becoming afraid of leaving your house is not a thing you ever plan on. It's something that happens to you. Has happened to her.

She is outside the ring now, but only a little. A block or two—she can hardly even see at this point, the fear blunting all of her senses, her vision drawn down into a tunnel, just randomly walking, casting terrified glances over her shoulder. She is stuck in the vise of these two intractable, immovable fears: people with guns that are really, truly after her, and all this open, weighted space where she is not safe.

Finally, the panic is too much. Another block and she is convinced she will be discovered, be seen, the buildings will topple on her, the street will open up in great heaving slabs of asphalt and dirt. The fear: so foolish, and no less real for it. Again, a knife-edged dichotomy—knowing something and still being powerless over it.

She dips into a bar she's never been to before, never seen, the red neon martini sign flashing on and off above the entrance. A disinterested doorman who looks up from his phone and just nods at her. Her phone, wallet, everything, is in the apartment. She has no money. She hasn't carried a purse in a decade. What would she do with it? Wear it from the kitchen to the bathroom?

The place is dark, a few hanging bulbs throw cones of dusty light. The backlit rows of bottles at the bar. There's a booth near the back of the room, a table there glossed in a single fist of light. She slides into it—even the tactile sensation of the booth, the tabletop smooth against her fingertips, is so goddamned strange. So familiar and so foreign all at once. Katherine feels a moment of relief that her back is against the wall. The panic retreats a little. Place is nearly empty. A few folks hunched over nursing their drinks. A pair of men play a lackluster game of pool near the back door.

She focuses on her breathing, counts backward from ten. Does it again. The jukebox plays something from her youth, something angular and bristling, local. A band she's played with, she's almost sure of it. Focus on that, Katherine thinks. The sound of it. Memories of when the world was large and unencumbered. The mic stand held around your fists. How the kick drum could be felt in your ribs. Breathe. Ten, nine, eight.

Near the front of the room, a woman turns on her stool and casts

Katherine with an appraising eye. Katherine puts her hands on the edges of the table when the woman peels off her stool and saunters her way. She's maybe Katherine's age—who can even tell anymore—and dressed much the same. Black shirt, black jeans, arms laced in tattoos.

"How you doing, baby?" The woman sounds like she was raised with a pack of smokes in her crib.

"I'm okay," Katherine says. "How're you?" The surrealness of the situation has constricted her to the most cloying politeness. Vicente Contrallo saying "No, please" behind her. The pistol shot. They killed him in the hallway. That's a thing that just happened. They killed a man she's known forever. Someone at the bar coughs up what sounds like a sizable portion of his lung.

"You drinking?" the woman asks, placing a hand on the back of the booth opposite hers.

"I'm waiting for someone," Katherine says. She should be running. She should be zigzagging through the ring, thinking of where to go. Or smashing through the ring, fearless, looking for Nick everywhere, anywhere. She should be more than she is. She asks the woman if she can borrow her phone, her voice cracking a bit.

The woman holds up a finger; it's a gesture that seems somewhat familiar to Katherine, brings up some distant bell-ring of memory. "I don't fuck around with my phone after work hours, but hold on." She walks back to the bar and hollers for the bartender, a man with a ponytail and a *Star Wars* T-shirt. The two confer. Katherine prepares to run.

But the woman comes back with a cell phone in one hand and a beer in the other. She sets both before Katherine. Stepping back to the bar for a moment, she grabs her own drink and then returns, sits in the booth opposite Katherine. Beneath the light, she's striking. A witch-wig of gray and blue hair, a galaxy of bangles on her wrists. Katherine has always admired women like this—ones willing to grow into and then remain the women they want to be. Katherine has felt for years devoured by expectations and disappointments. A woman trapped in amber. Every day she considers how Matthew Coffin's death, if it had happened some other way, might have been a freeing thing for her. That she might have lived an entirely different life. She could have been anyone.

But his death was not like that, and Katherine is who she is.

"Do I know you?" she says to the woman. Even as she speaks, there's a part of her that's trying to remember Nick's phone number.

The woman grins and leans forward conspiratorially. Her smile is dazzling, beautiful. "You're shitting me, right?"

"I'm sorry," Katherine says. "It's been a . . . it's been a day." She closes her eyes, feeling as if she might scream. They are after her son.

"It's Belle, Katherine! From Static Stars?"

Of course. Everything clicks into place. What'd been playing over the speakers. Katherine offers a smile that feels absolutely crazed as she points at the ceiling and says, "It'd been so long, but I *knew* I recognized this song."

Belle leans her head back and cackles. Their bands had played plenty of shows together. Belle, she remembered, would often be drunk by load-in, hours before the show even started, and would still manage to pull off guitar lines that could leave Katherine with her jaw open. The woman could play. More than once, Katherine had asked the promoter that the Blank Letters play before them, not wanting to get upstaged, something that had made Matthew furious. The two groups had cut their teeth amid the feeding frenzy that was the major label wars back in the day, with the Static Stars putting out one record on Interscope that never quite caught on. Nowhere near the meteoric rise and fall of Katherine's own band.

"I'm so sorry," she says now, wincing and pointing at the bartender's phone, "do you mind? May I?"

"Oh, go ahead," Belle says with a wave of a hand. She stands up, points at the bartender. "I'll give you some privacy. Just give the phone back to Gabe when you're done."

"You're the manager here?"

Belle looks at her, a little taken aback. She smiles, but there's some acid there too. The old Belle, that fuck-off spark still waiting to be lit. "I own the place, babe."

"Oh, God, I'm so sorry."

"Psh, it's fine," Belle says. "I'll just be right over there." Katherine watches as she saunters back to her stool with her drink.

Katherine fumbles Nick's number once, twice, and has to backtrack. Finally, she manages the number.

Nick doesn't answer. It goes to voicemail and she hangs up. She dials again.

Then, his voice steeped in caution, she hears her son say hello.

"Nick, baby, Nick—"

"Mom—"

"Nick, listen to me—"

"Holy shit, where are you, Mom?"

"Listen to me. There are people that came to the apartment."

"I know! I—"

"You have to run."

"I *am*," says Nick. "Where are you?"

"Hang up," someone says at Katherine's arm.

She closes her eyes for a moment, as if that might change anything.

When she looks up, the man from the apartment is standing before her.

"Mom?"

"Hang up." The man lifts the fabric of his coat. She sees the pistol in its holster.

"*Mom?*"

Belle comes over. "Everything okay, hon?"

"Everything's fine," the man says.

"I wasn't asking you, motherfucker."

The man turns to her. "Ma'am, you need to step back."

"And you need to get the fuck out of my bar. Now. Gabe, get Joey from the front."

And that's when the man turns to Belle and takes his pistol out, shows it to her. Belle backs up to the edge of the bar so smoothly that the ice in her drink makes no noise at all. It's only then that Katherine realizes the music has stopped.

"Get up," he says to Katherine, but she's frozen. The people at the bar are too; the men playing pool have disappeared. Joey, the doorman up front, finally peers up from his phone.

"Doorman, sit down on the floor, please," the man calls out without turning toward him.

"Me?" says the doorman.

"You, yes."

The doorman slides to the floor like water.

"Please tell me you hung up that phone," the man says. Katherine hangs up. He puts a hand on her arm and she stands on legs that feel as if they belong to someone else.

They walk to the front door, Belle muttering curses behind them. They step over the doorman and into a night filled, once again, with the sounds of the world. Katherine's vision swims, and she lets out a keening noise like some kind of animal.

For years, Nick has quietly insisted to her that the world is not a bad place, that she is safe. And now this.

The few pedestrians that pass them by cast quick glances their way and then look back to the street, unwilling to intervene. Perhaps his pistol is still out, she has no idea. Katherine raises her voice to scream, and the man, sounding weary, says, "Please don't. Please. I don't have the stomach for it."

She screams, so loud that it feels as if something integral in her throat will break. Traffic doesn't stop, the street is still mist-heavy, she's still a woman in a body being pulled somewhere against her wishes. Her scream is simply noise that is stacked and threaded among the other noises of the world.

The man yanks her forward, leading her to a black SUV around the corner. She doesn't get a look at the license plate. The man gets in the backseat with her. It has that new car smell to it. *A rental,* she thinks. *A government car. No, a rental.* Her thoughts pinball like this. She weeps.

The red-haired woman is in the driver's seat.

From his jacket pocket, the man beside her pulls out a black mask. She doesn't scream when he puts it on over her head. This is the summation of the world. Every bad thing come home to roost. Matthew and his unraveling, his terrible death, and now this. The two seem like waypoints to each other. A beginning and an ending.

But these people are after her son.

"We need the hand," the man says beside her.

She notes for the first time there is an element of despair to his voice. It's as if he has been waiting to be in relative privacy—the enclosed space of the vehicle—to say it. "Give us the hand."

"I want to go home," Katherine says. It's said with such pleading, such weakness, she hates herself for it.

"We need the hand."

"I don't have it. I don't understand you."

"Does Nicholas Coffin have the hand?"

"I don't know what you're talking about," Katherine says.

"Okay," the man says. "I understand. If that's how we have to do it."

They move.

HUTCH HOLTZ

Before any of it—before his stint in Rutherford Youth Correctional, where he met Tim Reed, before the two of them started breaking fingers for Peach Serrano, before some Crooked Wheel shitbags smashed his head into a van door—Hutch's dad, for a little while, would get together and play chess with this other vet, Leon.

Back when Hutch was a kid, this was, but years and years after his dad's tours of Vietnam were over and done with. The two of them, this guy Leon and Hutch's dad, had met at a pharmacy, of all places, his old man buying his heart pills, and they'd struck up a conversation waiting in line. Turned out they had been to some of the same places over there, had heard some of the same stories about some of the same guys. Hutch was ten, eleven, when Leon started coming over to their apartment with his chessboard—he was a big, grizzled fat man who breathed laboriously and walked with a limp; he'd lost a few toes not to a Bouncing Betty but to diabetes. Leon and Hutch's dad would sit in the kitchen for hours, Hutch listening to them talk while he read in his bedroom with the door open. The low murmur of their speech, the click of chess pieces. The thump of beer bottles on the kitchen table. His mom had been gone for a while by then, but the sound of the men in the kitchen reminded him of having two grownups in the house. It was a comfort.

His dad would always be pensive after Leon left, filling the rooms with his stony silence, picking things up and putting them down again as if he'd never seen them before. It was a curious friendship; after that initial conversation, they never talked again about Vietnam, as far as Hutch could tell. They hardly talked at all, really. Just played chess and drank beers. Maybe their shared history was enough. That knowledge of what they'd both been through.

The last time Leon came over, Hutch was at the kitchen table, working on homework. It was a Social Studies report on the Dominican Republic, and he had gathered all of his printouts together, carefully putting each one in its own protective sheet in his binder. One of those weird details that you remember. Leon was a widower, and he'd sometimes clink his wedding ring against the side of his beer bottle while he thought about his move. Hutch's dad that day had been staring hard at his lost pieces, pieces that Leon had collected on his side of the board.

Finally, that last game, Leon took his dad's second bishop and clinked his ring against the bottle again and said, "Dan, stop counting your dead, man. Move forward." He had a rattling, gravelly voice, like an idling semi.

Hutch's father had slowly raised his head, like he was waking up. "What did you say to me?"

"Stop worrying about the dead ones, man. You got more than enough pieces to win."

His father had looked hard at Leon then, and Hutch would never forget how his dad had raised one hand and run his palm slowly over the top of the board, knocking all of the pieces onto their sides, plastic knights and kings and pawns tumbling to the floor or rolling onto the table in their tight arcs. He'd stood up, the legs of his chair snarling across the linoleum, and walked out of the kitchen. Walked right out of his own apartment.

Leon had looked at Hutch and then slowly packed up his board, put his pieces in the little plastic baggie he'd brought them in.

Leon had cleared his throat and said, "Catch you on the flip side, buddy."

"Bye," Hutch said.

Then Leon had limped out the door. Hutch was just a kid at the time. He didn't know shit. He'd wonder later if it was the fact that there would be no reconciling Vietnam for his father, that he'd long held that war tight to his chest, held tight to his time there, let the war grow into his heart, become enmeshed there, like scar tissue. Maybe the trajectory of violence had influenced everything else in his life, inevitable as the arc and tumble of a bullet. Or maybe that was Hutch projecting his own history of violence onto him; his father had remained mostly unknowable to him.

Maybe, Hutch wondered, it was simply that Dan Holtz already had a great number of dead people populating his life, and he couldn't—or didn't want to—stop counting them.

So here's Hutch in the hospital, crazed and pained, gut-shot, hospital staff scrambling around him. Vision graying in and out. He's wheeled along the hall, lashed down to a gurney, as he's already swung on a paramedic. Someone asks someone else what his name is and Hutch thinks of his father running his hand along the top of the chessboard and walking out of the apartment, and he says, "My name's Leon, and you are a sore-ass loser," or maybe he thinks he says it, because next he's in a room and something's being inserted into his arm. He's hot, like fire has been poured on the left side of his body. As if the wound's being salted. He gestures feebly at the IV but he's still restrained.

"Oh, no thank you," says a nurse, patting him on the arm, like she's speaking to a young child. "We'll just leave that in there, sir."

Soon after, the pain in his body begins receding, like a tide drifting out to reveal the sand beneath. He's almost comfortable, actually, and with that some measure of lucidity returns. He remains tied down. People come by and peer at his charts. His shirt and pants have been cut from him. A doctor—he has the authority of a doctor, the dick-swinging grandiosity—stands before him and says in a loud doctor-voice that they'll operate on him now, and he should be fine.

"I been shot," Hutch says.

"Yes," the doctor says. "Not lethally, thank goodness. You're a lucky man."

He says, "Trade me places then," and the doctor laughs, and then he blinks again and the lights are above his head and he's being wheeled somewhere else.

Then a man stands over him, he has a mask over his mouth and nose, and speaks to Hutch like they're having coffee, asks him how he's doing and tells him to count backward from ten. He puts a mask on Hutch's face.

He makes it to six and then he's out.

Nurses. People in and out of his room. People with clipboards. The hazy shape of machines surrounding him. He comes back to the world incrementally, reluctantly. His vision seems coated in gauze. There's a window in his room, the blinds half-open, and he sees night, pure dark, through the slats. It's beautiful, that black and white delineation of blinds and nighttime.

"Water," he rasps to the nurse when she comes in, and she winces.

"Not a great idea, sir. We're keeping you hydrated through your IV, but swallowing water wouldn't feel great right now." She peers at his chart. "And we need you to pee first!" she says brightly. "I'll let the doctor know you're awake."

He remembers this from the time after the van door, the way care could sometimes feel like sanctimony. He shuts his eyes. He's got a catheter, an IV. He doesn't hurt, but it feels like the left side of his body is wrapped in a blanket. It's numb.

It comes back to him then that Tim is probably dead. The hand in the bag, that hot fever in his blood, the way that need to *hurt* had ripped through him like a wave. The ripple of gunfire around him as he ran. The parking lot saturated with the sound of fireworks. *Pop pop pop.*

Then he's no longer tied to his gurney.

He's floating again.

There's a man sitting in a chair. His face is underlit by the screen of his phone. Older man, white, bulldog jowls and a white flattop. Short-sleeve button-up and a pair of glasses that reflect the screen's light. He couldn't be more of a cop if it was written on his forehead.

He looks at Hutch over the top of his eyeglasses and puts his phone away in his hip pocket.

"Hey there, Mr. Holtz. Glad to see you're waking up." The man half-stands and leans over, extends a hand. He's a detective with the Portland Police Bureau. He says a name that Hutch loses immediately. His manner is folksy and friendly and absolutely none of it translates to his watery, watchful eyes. There's a pistol on his hip.

A nurse comes in and seems surprised that Hutch is awake again. "Sir," she says to the detective, "you'll have to step outside."

The man sits back down, his hands between his knees. "He needs to be interviewed."

"He just got out of surgery."

"And he was involved in a shooting earlier this evening. He's a suspect. Get your nurse manager in here if you need to, but I'm not going anywhere."

The nurse leaves and Hutch clears his throat. "Can you get me some water?"

"You bet," the detective says, and Hutch rolls over on his good side and beneath his blanket pulls out the catheter, wincing in pain as he does.

"You okay?"

Hutch rolls back onto his back. He takes the water, chances a small sip. It hurts going down, but nothing like the explosion he was expecting. He's still wildly doped up, of course. "I'm good," he says.

"Sounds like you ought to be playing the lottery. Missed any organs, grazed a rib without fragmenting it. In and out."

"Yeah, I feel very fortunate," Hutch says, and the detective laughs.

"You done with that?" He points, and Hutch nods. The cop takes the cup from him, sets it on the end table.

"Mr. Holtz, you're wanted for questioning in relation to a shooting outside of Pie in the Sky Pizzeria earlier this evening. You want to get a lawyer, we can wait, but you're not being charged with anything at this time." He reaches into his pocket and takes out his phone. "If you'd like to talk, I'll need to record it."

Hutch flexes his legs beneath his blanket. "You really a cop," he says.

The detective lets out a little chuckle. "I'm really a cop, Mr. Holtz."

"I'd like to see your badge."

He sets his phone on his chair and takes his badge out of his pocket. It's in a flip-wallet, with his ID on one side and the badge on the other. He holds it out and Hutch squints. The detective takes another step forward and Hutch rises, grabbing the detective's wrist with one hand and pulling him forward, onto the bed. The detective is not a small man, but Hutch has him pinned facedown. He hooks an arm around the man's throat and pulls him back, getting him in a choke hold. Pain natters in Hutch's side. He holds the man tight, counts. The detective is making gurgling noises, and then he's out, sliding to a boneless heap beside Hutch's bed. Hutch, wincing, pulls his IV out and then clambers out of bed. He reaches down and takes the cop's pistol and his phone. Bending down causes another starburst of pain. When he stands up, the cop's already stirring on the floor.

The nurse and another woman are standing in the doorway. Hutch raises the pistol and tells them to get the fuck back. They do. There's some commotion in the hallway, a voice over the intercom. A pair of people run down the hall.

Hutch hobbles toward the doorway. More people are running down the hall, full-tilt, shoes slapping on the floor. He holds the pistol tight to his leg and steps out.

2
THE EYE

OPERATION: HEAVY LIGHT

S/NF/CL-INTEL A-44/22—SECRET TRANSCRIPT—EXCERPT

DATE: XX/XX/XXXX

Q: Okay, so how long have you been involved with the program?

A: Well, Finch headhunted me, what? Nine months ago? Something like that. My hire date would be in the files.

Q: Tell me about it. The program.

A: Like, from the beginning?

Q: Yeah, in layman's terms. You know what I mean? Pretend I'm not Finch's boss. Pretend I'm just some guy.

A: Okay. Phew. We—there were a lot of meetings about this, long before I was around—where Finch wanted to create something, a program, with a sense of inevitability. Like, I've worked with formatted numbers, speech synthesis, phase-shift keying—all that stuff. That's—I feel super comfortable working in those areas, okay?

Q: Okay. And you worked with numbers stations a lot, correct? For various agencies.

A: Correct.

Q: Mossad. CIA. What about the KGB?

A: KGB was way before my time, Director Lundy.

Q: Okay, sure. Ha, I just assume everyone's an old fart like me. Anyway, we can confidently say that you're familiar with, I don't know, the nuances of relaying intelligence and data through a myriad of formats. Does that work?

A: That's exactly why I was brought on. That's why Finch hired me. And it's a key part of the program: making the means of arrival an *inevitability*.

Q: Tell me more about what you mean by that.

A: Well, Finch wanted a scenario in which there was no *option* to repel the data. You heard it, and even if you didn't understand it, it affected you.

Q: Like, uh, backmasking. Right? The Satanic panic when I was a kid, everyone worried that heavy metal had backward messaging, telling you to eat your parents and whatnot.

A: I mean, kind of, yeah. But not something playing backward. Something buried.

Q: Buried how?

A: Like buried underneath whatever you're hearing. Where something happened to your body, intrinsically, whether you wanted it to or not, whether you were even aware of it. Once you heard the thing. It was my understanding that was the whole scope of the project.

Q: A weapons delivery system.

A: A *clandestine* weapons delivery system, exactly. One the subject can't repel because, I mean, they're not even aware they're being attacked. In this case delivered aurally.

Q: Okay. Good. And how'd you settle on the Blank Letters song as a means of delivery?

A: Like, that particular song, you mean? Rather than just playing the original source material over a loudspeaker in a movie theater or something?

Q: Yeah. That song's got to be fifteen, twenty years old.

A: That was all Finch, sir. He was adamant.

Q: Tell me more about that.

A: We ran the source material's sound signature through a library of like, three million songs, and only twenty or so had the optimum tonal ranges and rhythms to thread the recording in. Only a few songs matched, had the right bumps—spaces in the song where it fit just right. We sent the list of songs to Finch and he listened to them over the weekend, I guess, and when he came in on Monday, it was the Blank Letters song. There was no discussion, that was it.

Q: Okay.

A: So, like, that was when it started. Over and over again, he started playing that song in the lab.

Q: But not with the source material included.

A: I mean, no, sir, we'd all have been screwed if that was the case. It was just the song. But his change was . . . really striking. Really immediate and really striking. Like, I'm not exaggerating when I say he literally put it on repeat, all day long.

Q: And do you think this was the start of Dr. Finch's . . . decline?

A: Yes. Oh yeah. It was day and night. The song fit the parameters of the project for sure, but he . . . it became unusual and then openly weird right away.

Q: Why is that?

A: Like I said, he just played it all the time in the lab. He told us he'd dreamt about the song. Would write notes trying to interpret its meaning. He studied up on the band on his breaks, just stared at photos of the band members like he was trying to figure something out. Right before he, you know, did what he did, he told me that he was "being haunted." Like, this is a man who's one of the leading voices of interpretive speech synthesis and intuitive AI in the last twenty years, and he's talking about ghosts and hauntings and stuff. He stopped shaving. His hygiene was, you know, not awesome. It got creepy really fast, and always with the song playing on his laptop, just endlessly.

Q: And then he was removed from the project.

A: I mean, he was removed from the earth, wasn't he? That's what happens when you, you know, shoot yourself.

Q: Okay, this is true. I appreciate your frankness. So, to get back on track, after Dr. Finch was replaced, the project resumed—with "I Won't Forget It" still as the means of delivery. What happened next?

A: Again, the emphasis was always on a pedestrian delivery. Something designed for a civilian population. And there were certain frequencies that we needed, repetitions in pitches and tone-shifts. Pauses. We had to fit all these puzzle pieces together. Like if you read the transcript of the source material, it might look like there's not a lot there, but there are certain pitches that repeat X amount of times. In the beginning he's kind of chanting, then he's crying, then he's muttering to himself, right? When the guy's talking, the words he repeats. Inflections in his voice. All of it had to fit perfectly into a song, you know? I know that it took a lot of work just to originally transcribe the source material, a lot of manpower and safety precautions, and when you look at a digital printout of the guy's voice, just the way it sounds, it's almost like a song itself at certain parts. There's dips and waves. But to get back to your question, we did try to just play the OG material at first. We ran the initial .wav file, not layered into any music or anything, on some focus groups—

Q: Is that what we're calling them?

A: Ha, yeah, that's some Finch-speak right there. Anyway, we ran the file on some focus groups and the results were good. It was intense. Like, right away. Immediately, subjects were dealing with stunned stereocilia, the optic nerve's glial cells going batshit, adrenaline levels through the roof. Amygdala in the red, just boom. They're just enraged. They have to be exposed to the file at a certain decibel level for it to take effect—like, if they heard it broadcast down the hall, it wouldn't work, right? But in the same room? Over a loudspeaker? Or with your ear pressed to your phone? You got lit up.

Q: So, why layer it in the song at all?

A: Well, because the original audio file is of a guy crying, right? Saying some pretty intense stuff. It makes more sense to layer it into a song that people are into. Can't really play the original audio over a loudspeaker without raising some eyebrows. I mean, at one point the guy's talking about making a necklace out of children's heads and stuff. It's, uh, a bit much.

Q: So keep it clandestine.

A: You got it, sir. Keep it veiled.

Q: Okay, to change the subject a bit. What do you think happened to Dr. Finch?

A: It's not really my place to say.

Q: I'm honestly interested. You worked with the man daily. Do you think he was, I don't know, maybe mainlining the source material? Microdosing little blips of it here and there?

A: Of the recording?

Q: Yeah.

A: Sir, I'm a scientist. And I'm into the work that we do. I appreciate it. I see its value. It interests me. I like working here.

Q: This sounds like you covering your ass, son.

A: I'm just saying, sir. I'm not going to pretend to know how it is men like you and Dr. Finch operate, or why you decide to do what you do. And I don't mean that as an insult. I just mean, I'm a scientist, and it's above my pay grade. I just want to do my research. What happened to Dr. Finch, why he grew so focused on that song, why it poisoned him the way it did? None of that's really any of my business.

Q: You just want to do your work.

A: I just want to do my work, man.

KATHERINE MORIARTY

The room is a room.

The room is a room among other, endless rooms. Four walls, a roof, a floor, the occasional sound of footfalls in the hallway. Katherine has spent more years in *rooms,* aware of their spaces, their containments, than she cares to think about. And that sense of containment has usually been such a salve to her.

But not now.

A pair of humming fluorescents cast everything in a cold and clinical pallor. A window reflects her own terrified face back at her. They've searched her and understood there is nothing to take. They've digitally scanned her fingerprints. They realized that she was having a panic attack, a true one, not something designed to create a diversion. A real, wide-eyed, hyperventilating, I'm-not-even-here-right-now panic attack, and a woman with a ponytail and a blue mask over her mouth and nose injected something into Katherine's arm and now the panic is a mutter. She doesn't feel high, just vastly distanced from herself. The fear is like looking at your body through glass.

She's not bound to this chair. She could get up and walk around, look for ways to escape. But she keeps herself rooted here. She sits. It's safer that way.

They want the *hand*? she thinks. What in Christ could that even mean?

Nick's hands? Have they . . . have they cut off her son's hands? No, she'd spoken to him and he was fine. Her thoughts are muddled from the shot, that's all.

She knows that some earlier iteration of her could have escaped. One that still had her band together, perhaps, her husband. One who had not seen the things she'd seen. Were she a woman still unafraid of telling record executives and handsy promoters to go fuck themselves. A woman who hadn't grown afraid of streetlights, of buildings, the yawing space between them—*that* Katherine would have at least tried to escape. But this one? No.

So she sits and thinks and waits for someone to come to her while she stays rooted to her tiny world. To this chair.

And eventually, the door opens.

The man in the doorway wears an off-the-rack charcoal suit, a rumpled undershirt. His is the face of every bureaucrat she's ever seen: a bit of jowls around the collar, features puffy with fatigue. The air of middle management about him, somehow, a mediocre car salesman. The room's light gleaming on the bald curve of his skull. He gently shuts the door behind him and pulls out the chair across from Katherine. He folds his hands on the table; there is the pale ghost of a wedding band on his finger. Katherine puts him in his early fifties, roughly her own age.

He smiles at her, pretending at calm, and his smile is the smile of every Good Cop she has ever met in her life. The smile of record execs and lawyers discussing contracts. The smile of every supposed nice guy trying to bed her, the smile the engineer would use to get her to do another vocal take when she didn't quite hit the notes right. Sometimes a Good Cop isn't even necessarily a bad guy, but a Good Cop always wants something from you. And this one? She hangs her arms at her sides and touches the warm metal of the chair there. Her world is the chair. It's that or go mad.

She says, "What do you want?"

He seems pleasantly surprised by this. "Well, I thought you knew, Katherine. We want the hand."

"I don't even know what that is. I don't know what you mean."

It's a room with the air of a shipping container, a warehouse. A place where things are stored. Like her. She wants her apartment, the pilled carpet, the record player. Her little guitar and her little desk by her bed where she crafts her little pop songs. The blessed terrain of the known. She is so afraid, she can taste the sour electricity of fear in the back of her mouth. She tries to keep the tremble out of her voice and mostly manages it.

"You're not cops," she says. "Military? ICE?"

He shrugs, looks over at the window for just a moment. "I mean, sure. Any of those. All of them. I'm David Lundy, Katherine. Hi."

"I want a lawyer."

He shrugs again. "I hear you."

"It's the law."

Another shrug, palms up. "I'm afraid the law is not applicable at this present moment. We want the hand."

"I don't know what you're talking about."

"Your son has something that belongs to us. It's very valuable."

"A hand? My son has a hand that's yours?"

Again with the shrug, a nod. "He has a bag, Katherine, and inside the bag is, yes, a hand. Okay? Are we communicating here?"

"I don't know of any bag."

But is that true? Had Nick come inside with a bag? One she hadn't seen before?

"We'll kill him, Katherine."

"No," she says, as if the word might deflect a bullet.

"We can do it, and no one will care, and there will be no consequences."

"I don't know what you *mean*," she says. Her voice breaks. She dips her head to her breastbone and closes her eyes and weeps. There is silence for some time—a ten-count, maybe more, and then the man slams his hand on the table in front of her and she jumps, lets out a startled cry. He does it again, and again, and finally Katherine is sitting there with her hands gripping the sides of her chair, weeping so soundlessly and fiercely it is difficult to draw breath. There is some small animal at work trying to stitch her throat closed, and the building is going to fall on her, it is, and here is this man, furious, slapping the table with a sound like a gunshot, and her son out there being hunted in the great teeming world.

David Lundy pushes his chair away with a squeal, stands and spins slowly in a circle, one hand on the bald dome of his head. "Get me a fucking phone," he calls. "Katherine, you're going to call him."

She nods. Yes, yes. She'll call him.

Lundy points a finger at her. "You call him or he gets a bullet in the mouth, you understand me?"

Yes, yes, she nods.

"Someone get me a goddamn phone," he calls again, and through the wavering prism of her tears, she sees him sit down before her once more. He leans back and folds his arms and waits. Watching impassively as she weeps and trembles in her chair.

Not such a good cop after all.

NICK COFFIN

Katherine was always the one who rooted the family to the ground. Nick, after all, was just a kid, and Matthew Coffin was forever in his own loose orbit around them. Sometimes touching down, often not. When Nick was older, he would come to loathe the idea of it—the "excess leads to success" rock savant shtick his father had cultivated, willfully or not. But as a young boy, it was simply the way things were. His father was mercurial, unpredictable, thrilling. A living trope in dark sunglasses and an affectation of distance. His mother was the glue. Always had been. Both within the band and the family. And how often the two were relentlessly intertwined.

Even when touring—and it's only now as an adult that Nick understands how wildly different his childhood had been in comparison to that of other children—his mother had held tight to one strict regimen: *the boy comes with*. Much of Nick's early years were spent in the back of a van or, later, a tour bus with the rest of the band, as well as Rich, their roadie and guitar tech, and Glenda, a friend that acted as a nanny whenever they hit the road. They'd toured for years, each tour getting successively larger, lengthier, more financially lucrative.

Rest stops, roadside diners, highways unspooling beyond the insect-spattered windshield. Sleeping on an air mattress on the floor of someone's home after his parents had spent the evening yowling their guts out. From basements and VFW halls to larger venues, until finally, by the time the second record came out, the band and its crew were being flown to festivals in Europe, and Nick's passport had become a careworn, beloved thing, scattered with a constellation of stamps.

He became accustomed to the cadence of touring at a young age, the strange rhythm of it, the repetition—the promoter with the plugs in his ears and the tattooed face that they saw every time they played Lexington, Kentucky, how he would say *What's up, my champion?* to Nick in the same funny voice, always pulling a ten-dollar bill from behind Nick's ear, folded in the shape of a diamond, which he would then press into Nick's palm. The same skylines of the same cities as they drove down the same highways. The skeins of sunlight rippling through tattered clouds, or a sky grown slate-gray and threatening snow. The quality of light depending on the time of year, the way it fell on his legs in the van. How he could tell what time of day it was by the sunbeams sliding slowly across the Econoline's floor. How you could read the grownups' moods by how they sat in their seats, their posture, how they talked to each other. How Doogy would play drums on the steering wheel for a hundred miles, for forever, until someone, usually his dad, yelled at him to stop. Arthur always with a book in his hand, talking up that evening's hosts and trading the book he'd just finished for another from that person's collection. Nick graduating from an air mattress to a folding cot as he got older, falling asleep in some back room while the grownups bullshitted quietly, the clink of glasses. The occasional groans and burst of giggles when someone dropped something. The pungent smell of joints drifting beneath the door. Toward the end, he'd sometimes had his own room when the record label put them up somewhere. Rags to riches to ruination, the drumbeat of his childhood.

Doing math homework on the side of I-5 while Rich cursed outside his window, changing a flat tire, the endless passage of traffic rocking the van. His father doing the equations in his head—*time versus distance versus will*—to see if they could make it to the next show on time. Matthew fishing through the metal lockbox that held the band fund, calculating how much a new tire was going to eat into their guarantee. The adults sometimes getting into ferocious arguments over which tape to play next, only to be laughing moments later, buckled over and cackling. When they were offered food from a promoter, Nick would discover from a very young age, particularly overseas and particularly at punk squats, it was *always* chili, almost always vegan, and without fail served from a gigantic steel cook pot, enough to feed all of the bands playing that night and their respective crews.

By the time he was old enough to understand such things, Nick realized that his parents were famous. Kind of famous. Pretty famous. It had taken place at some interminable point in his life. Their pictures would be in the newspaper of every town they went to. There were always people who wanted to talk to them at each city they visited, interview them. His father was both the guitarist and the band's manager—such as it was—and he handled both with a swaggering assuredness that often burst into frenetics. Usually without warning. As a guitarist, it made him formidable, fearsome, a fucking wonder to watch. Gesticulating wildly, mouth pulled back in a sneer, bucking his lithe frame as if being electrocuted, fingers cracking along the fretboard. Putting a foot through an amp to try to alter the sound, standing on stacks of monitors and leaping off. The smashing of endless guitars.

As a manager, though, Matthew Coffin's whole wild-man thing was less endearing. Had been, in Rich's words, "Fucking obnoxious, man. Because who cleans it up? He doesn't clean it up! I do!" Matthew Coffin had been known to skulk dressing rooms in a silent fury, that one vein throbbing in the center of his forehead as he strode back and forth, back and forth, silent save for the occasional curse more plosive than spoken. Known nationwide for his temper. Internationally. Known to shove promoters, members of other bands, fans if they got too pushy or insistent. Nick has heard many times the stories of his father knifing the tires of another group's bus after they'd taken the entire cut of the door. His father hadn't denied it, only insisted that it had been at a time when the Blank Letters were siphoning gas and counting quarters for groceries. If they hadn't been so goddamn good—his mother's haunting, gravel-to-honey yowl, his father's electrocution-style guitar playing, the buoyant, angular, veering rhythm section of Arthur and Doogy, his parents' college friends—no one would have worked with them. No one would've wanted to deal with Matthew Coffin's bullshit. But Nick was to discover—again and again—that rock and roll permitted or even sanctioned assholes, particularly men, particularly men who appeared at the mercy of their own tortured genius. Men hunting their own ghosts. Matthew Coffin ticked all those boxes.

But it didn't matter. The Blank Letters wrote songs that erased all the bullshit. Their debut album, *All Hail the Dirty Gods,* was put out by Slim Chance, an indie label out of Raleigh that'd been started by another college buddy of his parents, and they toured on that record for a number of years. The early tours were buoyed greatly by the fact that *Dirty Gods* stayed in the Billboard Top 50 for almost seven months after it came out. Absolutely crazy feat for an indie band at that time, and went a long way toward keeping them on the road and securing the purchase of the family's apartment in the Regal Arms.

When he was nine, the Blank Letters played a show at the Knitting Factory in New York, and the next day his dad got a call from someone at Geffen Records. Nick still remembers it. They were on the New Jersey turnpike. He was reading a Stephen King novel about a rabid dog (Nick was homeschooled, of course, and both Katherine and Glenda said it counted as English homework) when his father took the call. There had been some interest by major labels before—*Dirty Gods* by then was close to going gold—but this A&R guy was jubilant and insistent. He'd seen the show the night before, he said, and wanted to discuss potentially working together. His father had managed to sound both guarded and calm when he said, "Yeah, man, I'm the manager. You want to talk to someone, that's me." The rest was built into the myth of the band, the story told by his parents countless times as he grew up, hearing a hundred times how Matthew had slapped at Doogy's shoulders as Doogy drove down the freeway, the drummer casting frantic glances his way, mouthing *What's he saying, dude?*

A meeting was planned with the band and Geffen executives when they played LA later that summer. The LA show was phenomenal—even Nick, who was both young and by then more than a little bored by his parents' music—noticed the shift that night. They played all the hits from *Dirty Gods,* and a few new ones they'd written while on the road. It was the first time the band ever played "I Won't Forget It" live, and the response from the audience was ferocious. His mother had always quietly insisted that it was that song that had gotten them the deal. All the Geffen folks were there, and they unanimously agreed the band was mean as shit, the songs were unstoppable and infectious, and a new album would be a sure thing. Two weeks after the end of that tour, with *Dirty Gods* still at #55 on Billboard, the Blank Letters signed a two-record deal with Geffen for roughly 2.8 million dollars. *All Your Wasted Days,* their major label debut, would come out the next year, when Nick was ten, and would top at #5 on the Billboard charts this time. (This was before streaming and "all da downloads," as Nick would joke with his mother, and back when a band still had to sell a veritable shit-ton of physical units to land in the Top 10.) "I Won't Forget It," the second single on *Wasted Days,* was a #1 hit for six weeks in the US and #11 in the UK, and they made a ridiculous amount of money off of that song with licensing too. Deodorants. Neon-colored corn chips. Ads for basketball teams and golf championships, and, nearly twenty years after its release, a hybrid car. That song just snagged in people's heads like it came supplied with its own fishhooks.

All Your Wasted Days eventually went platinum. They toured hard on that record for the next few years. Countless festival and television appearances. Gone was the Ford Econoline with the temperamental AC and the tape deck that would randomly spit out *Marquee Moon* in the middle of a song. They had a bus now, and Nick had his own little bed with a curtain that he could pull open and closed if he wanted some facsimile of privacy on the endless drives. Crashing on floors wasn't a thing anymore. Nor were friends his own age, really. When the record first came out, the band toured for ten months straight supporting *All Your Wasted Days*. Nick had always been one of those kids who got along better with grownups; after *Wasted Days*, there wasn't much of a choice. His life was a flurry of highways and sound checks and green rooms, hotel rooms and diner booths.

He was twelve when his parents started demoing—reluctantly, and under contractual pressure from the label—the second album. *Knife Wounds,* his father wanted to call it, "because these cocksuckers are bleeding us dry."

They'd never finish writing it, of course, splitting up instead, still under contract with the label. Nick had never really gotten a straight answer out of his mother about what had brought it about—it was one area where she was uncharacteristically vague about Matthew's fault in the matter. "Just band shit," she'd say with a dismissive wave of the hand. "Label pressure, band shit, your dad and I going at each other's throats all the time. Being in a band with your husband's like being married twice, you know? And with two other dudes." Matthew talked about going solo, saying he'd get more done, to which Katherine, Nick remembered, had scoffed, wishing him the best of luck. "If you got another 'I Won't Forget It' in you, dear heart, be my fucking guest," to which Matthew had responded by casually punting a hole in the body of his own Martin acoustic resting on its stand—a guitar made of hand-hewn Sitka spruce, something that had cost him over three grand—on the way out the door. He hadn't come home for two nights after that one. It seemed to Nick like the dissolution of a friendship, the band breakup, but taken to the nth degree, given the money and fame involved, and his father's propensity for temperamental, fuck-it-all theatrics.

Their original A&R guy, long since moved on to another position in the company, was brought in as mediator between the band's lawyers and the label's lawyers. Matthew showed up for that first mediation session in LA shitfaced and sneering, wearing his sunglasses. They took a recess, where he and Doogy almost got in a fistfight in the hallway.

The next day, a consensus was reached. The contract for a second Geffen album would be fulfilled with a "scraps" record, a mishmash of compilation tracks, alternate versions of early songs, and live material, as well as the few demos that had been laid down before the breakup. It was a buyout, and it was either that or a "greatest hits" record, which would have given Geffen few options, given that they only had two albums. No one was happy, but by this time, with the band broken up and his parents in constant strife with each other, unhappiness had become commonplace.

The album was released shortly after Nick's thirteenth birthday. It was indeed called *Knife Wounds,* and it flopped. Cracked the Top 100 for a few weeks, lingering there like it was on life support. *Rolling Stone,* who had lauded both previous records, and fawningly interviewed the band, summed up *Knife Wounds* as "an obligation with a weak tracklisting, and populated with slapdash, tinny songs. The heart's been carved out of this band in the name of contract fulfillment." Meanwhile, *Dirty Gods* and *Wasted Days* were still, to this day, considered classics, nicely straddling the punk/alternative/rock spectrum broadly enough that they'd never gone out of print. Both records had long gone double platinum. There had been numerous documentaries made about the band, and there was a Blank Letters biopic in the works that both Geffen and the remaining band members were feverishly against.

And that was that. A pair of classic records, a third that limped along. A guitarist who'd thrown himself from a bridge. The three remaining band members had, each to their own degree, moved on.

His mother had, what? Two hundred songs on various hard drives in her bedroom? Always with the talk of putting them out sometime, "once I get my shit straight."

And he, Nick, was a man who helped people find achingly specific and rare things. As if in the hopes—and yeah, they were verging on some therapy-level shit here—that he might stumble upon that most specific and rarest of things: a reason for his father's death. Something concrete. Something that said, *I love you, Nicky, and I'm sorry I did you and your mom like this, man.* Nick, years later, still courting answers in the whirlwind. That single thing that might, once and for all, do away with the grand and goddamned painful mystery of it all. And at the same time, if he really wanted to till that ground, he'd look in Matthew's archives, wouldn't he?

It'd be too generous to say that Peach Serrano was a father figure. For one, he isn't all that much older than Nick, but beyond that, there's never been anything fatherly about the man. Nothing familial. Peach at his best is cordial and respectful, but Nick is smart enough to understand that that's reliant on Nick's own cordiality and respect. There is no warmth there, only expectation. Any small talk is born simply of the familiarity that comes with proximity. And Peach is a criminal. He doesn't know specifics, doesn't want to, but he understands that men like Hutch Holtz and Tim Reed are in his employ for a reason.

And now? Now, he should be talking in the past tense, shouldn't he? Because now Peach is just a spill of meat on the sidewalk in front of a dive bar. Peach has been removed from the equation. Nick's left the hand beneath a dumpster in Southeast Portland—let someone else field its nattering, deathly dialogue. His only job right now is finding Katherine. Where is she? He knows of only one place—home. The apartment. And she's not there.

He's supposed to be a *finder,* and he has no idea where to start.

The night is just the night, once again filled with rain and the endless noise of passing cars, light spilling from windows onto the street. He stands there ten blocks from his home, amid the buildings and cars and dripping trees. Well within Katherine's ring of safety, but there is so much *room*, so many places for her to be, and such a grand disinterest from everyone else and everything else, the world just wheeling along on its mad axis. He wants the world to stop, to freeze. He could find her then. If Peach were alive, he could call Peach and ask him for help. Peach would have at least done that. But Peach caught a round below the eye and spattered his brains on the window of a bar called Mercy's. So.

You're a finder, he thinks, tamping the panic down.

So find her.

He takes out his phone. Scrolls through his contacts.

Nick has still kept the number. He knows he shouldn't have.

It's the middle of the night in New York, if that's where he is now.

Nick pulls up the number, presses DIAL.

It's picked up on the second ring. "Yes," the man says. That same curious accent.

Nick says, "I need your help."

He can hear Rachmann smiling on the other end. "Hello, Nick. It's nice to hear from you. Please, tell me more."

JOHN BONNER

The night thrums with traffic. Bonner's flinchy, paranoid. After Pie in the Sky, the botched retrieval of the hand, Lundy's given them a new ride—the SUV had grown too hot. This one's a little less obtrusive—a black sedan—but with none of the protections of the SUV. Still, Bonner should feel better; they'd stopped too many hearts in the old one. Now he drives down Grand, heading south, evening lights all smeared along the avenue. He and Weils bickering, continuing their pointless endeavor.

Saint Michael is in the backseat, dying.

If Bonner ever had any doubt about the reality of the hand, or the scope of the Heavy Light program, it was obliterated within ten seconds of meeting Michael for the first time and helping him hobble into the car. All things were made real right then, made irrefutably true, and every cry of falsehood or exaggeration Bonner might have claimed was chopped off at the knees.

He's real, Michael, and he's fucking terrifying.

He wears a Blazers jersey and a black knit cap and wraparound Oakleys that, with his chalk-white skin and stone-carved cheekbones, make him look like a model from hell. Gazing out the window at the passing world with his hands folded in his lap, his breathing is labored and wet. Every once in a while, he'll clear his throat and run a rag along his lips; the rag will come away with something black as charcoal smeared in the folds.

Also, he thrums like a telephone wire. It makes the hairs on Bonner's neck and wrists stand at attention. It makes him want to grind his teeth. Being near Michael feels like worrying a hangnail until the blood comes.

And he's dying—Lundy's open about it, had told them as much as they stood there on the tarmac of Camelot, informing them that he had no idea how long Michael has but it could happen at any time, so act accordingly—and they've been sent back out into the world again to look for the hand. The Coffin kid's in the wind, but they have his mother in custody. Lundy's sweating her in a Camelot briefing room as Bonner and Weils chauffeur Michael around, hoping against hope. Driving around, randomly pointing out waypoints, as if proximity—the hand presumably somewhere in Southeast Portland—might jar something loose in the strange maelstrom that is his brain.

Michael says nothing. Just radiates his tinfoil discomfort. Coughs, wipes his lips with a rag. Alien and cold with his silence.

"We need more fucking agents," Bonner finally mutters, more to himself than Weils.

"It's Heavy Light, Bonner," says Weils. "It's not crowd control. We don't get more agents."

The crowd-control line jars him for a moment.

It's very possible there are statewide APBs out for the two of them now, their descriptions, cops combing street camera footage, trying to get a match on facial recognition software. Running the plates on the SUV, which, good luck running that up the chain and trying to get a straight answer. There's a manhunt likely underway for the killing of the civilian and the guy in the hatchback. This is what happens with undercover shit, in Bonner's experience—at some point, you run the risk of becoming dust in the cyclone. The project gets too big. Someone trips up. Four months after Brooklyn, after killing Sean Pernicio on the Williamsburg Bridge, and here he is. Wanted by local cops for a double homicide, and with something that feels very much like Death itself sitting in the backseat. The twisting pathways a life can lead you down sometimes. Bonner wants to blame his uncle, blame his handler, blame David Lundy, but he knows it's all him. Bonner's made his own bed.

Weils's face is tightly drawn. She's closed up even more than usual. She doesn't like being near Michael like this either. She doesn't like the detail they've been given. She doesn't like Bonner. Mostly, he thinks, she's pissed that she missed Coffin outside the bar. That the hand has gotten away from them again. Bonner would be smug about it—he likes her leveled down a bit—but there are dead people in the mathematics of it, a number of them, and that changes things.

"Alright, look. Where to, Michael," says Bonner, staring at the impassive lenses of the Oakleys in his rearview mirror. Those black lips, like he's been eating grape popsicles, or a pen he was sucking on exploded in his mouth. Being next to Michael makes him feel bad about himself, somehow, and doesn't Bonner feel bad about himself enough already?

"Michael," he says again, snapping his fingers, "how we doing, man? Any idea where we should be heading? You're the boss, where to?"

In the rearview mirror, Michael mumbles something. Nonsense words. Some private lexicon tumbling from those smeared lips. They've recently cut his wings again—as motivation, supposedly— and Bonner wonders if that's why he's so ragged and worn down. He's never seen them do it, but he imagines it hurts like hell. Nothing about Michael radiates, like, goodness or health. For a guy with wings, there is nothing pure or angelic about him. He's like the last clamorous sizzle of a raw nerve before it dies. Bonner's reminded of the rumor he's heard: One of the lab techs at Camelot, so she claims, knew a guy who'd been tasked with cutting Michael's wings off, back when he was with the DoD, before Michael had gotten passed on to Lundy. Bonner understands that rumors are rife in agencies like theirs, and half the time program directors rely on them as a kind of stopgap authority. A warning, head-on-a-pole kind of situation. *Take heed, peons,* and all that. But the tech swears by this one. This guy had, so the story goes, purportedly been the one tasked with sawing Michael's wing-nubs off, doing it for the twentieth time in a row or whatever, some ungodly number, there in some subbasement at Langley or DC or wherever they'd first kept him. And Michael had cursed the guy, the story went. Wept and cursed him. Said *something,* anyway. The tech had seemed fine, normal, had clocked out. Bought a lengua burrito from a food cart near his apartment, and then went home, fed his fish, sat down on his couch. Turned on an episode of *Antiques Roadshow,* then ran a pair of shearing scissors through his left eye into his own brain. Ran them all the way to the handle.

See, it was the *specificity* that unnerved Bonner. Rumors had a way of becoming garbled, like a lethal game of Telephone, even in intelligence gathering. Hell, *especially* in IG. But this one was so moored in that specificity: The guy that had hurt Saint Michael again and again had been cursed and then gone home and turned on *Antiques Roadshow* and ended himself. Bonner doesn't like how Michael makes him feel, but damn, he fears him even more.

"Michael," he says once again. "Please tell us if you're feeling anything. We're looking for the remnant, remember? Okay? Help us out. Help us find the remnant." He's speaking the way they've been taught—simple commands, regular reminders of mission objectives. *He has the attention span of a six-year-old,* according to Lundy. *Treat him as such.*

"There was a battle," Michael finally says, in that breathy, distracted way of his. He coughs again.

"A battle?"

"The remnant . . ."

Bonner waits, but Michael's already drifted off. There are a lot of police cruisers around, which makes sense—between the bar and the shootout at the pizza place, Weils has killed three people in the past couple hours. Plus, Christ, the maintenance guy at the Moriarty apartment. For a moment it chills him, the breadth of this thing he's involved himself in. Four dead men in as many hours, good God.

"Where is the remnant, Michael?" This comes from Weils, who doesn't bother to hide her disdain.

"A man was killed," Michael says, and Weils lets out a snort of contempt.

"And what else?" This from Bonner, who watches in the rearview as Michael dips his head in concentration.

"I am tired," Michael says.

"I believe you. I know you are, Michael."

"I don't feel well."

Bonner finds himself nodding. "I know, man. I'm sorry. We'd like to get you back to your room." *Back to your cell,* he almost says, then wonders if Michael would even notice the difference between the two words, if he's capable of grasping nuance like that. "Can you tell us anything else?" He wonders what Michael was like when they first found him, how different he must have been. This tremendously powerful, strange thing, and all they've done in the interceding years is carve him up, make him perform his inane parlor tricks until he's half-dead.

And how the hell am I any different, Bonner thinks. I'm right here. Driving him around. Making the same demands.

Michael puts the rag to his mouth, coughs into it. "He put it somewhere. He hid it, a thin man did. After the other man was killed." Weils casts Bonner a look; *this sounds promising.* "A man was shot through the eye. Above the eye." Michael clears his throat, a wet, clotted sound. Taps a long finger above his own eye. "Right here."

Weils says, "Where did he hide the remnant? The thin man."

And then a clicking sound is issuing from Michael's throat; he's gagging, a rush of blackness spilling from his lips in a torrent. Bonner looks back at him in alarm and nearly rear-ends someone, which would be a perfect capstone to this whole goddamn ruinous affair. A shootout with Portland cops over a fender bender, Michael dead in the backseat.

Bonner, angry and frightened, screeches to a halt, turns his hazards on amid a scattering of honks.

"Where did he hide it," Weils hisses. Insistent now. "Michael, where did he put the remnant?" All this while Michael chokes on his blood in the backseat.

Bonner curses, threads the sedan to the curb. He steps out and nearly gets clipped by traffic, then opens the back door where Michael is doubled over, coughing darkness into his cupped hands. Bonner goes to touch him, to lay a hand on the curve of his back, but he stops halfway. Fear and disgust rippling through him. Michael sits up and leans his head back, gasping. Drowning in front of them, some vital thing inside him ruptured.

"You okay?" Bonner says, sounding like an idiot in his own ears.

Michael's shoulders rise and fall as he gasps for air, that pale throat lifted up.

"Bonner," Weils says in the passenger seat. "Get in, we have to go."

"Weils, he's fucking dying right here, man. Right in the car. Come on."

Bonner crouches there in the open doorway. A single black line spills from Michael's lips down the side of his marbled neck. Bonner reaches in and gingerly takes the rag from his cupped hands. Tries to clean the blood from his neck as Michael stares at some interminable point on the ceiling of the car, shuddering for breath. Bonner just managing to smear the blood around, ink on plaster.

Weils leans back, catching his eye. "Get in the fucking car, Bonner. We have to go."

Michael gasps, takes a heaving breath.

"What is it?"

She tosses her phone on the dash. "The driver from the pizza place."

"Right," Bonner says, "the one you shot through the neck?"

Weils nods, ignoring the dig. "Camelot's monitoring local police chatter."

Bonner casts one more glance at Michael—he seems to be breathing again, managing it—and sets the rag in his lap, reluctantly getting back in the driver's seat. "So what about him?"

"He's at the morgue, and there's a bunch of cops there."

"Okay. And?"

She lets out a little laugh. "And he's up."

"The hell does that mean?"

"The guy in the car," she says. "The one I shot through the neck, like you said. He's up and around and attacking people, I guess. So let's go."

NICK COFFIN

"**W**hat is it that you need, friend?" Rachmann says. It's as if calling him in the middle of the night in New York is no bother at all. As if Nick last spoke to him minutes ago, rather than weeks.

He walks across an overpass. Below him is the freeway, a guardrail and a hillside of scree and weeds separating him from that sea of headlights. Nick keeps casting these furtive glances over his shoulder. Keeps remembering the black, dime-sized hole that suddenly appeared on Peach's cheek. The way Hutch sat curled over himself on the bus bench.

"I need you to help me find someone."

"Okay. And they're missing?"

Nick pauses. "What?"

"Do they want to be gone, Nick? This is what I mean."

He passes a tavern with bars over the windows and a couple standing outside, smoking. He waits until he passes them and says, "It's my mother. People with guns took her. Stormed in. Shot someone."

"Mmm," Rachmann says. He sounds unsurprised, unbothered, as

if such things happen frequently in his life. "I'm assuming it involves you somehow."

"It does."

"Tell me the details. I'll find as much as there is to find."

"This will cost money," Nick says.

He can hear the smile in Rachmann's voice, and somehow it calms him. "Of course," Rachmann says. He's a professional, after all. He is being hired for a job. The job's emotional freight doesn't interest him. "Why else would you call me, Nick? Everything costs money. Breathing costs money these days." He names a sizable sum, but certainly within the constraints of what Nick has taken from the bag.

"Fine," he says. "I can find things, you know? Things I can track down, stationary things. People—my mom—it's different." He's saying too much of the wrong things.

"This requires abilities outside of your particular field. It's wise of you."

"Okay."

"What is her name, Nick?"

Nick says his mother's name.

"Do you understand," Rachmann says, "that you might not like what I find? That there is that possibility?"

"Rachmann, I don't have time to fuck around like this. I'm sorry. She's out there, by herself. Do it or don't, but let me find someone else if you're going to play around."

"Okay. We'll begin. What have you done?"

Nick walks, night wheeling around him, wonders how to start. Finally, he says, "I find things for people."

"I know this."

"And tonight . . ."

Rachmann's silent, listening.

"Tonight, my boss, someone shot him in the face. Killed him right in front of me. I found a thing for him, was *given* it, and people want it, and they shot him. They took my mother. Because they want this thing."

"Perhaps we can broker a trade. You still have this item to offer?"

Nick looks helplessly at the smear of cityscape in the distance. "I got rid of it. I can't—it's difficult to be around this object. It's hard to explain."

Rachmann is silent again, and like a fool, like someone with no other choice, Nick steps in and fills the silence with all that's happened.

Some interminable time later, he's done with his story. Halting and messy as it is. He's in Old Town now, threading his way among bedraggled lines of homeless people camped out against the sides of shuttered buildings, while other businesses—bars mostly—do a brisk trade among the scattering of blue tarps and tents.

"This man who was shot in front of the bar, he's familiar to both of us?" Apart from Katherine, they have done well at not naming names.

"Yes."

"Your boss?"

"Yes."

"And he was shot by an unknown assailant."

Nick sighs. "Correct."

Sensing his annoyance, Rachmann says, "I'm being careful. You should as well. Where is the object now?"

"I'm not telling you that."

Rachmann is smiling again when he says, "If you left it somewhere, how do you know it's still there?"

"I don't. I'm taking a risk. This whole thing is a risk," Nick says, and comes close to hanging up. Simply walking to the police station and turning himself in. Telling them everything. *Just lift this weight from me.*

"You assume they were military, these people that shot our associate?"

"I have no idea, man. A militia? The mob? Cops? I'm calling you because I don't know."

"Alright," Rachmann says. "I'll call you when I have information.

Feel free to call around, exhaust other options. I don't demand exclusivity."

I have no other options, Nick thinks. He ends the call, dials his mother's number again. It goes straight to voicemail. He keeps walking. His heart won't stop hammering, won't let him breathe right.

KATHERINE MORIARTY

"You don't want him to die."

"No. Please."

"You understand we have that capability."

"Yes."

David Lundy pushes her cell phone across the table. They must have gotten it from the apartment.

"Call your son. Tell him we want the hand."

"I still don't know what you're talking about."

"It doesn't matter, Katherine. *He* knows. Call him and tell him to meet us."

She touches her phone with trembling fingers but won't tap the screen. Won't turn it on. Lundy watches her. "Katherine."

"How do I know you won't hurt him."

Lundy leans forward, grinning. "We will hurt him, Katherine. If you don't call him and tell him to give us the thing we need, this very important thing, he'll be hurt very badly. I'll see to it."

Katherine taps the screen. It comes to life, a rectangle of light. She runs a trembling hand beneath her nose. Types in her code.

"Get him to tell us where he is. We'll have people meet him, and then everything will be fine and you can go home." His voice is soothing now, a balm. So reasonable.

He keeps on. "Katherine, we know all about you. The band. Your husband's death. Living with your son. We know you write music for a television show, you live off royalties. Smart investments. We don't want anyone hurt. We're doing this to save people, I promise you." Still with that mad grin on his face, Lundy says, "I actually like your band, Katherine. I have all your records. Your music is very important to me."

She swallows, hears the click in her throat. It's not that she believes him. It's just that the world is so small, that it cannot get smaller than the chair she's in right now. There's no running room left.

She knuckles a single tear away and dials her son's number.

HUTCH HOLTZ

Hutch, in those months following the Gresham thing, slept a lot. Twelve, fourteen hours a day. Sometimes more. He was hurting a lot of the time, and sleep offered escape. But the dreams, Christ. He was inundated with them. Crazed, convoluted things full of death and misdirection. His father, dead a few years by the time he mouthed off to the Crooked Wheel club and met the door of a two-ton Ford passenger van, featured prominently in them. He was almost unrelentingly disappointed in Hutch in these dreams, and full of a dark merriment: Dan Holtz in his recliner, grinning and flipping through the channels while Hutch sat disemboweled on the couch. His father, keening a high crow's laugh from a rooftop while Hutch stood trapped in a bricked courtyard below, searching for an exit. His father a bent wolf/man hybrid that chuckled wetly right before he pounced. Most painfully, dream after dream of his father in his hospice bed, moaning as the painkillers slowly and irrevocably stopped working, unable to see or hear Hutch even though he stood right next to him, calling out his name.

Those dreams had been frighteningly realistic—his father's death had been piecemeal and drawn-out. Hutch knew that it was far from the passing the old man had wished for. Had he been given a choice, his pops would have opted for a round from his service pistol up through the roof of his mouth. By the end, he'd been both angry and ashamed of his condition, and any attempt at consolation that Hutch might have offered—even an understanding that yeah, cancer was devouring him, and yes, it was okay to be diminished and animal-like, drawn down into a human body that was capable only of occasionally moaning in agony—would have been rebuffed.

Hobbling out of the hospital now, he feels weirdly close to the old man. A kinship. The hospital has grown suddenly chaotic, full of alarms and staff running everywhere, indecipherable commands over the intercom system. People hardly offer him a glance as he palms the pistol and makes for the entrance doors. He thinks the old man would have been pleased at Hutch's brazenness. He'd been no fan of Hutch's work in life, that disappointment as familiar in waking as it was in dreams, but this bold escape? Goddamn would have put a smile on his father's face.

Not only that, but here he is, so much like him at the end, gritting his teeth through the pain, hobbling along, his guts in the most fragile array. All the good dope draining out of him. He has no idea what his back looks like—perhaps the wound is the size of a fist, or a silver dollar. Perhaps it is stitched shut. Regardless, he seems profoundly lucky: It's all mostly numb right now.

What *is* going on here, though? The waiting room of the ER is half full, the injured and their loved ones scattered throughout. He chances a look back at the door he's come from and sees nothing. Even the information desk is empty, the phone ringing. For the moment, they've been abandoned.

An alarm sounds then, loud. That's for him. Has to be.

A few people eye him warily from their chairs as he walks past, the electronic doors sliding open. Beyond the archway the night is wet, cold, spitting rain. There is a moment where Hutch feels like crying and walking back to his hospital bed, handing the detective his shit back and crawling under the covers, but it only lasts a moment. As ever, he's gone too far to turn back. He keeps moving further and further away from safety. When Tim shot Wesley in the head in the warehouse—a lifetime ago? A few hours? Hutch's trajectory was already mapped out by then. He knows it.

He heads toward the parking lot. His feet wet, rain in his hair. He gazes out at the parked cars, reflected streetlights shimmering on their rooftops. He finds an older car, another Datsun, and uses the butt of the pistol to smash out the driver's window. It takes him a bit of time. He spends a moment cleaning out the blued shards from the edges of the window and pushing the pebbles of glass out of the seat, onto the pavement. He uses the pistol to smash the housing off the steering column and hotwires the car, something he's known how to do since Tim taught him, a week after they got out of Rutherford.

The car rumbles, rattles, purrs beneath him. Three-quarters of a tank. His feet seek purchase on the pedals. Soon enough the dope will wear off entirely and he'll return to the wounded cage of his body. Exhausted, frail, hurt.

He taps the cop's phone. It's password-protected. He tosses it out the window and heads out of the parking lot. Hears another galaxy of sirens approaching. Presses his hand to his side. The fingers are dry, bloodless. No blood on his gown.

There's nothing left to do. Tim's dead, he's sure of it. Police after him. He's got some money in an ice-cream container in his freezer. Decent amount. He can go, get gone for a while, turn to smoke.

For what, though?

To heal enough so that in a week or a month down the line he gets raided by cops, shot down in the courtyard of some shit-ass motel?

Or he can do something that approaches benevolence and revenge both.

He can destroy the hand.

Kill it, as much as a thing like that might actually be killed.

It's no choice at all, really.

He heads south, toward Nick Coffin's apartment.

JOHN BONNER

The medical examiner's office is two stories of brick and glass. Modern, clean-lined, tucked behind a sizable parking lot that's sparsely filled at this hour, with high green hedges flanking both sides. The rear of the building butts up against an equally nondescript office building. Were it not for an ambulance and a pair of police cruisers parked amid the rest of the cars, Bonner wouldn't have a clue. Some part of him really had expected an old Victorian with turrets, maybe a black cat weathervane. You hear about the dead rising, your head goes in a certain direction. Thing was, Bonner had *seen* the man in his car, buckled in, seen the horrible wound in his throat, the spill of blood in his lap. Bonner would have sworn on his own life that the man was dead as hell, dead beyond any inkling of awareness, dead forever. According to the police radio, that isn't the case. They'd dropped Michael back at Camelot, and now here they are.

The plates in the flak jacket he's got on make him feel like he's wearing a set of phonebooks. He can't imagine trotting around in the thing, much less running. There's a beanbag shotgun stretched across his lap. Black ops or not, shortage of agents or not, they certainly have plenty of gear. Bonner has, perhaps not surprisingly, grown more reluctant to hurt anyone as the night's progressed. Weils has made it clear she doesn't have the same concerns. She jacks back the slide on her pistol, puts a round in the chamber, then casts a baleful glance at the shotgun.

"Subject's already dead, Bonner. It's not like you're going to hurt him."

The doors of the office are closed. No sirens, no alarms.

"You sure you heard that there was an emergency here? Everything looks fine to me."

Weils looks away. Quietly, she says, "If you make it through tonight, Bonner, I'm telling Lundy I want you sent back to Williamsburg. Or wherever. You can do whatever weak-ass filing job some FBI branch in Bismarck gives you. You don't have the touch for this, man."

Bonner sits a little straighter under the weight of the flak plates. "You shot a *civilian* in the face tonight. Tell me more about my shortcomings."

"A civilian who was aiming down on you."

"Two civilians!" Bonner says, holding up his fingers. "*Three!* There was the one in front of the bar too. And that old man in the hallway. It's fucking—It's not even unprofessional, Weils. You're rogue."

"I'm rogue," she repeats, the words like small bitter stones falling from her mouth. "I'm rogue, huh?"

"Four people dead. No hand. I'd say you're rogue, yeah."

Weils holds out her phone. "Call Lundy, tell him that. See how it goes." She waits, and when Bonner doesn't move to take the phone, she puts it away. "You are either stupid, Bonner, or *brutally* obtuse, because there is a dangerous lack of understanding of what's at stake here."

"Well, it's going to be a little hard to transfer me from a program that doesn't exist, Weils. I think that's the point, right?"

Weils snorts, shakes her head.

"I'm here for the duration," Bonner says.

She turns to him, and he sees that he's finally made her furious. "We caught *live fire* in that parking lot—from two different shooters—and you didn't fire a single round."

"It was in the middle of a traffic jam, Weils. I'm not—"

"You did *not* have my back out there. You're hurt that I don't trust you? Shit, I don't trust you for a *second,* Bonner. You're a desk monkey, man. Soft, afraid, unreliable. Makes you dangerous beyond words."

"Weils—"

A man staggers out of the doorway. He has no face. Just this pulped ruin, a wetness that catches and reflects the lights of the parking lot. Bloody sputum spilling down his shirt, a pair of eyes blazing through it all. Nighttime traffic is right there, forty feet away. The man-shape takes a shambling step onto the pavement and then swivels its head as if scenting the air.

Very quietly, Bonner says, "Is that a cop?"

Weils gently opens the passenger door of the sedan. The man—though a significant part of Bonner is having a hard time considering him a man at this point—just stands there, swaying slightly, as if he were some automaton awaiting further instructions. They hear a scream drift from the inside of the building. Weils sights down, using the top of the passenger door as a stabilizer. The shot rips through the night; Bonner flinches. The man staggers, catches himself on the wall. Weils begins walking toward him and Bonner, cursing, steps out of the car. Weils fires again and the man's head rocks back. He falls. She trots over, stands before him. There's a last dreaming twitch from the fingers of the man's left hand. Even from where he is, Bonner notes the look of howling vacancy in the eyes.

She dumps another round in his skull and Bonner flinches again.

"He was *eaten,*" he says, running over to her, his voice watery and small. "Look at that, Weils, that's a fucking *cop,* and he was *eaten, holy* shit, look at his fucking *face*—"

Inside the building comes the near-musical cadence of shattering glass. Someone screams again, and it is so purely anguished that the hair stirs on Bonner's neck.

Weils nods toward the building. "Watch that doorway." She pulls out her phone. Calling Camelot.

"It's me," she says. A pause. "It's happened. The ME's office, yeah. It's confirmed." She gives the address of the medical examiner's office, the very spot where they stand, and Bonner marvels at her calmness. He keeps stealing glances at the cop splayed out in the entrance. His face. His uniform. Has Weils been preparing for this all along? And Bonner just shuttling her around, a good little errand boy.

A shape shifts in the dark of the lobby and Bonner raises the shotgun, then curses and slips the strap over his shoulder, instead drawing his pistol. This, at last, garners the slightest nod of approval from Weils. She keeps her phone to her ear and holds her own pistol out, scanning the parking lot behind them.

"Tell Lundy," Weils says, "we've got a fever house. It's confirmed. We're at room zero. He needs to let Langley know." A pause, and someone runs by inside, lit up in the half-light of the lobby. Down a stretch of hallway and gone again.

"Listen to me. Heavy Light is done," Weils says over the phone. "Every concern about the remnant," she says, and Bonner can hear the panic in her voice now, the humanness in it, finally, "is realized. It's worse than we thought. DoD, State needs to be notified."

A spill of bodies suddenly bursts from the hall and floods the lobby, smashing against the front doors in a shower of glass. They tumble through, falling to the ground, Bonner and Weils backpedaling. It's two cops and a woman in a white smock and a hairnet, and then, crouched low, there he is, the driver at the pizza place—long, greasy hair, naked body scattered with stick-and-poke tattoos. The last time Bonner had seen him, a few hours before, he'd been wearing a leather jacket and a shattered jaw that hung wrong. And now here he is, cadaver-gray, an incision halfway down his chest. His face freshly slicked in gore, jaw snapping even through its strange lean. The four of them stumble and then sprint toward Bonner and Weils, all four with that same vacuous, deathly glaze on their eyes. One suddenly peels off toward the street, the other three coming for them. Bonner fires off a volley of shots—it's finally happened, he's firing his pistol. He backpedals and for a second feels Weils's steadying hand on his back. He manages to land a round in one cop's shoulder. It spins him but a second later he's up and sprinting toward them again.

Bonner and Weils turn and run.

Two cops, a criminal, and a medical examiner. Sounds like the beginning of a bad joke. Bonner and Weils jump in the car, lock the doors. The windshield is slapped by pale, bloody hands. The eyes of the dead—if that's what they are now—are depthless but filled with a certain concentration, a singularity of purpose. Bonner looks at them and understands that you could plead with those eyes the rest of your life and never see anything reflected back at you. One of the cops actually tries to bite the windshield, smearing bloody saliva against the glass.

Bonner sets his Glock up against the window, his chest heaving. An inch separates them. His hand trembles; the barrel clicks against the glass.

"You fire that, we're dead," Weils says. "They'll get in."

"I know it," Bonner says. "What the fuck is a fever house, Weils?"

"Just drive."

A woman runs out of the doorway and through the parking lot. She's in a green smock. She wears one shoe. Her hand is covering her forearm. She's alive.

She's screaming as she runs toward the street.

Oh, *now* people are starting to scream, Bonner thinks.

Now people are starting to notice.

SAINT MICHAEL

Decades spent in various cells. Days upon days upon days. The window, the bed, the ceiling, where commands are relentlessly issued. Decades spent here, alive like this, freighted with the ownership of all this. Flesh. Eyes. Fingers. The wings they cut from him.

Michael beyond here, Michael without the stones of time and place stacked upon his neck, *that* Michael's a shapeless thing, a vessel of light, of a particular *thereness*. But he's been given wings here, charged with watching. Waiting. It's a profoundly unkind world, this one. "Terrible but it's true," to quote David Lundy. *Terrible but it's true,* a thought that ricochets endlessly throughout his mind these days. Michael sees what he sees, sees what is given to him. It's the exacting price for being here, the visions. The knowledge of them. To tell his captors of the visions is no matter. Easy. A necessity, even.

They've assigned his name to him, assigned meaning to it. Something they made up. "Saint Michael," they call him. They call him that, they saw the wings from him and laugh about it, put this name upon him. Decades of this. Days upon days. Demanding and cutting. Michael does not really understand time, how it works, but knows that even if he understood it, he could not stop it. Time is a hallway with death at the end.

For many years he has told himself: Those that cut the wings from him incur a great debt. Those that hold him to the floor and hurt him incur a great debt. He's grown to wish vengeance upon them even as he knows a wish for vengeance incurs a debt itself. This seems, to him, the trapping of man. Of life itself. That what you wish upon others comes back against you. Terrible but it's true.

He was found, Michael was, as he was supposed to have been found. Wounded, winged, befouled with so much heaving life. Found where he was supposed to be found and brought to a gathering of rooms by men in uniforms. Hurt. Moved and hurt and moved and hurt. Demanded upon. Years of this. Decades.

He is eager to die now.

David Lundy stands before him. David Lundy demands sights from him now, more frequently than ever. Michael tells him of his meager visions but time is bringing him closer to death. Something they both know. Michael is weak, tired. He is hurt for his visions and hurt when he's unable to provide them. This too seems a trapping of man—this brazen cruelty. You are hurt either way. You are hurt no matter what you do.

He's become a thing that wishes vengeance now, and perhaps that is something he's been meant to learn.

Perhaps he's been meant to become this.

Michael knows what he knows, has always known it:

He knows of the hand, the voice, the eye. The remnants. Knows that a lesser devil might someday come forth, were certain conditions to align, allegiances and oblations made. All through here, shot through this place, there would be a grand leveling of the world. He knows that such a thing is near.

"Listen to me, you cocksucker. I am done fucking with you," says David Lundy, standing over him. "How do we stop it?"

"What?" Michael says. It hurts to talk now. His voice is small.

"I've never gotten a straight answer out of you," says David Lundy.

"In all this time. In all these years. *We have a fever house,* Michael. It's here. The hand got away from us, and people have died near it, because of it. And here we are. So what now?"

David Lundy sounds afraid. He strikes Michael.

Certain men might position themselves to become devils, were they willing to do certain things. To themselves, to others. Perform certain actions, and be willing to wait for a time in a kind of wretched half-life. Willing to promise fealty. These are things that Michael could say. But he says nothing.

David Lundy points a finger at his face. There is Michael's blood on David Lundy's knuckles. His body feels hot, cold, sick, dying, pained. One lesson he's learned is that they are truly not meant to come back here. It hurts here.

"Tell me what we do to stop it," says David Lundy, "or I shoot you in the fucking head and see what comes out the other side. I'm so tired of this dance we do."

Michael could tell him that this is not the thing he should worry about. That David Lundy should worry what happens when the remnants—the hand, the eye, the voice—are used all at once. That someone has placed himself in a position to come forth, has promised fealty, made offerings. That when this happens, darkness will spill forth. It's a matter of closeness now. An inevitability to it.

Michael could say all this, but he only says two words. Two words. He is eager to be done here. Let me walk the dark hall, he thinks.

"Start talking," David Lundy says, "or I'll saw your fucking head off myself." The remnants, the remnants, the hand, the voice, the eye. Use them all at once and here comes the seepage, the devil stepping forth, the grand and yawing darkness. It has been Michael's purpose to witness this. To see.

He says two words only.

Saint Michael smiles with blood on his teeth. He says, "It's begun."

NICK COFFIN

Sirens rip up the night. Sometimes close, sometimes a susurration in the distance, but by now a regular feature of the night's unraveling. He has nothing to do but wait for Rachmann's call, and has no idea what to do beyond that besides occasionally call his mother's phone—voicemail, always—and walk aimlessly, furiously. It's not safe to go home, of course, but beyond that, he has nowhere to go. He has nothing but his adrenaline and the image of Peach Serrano's brains spilling out to guide him. The bullet holes in the hallway outside his apartment. It's enough to keep him moving.

Nick's standing before a parking lot at the edge of the Pearl, not far from the loft where his father spent his last crazed months, and is considering getting a hotel room—he has no shortage of money, at least—when his phone vibrates in his pocket.

Katherine's name on the screen.

"Mom?"

"Nick? Oh, God."

"Mom, where are you?"

"Nick," she says, "I'm with some people," and then there's a man on the line, saying his name.

"I want to talk to my mom," Nick says, hating the petulance in his voice. "Put her on, now."

"Absolutely, Nick. We want to reunite you two as soon as we can. I'm Officer Lundy, with the Oregon State Police. Your mom's okay, she's not hurt, but there's been an incident at her apartment and we had to get her out of there."

He's reminded of the officer in the hallway, the cops surrounding his building. "The State Police? Let me talk to her."

"Katherine's in the other room now, Nick, with my colleagues. We're taking her statement. She'll be done in a bit. She wasn't involved in anything, but she's been a witness to a crime. I don't really want to interrupt the other officers." The man has the mellifluous voice of a talk show host. "But we're more than happy to come pick you up. Your mother's worried about you. You're not at home, are you?"

"Is she safe?"

"Absolutely, sir."

Nick looks at the traffic peeling by him. A couple walk past, the woman cackling at something the man says into her ear. "I can meet you," he says.

"I really—I'll be honest, Nick, I don't think that's a great idea. We want to get you and your mom together as quickly as possible—"

"What is this really about?"

"We're still investigating, but it appears there was a shooting of some kind in your building. Possibly in your apartment. You might— and again, let me be honest—you might be in some danger. We'd really like to come pick you up."

I'm with some people, she'd said. Not *the police. Some people.* "Let me talk to her and I'll tell you where I am."

There is a pause, and then the rustle again. His mother says his name once again, and he was a fool to have missed it—that tremble, the waver in her voice. "Mom, these guys want to pick me up. Should I meet them at Rizzo's or the sushi place?"

There is no pause. "Sushi place, definitely."

"Shoyou?"

"Yeah," she says.

"You sure?"

"Definitely, Nick."

"Okay. I'm so sorry, Mom."

"It's okay."

"I love you. I love you so much. Can you put that guy on, please. We'll fix this."

"Listen," Nick says when Lundy comes back on. "Meet me at Shoyou Sushi. It's right off Burnside. Northwest Twenty-sixth and Everett, I think. I'll be out front."

Nick hangs up.

They have worked for months at expanding Katherine's ring of safety, that area in which she feels safe enough to move, to breathe, to not feel a hand tightening around her throat. Sometimes they are able to go a block, two blocks beyond what they've done before, and other days the ring is smaller, withdrawn. She and Nick, navigating their small section of the city together, Nick talking brightly—practically chirping—at every passing detail, as if he might buoy and distract Katherine with his incessant talking. And often it worked. Other times, she'd curl into herself, squeezing his arm, her face tightened in panic. The last time they'd gone out—three nights ago? Maybe four? They'd gone past Twenty-sixth, the condos and boutiques giving way to apartment buildings as old as theirs, scattered among million-dollar Victorian homes, until something inside her suddenly shifted and she had gripped his arm and said plaintively, "I can't, Nick, oh God. I'm sorry, I can't."

They'd turned around. No question. He'd wanted to bring her to a place to sit down, drink some water, gather herself, and the first place they came to was Shoyou, with its little conveyor belt that ferried everyone's sushi around on trays, but that place had been too close to the edge of the ring, and they had wound up at Rizzo's instead, the Italian place right next to the apartment, where Katherine had wept with frustration and shame over her glass of red wine.

Her message in choosing Shoyou, a place she cannot, will not go: *These men are not safe.*

And she had said *some people,* hadn't she? *Some people.*

And yet. What if she was just taking him at his word?

He stops and closes his eyes. Fear striding up and down his backbone, hammering on all his vital organs. His heart won't stop thundering. Sirens everywhere. Nick begins walking again, even as a voice clamors inside him that he's done the wrong thing. Has truly damned her. He's only gone a block when his phone lights up again. This time it's Rachmann.

"I have news."

Nick lets out a shaky breath, resists the sudden urge to weep. "Okay."

"It's of a sensitive nature, Nicholas. This will be costly."

"I have money."

"I believe she's been taken by an organized group. Possibly sanctioned and funded."

Nick blinks. The words don't track. "What does that mean, sanctioned?"

"It means a government agency of some sort."

"Jesus Christ, man. I called you because I needed help."

"This is me helping you. I don't know specifics yet—hopefully soon—but I came across an interesting piece of information. Something to do with audio/video manipulation in test subjects. The information's a few years old, little details, but I thought it was interesting. If I can reverse-locate it, we'll be somewhere."

"Rachmann, man," Nick says helplessly, "I don't know what you're talking about."

"I think your mother is possibly linked to a US-funded 'ghost agency' doing psychological or counterterrorism research."

"Sure. Right."

"One of the weapons being developed by the agency is buried within a song called 'I Won't Forget It,' by a band called the Blank Letters." Rachmann waits pointedly. "I'm assuming you've heard of them."

Silence from Nick. He can't make sense of it.

"The weapon is not the song itself, apparently. The song is the delivery system. I have no idea what kind of weapon it is, what it does. This is only a small, single blip of intel I've managed to gather, and I had to call in a number of favors to locate it. But you see why I contacted you."

Nick laughs, incredulous. "I don't see why, Rachmann. What does my parents' shitty song have to do with any of this?"

"This I don't know."

"So do they want her or me? These people?"

"I don't know that either."

"Jesus Christ. Okay, great. Thanks for your help."

"But I will find out. And then," Rachmann continues, "there's the chatter I've come across in conjunction with the hand you mentioned. All unsubstantiated."

Nick lets out another maddened, frustrated laugh. "Okay."

"Have you . . . Is there any chance you've heard of a government asset nicknamed 'Saint Michael'?"

"No. I mean, I'm not really up to speed on my government assets, Rachmann."

"The only mentions I've come across of a hand bring up talk of this Saint Michael. I've found a few transcript excerpts, things of that nature." Rachmann clears his throat. "But the hand has been mentioned."

"It has," Nick says flatly.

Rachmann pauses. Finally, he says, "I have a concern here that you'll think I'm trying to deceive you. This isn't the case. It's outlandish, yes, but I'm happy to show you this intelligence in person, and how I retrieved it."

Nick thinks of Rachmann back in Brooklyn, saying *Some of these agencies are legitimate, and others are . . . operationally black.* "What intelligence?"

"The intelligence that states that Saint Michael is part of a clandestine remote viewing program."

"A what?"

"A psychic program," Rachmann says.

Nick just laughs. The world falling apart around him, and he's chosen Rachmann, of all people, to put it back together for him. Rachmann and his psychics. His black ops counterterrorism programs.

"So what now?" Nick asks.

He can tell Rachmann is grinning on the other end of the phone. "I have a plan," he says, "if you would care to hear it."

KATHERINE MORIARTY

She sits there, waiting for Lundy to return. *I'm with some people,* she'd managed, the vast relief at hearing her son's voice, the centering nature of it, and now she waits for these people to do whatever it is they've decided to do to her. What matters is Nick. The world is big enough to swallow her, to flatten her, if she lets it.

One thing she has learned when traveling the ring, when the weight of all that concrete and steel, the vast unblemished space of the sky threatens to undo her—the thing she's learned to do is to walk back through the years to a time when she was assured and unafraid. It is a small, minute mechanism butting up against a vast and terrible predicament, and does little to alleviate the agony of the situation itself, but it works much of the time. It gets her out of the present moment.

And dear God, if there has ever been a need for that, it's now.

She'd met Matthew Coffin while majoring in English at UCLA, following an ill-conceived idea of getting a degree in journalism. She wanted to be a music journalist, she'd decided, after finding punk as a kid. Writers like Lester Bangs and Legs McNeil her avatars, her guiding lights through the world. Just the offhanded *coolness* of it, the way they managed to insert themselves into their writing, into the movement itself. Their clear love for what they were witnessing, veiled through the cynicism and world-weariness. She was covering a show for the college paper, a little two-hundred-word write-up that at least got her into the club for free, where she knew the bartender, who was always comping her drinks with the unrequited hope of hooking up later. LA was as beautiful and dirty as it ever would be in those years, punk still blowing up, still radio-heavy, still running at least a little roughshod through the music industry, A&R guys occasionally dropping into small-time venues with the whisper of cash and contracts, happy to toss some big promises out there.

It was a Tuesday night in Silver Lake. The crowd was light, one of those shows where half the audience is made up of the band members. After getting her pint from the bartender, she made her way to the small stage, where a group was already mid-set. And within seconds, it was one of those things where the music—more specifically, the guitar player—wove its way through her, Katherine finding herself both rooted to the ground and transported elsewhere. This guy, Jesus. Just the ferocity with which he attacked the guitar, arching his back, skinny arm flung up, his fist inches away from grazing the spackled ceiling of the club and massacring his hand. His guitar strap had been a length of silver duct tape, she remembers. The band was good because *he* was good, the way one person can electrify an entire room. At the end of the song the place had exploded in applause, Katherine already knowing that she'd be hitting up the band for an interview—whether the school paper would run it or not, she could shop it to the weeklies, and who the fuck *were* these guys. She'd buy their merch even though she was broke. Was the guitarist hot, Katherine wondered distractedly, not even sipping her beer, just staring. No, she decided, not really—emaciated, with a heavy brow and one of the truly ugliest haircuts she'd ever seen, he looked like some stitched-together scarecrow heaving and roiling about on the stage. Jittering and flailing and never missing a note. The band burst into another song and their eyes caught for a moment—at least Katherine thought so—and as if in response he jabbed the guitar out toward the audience, coming within inches of running the headstock face-first into a longhaired punk in the front who was banging his head, oblivious, one arm raised, the whole thing sending a judder of electricity through her.

It was only the band's fourth show, she'd find out later, and less than a month after she hooked up with Matthew Coffin, the group—having never even decided on a name—split up. The two of them spent most of their time at the apartment Katherine shared with another UCLA student, a woman named Ming who was studying ornithology and was hardly ever at home. Matthew seemed to luxuriate in amenities like hot water and coffee that didn't come from paper cups at the bodega down the street. He had a closet that he rented in a resoundingly sketchy loft in Hollywood for sixty-five dollars a month. It held a mattress, his amp and guitar, and a duffel bag of clothes.

Prowling her apartment in his underwear, those stick-and-poke tattoos like ink spills on his alabaster skin, he seemed half feral to her. Skeletal, underfed, that great dark mass of hair, the calculating intelligence behind the eyes. Sipping espresso from one of Ming's oversized coffee cups, the sun shining through the window in neatly delineated slats on the countertop. She would leave him to go to school, some part of her—okay, *most* of her—wanting to stay in bed with him, finding herself ravenous with this man in a way she had never been previously with anyone. Just the way they fit together, it spun her. Matthew—never Matt—had been like some drug for her in those early days, dizzying and insistent.

Coming home from class one day, she discovered him shirtless on the couch with an acoustic guitar he'd picked up somewhere. It wasn't Ming's, and certainly not hers. A beaten thing with a few faded, nearly illegible stickers on the body. She sat down in the rat-tan chair next to the TV as Matthew lit a cigarette, one eye squinting against the smoke.

"Where'd you get the guitar?"

"Ah, this lady gave it to me."

Katherine smiled, annoyed at the rip of jealousy that moved through her. "A lady, huh?"

"Yeah," he said, "I saw this lady doing palm readings on La Cienega and I went in and she read my fortune. And then she gave me this guitar."

"She gave you the guitar?"

"Yeah." He shrugged, as if such things were commonplace in his life. "She said I had some good luck coming with it. Really cool of her, to tell you the truth."

"You believe in that stuff? Fortune-telling and psychics and all that?"

"Oh, hardcore," Matthew said. "All of it."

He started playing something then. It was clearly something he'd been working on; one of those rare times she'd sensed any studiousness about him. Head dipped, bobbing both his foot and that ragged head of jet-black hair in time with the beat. A snarling punk thing made almost buoyant, jubilant, with the fact that it was being played on the acoustic.

"That rips," Katherine said. She meant it.

Matthew nodded in appreciation, played one more verse—she assumed it was a verse—and then let the final chord ring out. He'd looked at her then, Katherine feeling almost prim under his assessment. Shy. "You play anything, Kat?" Not even her mother called her Kat.

"I played the clarinet in middle school."

He smiled. "You any good?"

"I mean, it was middle school, so."

"Why don't you sing something."

"Oh, I can't, man." She had felt heat rise to her cheeks.

And then Matthew had done something that made her inch, to her everlasting surprise, a little closer toward love. It had made her reconsider him, reconsider what she'd thought were the confines, the depth—or lack of depth—of his interior life. He had scooted onto the couch closer to her, their knees almost touching. He put the guitar to the side and placed his cigarette in the ashtray and leaned forward. "Could you maybe try," he'd said. "Because you just got that look about you. Let's see where our luck goes. Please."

Katherine had slowly reared back, she remembers, the fibers of the chair creaking a little. She was off-put by his intensity, the sincerity. Unnerved by it. But that's how he did things. It was *me me me* until what seemed like his last breath, and then he turned that searchlight on you, and that door you swore you could manage to close forever opened an inch.

"What look is that," she said.

"The look that says you're going to do just flat-out amazing things, Katherine. Let's just write a song, fuck it. Tell you the truth, I got a feeling."

I got a feeling.

Those words would change her life forever, wouldn't they? Those words would give her a son. Make Matthew her husband.

I got a feeling.

And he'd been right, hadn't he?

"Play that song again," she'd said, and he'd grinned that boyish, chipped-tooth grin, and she'd started singing, whatever came to her mind. Nonsense words, really. But her own voice had surprised her, how well it fit in. Diamond-edged, a sandpaper rasp that fit so well against the angles of his guitar-playing. Within a week, they had four songs written. Two weeks after that, they had their first practice with Arthur and Doogy in a warehouse in Highland Park, the sound of rats skittering in the walls between songs. A month after *that* they played their first show, a six-song set at Raji's that fucking wrecked the place and left people with their jaws hanging open. Katherine formally dropped out of UCLA the next morning, hungover and happy and sure in a way that she has maybe never been sure of again in her entire life.

John Lundy comes in, red-faced, turgid, grinning with rage, wiping blood from his hands with a paper towel.

"So, we're meeting your son at a sushi place." He tosses the paper towel in a dented metal wastebasket by the door. There's still blood in the creases of his knuckles. "You like sushi, Katherine?" He folds his arms, peers up at the ceiling, as if deep in rumination. She sees what looks like a . . . USB stick on a cord around his neck, the shape of it dimly visible through the material of his dress shirt. "I'm just wondering why your son thought this place—Shoyou—was a good spot to meet up. That wouldn't be a code or anything, would it? An ambush, maybe?"

It takes a moment for her to even decipher what he might mean. "An ambush? Look at me, dude. I think you're, you know, overestimating—"

"It's a little suspect, is all."

"He's a fan."

Still grinning, furious. "He's a fan?"

"They got a conveyor belt there, it brings everything around on little plates. He's loved it forever. We've gone there since he was tiny."

"You better not be fucking me, Katherine."

"I'm not."

"You'll regret it, I promise you."

"I believe you," she says, as sincerely as she can muster.

"Good," Lundy says. "That's a start."

HUTCH HOLTZ

Hutch gets spooked driving toward Coffin's place. Too many cops. Too many sirens, too many emergency lights caught in his peripheral vision. And things just feel *off:* People running down the sidewalk randomly. A busted window of a Subway, someone kicking it in and no one doing anything about it, even with cops driving all around. He's reminded of the protests the previous summer, when the whole city seemed intent on marching all night every night, cops in lockstep, munitions and flash-bangs being fired into crowds. Whole neighborhoods rank and choking with tear gas. Tonight has that same weird, dangerous feeling, things beneath the skin just barely tamped down.

So Coffin's place is out. It's just too close to the nexus of that feeling he's got, that *offness.*

Instead, he drives just to drive. Just because there's nowhere else to go. The pistol rests in the little pocket of gown between his legs. He slowly passes an accident, a pair of cars pressed together amid a wash of buckled safety glass and shards of plastic. One car's hazard lights blink idiotically. There's no one around—both drivers are gone, no cops, nothing. Like it's been there long enough that even the gawkers have taken off. His wheels rasp over the glass. It's as if ghosts have taken over this pocket of the world. Hutch doesn't get it, but it's unnerving as hell.

And he has arrived, finally, at pain. Bumps in the street bring about clenched teeth and whimpers. He's afraid to reach back and touch his wound.

Night mist washes over him through the broken window. Cools him. His conviction to destroy the hand is vanishing. Hutch wants instead to lie down and sleep—forever, preferably—but then imagines parking at his apartment complex, walking past his manager's unit, the slow clack and clatter of the elevator up to his place. Locking the door. Trying to push something in front of it, lest they—and there are suddenly a multitude of theys—come for him. Then lying down at last, the sweet relief of it.

And then bleeding to death in his bed, most likely. Going to sleep like that, the slow dark pull of it, and never waking up. He has to admit, there's a certain allure.

But he'd be stopped before that ever happened. Even on a night like this, with this strange pall across the city, he's still a shoeless man in a hospital gown, carrying a pistol. He's assaulted a detective, is wanted for his involvement in multiple shootings. Hutch goes to his apartment, he's coming out in cuffs or a body bag.

He pulls to the curb on a sleeping street so like the one they visited right before this shitshow started. That surprised man with his groceries, Tim and Hutch getting the money from him with a few easy words, an implied threat. Hutch leans his head against the steering wheel. The air chills him. The gun a weight in his lap. He reaches back, wincing, and finally touches the wound at his back. This time, yes, his fingers come away red. Seeping through the bandage. Stitches, if he ever actually got them, pulled apart.

He starts the car with shaking hands and turns the radio on. Searches the dial while he drives, tries to find himself a sad song.

———

Don's house is as they left it, down to the blur of treads from Tim's car still on the lawn.

He pulls into the driveway and turns off the engine. He steps out, hearing nothing save for the cooling engine, the briefest stir of leaves in a gentle wind.

Everything black now, full night, and he gently opens the back gate with the pistol held out before him. Here, in Don's home, he'll find the man's phone with Peach's number in it, perhaps even Nick's. He'll find out where the hand is, if the hand is a retrievable thing.

If it's not, fine. He can sleep. Sleep in Don's bed, why not. The last place anyone will look for him.

Though there is, of course, the small matter of Don himself, the way those eyes had met his in the final moments before Hutch had left the house.

He's wondered sometimes, at calm moments in his life, with a little folding money in his wallet, and no particular aches anywhere, if he would go Baptist when death came near. Quaking and wailing, begging God, petitioning forgiveness, lamenting all those broken fingers and eye gouges, the two—three now—lives he's ended. Regretting the mayhem he and Tim brought into the world. But so far, there's little sorrow and even less regret. Death seems mostly a matter of being tired.

And really, who ever dies the way they envision it?

He walks around the back of the house once more, steps into Don's bedroom and quietly shuts the door. His body feels cold as river rocks, stones at the bottom of the sea. All these disconnected parts of him. He can hear the television, see the thinned light of it shifting through the doorway. The penny-stink of blood is still here, lessened none for the time he's been gone. He stands in the darkness, breathing. Finally his eyes adjust enough that he sees Don's phone on the nightstand. He walks over—grateful now for his bare feet— and picks it up. It's thumbprint-activated, luck stacked on luck. He sets the phone on the bed.

Something scrapes along the floor in the next room over.

Hutch pauses, frozen. His scalp tightens. He breathes, walks silently through the doorway and down the short hall that leads to the living room.

The blood-soaked couch where Don's corpse sat is empty.

In the trembling television light, Hutch sees a trail of gore, black and lacquered, that leads from the living room to the kitchen. The same sitcom is on the screen, a marathon. The sound is low, the riot of a canned laugh track reduced to murmurs. The lasagna on its familiar plate, dripping great, frothing strands of cheese, talking to a crying girl in a beret. This juxtaposition feels like something culled from hell.

"Don?"

The straight razor Don tried to sever his hand with rests on the coffee table. Hutch stares at it for a moment and then says Don's name again, his voice coming out in a tremulous croak. A little boy's voice. The hand holding the pistol is slicked with sweat. Heading toward the kitchen, he gingerly steps over the blood on the floor. Through the doorway he can see a table, a wooden chair. Another chair overturned. The television behind him goes black, some night scene on the screen, and the room is thrown into darkness. Hutch freezes.

Another scrape in the kitchen. A dragging foot, perhaps.

"Yo, Don, what the fuck," Hutch spits, stepping forward, playing at bravery, his free hand reaching in and swiping at the wall maniacally for a light switch. He finds it, finally, and good clean light fills the kitchen. A light pure enough to make him wince.

Don stands in the middle of the room.

One hand dangles from his wrist, wavering like seaweed in the tide, twisting and spinning from a single stretch of skin. Gore darkens his pants, smears across that pale old man belly. Blood tacky in the matted hair of his chest. His head rests at an angle, like an inquisitive dog. His eyes focus somewhere above Hutch's shoulder. Death clouds the room, and Hutch aims the pistol at the loose white mass of Don's body.

"Don?" It comes out in a breathy whisper. And then, ridiculously, some part of him insisting on some answer: "The hell happened?"

Don opens his mouth. All those yellow teeth beneath that mustache. Hutch thinks he's about to speak, but all that comes out is a ghastly rush of noise.

He takes a staggering step forward.

And Hutch takes a step back, butts up against the doorframe. Starts to raise the pistol.

"Don't do it, man. Don, stop. I mean it."

Like he's going to listen, right. Like Don's a thing that can hear anymore. Can understand.

Don moves, bends low suddenly. Hissing like a cat. Eyes unplugged from any ounce of life or care or knowledge.

Hutch backs up, retreats into the other room, feet sliding through the blood on the floor, and Don, he follows.

He's become a thing that *skitters*.

He holds Don's severed hand in his own. Uses the thumb to unlock the screen on Don's phone. The television cuts to a commercial where a teddy bear jumps from a plane onto a field of diapers. There's a ring of teeth marks on Hutch's forearm that wells with blood. He scrolls through Don's phone, leaving smears of blood on the screen. Don's brains stipple Hutch's face. The body lies in the kitchen. The gun is in his lap. Don's hand, finally loose of its last tendril of hanging skin, he puts on the coffee table.

He stands there, wills his legs to stop shaking. He picks up the remote and mutes the television.

Scrolling through Don's contacts, he finds NICK and PEACH. Peach's number gets no answer. Voicemail.

Nick answers, though, and Hutch, even through the glaze of terror and exhaustion that has settled upon him, knows something is wrong.

"Nick, it's Hutch."

"Hutch? What the fu—Are you okay? This is Don's phone?"

"I'm good," Hutch says, looking down at the towel he's pressing against his bloodied arm. "Where's the hand, man?"

Silence draws itself across the line. Finally, Nick says, "Something's happening with it. It's—These people took my mom. They want it."

"You have it still? You didn't give it to Peach?"

"Peach is dead, Hutch. They shot him. Right in front of me."

Hutch blinks at the TV. "Who did?"

"I don't know. They sniped him in the face. I ran."

"Listen to me. You've got to get rid of that thing, Nick. It's poison."

"I did," he said.

"You destroyed it?"

"I mean, I got rid of it."

Hutch closes his eyes. "Got rid of it how."

Again with the silence and then, "I hid it."

"That's not going to work. You know that's not going to work, Nick."

"I couldn't stand to be around it anymore," Nick says. "It's just . . . It was fucking with me. It's too much."

"They got your mom?"

"Yeah."

"And they want the hand?"

"Yeah."

"Tell me where it is. I'll take care of it."

He can hear Nick breathing on the other end. "I think they might kill her."

"They won't kill her. They think you have it. Keep them thinking that." God, he's tired. Hutch lifts the towel and looks at his arm. Remembers how Don had leapt before he'd even fired a shot, had latched onto his arm, gripping it, nails digging into the flesh on each side. The galvanizing burst of pain when he bit down. Those eyes empty as anything. Then Hutch putting the barrel of the Glock against Don's temple, the spattering of brains.

Squinting in the poor light, he swears he can see the bite bubbling. "Where is it?"

"I put it under a dumpster. On Twenty-fourth."

"Southeast?"

"Yeah, Southeast. Right off Marklin, I think. Marklin and Twenty-fourth. A brick apartment building, under a blue dumpster next to some garages."

"I'll get it. You do what you need to do, but I'm getting rid of it."

"Okay."

"Don's dead too," Hutch says. He lets out a little laugh that turns into a cough, and a slow fire throbs in his guts until he stops, tears leaking from his eyes. "He died and he came back to life."

"What?"

Hutch says it again.

Nick is silent. As if such a thing needs a response. As if there is one.

Hutch hangs up and after a moment pushes himself up from the couch, crying out. His back is throbbing and hot, wet. His arm aches as if the bone itself has grown molten.

He picks up Don's hand and walks with it into the kitchen. Sets it down on a cutting board.

He saws Don's thumb off with a bread knife.

Stepping over the man's shattered body, he heads to the bedroom. Pulling the hospital gown off will hurt too much, he knows, but he finds a pair of sweatpants in Don's dresser and puts them on standing up. Shoes are a lost cause; Hutch is a size 14. But he finds a pair of slippers and a windbreaker in the closet. He turns on the bedroom light and looks at himself in the mirror on the back of the closet door. In spite of it all, he starts laughing until the pain seizes him: He looks like a maniac. Looks like what he is: an escapee.

He puts the gun in one pocket of the windbreaker and Don's phone and his severed thumb in the other.

And then Hutch Holtz walks out the front door of the house, his arm screaming, his hand gently tracing the guardrail down the steps.

SIMON OSTERBERG

"**M**an has a fucking *tent*, you think it grows on a tree. It must, right? Easy as that. Think the possessions inside the tent are fucking garbage. Think a man just has his possessions that he gathers, think he can just snap his fingers and they reappear, like that? Man who has next to nothing to begin with, you fucking *cop*, you think he can just snap his fingers and there they are again? You live in a magical world like that? Because I *don't*. Alright? Not *me*, I don't."

Simon Osterberg limps down a nondescript residential street in Southeast Portland, this acidic monologue in his head. It's raining again, and Simon with nothing now. No protection whatsoever. Clothes on his back and barely that: Not even a jacket to his name, because that was, you guessed it, in his tent. Earlier that day, he had come back to the camp to find that the cops had once more raided the place. Simon has been in Portland eight months after coming here from Bend, and previous to that, the LA/Orange County area, and this is the *fourth time* he's gotten his shit raided by the Portland police in their sweeps of homeless camps. Difference is that he was there when it happened the first three times, and able to grab his stuff and fold up his tent before the whole group of them, thirty or forty people, got ousted, told to get the fuck out. Go somewhere else. It feels like a war much of the time, and the war really just came home to roost this morning, when Simon came upon the shredded remains of the camp, garbage everywhere, their public area reduced to stomped mudholes. Whole place empty, feeling like a battlefield, whole area with a sense of life to it that's just been vacated. Food containers, garbage bags, a sodden green sleeping bag wadded in the mud like some cast-off skin. His tent—and, almost certainly, everything in it—has been tossed, he's sure. Supposedly it's all been taken into custody, and he can visit the police station if he wants to get it back, but no one Simon knows has ever successfully done so. It's always, you walk into the precinct, tell them where the sweep happened, and they're like, *Describe your belongings.* Looking at you like you're a piece of shit. And it's always like, *Well, it's trash to you, but not to me.* How do you say that to a cop? And get them so they understand it? And then they inevitably want ID, if only so you can sign out on the shit, and Simon doesn't have ID, hasn't had ID in, what, two years? At *least* two years. He knows plenty of fools who have fake ID, IDs they've lifted out of cars and things, IDs they've found or been given, but hardly anyone he knows has their real ID anymore. Hard to hold on to shit like that. Hard to hold on to anything out here, damn. Forty-two years old, off hard dope for thirty-two days, and just walking aimlessly now, imagining the smug cops in their yellow coats and rubber gloves as they toss people's special, private, valuable shit into a garbage truck they bring along. Man, the things he'll say the next time some cop tries to hassle him. Fuckin' heads will *roll.*

"Like, what, snap your finger, clothes and books and shit just appears? Had a full unopened thing of Handi Wipes in there, man, you just roll through and there's my life, torn apart. My *books* were in there, asshole."

Simon is limping the more he walks because of his bad leg; the more he walks on it the worse he feels. Just the way of things. It's raining now, it'll be raining all night, probably, and there's no way he's getting into a shelter this late, and things are already off, man. The whole night feeling like it's spinning on some new, terrible axis. Sirens all over the place, and maybe ten minutes before, he seen a guy hit another guy with a whole bicycle right in front of the convenience store, the one where Wheelchair Steve got held up that one time, just lifted up the whole bike and wham! Smacked him with it, then started bringing the wheel down on the guy's head when he's all fucked-up lying on his stomach. Again and again, Simon just turning straight around and heading back the way he came, not even messing with it. More sirens, the slap of footfalls echoing out of the mouths of alleyways, faint smell of smoke in the rain, things are just feeling sideways, man, the whole thing. If he had a tent, he'd be just sleeping it off, ducking down and waiting for the feeling of the world to change to something different, more manageable. But yeah, no tent, so here he fucking is.

He's limping along, still muttering, when he stops at the side of an apartment building. Brick, two-story, a couple dumpsters, a little parking area, Simon *feeling* something there, tilting his head like a dog hearing a whistle.

"The hell," he breathes, exultant. Stands there feeling some red thread run through him, loosening him up. Stock-still beside the dumpster, Simon stretches his fingers wide, his lips pulling back in a grimace, any number of images flitting through his mind. The wadded, wet sleeping bag stomped and mud-lathered, the flash of the police and their yellow slickers, their purple latex gloves, their contempt, Simon imagining one standing before him, that flat-topped one he remembers from the last time, the red river of his throat as Simon gnashes and bites, them always being like *Describe your belongings,* like you're just shit, Simon imagining the guy falling and him falling on top, gnashing, the world a red river to bite through.

He crouches, unaware of his injured leg now, bends down, sweeping his hand beneath the dumpster there, convinced beyond words that he'll find something important hidden beneath it, that he'll be rewarded with some vast and unknown treasure.

3
THE VOICE

OPERATION: HEAVY LIGHT

S/NF/CL-INTEL—CLOSED—A-55/76

RESTRICTED—HIGHLY CLASSIFIED—INTER-
DEPARTMENTAL NOTICE ONLY—CLOSED—DESTROY UPON RECEIPT

DATE: XX/XX/XXXX

SUBJECT: Transcript and analysis of field recording of Opera-
tion: Heavy Light objective/asset—RESTRICTED—CLOSED—
CLASSIFIED IN-AGENCY PERSONNEL ONLY—DESTROY
UPON RECEIPT

(S/NF/CL-INTEL-CLOSED) Below is a transcript of the
found field recording on the hard drive located in a storage closet in
Program Director Jerome Finch's laboratory, where sound modula-
tion experiments were taking place as part of a top secret Department of Defense umbrella program working in explorations of sonic
warfare/psychological control opportunities.

(S/NF/CL-INTEL-CLOSED) It remains unknown where the
recording originated from. Also unknown is how old the recording

is, who the Subject is, or if the Subject's voice has been modulated in some manner. As noted, Director Finch is no longer available for questioning (see Memorandum A-19/13). Remainders of his staff have proven to have limited knowledge of the recording's origins, and have been removed from inter-departmental questioning after debriefing.

(S/NF/CL-INTEL-CLOSED) Also unclear is if the Subject is addressing an individual on a telephone or device, or someone in the recording's proximity.

(S/NF/CL-INTEL-CLOSED) The recording is a .wav file found on a hard drive in the Dynar Laboratories located in Beaverton, Oregon, a suburb of Portland. Dr. Finch was the director of the umbrella program, working under the command of ARC Agency Director David Lundy, and within the confluence of the OPERATION: HEAVY LIGHT program.

(S/NF/CL-INTEL-CLOSED) The recording is 00:59 seconds in duration. A single "bump" in volume can be heard approximately 00:09 seconds into the recording; investigators have surmised this might have been caused by the Subject bumping the microphone or someone dropping something near the recording device. The Subject speaks in a monotone; linguists have noted inflections in certain words and glottal stops, as well as an overall "accent," that place the speaker as residing and having spent significant time in the Pacific Northwest, though this remains speculative. Based on a variety of factors, it is believed that the voice throughout the entirety of the recording—as well as the Subject weeping from 00:29 to 00:50—belongs to a single individual, though, again, it remains possible that other nonspeaking individuals were present.

(S/NF/CL-INTEL-CLOSED) See Departmental Report PRI-3321-6, *Physiognomic and Physical Effects of Base Field Recording on Subjects* and Memorandum A-20/22 regarding effects upon the listener when hearing the recording. This experience forms much of the operating principles of OPERATION: HEAVY LIGHT, and should not be overlooked.

(S/NF/CL-INTEL-CLOSED) Transcript of the recording in its entirety is as follows. Recording begins mid-sentence.

00:00–00:29:—if I tell you to sever the head of your neighbor, yes, to dine in the bowl of their skull, you do it, and we might call that fealty. If I tell you to make me a necklace from the heads of your children, to make me a red veil from their latticed veins that I might lay on my brow, you'll curtsy on bloody knees and crow, 'Yes, Father!' and you'll ready the knife. And we might call that fealty as well. I say cut out your eye, you slice away. Take your hand off at the wrist, you whet the blade and get to work. That too is fealty. You understand? Yes? Make me a king's house from this whole place. How I use your voice now, how I speak through you, the sorrowful jaw working just so. How you might remake the world for me. A king's house among all the leaning world. You shall make me a house of fever and wounds. A house of beetle and crow. A house of worms. A house of hounds that savage forever at the belly of love and take root there, devouring.

00:29–00:50: SUBJECT weeps.

00:51–00:59: Cut here, here, here. Avail yourself to me. Make me a house of fever and wounds, where all rooms are ghastly and dark. Do it. Make me a king's house, and you will have all you ever wanted.

(S/NF/CL-INTEL-CLOSED) END RECORDING

JOHN BONNER

Bonner remembers clearly the first time he sat down in front of David Lundy. In Camelot, maybe ten o'clock at night, Bonner having already been there a few days, wondering just when it was he was going to be briefed on agency protocol and objectives. It had felt show-offy at first, the boss trying to keep his agents on edge; after months of working with Lundy, he's since come to realize the man just has no schedule he sticks to, sleeping like a vampire in his office half the time. He lives and breathes ARC, but as a program director—at least when it came to Bonner—he was terrible from day one.

Lundy had steepled his fingers in front of his chin like some arch-villain. Bonner sat there, still ego-stung from what felt like a demotion, the run-down barracks quality of Camelot itself, and him still more than a little heartsick over Pernicio. The building's overhead lights lit up Lundy's red face in unforgiving detail. Bonner heard the dim squawk of a fax machine in another room and marveled at the fact that a black op was using fucking faxes.

Lundy had pushed a sheaf of papers around on his desk, kind of edged the corners of them straight, then went back to steepling his hands. "John," he said, "tell me why you're here."

Bonner had adjusted himself in his seat. Shooting for a neutral tone, a voice that he wanted in no way to belie the rage, contempt and fear he felt, he'd said, "I've been promoted to a field agent here at ARC."

"And why is that?"

Bonner's eyes had cut to the edges of the room. Lundy saw it, waved a hand dismissively.

"Nobody's listening, man," he said. "And if they were, I promise they would not care about you."

"My handler at DoD thought it best that I get transferred to a black op."

"Why's that?"

"He just thought it was best, sir."

Lundy nodded, pursed his lips. "So they picked me. They picked my op. And now here you are."

"I guess so, sir."

Lundy picked up the sheaf of papers on his desk, made a show of thumbing through them. "An MS in data science from Columbia, did your little stint at Camp Peary learning how to be a spook, with the State Department for a while, then data analytics for various agencies for the past seven years. Briefly overseas for 'analytic fitness and military strength assessments for rebel-controlled areas' in the Kandahar region, which is fucking word salad as far as I'm concerned, and you've never been with an outfit more than eighteen months." He peered at Bonner over the papers. "So you're homeless, basically. And this is a new dog pound for you. My question is, why don't you have any friends, John?"

Bonner, still hoping for nonchalance, felt his stomach drop. Here was Lundy casting him as an outsider, a fucking pariah. Here it was. "I have admittedly niche but varied skills that allow me to move throughout the strata of a lot of agencies. I prefer to look at it as an asset, sir."

"You're a fucking temp, you mean."

"Well, I'm a specialist."

"Uh-huh."

Bonner smiled, a kicked dog baring its teeth. "Like I said, it's been considered a strength up to this point, sir."

Lundy nodded. "The strata," he said dryly. He went back to the paper. "An only child. Father an investment banker, dead of a heart attack when you were twelve. A mother who clerked for the Supreme Court some thirty years ago and then went into a highly notable career in corporate law. One uncle who runs a wildly powerful lobbying firm for nuclear energy, and another one who, hey, look here, is the CFO of one Terradyne Industries, arguably the largest defense firm on the planet. A lot of dictators have been installed in a lot of third-world nations using Terradyne-manufactured gear, wouldn't you say? And they've got their finger on the pulse of pretty much every weapons delivery system being created on the fucking planet in some way, shape or form." Lundy had set the papers down and fixed Bonner with a face screwed up in mock confusion. "You got to excuse my ignorance, John, but what the *hell* are you doing here? You're a one-percenter, son. You ought to be on a yacht somewhere. Have some college dropout feed you grapes while you catch some sun."

"That's . . . highly specific."

Lundy laughed joylessly. "What I'm saying is, you're slumming. Coming from a family like yours, with the connections you have, and you get passed on to me? Feels like you've been hung up somewhere. Put out where you won't bother anyone."

Bonner was surprised to find relief in the fact that Lundy had put it out in the open like that. "Well, I'm not happy about it either."

"Happy?" Lundy spun his chair around, hit him with those frank, assessing eyes as he put up a leg on his desk. "I don't give a shit if you're happy, John. I want to know if you're getting tucked in at night."

"I don't know what you mean."

"I mean, how close are you to your uncle Jack? You two talk on the phone a lot? Sit down and watch football on Sundays? Have each other over for dinner?"

"I'm confused."

"Are you?"

"You think my uncle put me in a black op agency because . . . why?"

"I don't know what you did that was good enough, or bad enough, to get you transferred into my show, but I think—and I'm not dumb enough to ask you to tip your hand here, John—I think I'm going to watch you real close. You know what I'm saying? The fact that Terradyne's got their hands in just about every marginally developed country's weapons market is not lost on me." He'd taken on the cadence of a man explaining something to a child now. "So I'm telling you, John, that this is a compartmentalized, top secret op we're running, and I find it concerning that I get saddled with you, just as I hit these other snags, like losing one of my remnants. I am alarmed by that, and I hope you're not running any of this highly classified information through any pipelines to, say, a third-party defense firm that's run by one of your relatives." He splayed his hands out and offered Bonner an eat-shit smile. "Might you understand me now?"

The thing was, he did. He didn't want to understand, but he did.

Truthfully, he wondered if Lundy was right.

If his uncle Jack was making him a mole without him even knowing it.

KATHERINE MORIARTY

In their infinite wisdom, it's been decided that Katherine is to be moved somewhere else. Another facility. The why is unknown, at least to her, but in the interim they've let her travel the short distance down the hallway to a bathroom. The same cement walls and floors, a steel toilet where the sound of her piss reverberates shockingly loud through the empty room. A man in army fatigues stands outside the door. She'd been too frightened to see if he had a gun. And even if he didn't, what was she going to do? Throat-punch him? Slide down the toilet? The bathroom is a box with a narrow wedge of window set up high in the wall. She'd never get up there, much less make it through. And then what? All that world beyond the glass, then what?

The man who'd spoken to Nick, who'd threatened her with his life, he has a name. It's a name that she rolls around in her mouth like a stone. Like a bullet, or so she tries to tell herself. *Lundy*. She insists she'll remember everything. He *looks* like a Lundy—windburned and jovial and cruel. Those eyes, she gets the same sense from them as when she was a young girl exploring the woods beyond her grandparents' house and would come across something under a rock she'd lifted up. A centipede, something many-legged. It's not disgust, exactly, what she feels when she looks at him, but close to it. Something grandly unnerving.

She finishes peeing, wipes, goes to the steel sink and washes her hands with gritty pink soap. Holds her hands flat against the countertop to root herself there. Thinks of her bedroom again, her instruments, the computer. Her records. These beloved *things* that hold her tight to the ground.

She steps out and sees that the man is indeed armed with a pistol on his hip. They walk a corridor the length of the building, their footfalls loud in her ears. He walks behind her, tells her when to stop. He knocks on a door, and there is Lundy, in a large office. Computers, a bookshelf filled with folders, a cabinet on wheels. Nothing on the walls. It has the air of impermanence, this place. Something hastily pieced together. Lundy stands up and tells her to hold out her hands. The soldier zip-ties her wrists in front of her.

Lundy spends a moment looking at her and then says, "You're not going to say a word, Katherine," and something is put over her head. Another bag. She's sat down in a chair. She can feel the closeness of the room, smells copier toner, Lundy's aftershave.

"You got her phone?" Lundy says.

"We have it," says a woman.

"Where the fuck is Weils? She call in?"

"He's not there."

"What do you mean? He didn't show up?"

"Nope."

Louder, singsongy, "Katherine. Katherine, you lied to me. What was this bullshit about a sushi place? You two got a little code going on? You and your son? You think this is cute?"

Somehow—God—somehow it's better with the bag over her head. To be small like that. To be cocooned in darkness and call it safety. She hates that she's grateful for it.

They stand her up and she's walked out into the hallway, to a door at the end of the hall. The door opens, and the coolness of the night—it *feels* like night—moves against her skin.

"You can't take me anywhere," Katherine says, and it comes out so weak and mincing she might as well be talking to herself.

"Get her on the plane," Lundy says from behind her. "Michael too, dead or not. I don't give a shit at this point. Strap his ass down in there."

They stop. The hand on her arm lets go. "This isn't containable, David," a woman says beside her.

Lundy: "Do you have the parking spot with your name on it, Diane? Or do I?"

"Sir," the woman says sharply. "We have a confirmed fever house. A massive spike in assault, DV and drunk in public calls on local police scanners over the past hour. We know what those are. We know what it must mean. It's because of the hand. We know how it—"

Thundering now, right beside her, enough to make Katherine shrink down, Lundy roars, "Diane, shut the *fuck* up."

Softer: "I'm just saying, David. Please call DoD."

"I'm not calling anyone at DoD, and neither are you. Is that clear?"

After a moment: "Yes."

"Are we absolutely clear, Diane?"

"Yes, sir."

"You talk to me like that again, call into question any of my orders, and I swear to God—"

Katherine rips the black bag off of her head and runs.

She's on some kind of base, a concrete field full of stadium lights and boxy buildings. An air tower in the distance. Her feet slap the pavement; her bound hands slowing her, but for a moment, even with her heart in her throat, the scent of the night is exhilarating.

Her sense of freedom is short-lived. She's grabbed by the collar of her T-shirt—she hears the snarl of ripping fabric somewhere—and falls to the tarmac, rolling. She screams in frustration, and is hauled to her feet, weeping. Her shirt's ripped at the sleeve, an elbow blood-ied. She tries to strike the soldier who holds her. "Careful," he says.

"Lucky you didn't get shot, Katherine," Lundy calls out.

She is pulled back into Lundy's orbit and he bends down and sticks a finger in her face. "Do that again and you're more of a risk than you are a value. I hope you understand what that means. Please tell me we understand each other."

She nods her assent. The tears burn down her cheeks, her face hot with shame and rage.

"Where the fuck is he, Katherine? Where's your kid?"

"I don't know," she says.

"Psh. You know."

"I don't."

He spends another moment staring at her, his eyes pinballing around her face, and then he stands back, clapping his hands against his thighs.

"On the plane," he orders, and the bag goes over her head again. She's led toward the next place. The next inevitable room.

This time, when the bag goes on, there is no gratitude, no peace in the shrunken, darkened world they've given her. Instead there's anger, and it's an ember, a coal she blows on. A small thing she draws into herself.

SAINT MICHAEL

Once, one of them said, *Were you born.*

She had to tell him what that meant, such was his confusion.

No, he had said. Not like a child is born. *No.*

This he remembers well—the early days, when his strength had not flagged, before they had culled his wings from him the first time. They had recorded him, back then it had been a boxy machine that whirred and clicked in the center of the room. A room like this one, and the one before. Recording him has always been one of the few consistent things. The recording and the pain, the demands that he describe the visions that come to him. The lengths of aloneness in between. Those are the things that repeat here.

Michael lies on his side on his cot. He looks at his hand; tendrils of steam rise from the back of it. He breathes a shallow breath.

He looks forward to the ending of pain.

Two men in white coats enter. They stand there a moment. "You're not doing well, are you," one says. They push a thing between them—he thinks for a moment and the word comes to him: *gurney.*

Michael doesn't answer. He's no longer indebted to answer them. The process has begun. What follows next is an inevitability. His duty—that's not quite the word but the closest he knows—has been fulfilled.

Michael is familiar with these men by face, but has such a difficult time with names, all of these distinct collections of sounds, just for one person. One of these men has always been calmer than the other, has treated Michael with something close to kindness. Most of them, their deference is based on what he is and what he might do to them. Then there is David Lundy, who has been with him all this time, whose name he knows well, and who only wants things from him. Only takes. Only cuts, or insists others cut.

Michael wheezes and coughs, and something oily and dark—not quite blood, but something like it—spills from his lips onto his pillow. That he has blood of a sort does not mean they can revive him. He is heartless in a biological sense. He does not eat or drink.

"Jesus Christ," the unkind one mutters. "Get up."

He coughs again, closes his eyes.

"I don't know if he can," the other man says.

"Well, I'm not touching him."

The kinder man steps toward him, gingerly, as if Michael is an animal he doesn't quite understand—and this is a true thing, in its own way—but he lays gentle fingers upon Michael's shoulder. Michael allows himself to be touched, and rises to a sitting position on his cot, his body quaking. He coughs again. Wracked with the nearness of death. The hallway's end.

"How do you do this," Michael asks. He coughs again, and a mist of black expectorate dots the man's hand. Michael is surprised when the man doesn't pull his hand away.

He smiles. "You just stand up, Michael. You just do it."

But that's not what he means. He means it all—life, the endless brutality of the people here in this building, in every building, how he is shut in a room for weeks at a time until they need him again. The way that the inflicting of pain makes people—and as death strides toward him he has become as close to a person as he will ever be, after three decades or more spent in their rooms—want to inflict pain on others. That terrible and simple equation.

But he is tired, and he lets himself be stood up.

They load him onto the gurney, where the kinder man takes some care in strapping him down.

Michael wants to ask if they will cut him after his death. Explore his insides, his workings. But he's too tired, and he already knows the answer.

Rolled from his cell along a hall, the lights strobing along, dark and light, and then outside where he smells fresh, rain-laced air. Sees the dark, wheeling sky huge above him. Overhead lights like great searching eyes. He is pushed up a ramp, into a large airplane. Placed then into his own small cell, a room just large enough for the gurney, a bit of space on each side. A door that locks with a keypad. A small window inset into it. They do not unlash him.

The reckoning has begun. The very thing he has become to bear witness to. It is a taste in the air, this knowledge. A dark thread of ruination that feathers his mind, touches it. A great wheel is in motion now.

He feels the plane turn on the runway and then the slow lift as it pulls away from the earth. His own wings have never been allowed to grow to their full length, not since that first time. Always sawed down to the nubs. He wonders distantly if flight might have been a thing he was once capable of. Michael coughs, spits black. Occasionally a pale head walks past the window.

His breathing is labored and difficult. He is eager to be done of this place. Back to the grand striations of nothingness, the yawing light and dark. The endless silence.

A face at the window now. The door beeps and David Lundy comes in. He is smiling. Unbothered or perhaps happy to see the dark oil of Michael's life spattered around him, wetting his sheet.

"Michael," he says, "how you doing, bud?" He steps in the narrow wedge of space between the gurney and the wall and peers at Michael as if considering an interesting animal. "It's quite the road you've traveled, isn't it?"

Michael coughs, breathes. Turns his face away.

David Lundy leans close. "Michael, you've outlived your usefulness. I cannot wait—and I mean this, honestly, after all these years—to cut you open and see what's what. Get down to the nuts and bolts of it. You are, in your way, tremendous."

Michael flexes his hands at his sides. He coughs again, and more of his insides spill out onto the pillow he rests his head on. Spill off the side of the gurney, spatter to the floor.

Lundy laughs, softly claps his hands. "Christ, you're just *liquefying*, aren't you?" He lifts a finger, points up to the ceiling. "Very glad we're getting this all on tape. Very glad. We're going to reverse-engineer you, my man, do you know what that means?"

"I always told you. What I saw."

"Yeah," Lundy agrees. "And a fat fucking lot of good it did us, Michael. I've got a hand that turns people into fucking *zombies* when they die near it, and I've got my little recording, and I've got *you*. My life's work. My trifecta of bullshit."

Michael coughs. Shuts his eyes. "The remnants," he says.

"Yes, the two remnants. The hand and the voice. Bane of my goddamn existence, Michael."

Michael, his eyes still closed, says, "There are three."

A momentary pause. "Three what?"

"There are three remnants. Of the devil dead."

"Oh, bullshit," David Lundy says.

Michael lets out a groan and blackness spills from his mouth like water from a grate. He gasps three, four times. "There is the hand, and the voice." Michael turns and looks at David Lundy. The eagerness of the face above him. The glittering eyes. The *need* there. "And," Michael croaks, "there is the devil's eye, and his sight laid upon you tells the nature of your death, and what comes after death. And when all three remnants are used together—"

But Michael doesn't get to finish. David Lundy leans forward, one hand gripping Michael's wrist. "What do you mean, an *eye*, Michael? There's a fucking *eye* out there and you never told us? After all these years?"

"Let me tell you now," Michael whispers. "I will tell you of it."

"Goddamnit," David Lundy hisses, and leans forward, leans his great pale head over Michael's. And the straps lashing Michael to the gurney give way with a sound like someone slapping a wall, and Michael, flesh now bubbling in great red welts, his face a painted rictus of black oil, wraps his hands around the globe of David Lundy's skull. "You and I have incurred a great debt," Michael gasps, and the bones of David Lundy's head crack like a breaking dish beneath his hands, and he squeezes still, squeezes until all the man's dark and clotted life spills out onto Michael's upturned face and David Lundy issues a last gurgling scream thirty thousand feet in the air.

JOHN BONNER

"So we just sit here," Bonner says. "After what just happened. We've got to do more than this, man. There's got to be something."

They're parked across the street from Shoyou Sushi, its windows dark at this time of night. The restaurant's in that no-man's-land between the Pearl District, its boutiques and tea shops, and the gnarled decay of Old Town. Class divisions butting up against each other in stark relief, but at this time of night, the streets generally quiet. Light traffic, a few tents in front of an abandoned glass shop a block over. There is blood still smeared across the sedan's windshield. Bonner's hands won't stop shaking.

"He's not going to show," Weils says, and dials Camelot again. She speaks briefly, asks if Lundy has called DoD yet. "Well, if he hasn't told you yes, then that's a no," she says into the phone. "We're heading back."

Making their way toward the highway that will take them to Camelot, Bonner sees a bloodied man give a looping roundhouse to a woman that spills her into the street. Before she is even on the ground, the man is on top of her, biting her face and neck, biting at the hands she holds up to protect herself. Bonner slows.

"Jesus Christ."

"Don't even think of stopping," Weils says.

Another man, not twenty feet away, shirtless with a cigarette in one hand, films the entire thing with his phone.

"Weils."

"Don't stop," she says. "There's no time. It's happening whether you stop the car or not."

He shoots wiper fluid on the glass, smears some of the blood away. His stomach roils. They'd simply driven out of the parking lot of the medical examiner's office. No shooting through the wind-shield, no zombie-movie heroics. They'd driven away, the bodies parting, scratching at the roof, slapping at the windows. How long would that remain an option? Just driving away? The woman's a hunched shape in his rearview mirror, the man still bent over her.

Toward Camelot, then. Wishing for another chance at that night on the Williamsburg Bridge, Pernicio's neck notched in his arms just so, the peppery burn of tear gas all around them.

The way that man bit at her fingers, at the upturned palms of her hands. Good God. What has he done? What has he become a part of?

"Lead helped," Weils says suddenly, making him jump.

"What?"

Her face is carved from stark planes of shadow and light as they drive down the highway. "We kept it in a box. The hand. It helped quiet the voice, right, the way it tried to reach out. You kept it in a lead-lined box, and you changed guard shifts every six hours, and no one took it out and messed around with it, tried to study it. And it stayed contained. Mostly. You'd get maybe a headache, some dark thoughts on some days, like afterimages. But that was it. It worked. But then someone—Seaver, a new guy like you, Bonner—just had to take it out of the box. Just had to see what the fuss was about, right?"

Her hair obscures most of her face. "That's the thing about the hand. About darkness in general. Everyone thinks they're exempt. Nobody thinks they'll be the one to tip the whole thing over. But Seaver took it out of the box, and it played him."

Bonner keeps driving.

"Lundy," Weils says, "he wondered what would happen if someone died because of the hand. Died or killed someone. We knew the hand got people that way, pushed that idea into your head. *Kill someone, kill yourself.* Over and over again. Like a broken record. Or gas, maybe, how it fills a room. So Lundy wondered what would happen if someone actually did die under its influence. There were rumors, never verified. But now we know. A fever house is what happens. That was his pet name for it. 'What's a fever house look like, Samantha? Care to guess?'" She looks at him, and in the weak light of the dashboard, the passing streetlights, her face is haunted and drawn. Bonner sees the weight of things upon her. Sees Weils for herself, as she is. Maybe for the first time. "It was me that started it," she finally says. "By shooting the driver who woke back up."

"The other guy had run off with the hand by then, Weils."

"Not far enough. Maybe if you stay near it for a while, it's stronger. Like fallout."

"We don't know enough to say for sure."

"It was me," Weils says. "I know it."

"It was bound to happen sooner or later."

"Maybe."

"It's fucking *demonic*, Weils. It *talks*. Gets in your mind. It was bound to happen. How long's Lundy had it?"

They take the off-ramp that will lead them to the base. She sighs, picks at something on her slacks. "DoD had it for a while, then they passed it off to the State Department because that's who Lundy was working with. He's had it for a few years. Michael, he's been talking about it forever, though. Ever since Lundy landed him, Michael's been talking about the hand. It's been passed on from one agency jurisdiction to another, everyone bickering over it. But like Michael, they've kept it under wraps so far. The hand's how Lundy got Heavy Light approved and funded, and here we are. Mission objectives: Study the hand and harness the recording as a doomsday device. And then Seaver loses the thing and we're scrambling."

Bonner turns and stares at her—starts to swerve and feels the shudder of the warning bumps beneath the wheels—and says, "What?"

Weils looks at him. "What?"

"What do you mean, 'harness the recording'?"

Her laugh is a sharp bark. Cynical as hell. "What did you think the recording was for, Bonner? You got briefed on what it does. Why do you think they're putting it in a song? It's a weapon. Get a radio station in Kabul or Moscow to play that thing, see what happens. God, get a drone to play it over the capitol building at Pyongyang and watch the blood fly. Lundy's whole career has been leading up to it. That's what Heavy Light's been about. Use Michael to find the hand again, and then start using the recording in the field. Or everywhere."

"Everywhere?"

She shrugs. "There's rumors that other agencies want to just greenlight a saturation campaign. Tap into global satellites. Play it on every phone on the globe simultaneously. Protect enough of the command structure and then watch the world burn."

"Fucking *why?*"

Another one of Weils's shrugs. "You get a toy, you want to play with it. It's just a rumor."

"How do you know all this?"

"You'd be amazed, Bonner, the things you're privy to when you stop fighting the current."

"Is that what I've been doing?"

"Entire time you've been here. Full of judgment. Nose up. Like this is all some punishment." Any supposed connection they might have had a moment earlier, any notion of Weils softening, is gone.

The night spins past. Closer to the base, traffic thins, gives way to great stretches of scrub grass, concrete dividers. Cyclone fencing. Immutable, endless dark.

They arrive at Camelot. The soldier at the guard station eyes them suspiciously as Bonner holds out his badge. Unhappy with the blood on the windshield. Wanting to call his CO, Bonner's sure, until he gets a look at their faces, their clear unwillingness to brook any shit.

The gate peels back.

They make their way past the barracks, the motor pool, the hangars. Admin buildings. Shapes limned in the darkness. Camelot's at the far end of the facility, their decrepit hangar, their sad little gathering of stick furniture.

This part of the base is dark. All the lights are off. The plane's gone. The hangar's left empty, the bay doors wide open.

The sense of abandonment about the place is so strong it might as well have a taste.

Weils gets out of the car. Takes a few steps and slowly spins around. Heads to the main building housing Camelot and types in the code and opens the door. She peers inside and steps out just as quickly.

"They left," she says.

The crisp fall air is tinged with the faintest ghost of diesel and oil. A cold wind rattles the chain-link fence. The stringed lights of the runway out there in the distance.

"What do you mean?" Bonner calls. "Who left?"

"The whole team. Offices are empty. The hangar."

"Lundy left? He fucking *left*?"

"Lundy's running, Bonner. It's a fever house. He fucked up."

"Where's he going to run to? He's what, gonna outrun the State Department? Outwit the Department of Defense, that's his big plan?"

Weils chews her lip, looks at him over the roof of the car. So much at play on her face, so much going on there. "You still got those plates in your vest, Bonner?"

He looks down, touches the vest he's kept on this whole time. "Yeah, I got plates in my vest, Weils."

When he looks back up, she's got her gun out. A silencer at the end.

She's aiming at him over the roof.

Fucking Weils.

She shoots him in the head.

NICK COFFIN

Too young to even buy beer when he met Peach Serrano for the first time, but old enough to know that he was no one to casually mess around with. No one you really wanted on the periphery of your life: You either wanted him dedicated to you, for your own safety, or you wanted to steer way clear.

Nick was a busser at Chadwick's, an upscale seafood place downtown, doubling sometimes as a dishwasher when they got slammed. It was cool—he had moved out that summer after graduating high school, figuring maybe college, maybe not, but in the meantime he'd landed a job that was enough to rent a studio apartment on the Eastside, an intentional thing to get some distance from Katherine, figuring it would be good to have the Willamette River between them. Mostly it was a cush job; tips were good, staff was a mix of world-weary old-timers and young dumbasses like him. He got to sleep in, his coworkers liked to party. Life and its demands could wait. And if his mom was a weight on his heart, she had enough money to take care of herself and was still—in the confines of her apartment, at least—clear-eyed and wise.

The night he first met Peach—the night that Peach, in his own way, became minorly indebted to him—they were slammed. Nick running from table to table in his dress shirt and little black bow tie, Adam's apple bobbing like a fish on a lure, a kid skinny like a Gorey drawing, already sweating an hour into his shift. It would be crazy for the next three, four hours, with Nick bussing and then doing whatever prep and dish-work he might be asked to help with.

As sometimes happened, he was tasked with laying out silverware and all the other various accoutrements after the guests had already been seated; it happened occasionally, not a big deal, but some of the customers acted shocked and put-out. This particular night, Nick went over to the table in question—it was a window seat, high-profile, either a reservation or the guy had palmed some cash to that night's host, a severely unfunny older man from Jersey City named Stewart—and began laying his little wrapped collections of silverware, his starched crown-like napkins, lighting the new candles with a long barbecue lighter, always feeling a little silly at the forced intimacy of it. Most people would wait for him to finish before continuing their conversation, everyone's faces etched in tight, loveless smiles until he took off.

That night, though, these guys, they hadn't waited for him to leave before they started talking again. One guy, smaller, wearing a nice charcoal-gray suit that showed off his gym biceps, a pink tie, little product in his hair. The other guy with inky black hair that brushed his shoulders, his face sharp and drawn. Rodent-like, Nick thought. Wore a scuffed, road-worn leather jacket—into Chadwick's, which meant more folded money into Stewart's hand, because suit jackets were required here—and a pair of black jeans. Nick, readying the table, swore it looked like the man had been crying. They vibed closer in age than not, these two, but there was something about them that made Nick think father and son, something like that. Something proprietary. Boss and employee, maybe. Whatever it was, they gave absolutely zero shits about Nick setting their table for them, just plowed forth.

"I'd like to roll up there and lay some fire down," the one in the leather jacket said. Practically rocking in his seat with anxiety.

"Yeah, you can't do that," said the one in the suit. "You just can't do it."

"They shut his head in a door, man. Caved his fucking head in."

"I know it. And he doesn't want retribution."

"He doesn't know what he wants," the man said, and then looked up at Nick with those bleary eyes. "Can I get a beer, please?"

"Absolutely," Nick said, "I'll let your server know right now."

Busy, busy, the clatter and howl of the place. Volume increasing gradually as wine began flowing throughout the dining room, Nick already dreaming of the ensuing tips. Barring tragedy—more tragedy than he'd already experienced—he'd be set for life financially, Katherine had already told him as much, but making rent on your own, eking it out via your own sweat, it was a different feeling.

He kept an eye on the two at the window table. Both of them with their own unique magnetism, their own pull. Both thrumming with a kind of danger, a menace, that Nick found himself drawn to. Actually found himself thinking of his dad, how Matthew would have probably enjoyed drinking with these guys. And drink they had—over the course of an hour and a half, the one in the suit had put away a four-hundred-dollar bottle of red, the one in the leather downing almost an entire six-pack of imports, just one after the other, *boom boom boom*.

During a brief break in the madness, he'd hit up the men's server, a blond woman a few years older than him named Melanie, who ran the floor with a cold efficiency that belied her cheerleader looks. "You hear those guys talking at the window there?" he said.

"Who, the fucking wannabe gangsters?" Melanie said, waiting at the bar for her tray to get filled. She rolled her eyes.

"They're gangsters?" Unable to hide the awe in his voice.

"The one who looks like he eats cigarette butts? He keeps talking about his friend that got put in the hospital, and the other one with the glue in his hair keeps saying, 'You can't kill em, Tim, it ain't on you, it's my call.'"

"Wow," Nick managed.

"Yeah," she said, "give me a fucking break." Then, looking him up and down, as if seeing him for the first time, she said, "Nate, right?"

"Nick."

"Nick, we got a bunch of campers at table twelve and we've still got a wait-line out the door, so why don't you go take their shit. Maybe they'll get a clue."

Finally, over two hours after they'd entered, the place still wailing, Nick watched as the one in the suit dropped a stack of cash next to the bill, and the other one staggered to the bathroom at the rear of the restaurant.

When he reemerged, Nick saw something fall from his jacket, there by the bar, the lights dim in that part of the room. Guy didn't even notice, just kept on. Nick, his heart suddenly thudding woodenly in his chest, walked over without a word and scooped it up, placing the matte-black pistol in his dish bin, putting a dirty plate over it. Stalking into the kitchen—still with his heart whamming against his ribs—he'd put the bin beside the dishwasher and tucked the gun into the front of his pants, pulling the tails of his dress shirt over it.

He ran out the back door then, thinking about how crazy it was, how stupid, and then circled around to the front of the restaurant. He'd be fired at least, if not arrested, this was so actively idiotic, but he caught the two of them at the end of the block, the one in the leather jacket walking with his head down, staggering a little as he went. The zombie-stomp, his mom called it, no stranger to a few drinks herself.

"Excuse me," he called out, his voice tinny and dumb-sounding. Out in the open, he could smell the grease of the dish pit on himself. The two men kept walking.

"Pardon me," he called out again, louder, and the one in the gray suit turned to him then, a little hunched, ready to strike if he had to. It thrilled and scared him at the same time. The one in the leather jacket, red-eyed, his face hanging blank and uncomprehending, turned a few seconds later.

"He dropped something," Nick said to the one in the suit.

"Who did?"

Nick lifted his chin toward the man in the leather jacket, who blinked owlishly. "He dropped a gun."

"Bullshit."

"I got it right here," Nick said, gesturing at his front. "I just didn't want to, you know, pull it on you guys."

The one in the suit looked over at the other man. "You fucking dropped your gun?"

Eyes still at half-mast, the other man patted his pockets. He grimaced and blinked, a pained, almost shy look on his face. "Yeah."

His mouth knit into a tight colorless line, the one in the suit said, "Give it to me," and Nick carefully pulled it from his waistband and handed it over, grip-first. The man quickly released the clip, saw that it was loaded, and let out a hiss of disgust. "You dropped a loaded piece in a *seafood* restaurant, Tim? How many people in there? How many felonies you got hung on you, man? You get *your* head shut in a van door, you fucking maniac?" He effortlessly put the pistol somewhere inside his own coat, and then turned that searchlight gaze on Nick. Nick with a flush of recognition then, that sense of being seen; it was like being near an electric current, and again he was reminded of his father. "Thank you, my friend, I appreciate you and what you did."

"No problem," Nick said. "Have a good night."

And the two had turned and gone on down the sidewalk, the one in the suit with his hand gripped loosely around the collar of the other, Nick hauling ass back to the rear of the restaurant, hoping he hadn't just lost his job.

It was an anecdote he told to a few people at work the next couple nights, a good story, but not an amazing one. Perhaps, Nick thought, if the gun had gone off, shot out a light, nailed Jersey Stew in an ass cheek, something. It was maybe five or six days later when the same guy, wearing a navy blue cashmere sweater and pressed slacks, a small diamond glittering in one ear, got a table at the front window again. This time, he saw Nick and motioned him over straightaway. "Whyn't you have a seat," he said.

Nick's face flushed with pleasure. "Ah, thank you, sir, I can't, I'm on shift right now."

"Who's gonna complain? Stew? Don't worry about Stew."

"No, sir, it's just my manager," Nick said, even as he slid into the seat opposite, gently laying his empty tub at the side of his chair.

The guy leaned forward, put his arms on the table. "What's your name?"

"Nick."

"Nick, my name is Peach, and I wanted to come in here and thank you personally for what you did the other night." He held out his hand and they shook, Peach's grip rough with callouses. "A lot of people would have fucked that up."

"You're welcome."

"They would have freaked out. Would have reported it to their manager, even the cops. Even guys that would have given it back might have pulled it first, and that guy I was with, he probably would have broken your arm or some shit. Lives a lot in his feelings, you know? And he's going through a time right now. Him getting busted with a piece, given his particular history with law enforcement? Would have been a bad situation."

"Okay."

"I'm just saying, you handled all that exactly the right way, and I owe you."

From the corner of his eye, he saw Melanie coming toward the table. Smile like a knife scar on her face, taking in Nick sitting at a front-window table with a customer, his fucking *dish tub* right there on the carpet.

"It's cool, he's with me," Peach said, before Melanie could even speak. She nodded briskly once, and in a voice bright with false cheer said, "I'll let Maxine know," turning on one heel and stalking away.

"Who's Maxine?"

Nick, his heart fluttering, said, "My manager."

"Ah, shit," the man said, wincing, a small smile at play as he leaned back in his chair. "We're in for it now."

"I should go."

"Tell Maxine you quit."

"What?"

Leaning over, the man pulled his wallet out of his pants and counted out a crisp sheaf of hundred-dollar bills. "That's a grand, brother. Fucking quit. Tell her to fucking beat feet. Tell her you got things to do."

"I like Maxine," Nick said, smiling in spite of himself.

Peach shrugged. "You don't have to be a dick about it. Just walk away. I got guys on the payroll, I'll find something for you to do."

Nick, his hands sweating in his lap now. He let out a laugh that he hoped didn't relay his profound awkwardness. "Sir, I don't know you. I appreciate it, but I can't."

Maxine, across the room, daggers flying from her eyes, started walking toward them, until Stewart gently cut her off, taking one of her elbows and whispering into her ear. It was like a work of art.

"Cool," Peach said, watching the whole thing unfold. "You say so." He pushed the neat stack of bills toward Nick, and then took a business card from his wallet and threw it on top of the money. "You ever need anything, though, just give me a ring. I'll see if I can help you out. My man was in bad shape the other night. People help me out, I don't forget it."

He went over to the Regal Arms a few nights later. He and Katherine with a standing hangout time, every Thursday. Go for a walk, even if the weather was shitty, try to expand the ring as much as she was able to. Then go grab sushi, pizza, his mom getting gently spritzed on a couple glasses of wine, Nick there to help her avoid her dipping her toes too deep into the bad memories of the past. He could tell that Katherine had grown more insular since he moved out. He seriously doubted that she was leaving the apartment much at all when he wasn't there, even just to pop down to the convenience store a few blocks away for a bottle of passingly decent wine or some woefully overpriced toilet paper.

He walked into the lobby that night, same as ever, that familiar sense of home rattling in his breast—how many thousands of times has he walked through these doors, gone to the elevator and then decided to take the stairs, knowing it would be faster? Stared at these light fixtures, this dark molding? Nodded, just like he did now, at Mr. Contrallo, coming out of some unit or another, gently muttering to himself. That familiar scent in the stairwell—carpet cleaner trying its hardest to cover up the tinge of mold, age, the passage of years. Then down the hall to his mother's place—*his* place, really, given that Katherine kept insisting she'd do something with his room at some point, but just hadn't gotten to it yet. Then the knock on the apartment door, still weird after living there pretty much his entire childhood.

Still thinking about that guy, Peach, the weight of the pistol in his hand, he'd knocked on the front door to the apartment and opened it up to find a bloody footprint on the carpet. A scattering of them really, red smears that led from the bathroom to Katherine's bedroom, where he could faintly hear music playing.

"Mom?" he called out. The way his heart just dropped into his feet, that cold feeling rushing through him.

"Hey," Katherine said, sounding weary, tired. "I'm in here, hon."

He found her lying on her bed in a pair of sweatpants and a T-shirt. One foot was on a stack of pillows, wrapped in a coral pink hand towel that was spotted with blood.

"Think I had too much to drink," Katherine said sheepishly.

"What happened," Nick said, already putting it together.

"Stepped on a wineglass in the bathroom."

"Shit."

"Yeah."

"Can I see?"

Katherine winced, her wet hair still fanned out on the pillow. "So dumb. I just stepped right on it."

Nick gingerly peeled off the towel, his mother's face tightening in apprehension. He tried not to look alarmed at the red, slashed mess that was her heel.

"Is it bad?"

"It's fine," Nick said, a little queasy. A shard the size and shape of a ping pong ball, wickedly curved like that, was still embedded in the flesh, along with a bunch of other smaller pieces. Nick, eyes furrowed, grasped the bigger piece and pulled it out, Katherine hissing in surprise. Blood spilled from the mouth of the wound.

"Oh fuck," Nick said.

"What happened? What did you do?" Katherine sat up, trying to see.

"Don't worry about it."

"What do you mean, don't worry about it? Did you just pull a piece out?"

Nick wrapped her foot in the towel again, his mind a scramble as he understood how difficult this would be.

"We have to get you to a doctor, Mom. An ER. There's an Urgent Care down on, like, Hoyt, I think. By that vintage place. I'll call us a ride."

Katherine had lain back down, her throat working one time as she swallowed and said, "I can't, Nick."

"Why not?"

Katherine's eyes cut to the window, shame tightening her voice. "I can't go down to the frigging Pearl, Nick. We couldn't even make it to the record store last time."

"This is different. This is an emergency."

She'd looked at him then, her eyes wild, fierce with panic and a steeped anger of her own. One that he found himself rarely witnessing, even more rarely receiving. Meanwhile, her foot was still bleeding, the bottom of the towel growing fire engine red, Nick regretting like hell that he'd taken that big shard of glass out. He pressed his hand against the towel, the bottom of her foot.

"Ow."

"Mom, come on, we have to do this."

"I *can't.*"

"Mom."

"*I fucking cannot, Nicholas! Alright?*" Jaw jutting, hands curled into fists at her sides.

Nick stood there, helpless, knowing that someone couldn't die from a cut foot, but what was there to do? Have him dig all the glass out himself? Stitch his mother's foot up like a 1920s sawbones? Maybe ply her with whiskey first, give her a stick to bite down on? In twenty minutes, she'd be fine, right? The bleeding had to stop eventually.

But it revealed that deep-set thing that he'd wanted to run from so badly: Katherine was at the mercy of the world. Something happened to his mother whenever she had to leave the house. Mental, yes, but physical too. And given the choice, she'd rather bleed.

She'd rather bleed than go out there.

He'd taken a deep breath, walked into the bathroom and back, gently replaced the blood-sodden towel with a fresh one. Katherine by then was gently weeping with her face turned away from him.

Stepping into his own mostly cleared-out room, a tremendous moment of sorrow and regret had ripped through him. His mother had had everything taken from her. Piecemealed out. A career, a husband, now a son, all moved on in one way or another. Time, in the confines of Katherine Moriarty's life, simply took and took, gave nothing back. He put his hand in his pocket, felt the edges of his phone. His mother immobilized at the notion of a twenty-block car ride to save herself.

Again, that galvanizing notion: *She can't fix herself. She would if she could.*

He exhaled, the apartment still as a tomb, and he fished out the business card that Peach Serrano had given him. Dialed the number.

The man at the end was chewing something. "Yes?"

"Hi, is this Peach?"

A momentary silence, Nick plowing through it. "Uh, this is Nick Coffin, the guy at Chadwick's. Chadwick's, the other night—"

"Nick, yeah." Peach swallowed. "How you doing, man? What's up?"

Nick closed his eyes. "Well, listen, you know how you said you might be able to help me out?"

"I do."

"I have a favor to ask you."

Nick had imagined any number of things when Peach had said, casually, as if people called for such a thing all the time, that he'd be sending someone over. *Be like thirty minutes,* Peach had said, *your mom going to live for that long? Or do I need to tell my guy to hustle?* He'd imagined a doctor, again like something from the Old West, harried and exhausted from riding his horse all night. Or a man in a lab coat, stentorian and severe and loud.

He was not expecting to open the front door and see the man in the leather jacket from the other night, with his hair now tied up in a dark ponytail, carrying a paper grocery sack. Clear-eyed with sobriety and ferociously chewing gum.

"What's up," he said by way of greeting, and walked past Nick into the apartment like he'd just bought the building. Katherine, by then informed that someone would be coming over to help, had awkwardly moved herself to the living room, where she lay with her wrapped foot hanging over the arm of the couch. They were on their third towel.

"How you doing?" the man said to her, setting the grocery bag on the coffee table and starting to pull out the contents, Nick looking for the shape of the pistol on him somewhere. "Stepped on a wineglass, huh?"

"Yeah."

"Sucks. It hurt?"

"Oh yeah," Katherine said.

"Happened to a buddy of mine once, kind of. My buddy Hutch, he's huge, right? Like six-three, six-four, just an animal. Gets hammered one night, walks right into this chandelier, the thing was hung way low." The man stood up then, performing all the actions of that night—the stagger, the collision, cupping his hands to his head. Nick distractedly wondering if this Hutch was the one who had gotten his head shut in a van door, the one that this man wanted to exact revenge for. "Glass all in his hair and shit, just this close from his eyeballs. It was wild. He turned to me and he's all 'Tim, am I bleeding?' and there's a lightbulb, I shit you not, sticking straight out of his forehead like a finger, like this long." He bent back to the grocery bag, took the last thing out—a small glassine vial of something—and then folded and refolded the paper bag until it was flat. He put the bag under the coffee table, Nick finding himself pleased at the man's efficiency, his fastidiousness. "Anyway, let's get this thing cleaned up, get the glass out, get you stitched up."

The man took in, finally, Nick's hovering, worried presence, and seemed to assess him. Nick wondered if he remembered him at all. "What's your name again?"

"Nick."

"Nick, I'm Tim. I see you all got a record player over there."

"Yeah."

"You got any metal shit? I'm in a mood."

"Uh, I don't know."

"Why don't you go check," he said softly, "make us a stack of the good shit. You can be DJ." Turning to his mother, he asked what her name was, and she told him, sounding small and tired.

"Katherine, Tim. It's very nice to meet you. I've done this plenty of times, so it'll be chill, okay?"

"Okay," she said.

Nick, inanity rattling in his own ears, uselessly thumbing through the stacks of records over by the stereo, said, "Were you a combat medic or something?" Tim opening up packages of gauze, a small sewing kit with a red cross on the front, and what looked to be some medical-quality stitching in an air-sealed plastic bag.

"A what?"

"Were you in Iraq or something?"

"Iraq, like the war?"

"Yeah."

"First one or second one," Tim said, sitting on his knees before Katherine's foot, shaking up a bottle of hydrogen peroxide.

"I don't know," Nick said helplessly.

"First one I was in school," he said, "second one I was in prison," and Katherine, to Nick's surprise, laughed out loud.

Tim laughed too. "I'm just fucking with you. I wasn't in prison for that long. But no, man, not a vet or anything."

"How do you know how to do this?"

Tim paused, seemed to think about it. Katherine was still smiling at him over her own bloody foot.

"I don't know," he said. "I guess it's just, you're not the first person that's ever asked me to stitch them up."

Katherine said, "Get calls like this a lot, huh?"

"I mean, you're not the first, let's say that."

Thirty minutes later, Katherine had hobbled back to her bedroom with a giant white wrapping around her foot. The lidocaine still doing its numbing work, sixteen surprisingly tight and adept stitches over three separate cuts. The murmur of the television could be heard through her closed door, and all evidence was gone of Tim's visit. Nick took a break from scrubbing the blood on the carpet to call Peach.

"I just wanted to say thank you," he said.

"Of course. My man in there said you were kind to your mother."

"I mean, I guess so."

"That's important. Loyalty, sticking by someone. I got a thing right now, one of my guys, an employee, he got hurt. I got to figure out what to do about it, or if there's anything *to* do about it, you know what I'm saying?"

"Are you talking about Hutch?"

A pause. "How you know about Hutch."

"Tim was talking about him."

"Of course he was. He's busted up about it. Those two, they grew up together."

Nick, thinking of the thrill that ran through him when Peach had motioned him over, thinking of how his own father would have been drawn to this man. Both of them shot through with that same kind of allure, charisma, and with all of that moving through him, Nick just threw it out there: "You still need any help?"

"Like what?"

"I don't know. Like finding the guys that did it?"

Peach had paused and Nick, sputtering, filled in the silence: "Not like I would *do* anything, I'm not, that's not what I do, but finding someone? I bet I could do that. I bet I could help you like that."

"I mean, I don't need—I know where these fucking guys are, believe me. But you're good at finding shit, Nick? Because I collect things—stuff, I value the thing and the thing that that thing represents, you know? I got a whole theory around it—and sometimes I just don't have time to track everything down, okay? I'm a collector, but I also got a life, you know? Is that something you might be interested in, Nick? Helping me find things?"

Nick swallowed, missing, maybe, that bit of danger thrumming in the background of his life now that his dad was gone.

How a handful of words could change your life. Staring at the blood on the carpet, Nick had said, "I mean, yeah. I could try, Peach."

INTERVIEW EXCERPT

Rolling Stone Magazine

Issue #980

August 11 20XX

Pgs. 35–47

Arthur Renfrew, wiry and bespectacled bassist for the Blank Letters, lights a cigarette while waiting for the ATM to dispense his cash. He's in Raleigh, North Carolina, the rest of the band loosely clustered around him, waiting their turns. They're a block away from the club they'll be playing at later tonight, and it's a balmy, humid summer evening, the four of them in black T-shirts and shades. After collecting his money—"They let me take out $500 at a time now," Renfrew says with an offhanded grin, the joy obvious—he discovers that another $20,000 has been deposited into his account, a result from the band's debut album, *All Hail the Dirty Gods,* recently going platinum. This, he says, is a far cry from the band's first decade as a group, monumentally so. Lighting up a cigarette, one foot cocked up on the brick wall, Renfrew waits for the rest of his bandmates and says, "We were so fucking broke, man. We played a show at this movie theater in Scotland on our first UK tour? It doubled as a venue and they showed *The Rocky Horror Picture Show* before we played. I remember it being not a great show. We hadn't eaten since playing at a squat the night before, right? So the theater at the end of the night, they got rid of all the popcorn that no one ate during the movie, these *huge* plastic bags of neon-yellow, salty-ass popcorn. Each bag was almost as tall as a person. And they gave them to us— we fucking begged for them—these three giant, people-sized bags of bright yellow popcorn, and we loaded them up in the back of the van like bodies. Just totally dejected, you know." Renfrew laughs, pulls a drag of his smoke. "I think we got paid like thirty bucks for that show."

"Thirty euros," vocalist Katherine Moriarty offers, lifting her sunglasses and peering at the receipt the ATM has spit out.

"Right," Renfrew says. "I don't think it was even enough for gas."

"It was enough for gas," says Matthew Coffin, and it'd be impossible to ignore the defensiveness there, feigned as annoyance. Guitarist, backup vocalist, and co-founder of the band with Moriarty, Coffin also acts as the band's manager, a role he's taken on, he says, out of necessity. "No one else," he says, with a barely concealed bravado, "will put up with our shit." It all seems a little self-effacing and perhaps a bit of a put-on: the band's currently in the midst of a seventy-two-date tour that will continue to take them all the way across the US for the next three months, and they're making a lot more than gas money these days. Their last show at the Roseland Ballroom on Manhattan's West Side sold out so quickly the band added another two New York dates. It's difficult to gauge how this has affected the four of them.

"On one hand," says drummer Doogy Almoth, flipping his lime-green mohawk over to another side of his otherwise-shaved head, then smoothing it down with a ringed hand, "it's insane, it's every-thing we've ever wanted."

The band, flush with spending money now, heads back to the venue where they'll begin sound check. The show isn't for hours yet, but they seem buoyed, energetic, the cadence to their steps like that of teenagers. Moriarty slaps Coffin on the derriere and then leap-frogs over him, laughing her gravel-and-honey laugh and nearly faceplanting on the pavement when she lands, the group drawing bemused eyerolls from fellow pedestrians. "On the other hand," Almoth continues, "now there's five million people in your face every night telling you how to do what you very obviously already know how to do. It can be a little maddening."

When asked what he means—is he talking about label folks, pro-moters, A&R reps—Almoth hedges a bit. "I don't want to get into anyone's shit," he says (drawing a loud call of "I will!" from Coffin), "but it's just a struggle to navigate all this extraneous shit when it's like, 'I want to play the drums, I want to write songs, I want to fuck-ing perform,' you know? We're a live band, first and foremost. Any-thing beyond that, I've got, like, diminished interest in it personally."

It's a sentiment that the rest of the band echoes. Formed in LA in the waning days of the indie-punk explosion, the Blank Letters, for a brief window of time, seemed to be branded as the sole resuscita-tors of the genre, bringing the entire notion of "alternative music" back into the national spotlight. It seemed possible, even if it didn't happen that way; similar bands signed in the wake of the Letters's ascendancy have failed to generate much interest. But not so for the Blank Letters. They've got their finger on something, clearly; they've sold out the majority of the slots on this tour so far, and last week were on *Late Night with Conan O'Brien*, where they played their radio hit, the ferociously catchy, bombastic, Moriarty-penned "I Won't Forget It."

"I just think we're in the right place and we work hard," Coffin says, pitching his cigarette to the curb before heading through the security entrance, Coffin showing his backstage pass and ushering everyone else through. "I love this shit, personally," he says, gently putting a guiding hand on Moriarty's back as she walks into the green room that the promoter's provided the band, where the Letters's roadie, Rich Soto, is already stringing the band's guitars in preparation for sound check. "I feel like we've been working for this our entire lives."

Meteoric rise or not, the majority of the group has put in the hours. Coffin's spent the past fifteen years in countless LA bands, few of them truly getting off the ground or touring with any considerable success, while Moriarty, who writes "about a third" of the music and nearly all of the band's lyrics, is a journalism dropout via UCLA, with the Blank Letters being her first and only band. Almoth's worked in LA as an exterminator, a bus driver, a roofer, and a line cook, and Renfrew, as recently as six months ago, was still washing windows in Century City. For all four of them, the band is now a full-time job.

There is, admittedly, a tendency for the band to sometimes get in its own way. The group's label, Interscope, is still owed another album as part of their recent two-record deal, and the follow-up to *All Your Wasted Days*, their major label debut, has been slow in coming. The band, for the first time since the interview started, gets notably more tense when the new record is brought up, Almoth going so far as to sigh expansively and crack open a Heineken from the cooler in the green room—part of the band's surprisingly detailed rider—and earning a shrewd warning look from Moriarty. Coffin puts it bluntly enough: "Fuck the fucking record. The fucking record'll be done when it's fucking done." When quizzed about why it might be taking so long, he simply waves his hand.

"You can't force songwriting," Moriarty says, stepping in for her husband, "it's not like other, more tangible, physical art."

Coffin agrees. "You force it and it dies. All the soul gets carved out of it. It has to come organically or not at all."

When asked if they feel any pressure to give the label something, there are veiled looks around the room until Soto, sensing the unease, breaks wind explosively, the band exploding in revulsion and laughter. "We'll get there," Almoth says soothingly, tapping out a little rhythm on his beer bottle.

The room's energy changes once more when Moriarty and Coffin's son Nick is brought in by his nanny, Glenda, a heavily tattooed friend of the band's from Moriarty's UCLA days. Nick, ten, seems perfectly at ease in the green room, shyly smiling and high-fiving Renfrew before going over to his mother, who absently smooths over his hair. Another way in which this is an unusual band: Nick tours with them, and always has.

"That's the thing that people don't get about us," says Coffin, still annoyed at the new album being brought up. "We've been around for a long time. We're not, like, a bunch of twenty-two-year-olds, all star-struck by this shit. We're lifers, right? I'll fucking smack a promoter in the mouth if they try to fuck us, I don't care."

"Looking good, Matthew," calls out Almoth, to the delight of the rest of the band. But Coffin is undeterred.

"I'm serious. The thing that I always want everyone to understand—my son, my wife, my bandmates—is that no one's going to come and rescue you. You have to claw for every fucking inch you ever get. No one's going to save you. I'm one of the greatest, most incendiary guitar players of the last fifty years—no shit, I'm serious—and that's all me. I did that. I made myself into that."

It's a tactic that seems to be working. The show that night—four thousand screaming, moshing, fist-pumping fans—goes for nearly two hours, the band playing nearly every song on *All Your Wasted Days* and *All Hail the Dirty Gods*. When Moriarty and the band come out for their encore—"I Won't Forget It," of course—she dedicates the song to her son. "This one's for our boy, Nicky," she says, "who we're raising to be a decent man, to fight the power." Then a throaty chuckle, a hand over her brow as she stalks the stage before leaning toward the crowd, a moment of intimacy. And quieter, wink-ing to the audience, she says, "Except for us, Nick, please, listen to us, man, it's fuckin' way past your bedtime, dude."

And then the four-count on Almoth's sticks, and Renfrew comes in with that bassline, and Moriarty lifts her face to the stage lights and pushes the microphone out toward the crowd, and a moment later, four thousand people are scream-singing along with her.

HUTCH HOLTZ

Hutch passes more emergency vehicles, finds that this part of Burnside has been completely cordoned off. Another accident of some kind, a wash of red and blue lights, caution tape thrown up. People milling about with their phones.

Hutch sees his first emergency responder in a hazmat suit. Ghostly as an apparition. He turns onto a side street, threads his way among the brick apartments and old, piecemealed Victorians of Southeast. He parks at Twenty-second and Marklin, the street shaded with dogwoods still dripping from earlier rains. His legs stiff, he walks like an old man. Holds the pistol in his fist inside his jacket pocket.

Twenty-fourth and Marklin is just as Coffin said it would be— another two-story apartment building, brick and cement, the upper-floor walkway laced with black iron railings. Maybe a dozen units, no lights on. Hutch hasn't felt a thing on the approach here—no snarl, no whispering insistence that he wreak havoc upon himself. He turns the corner onto Marklin and here's the back of the building, three garage doors and a dumpster. He hears footfalls and turns, staggering, but it's a woman who runs past without even noticing him, her head turned, fleeing from whatever's behind her. Hutch leans against the brick beside the dumpster and then crouches—gingerly, groaning—and peers beneath it. If the hand was ever there, it's gone now.

He stands up, takes out Don's severed thumb and then his phone. He presses the thumb to the screen once, twice. It comes to life. He scrolls through Don's contacts, looking for Coffin's number again, when a man lurches from around the corner and collides against him, the two of them falling to the pavement in a spill of limbs. Hutch's head bounces off the cement, hard, and his vision grays. The man—small, with a widow's peak and a dark goatee—is already biting at him, his teeth snapping together inches in front of Hutch's face. Hutch puts up his arm and the man bites through the thin nylon of Don's windbreaker. His eyes are threaded with starbursts of red veins, the pupils huge. He shakes Hutch's arm in his mouth like a dog.

Hutch digs a thumb into the jelly of the man's eye, the nail finally disappearing into the iris with a febrile give, a spill of watery blood. The man doesn't recoil, doesn't scream in pain. He clamps down harder on Hutch's arm, teeth gnarling against muscle. Hutch grunts and punches him in the head, three, four times. The man's hands skitter across his face and find his throat. Hutch can hear the clicking of his windpipe constricting as he scrabbles for the detective's pistol. It's snagged in his pocket, won't come out. His vision swims with stars. He fires the pistol blindly through his jacket pocket and the man goes rigid, his hands finally loosening. Hutch pushes him off, air screaming through his bruised windpipe, and he rips the pistol free in a snarl of torn fabric. The man's on his elbows, already rising, and Hutch sits up and shoots him twice in the face. Hardly hears the gunshots through the blood throbbing in his ears.

The screen of Don's phone is cracked. He looks for the thumb and can't find it. His back wound has fully opened up. His arm where the man bit him now feels coated in a pulsing fire. Join the fucking club, he thinks. The man lies with the upper half of his body splayed in the gutter.

Hutch rises, staggers back to his car. Lights have come on in the apartments. The movements necessary to simply sit in the driver's seat are absolute anguish, and once he's managed it he grays out, drifts away for a moment with the pistol in his lap. Comes back when Don's phone begins a harsh, metronomic screeching. He reaches over—Jesus, his guts are an utter slick of blood now—and with his good arm fishes around for the phone.

An emergency alert. White text on black, the words pulsing and too bright. He squints.

A county-wide emergency, telling everyone to stay indoors. Call 911 if they witness a crime or injury. Get inside as quickly as possible.

Hutch fishes for his keys but can't find them. The heat from his arm climbs into his heart through a veering staircase. Dark thoughts swim through him. Dim shapes spied through a red veil. The phone's screeching continues. The street beyond the windshield is a pure and unbridled dark. Only the white corona of streetlight above him, like some judgment.

He squints against it, his bloody hand raised before his eyes.

NICK COFFIN

What Rachmann says is that if you want to meet this woman, she doesn't come to you. You go to her. There's no way around it. She won't talk on the telephone. She's paranoid of the phone being tapped. Given her history.

"What does that mean?" Nick asks.

"It means we fly to Los Angeles."

It's one in the morning and they're in the airport, nursing vending-machine food and paper cups of coffee. Rachmann, who Nick had last seen in New York, had met him at the airport, three hours after their conversation.

"How'd you get here in three hours?" Nick had asked.

"I was in Seattle."

"Lucky for me," Nick said.

Rachmann had shrugged, hoisted his bag over his shoulder as they began walking to the terminal to buy their tickets. "I was in Brussels yesterday, so yes, lucky."

There's little to understand—it's just Rachmann, and perhaps a bit of good fortune turning Nick's way. He wants to believe that there are vast mechanisms at work here, destiny bending toward him, helpful and kind, but knows it's not true. There is luck and there are choices, and that's all.

Nick had stopped Rachmann in the middle of the airport and handed him ten thousand dollars wrapped up in a plastic Safeway bag. They'd purchased their tickets with cash and then walked to their gate.

Now they sit among a scattering of other people awaiting their flights. Restless, tired, bundled in their bucket seats. The glow of phone screens.

"Does she know we're coming?" Nick asks again.

"She does," Rachmann says. "We've made an appointment." He looks at his phone and then smiles at Nick. "A very early appointment."

"And you think it's an agency that has my mother. An actual government agency."

"I do. And I think that's why she's safe for now."

"You know the government greenlights assassinations all the time, right? US citizens or not."

"She'll be fine, Nick."

Nick recalls a moment—not even six months ago, probably—where he and Katherine had each nursed a beer back at the apartment after another failed attempt at expanding the ring. It had been a clear, unseasonably warm night, and Katherine had simply shut down. Just took one step too far, or the sky looked a certain way, a car horn honking a little too close. This one particular street not offering the right sense of escape or expansiveness to her. Who could say. Whatever it was, it had simply been too much. She'd hit her wall.

Katherine had been uncharacteristically withdrawn on the walk back; kicking herself, Nick could tell. There were times where his frustration at her mounted, where he wanted to just tell her everything was fine, why couldn't she understand that? There were so many things to be afraid of, but the city wasn't one of them. He had, so far, avoided such an outburst, but Christ, it felt close sometimes.

Ungenerous, yeah. Unfair as shit, certainly. But Jesus, who was the parent here? She had put the Clash's *Give 'Em Enough Rope* on the turntable and stood in the doorway that separated the living room from the kitchen. Shoulders hunched, one leg cocked, moving only to lift that beer bottle. Her jaw working, eyes drawn to some place far from the apartment. Nick had walked over, peered at the album jacket, the blown-out halftones and large blocks of color, trying to figure out what to say to her. Remembering that moment when she had seized his arm with both hands and stopped on the sidewalk, a man behind them abruptly pivoting and walking past, hearing the stutter-step squeak of his shoes as he changed course, Katherine just going, "No, I can't, I can't, I can't, okay, I can't—" her voice raw-edged with panic. With real terror.

Behind him, in the living room, Katherine had surprised him by speaking, Nick actually flinching a little. "This is not something I was planning on."

"Oh shit, I know, Mom." He turned, held his beer bottle to his stomach. Some kind of talisman. Protecting himself. Either against the enormity of her pain, or to keep himself kind, he couldn't say.

"I did not plan on being a fucking shut-in, you know? That was not on my dance card."

"I know, Mom. We can keep trying. And there's, you know, therapies we can try. People get better."

She had tilted the mouth of the bottle toward him and winked, no humor in it. "Got to go to the doctor to get therapy."

Nick frowned. "Not anymore. Just jump on your laptop now, you know?"

"Maybe." Katherine, telegraphing as ever, *You don't understand. You don't understand, I'm different.*

"I'm just saying. I'll do this with you until you're an old lady—"

A small smile. "Watch it."

"—but maybe it doesn't have to be just you and me."

She tilted the bottle to her lips and Nick could see then, in that brief moment, the woman his mother had been, her own history snared tight within her, the body she inhabited such a cage now, fear tethering her so tightly to the ground. To these rooms.

"I ever tell you the time I went to see the Clash?"

"With Dad?"

"No, this was before I met your dad. I was still in high school. They were playing with the English Beat, which was my friend Jerome's favorite band. Just loved 'em. We were walking to the Palladium, sixteen years old, the bands were playing like a week of shows together, and I had this safety pin through my ear that just *throbbed*. Nobody was really doing safety pins anymore, at least not in LA, but I was going through this UK phase, Soo Catwoman and Siouxsie Sioux and all those girls, and so I had this safety pin through my ear that was just dripping pus—"

"Jesus."

Katherine laughed, coming back into herself a little. "I know! And it was all I could think about, was how bad it hurt and how, if someone whacked it in the pit, I was probably just going to pass out, just die right there. But how could you not dance to the goddamn Clash, right?"

Nick, smiling, "Right." His mother, moved by music even now, shaken to her core by it.

"So I'm thinking about that, and we're walking to the Palladium and we took the train in and Jerome squeezes my arm"—Nick flashing for a moment to Katherine gripping his biceps, *I can't, I can't, I can't*—"and I kind of come out of it, right?" Her eyes bright, she chops a hand at him and says, "And there's this guy *right there,* standing right in front of us, and he's got a stiletto."

"Oh, shit."

"Right? And Jerome, he's just seized on me, this was a tiny Black gay kid who liked *ska,* okay? And he stops, and I just, we had to *go.* You know? We had to get to the show. And this guy with the knife, he kind of wiggles it around and he's like, 'Pass it over,' and I'm thinking, 'I got T-shirt money in here, I got beer money if anyone will buy us beer, I got train fare.' And there's no fucking *way* I'm passing it over. And so I kind of just put my hand over Jerome's hand on my arm, like he's a gentleman helping me ford a mud puddle after he's dropped a handkerchief across it, and I just go 'Fuck off,' and that's that. We just walk right past the guy, Jerome and I both kind of laughing, freaked out, and we make it to the show." Another tilt of the beer bottle. "Which, I'm happy to report, was amazing, *and* they played 'Death or Glory,' *and* Jerome got a guy's phone number at Oki Dog later that night, *and* we both got so shitfaced that we threw up waiting for a train home. A win-win." She thought about it for a moment. "A win-win-win, really."

"You're lucky you didn't get stabbed."

She nodded. "No, you're right. But my point is," and here her voice had cracked, this rage and self-loathing just under the surface of this entire story, just waiting to bubble up, "my point *is*, Nicky, I just cannot believe, down to my marrow, that the girl who laughed off a stiletto now can't leave her fucking apartment without feeling like the entire planet is going to drop on her." She leaned back and set her bottle down on the coffee table with a clatter. "I'm just . . . this is not the world I planned for myself."

She'll be fine, Nick.

He has to believe that Rachmann's right. What else is there to do?

Going to LA seems like a profoundly bad move—leaving the city at all feels dangerous and stupid—but there's a risk no matter what. It's very likely, Rachmann has pointed out, that if someone *has* ID'd him alongside Peach when Peach was killed, Nick is wanted for questioning. Plus there is the shooting in his apartment to consider, and the fact that he ran.

The minutes peel away. By the time they board the red-eye flight to LAX, Nick is convinced that he is making the wrong choice. He calls his mother's phone, finds himself hoping that the stranger will answer, this man obviously pretending to be a cop. Let's do *something*, Nick thinks, to move this intractable setup forward somehow. But it goes to voicemail, and he doesn't leave a message.

They find their seats. Rachmann grips his armrests.

"You okay?"

"It's not my favorite thing," Rachmann says. "Flying."

"We'll be fine," Nick says. He thinks, Surely we'll be screwed some other way, Rachmann. Nothing as pedestrian as problems with an airplane. That's not our lot.

The plane pulls itself from the tarmac, a bullet hurtling through the thinned air, and there is, for the next while, nothing he can do. It's as close to peace as he's come since Hutch's phone call, and in his exhaustion, he falls toward sleep gratefully.

When he wakes, they've landed. It's still night, morning hours away.

He wants to ask if Rachmann is worried about Peach's death—Peach's murder—but why would he be? Peach is one client among many. It's Nick that's the hunted one. Nick's the rabbit in the brush.

They grab a Lyft out to Venice Beach. Sleep still drags at him and he wonders if there is some kind of psychic hangover at play, after having been near the hand. Rachmann chats with the driver for the twenty-minute ride, keeps up the pretense that they are tourists visiting their girlfriends who are here for work, and when they're let out a block away from the boardwalk, Rachmann and the driver bump fists. Nick's rage at the man's compartmentalization increases. Motherfucker has no clue, and no concern, about what is at stake. His mother's head could be in a duffel bag right now and Rachmann would pocket his ten grand and move on to the next job. Rachmann fishes a pair of dark sunglasses from his jacket, because of course he does. Still pure night out. Nick, meanwhile, is ready for a shower and a cup of coffee. Ready for a weeping jag. Ready to get this over with.

The hotel's on the beach, right there, touristy and expensive and slathered in pastel swaths of color and odd angles. Rachmann's gotten them rooms across from each other. Nick's room is all Ikea furniture and a mattress filled with what seems to be slats of cardboard. A seagull stands on the sill of his window, cocking its head and looking at him with an accusatory eye. Nick, projecting.

An hour later he meets Rachmann in the lobby. Rachmann is sitting in a modernist chair that looks made of carelessly folded canvas and steel. He drinks a smoothie out of a plastic cup, his leg jostling like mad. Nick has no idea where he got it—there's no café in the hotel. He realizes that Rachmann has become, in his own way, Nick's procurer. His finder. It seems dangerous to think of him as more than that.

Rachmann sees him and unfolds himself from the chair. Puts his sunglasses on. "You ready?"

It's hours before the T-shirt shacks and surf shops open. The boardwalk empty, caricaturists and spray-paint artists all snug in their beds right now.

He is in California, he is on the Venice boardwalk, and even at this ungodly hour a man slaloms past on rollerblades. He is wearing small, lime green bikini briefs and a stenciled T-shirt that says DEATH IS THE ONLY ANSWER.

The shop is small. Wooden shingles, a purple door. The store window has a bevy of jewels and feathers on a crumpled velvet blanket. Crystals, things in stoppered bottles. Something snags at Nick as they stand there. Maybe just the idea that answers supposedly lie beyond the door here. He's going to save his mother by talking to someone who traffics in potions, crystals? Books about magic? He's given Rachmann ten thousand dollars and this is what he's bought with it? Plane tickets to the Venice boardwalk.

The door is unlocked and a bell jingles as they walk in. The narrow shelves on each side are crowded with books, more crystal displays, dreamcatchers, figurines. Incense, this early, is already heavy in the air. New Age pan flute music wafts from overhead speakers. Everything dark, cave-like, gilded in soft edges.

A woman pushes through a beaded curtain behind the counter. Nick's expecting someone who plays the part—jeweled fingers, a patterned shift, perhaps a headscarf, a cultivated air of mysticism. But this woman looks like someone's grandmother from Orlando. Silver bouffant, leathery, sun-ravaged skin. Beige shorts and a hot pink T-shirt that says *SWEET* in cursive. A turquoise fanny pack snug around her waist.

"Help you?" Her voice is as gasoline-soaked as Nick expected.

"I'd like a reading," Rachmann says.

A small smile. "You're up pretty early, sunshine. You got an appointment?"

"My money talks."

Nick glances at him, confused, but the woman is already gesturing for them to follow her through the curtain, laughing a little as she does.

The back room is small and windowless. Boxes of merchandise and fragile, leaning towers of packing materials. In the middle of the room there's a card table covered in a thin shift, run through with skeins of glittering thread. Framed posters for magic shows and old circus acts hang on the walls, crowding the room even more. He and Rachmann sit in a pair of folding chairs at the table. When the woman scoots past him to sit in the chair opposite, Nick catches a whiff of cedar and perfume.

"Smoking an issue?" she says.

"What's that?" says Rachmann.

"You care if I smoke?"

"Oh. No."

"I'm Beverly."

"We're using names?" says Rachmann, a droll smile on his lips. He still hasn't taken his sunglasses off, and Nick, to his surprise, feels a tinge of embarrassment.

Beverly laughs. "There's no obligation here. You came to me."

"Alright."

She pulls a cigarette from her fanny pack and lights it. Tosses the pack on the table. For a moment she sits there smoking and looking at them, the cigarette in two fingers near her mouth. "Give me the money."

Rachmann pushes an envelope across the table. She folds it in half, puts it in her fanny pack without counting what's inside, then smooths the shift over the table again. She says, "I can give you ten minutes."

"That's fine," says Rachmann. "We'd like to talk about the operations you were involved in."

Beverly blows a jet of smoke at the ceiling. "Which one?"

"I don't know. All of them? Moon Spoon?"

Nick looks at Rachmann. Rachmann finally takes his sunglasses off, puts them in his pocket.

"Moon Spoon was a joke," Beverly says. She peers at both of them, her gaze finally settling on Nick. "I don't know what you know about it, but the best thing was the name, and the name was terrible. This was during the Gulf War, the first one, and for Moon Spoon they had us on a farm in Kentucky—a little farm outside of Brickville, Kentucky, just insufferably hot. I slept on the second floor and all they gave me for it was a tiny little box fan. We were supposed to locate troop and supply movements of the Iraqis. As if Saddam's people weren't running everything straight down Highway 80 out of Kuwait."

Nick says, "The Highway of Death."

She's a little surprised, and spends a moment looking at them again. "How old are you two?"

Nick tells her his age. Rachmann, he learns, is three years older.

"Jesus, I'm ancient," Beverly says. Her laugh is harsh and smoke-filled. "What kind of trouble are you in?"

Rachmann presses forth. "So Moon Spoon wasn't successful?"

Beverly takes a drag, blows smoke against the ceiling. "Well, there wasn't anything to find. Like I said, everything got thrown straight down 80. There's wasn't anything for us to see."

"How'd you get cherry-picked for remote viewing ops, anyway?"

She shrugs. "I applied."

They smile politely.

"Seriously. It was the seventies. There was an ad in the paper. They paid fifty bucks for that first analysis session. Maybe two hundred of us in a rented hall, freezing our asses off. This was back when I lived in Jersey City, and they just had us do some quick tests, to kind of cull the herd, right? There were maybe six of us left by the end of it, six who had actually produced results, or close enough, and those six of us got our fifty bucks and then a guy who said he was with the US Army bought us lunch and gave us a pitch. Sandwiches, I remember that. Turkey. I didn't care what they were talking about; I was hungry. I was sleeping on a couch back then, living with, like, five other people, and the guy whose name was on the lease was a creep. There were bedbugs. I was twenty-one. Food and a place to live? A stipend? Sounded pretty good to me. It beat handing out flyers on the street, which was what I was doing at the time. Remote viewing's the easiest job in the world if you can do it." Beverly shrugs. "And we came cheap. Put a bunch of us in a trailer on a base somewhere, give us some TV and cigarettes—they gave us plenty of Miller Lites, but wouldn't let us smoke dope. But yeah, get a handler that's not a total shit-for-brains and see what happens. Sometimes we got solid results."

Nick raises a finger. "Can we hold up a second? What's remote viewing?"

Beverly looks from Nick to Rachmann and back. "Where'd you get this guy?"

"I mean," Nick says, "I have a general idea, but—"

"Can you just go ahead and fill us in, please?" Rachmann says.

"Well, it's finding targets with the mind. Sensing the precise location of an object—be that a person or a building or a weapon, pretty much whatever you're told to find—using solely your mind."

"And this is a real thing?"

Beverly tilts her head. "Well, that's rude."

"I'm sorry, I'm just—"

She waves a hand at him, smiling. "I'm messing with you, man. It's as real as any other intangible thing is real, okay? Best answer I can give you."

Rachmann says, "I'm going to run some things by you, Beverly, and I'd love it if you could just let me know what your take on it is. Kind of a speed round, yes? I know you're busy."

"Shoot," she says.

"Operation: Low Tide."

"Oh, that one sucked too. Run by another shit-for-brains, but we were stationed in Santa Monica for that one, which was what made me fall in love with California." She ashes her smoke. "I'm from Lodi originally, and Santa Monica in the early eighties was a far cry, let me tell you."

"What was the purpose of that op?"

"That one was cocaine. This was before every cigarette boat off the coast of Florida was loaded with coke, back when it was coming in on the big ships. But Low Tide got pulled pretty quick."

"Why's that?"

"Our results sucked, honestly. All of my visions, personally, were murky. Scattered. They wanted boat numbers, coordinates. Specifics. And we were pressured to deliver, even if we didn't actually see anything. It was pretty terrible. A guy named David Lundy was the one running that program. Just a monumental prick. I saw him hit my friend Marcus with a phone book once when he messed up on a viewing, and since it didn't leave a mark, no one believed him. I couldn't stand the guy. But Low Tide got shut down, and then all the little boats started bringing in dope anyways, so there wasn't much point."

"David Lundy was the director of that program?"

Beverly nods. "That was him. Like I said, a prick."

"Operation: Raw Power."

"Don't know it."

"Operation: Lace Wing."

"Don't know it."

"Okay. Ever hear of someone called Saint Michael?"

Beverly pauses.

"I mean, yeah," she says quietly. "Heard of him for sure."

"Who is he?"

She shrugs, ashes her cigarette. "Well, he's a cipher, if you believe in that sort of thing."

"What do you mean?"

"I mean he's the boogeyman, right? The monster in the closet. The one they hung over our heads if we screwed up. *Michael gets it right, be more like Michael. You want to stay in Marlboros and Twinkies, do what Michael does.*' Which is a true thing Lundy said to me once. Saint Michael's the one that let Lundy keep his security clearance after Low Tide."

"How so?"

"Saint Michael," she says, rolling her eyes, waving her hands like fluttering birds. "Oh, Saint Michael's become this myth, but there's always some truth to something like that. A little kernel of it. Michael, he could *see,* man. He had clarity."

"More clarity than you?"

"Oh, absolutely. I don't mind it. Lundy was ambitious, right? You saw the way the guy handled people in some little satellite office in Santa Monica, the way he worked people, just stomping them into the dirt if they didn't produce, and you just thought, 'This guy's got big plans for himself.' This was, God, over thirty years ago, and nothing I've heard about him in the interim has changed my opinion. Low Tide bombed but then he found Michael—that's a whole other story right there—and then the thing with the studio happened and Lundy suddenly had a golden key. All the funding he wanted. Shit, they tailored a program for him after that."

"What do you mean, the thing with the studio?"

"Michael found a bomb in an LA news studio before it went off. Saw the whole thing. Even told them what desk it was under. Gave them hours of notice in advance. Some right-wing fringe group destroying the liberal media and all that, I don't know. But after the studio thing, Lundy was untouchable. I was already put out to pasture by then. Gently retired to palm-reading and tarot cards in Burbank. But I knew people that knew people, and we'd talk sometimes."

"So David Lundy is Michael's handler."

"That's my understanding, yes," Beverly says. "At least he was."

"So who is Saint Michael?" Nick says. "I don't know any of this stuff."

"It's not a question of who," Beverly says. "It's a question of what."

"What does that mean?"

Beverly sighs. She opens her fanny pack and takes out Rachmann's envelope. Thumbing through it, her lips move slightly as she counts. The part in her hair is a precise white line. She puts the money back.

"Saint Michael—that's what they call him—was found in the corner of a truck depot at, if I remember correctly, Thule Air Base in Greenland. This was in '85 or '86. If you believe the stories, he was naked, bloody, couldn't talk. Hiding behind a bunch of pallets. Like he just appeared there. Nobody knew how he'd gotten inside— closest notion was that he'd smuggled himself in under a truck carriage or something. Some poor MP found him and tried to put cuffs on him. Thought he was a vagrant, on drugs or whatever. Michael broke the MP's arms, almost ripped his jaw off, supposedly. Within a week he was growing wings. Like real, actual wings, and then he tells one of the officers on duty that his kid's at home playing with a gun. Michael convinces this guy, right, and the officer freaks and calls his wife. Wife has a shit fit when she realizes it's true. Kid's sitting there playing with a service pistol in their bedroom."

"This is a true story?"

Beverly shrugs. "It's a story. But it's a story I heard for years and years. Part of Saint Michael's lexicon, right? His mystery. His *allure*." She lights another cigarette.

"So," Rachmann says, "Lundy runs a bunch of you remote viewers who are, how do I say this? Mildly successful at best."

Beverly shrugs. "Truth hurts."

"But he also runs this Saint Michael, who is . . . what? A genetic experiment? A super soldier?"

"An alien?" Nick says. Resigned, for the next few minutes at least, to go with it.

Beverly shrugs. "All of the above? Who knows? I never saw him in person. This is just the stuff you hear drinking some pinot grigio while you chat with your girlfriends over the telephone."

"Okay. What else did Lundy run? What other programs?"

She taps a front tooth with a fingernail, the cigarette's smoke wreathing her head. "I know what you're asking me. It was way after my time."

Rachmann nods slowly, smiling. "What am I asking you?"

"You're asking about the hand, and the recording they found. The remnants, they call them."

Nick swallows, his throat clicking.

"Okay," Rachmann says. "Tell me about them."

"All I know's what I heard. For all I know, it's stuff that Lundy put out into the air on purpose. He could be like that."

"Okay, fair point. But let's say it's not just Lundy's misinformation. Let's say it's for real."

"Well, what I heard is, for one, they got a recording of the devil."

Nick slowly takes in a breath. Holds it.

Rolling the edge of her cigarette on the rim of the ashtray, Beverly says, "Supposedly, if you hear the recording, you go nuts. Clawing at your own face, attacking people. All that."

"What did it say? On the recording?"

"Well, I never heard it. I mean, obviously."

"No one ever told you what it said?"

"The rumor was that it was just some guy talking. But spooky shit. I mean, the guy wasn't ordering pizza, if that's what you're asking."

"You think it's real?"

Beverly rubs an eyebrow, looks pained. "I couldn't say, man. I just did my work, saw what I could see, tried to steer clear of Lundy."

"And what about the hand?"

"Just rumors. Again, this was all after I left."

"Okay."

"Look, the hand . . . the hand was way after I was involved with anything. Saint Michael's been around for a long time, but I've only been hearing about the hand for the past, I don't know, ten, fifteen years or so. But what I *heard* was that it was supposed to be a cut-off hand, and it belonged to the guy on the recording. The voice. Like he died and they chopped him up, and the hand could make you crazy too. Just being near it."

"So you never saw it."

She frowns. "I just drank my Hamm's and smoked my Marlboros and watched *Three's Company* and checked out the men on the base. If anyone tried to bring me near a cut-off hand? I'd have hauled ass back to Lodi, snow or not. Like I said, I was already here in Venice when I heard about it."

"What else?"

"I heard," she says, with a hint of defiance, a hint of *You asked for it, so here it is,* "that it's a devil's hand. That it's a devil on the recording too, talking about end-times or whatever. Or the devil is in the room with the guy who's talking. Something like that. The story always changed. There's *two* hands, there's *one,* it's just a *finger,* you know. Stories. But the version I heard most is that the hand and the recording belonged to some devil that died and got chopped up, and either one of them can make you insane."

Nick stands up. Walks out with a grimace of apology.

"I don't know if it's true," she says to his back.

He walks through the beaded curtains, past the counter and out the front door, into a night full of the glittering sea, strings of lights hung along the boardwalk. He stands with his hands at his hips, looks out at the nickel moon hanging above the water. Dawn is coming, bluing the horizon line.

Rachmann comes out and stands next to him. Spends a moment looking at the sea as well. Without turning to him, Rachmann says, "We'll get her back."

"Just give me a minute, man," Nick says. And Rachmann does.

The sound of the surf. The sea and sky, these two hard dark lines meeting. Finally, Nick turns to Rachmann and says, "This is so stupid. What are we doing here? A psychic? *Devil's hands?* Come on."

"Let's give her some more time," Rachmann says softly. "Come back in. Please." He smiles out at the water, then turns and gestures at the shop. "Perhaps, Nick, if you've come across a severed hand that makes you want to kill just by being near it, you'll reconsider the possibility that the stories put forth by a tarot card reader really are not quite such a leap. Logistically speaking."

"Okay," Nick says. "No, okay, I hear you."

They go back in.

Beverly's eyes fall on Nick again. "I'm just telling you what I heard."

"I know," Nick says. "I just needed a minute."

She stares at him as she smears her cigarette into the ashtray, and then points a finger at him. "There's a man in Mexico I want you to look up. Last I heard he was in Mexico, anyway. In a border town called Colina Roja. He's a collector. He'll corroborate what I said. Old guy, old as hell, and he collects occult things, dark-leaning things. Okay? I've met him before and the guy can make your skin crawl. He's come to the shop and bad things happened to me for weeks afterward. I won't even tell you about the things that I seen when I gave him his reading. But you'll want to meet him. His name's Herman Goud."

"Alright," says Nick.

"So the thing about Goud is, he's neck deep in the remnants, and I've heard that he has an eye too."

"An eye?"

"Like another actual remnant from the same man, devil, whatever. Along with the hand and the recording, there's a devil's eye. And this is new, within the past couple years he's gotten this thing."

"Herman Goud," Rachmann says.

"That's right."

Nick turns to Rachmann. "Have you heard of him?"

"No," Rachmann says. "But I'll find him."

Beverly looks at her watch. "Time's up, boys."

"The hand," Nick says, leaning forward. "I had it. I found it."

"Nick," Rachmann says.

Nick stands. Holds out his hands plaintively toward Beverly, who shifts back in her seat a little. "These people came, looking for it. And they took my mom. She's not . . . You think this David Lundy took her?"

"Sweetie, I don't know," Beverly says quietly. She motions for him to sit again and he does, scooting his chair forward. She reaches her hands across the glittering table, and Nick takes them in his own. He's aware that moments ago he was belittling her supposed visions, the things she's claimed to have seen and heard, and now he's courting them. Desperate for them. Her hands are warm and rough, the fingers taking that slightly curled, blunted shape when arthritis has begun to encroach upon the framework of the bones. Beverly closes her eyes and dips her head down. There is, once more, that knife-line of pale scalp. The tanned, freckled skin of her shoulders beneath her T-shirt. He feels a wave of tenderness toward her; the feeling surprises him. That there is space for that in his heart at this moment.

"Think of her," she says. "Picture her."

He does. He tries. There is the "her" he sees—diminished and frightened, contained in the walls of their apartment, the worry lines carved into the seamed corners of her eyes. But to consider that as Katherine's totality would be to diminish her. Like calling a star a light in the sky and nothing else. There is the Katherine who is afraid, yeah, but also Katherine the singer, the dervish of the stage, and Katherine of the wry pun. Katherine desperate for coffee in the morning, Katherine who can't help but start laughing uncontrollably at scary parts in movies. Katherine who wears her husband's death like some kind of ill-fitting shirt, one she can't loosen or take off. Katherine who has told him as they walk the ring, as they try to expand it slowly, a block at a time, "I know you could be doing anything else, Nick. I want you to know I value it. Thank you." The

Katherine who will order them a pizza in a horrific De Niro impression and then give them Nick's name and make him go pick it up. These and hundreds more. We contain multitudes. Nick knows it. To imagine her as simply a mother is to halve the totality of her life.

He tries to picture her.

But Beverly looks up and shakes her head. "I'm sorry, hon. I'm not getting anything. It's like that sometimes. I could tell you something, but it'd just be me blowing smoke."

He feels a crushing moment of disappointment and tries to shake it off. "No, thank you. I appreciate it."

They step out onto the boardwalk. Rachmann insists on putting his sunglasses back on. He zips up his jacket and says, "It's not all for nothing."

"Bullshit."

"Nick—"

"You told me she could help, Rachmann."

"And she did. We got something, didn't we?"

Raindrops begin darkening the cement at their feet.

"What's that?"

"David Lundy," Rachmann says. "And Herman Goud. We have names, Nick." He turns, tilts his head. Nick's own helplessness is reflected back at him in Rachmann's lenses. "Let's go back to the hotel. I need my computer."

KATHERINE MORIARTY

Something has happened on the plane.

They're in the air. Have been. She heard a single scream fill the tight hallway of the aircraft, just once, some minutes ago, and now it seems that Katherine has been forgotten. Left alone and unattended. What exactly has happened, she doesn't know. But nothing good, clearly. She takes the bag off her head.

It's empty, the small room she's in. More of a closet. There's a single chair of molded plastic mounted to the wall. No window save for the one in the doorway, but she can still feel the drag of the plane knifing through the air. There are no weapons she can think of, just this useless black bag in her zip-tied hands.

She tests the door. It opens, and she peers down the hall. It's cramped. A pedestrian, unlovely carpet, everything else metal, curved plastic. There is a pair of doors on each side of the hall and then it opens up into a kind of wider seating area. Beyond that, the sealed cockpit.

Katherine sees a pool of blood leaking from beneath one of the doorways. Blood, right there, soaking black into that inoffensive, sky-blue carpet.

Katherine closes her eyes, breathes. To witness more means taking ownership of what she's seen. A part of her understands she can lean into the smallness of her world right now, fall into it, use that constriction and terror as a salve. Think about nothing, just feel. Instead she opens her eyes. There is Nick to consider.

Like the door in her room, there's a small window set in the one from where the blood seeps. She creeps along and peers in. People rove about the room—it's larger than hers, enough space for a bed. Some of the people inside argue and gesture, the sound somewhat muted through the window. There is a white blanket over a gurney in there, where blooms of dark blood flower on the sheet. A spatter of ink like a child's painting drips down one plastic wall. Other spatters as well, people walking all through the mess of it.

She spies a leg on the floor behind the bed, clad in a blue suit. Brown shoes with the heels up. Lundy's body. The pale starfish of a hand near a gurney wheel, that tan line of a missing wedding ring.

The woman Lundy had yelled at, Diane, spots her. Backpedaling, Katherine bounces off the opposite wall, but where is there to go? She's on a fucking airplane. The door opens and Diane steps into the hallway, a few men behind her in their suits, bristling with severity.

"Don't you touch me," Katherine hisses, her zip-tied hands held up before her.

"Get back in your room, you idiot," Diane says wearily. Katherine readies herself, but the woman just rolls her eyes and walks away, toward the cockpit.

"Where are you taking me?" Katherine calls out.

The woman looks back at one of the men, who pulls a pistol from his jacket as if he's bored. "Get in your little seat," Diane says to Katherine over her shoulder, "or I'll throw you out of this plane myself."

The man lifts his chin toward Katherine's door.

"What happened?" Katherine asks. "Is that Lundy? That blood?"

"Get inside," the man says.

"What's a fever house?"

Gently—considering especially he has a gun, there are two dead bodies, and Katherine's hands are bound—he turns her by the shoulder. She goes back into her plastic room.

The plane descends. Every grand plan has been whittled out of her by then. No hero will suddenly appear. There are no hidden resources within her. She is at the world's mercy, and Lundy's earlier proclamation—that she's lucky she didn't get shot—rattles inside her like a wasp in an upturned glass.

Her ears pop; she feels the jounce of the wheels as the plane dips on the runway. It slows, turns. Her palms sweat. She concentrates on her breathing.

And then she waits.

Counts to a hundred, counts to a hundred again. Calls out "Hello?" but is met with silence.

She stands, opens her door again.

Sees light spilling into the cabin; further down the aisle, she sees that the cabin door's been opened, the sense of pressure different now. She walks forward, peers in the window of the room again; there is still the body beneath the sheet, the shape of it constellated with black spots like a growing Rorschach, and there remains Lundy's foot, his hand.

Katherine's throat begins to close and she shuts her eyes and breathes, presses her brow against the steeple of her clasped hands. Counts to ten backward, realizes she is stepping in blood that has seeped from beneath the door, that they have all walked in it, left footprints all up and down the cabin. She is marveling at this when a cylinder rolls toward her, the rattle of it, how pale yellow smoke billows from one end. She looks up, sees a black-clad man in a gas mask aiming a snub-nosed, squat rifle at her, and then there is a brilliant flash and a sound that she can feel in her teeth, in the architecture of her bones, and then there's nothing.

Katherine sits at an old steel desk, pitted and scratched. Graffitied. The floor is glossed cement, the overhead light bright and unforgiving. No windows, no emergency exit signs, no posters that dictate one's rights.

She counts to sixty and wonders if it is a minute, or longer. By now, she should be familiar with how time can grow elastic. She has to piss again.

Eventually the door opens and two men step in, pull up chairs across from her. The anguished desk between them. Both men wear suits. One man is small and wiry, the other is large, big-eared, has an earnest face. The small one carries a clipboard, a manila folder.

"I have to go to the bathroom," Katherine says.

"This won't take long," says the larger man.

"Your guy could have broken my jaw, tackling me like that."

"Katherine," the wiry one says, dread shirring through her when she hears her name fall from his mouth, "you're lucky we didn't kill your ass dead when we cleared that plane."

"What happened to Lundy," Katherine says.

"We were going to ask you the same thing," says the wiry one.

The larger one clears his throat and says, "Director Lundy is no longer involved in this situation."

"That's one way of putting it," she says dryly, and the wiry one laughs.

"Your case," says the larger man, "is now under the jurisdiction of the State Department. I'm Special Agent in Charge Monahan, this is Agent Willis."

Willis pushes the clipboard her way. There are papers. There's a pen attached on a little chain.

"Ms. Moriarty," Monahan says, "I'll be blunt. You're being charged with one count of conspiracy to murder US citizens or US nationals, one count of providing material aid and support to terrorist organizations, and one count of using and carrying firearms or explosive devices during crimes of violence. This, again, comes directly from the State Department. It's a federal case, and if you're convicted, you're looking at a life sentence. The US has taken a hard stance against providing succor to terrorists."

Her mouth is dry. She feels the slow thud of her blood traversing her body.

She looks at them, waiting for something else to happen. Finally, her throat clicking, Katherine lifts her chin toward the clipboard. "I don't even know what this means."

Monahan smiles. "Well, simply put, it means you're in deep shit."

"It's a lie."

Willis lets out a little incredulous laugh. "I mean, no. No, Ms. Moriarty. We have witnesses. Photographs. Recordings. Profound amounts of physical evidence. This is not a circumstantial case."

"I've never fired a gun in my life."

Monahan shrugs, perfectly at ease. "We have footage of you holding explosive devices, storing them in your home. Hiding them for known terrorist organizations. Funneling cash and resources. Your apartment is a documented waypoint for terrorist activity. More importantly, we're *very* familiar with the depth of your son's involvement with these organizations. It's bad for you, Katherine, I won't lie. But it's much worse for Nick."

"I want a lawyer."

"Oh, you'll need one."

"Lundy already tried this," she says. "It didn't work."

A twitch in the eyes from Willis. "Tried what," he says, smiling.

"Threatening me."

Monahan shrugs again. "It's not a threat, Katherine. That's a federal indictment in front of you. You're free to look at it. The evidence against you is damning. Your son, though? Did you know the Department of Justice is starting to vie for federal executions again? Can you imagine?"

She opens the folder. A mountain of legalese, her name—

MORIARTY—in all caps threaded throughout. An evidence list at the very end, citing supposed photographs and videos, phone calls, corroborating witnesses.

"What do you want?" she says. Her voice is watery, weak, someone else speaking for her.

"I'll be straight with you," Monahan says, clearly enjoying himself. "You've been left behind as an offering. Okay?" He rests his cheek on his fist and smiles. "The agency that apprehended you was working illegally, and trafficking in very dangerous materials."

"The hand."

"Sure, the hand, okay," Monahan says. Willis licks his lips, shifts in his seat at the mention of it. All kinds of tells with these men.

"Point is, David Lundy? He was missing a very important piece of evidence upon his person when we found him."

"What was it?"

Monahan stares at her for a moment, then says, "A USB stick with a document on it."

Katherine shrugs.

He nods, as if he'd expected as much. "Anyway, we found him with his head pretty much pulped on that airplane, Katherine, and he was next to another guy who is—or was—a *very* high-yield government asset, okay? And *he's* dead too. And all the other agents that worked in Lundy's agency that were on that airplane? Doing all this illegal shit? They're gone. We just missed them on that tarmac, and now they're in the wind. You follow me so far?"

"Yes."

"But who was left behind, Katherine?" asks Monahan.

"You were," Willis says.

"A little consolation prize," Monahan says.

"So I'm a scapegoat," she says. There's a freedom in it, a yawning breadth of space opening up within her. She's leapt from the chasm into the darkness. No, she's been pushed.

"You're not a scapegoat," Willis says, leaning his little rat-face toward her. "You're just in the fucking way."

"Make it easy on yourself," Monahan says. "Where's Diane Ro-driguez?"

"Diane? The woman from the plane?" Katherine says. "I don't know."

"You better know."

"I don't. I saw the bodies in there, on the plane, and she told me to get back into my room and then we landed. They had guns. It's not like she told me her, her *plans*, you know?"

Willis reaches into his pocket and pulls out Katherine's phone. He pushes it gently across the table.

"You can still help yourself, Katherine."

"How?"

"Call your son. Tell him to meet us."

"Why?"

"Why what?"

"Why should I tell him to meet you?"

"Because we need the fucking hand, Katherine. The hand or the recording or both. Anything."

"What recording?"

"Jesus Christ," Willis mutters into his lap.

"If I'm already this screwed, if you have all this evidence against me—what's the point of cooperating?"

Monahan seems surprised at this. He rears his head back, squints at her. As if she's missed some integral point. "I'd think that's obvi-ous, Katherine. Because you love him, and you want him to live."

SAMANTHA WEILS

Picture it, then: Weils, abandoned.

Weils with a rageful heart, a silencer tucked into her coat.

Holding on to a thing like that, wondering if it would be needed, unflinching when it is. Threading it onto the barrel of her pistol and doing the thing.

Camelot empty, Lundy gone. Leaving her with Bonner.

Weils peering around after the shot, pivoting and whirling in the sudden absence of sound. Wondering if anyone had seen John fucking Bonner—scourge of her life, albatross of her career, rich-boy anchor lashed around her legs—drop, head-shot, onto the pavement on the other side of the car. But no, this part of the base is now a no-man's-land of cracked tarmac and empty, tucked-away buildings. The razor wire coiled above the fencing catching glints from the arched sodium lights overhead. The sense of abandonment here is irrefutable.

She's been left behind.

She walks over to Bonner's body, unscrewing the silencer and slipping it back in her coat pocket, the pistol in its holster. Crouching down beside him, she sees reflected light snag in the curve of his eyes, the red thread of blood spilling from his temple. Weils takes out her phone, some part of her still expecting Lundy to have called, given her a location, given her something. But there's nothing there.

She knuckles a single tear away, bouncing on her heels a little. She rifles through Bonner's pockets. Takes his pistol, his spare clip. Wallet, keys. Her mind is not well, vengeance and sorrow in this mad roil.

She gets in the sedan, throwing Bonner's shit on the passenger seat. Calling Lundy's phone one more time—almost desperate to hear his voice—like if she says the right thing, none of this will have happened, the hours will be exhumed and pulled back, Lundy will call her with instructions. Will once more include her into the fold. But she doesn't know what those right words might be. She hears his voicemail, hears Lundy vaguely annoyed, telling the listener to go ahead and leave a message. She hangs up, tosses the phone on the passenger seat. All that sorrow, that heartbreak and rage at work inside her. She puts her hands at ten and two on the wheel and heads toward the base's exit.

Heart-busted and left behind, she goes out into the fever house.

No summers off, no breaks, means that Samantha Weils graduates from UVA with a degree in criminal psychology—on a free ride too, thank you very much—and gets herself fast-tracked into the spook life with almost astonishing ease. It happens like this: From UVA to CIAU—CIA University, which she is amused to discover is a real place—in Chantilly, Virginia. And then from CIAU to Camp Peary—the Farm, Lundy-mandated and Lundy-arranged. *Boom boom boom.* Things just dropping for her domino-style.

Like, *thirty hours* after graduating from UVA, she's headhunted by the feds.

This is at work, mind you, slinging drinks at a tiki bar in Belmont, spearing mai tais with little paper umbrellas, a plastic orchid in her hair, wearing a low-cut tank top for better tips. The notion of being headhunted is not unusual to her: coming from the wrong side of the tracks as she is, born into abject poverty, with her father's numerous convictions and an endless stretch of federal time ahead of him. Weils has long capitalized on the allure she holds for certain institutions. She's far from surprised when a hard-faced woman with an ink-black bob and a severe charcoal skirt and jacket orders a coffee from her at the bar and then pushes a business card Weils's way.

"I'd love to talk to you when you have a second," the woman says.

Weils smirks, looks at the card. She's been thinking law school, corporate law, a DC think tank somewhere that focuses on criminal reform. She wants nothing to do with street-level crime, nothing that will take her into the orbit of men like her father. She's thinking law as *overarching idea,* big picture style. Reform as an abstraction. Given her history, she has a stolid, no-nonsense belief system regarding crime and recidivism that's often at odds with her liberal peers. It's not that she's pulled these ideas out of the blue, though, not with her old man arrested, what, a dozen times over the years? More? Assault, Possession with Intent, DV, Reckless Endangerment. How many times did CPD take him in and let him go? How many week-long stints in county lockup did he do, the house so blessedly quiet in his absence, only to have him stomp back in, seething with an unspoken rage? Not even waiting to score again, just getting right on the phone to this connection or that, and usually leaning on Weils's mom for money to do it. She and her mother watching the whole thing play out one more time. The old man daring Weils or her mom to say a fucking thing, say one word, see what happens.

Anyone who believes recidivism works should take a look at her old man and his collection of bodies.

The card has the woman's name—*DIANE RODRIGUEZ*—in embossed script. A phone number with a Virginia area code. No title, certainly nothing that says, like, "Spook Recruiter," but with her degree in criminal psychology, and even working in a bar here in Charlottesville, gauging the sway and pull of government folks and how they carry themselves has become a kind of sixth sense. The Beltway is not far from here; the whole area is constantly inundated with lobbyists and feds and poli-sci dorks.

"That'll be two dollars," Weils says, and this Diane Rodriguez pushes a five over, tells her to keep the change. Weils thanks her, hits the register, drops the three dollars into the tip jar. It's early in her shift and she likes the look of this woman's face, the way she squares her shoulders against the world. There's a hardness there that Weils recognizes and appreciates. This woman reminds her of a more put-together version of her mom, honestly, so she comes back from the tip jar and puts her elbows on the bar and says, "What do you want to talk about?"

"Diane," the woman says, holds out her hand. Weils puts her at her early forties.

"Hey," she says, and shakes Diane's dry, papery hand. "Samantha."

"I want to let you know, your professor gave us your contact info."

Weils grins, surprised and pleased. "Which one?"

"Arnsdorf."

Her grin widens. "Professor Arnsdorf gave you the name of the bar I work at?"

"Well, that part was me."

"Okay. I mean, I'm flattered. I think. What's up?"

"You have plans, Samantha?"

"Like for the night?" Weils playing dumb. Loving it. Loving the whole thing.

Diane leans forward too, drops her voice a little. "I'm running a program—well, quite a few programs, actually—over in Chantilly. I was wondering if you might be interested in enrolling."

"This is Spook School?"

Diane winces. Seesaws her hand back and forth. "I mean, it's a university that's operated by the Agency—"

"The CIA."

"—that runs a bevy of classes for people interested in working in the intelligence field."

"Yeah, we just called it Spook School."

Diane shrugs expansively, leans back. Cups her coffee with both hands. She has a small, discreet wedding ring, nothing flashy, and Weils likes her even more. "Sure, okay. We got your name from your professor, and I looked you up. Your thesis was solid, Samantha. Your grades. All of it looks good. What are you picturing, career-wise? Behavioral analyst? Profiling?"

"I mean, I just graduated yesterday."

Nodding, Diane says, "Fair point. But like I said, I looked you up. Seems you're not one for sitting around."

"That's true."

"So, seriously, have you ever considered fieldwork?"

"Me?"

It's Diane's turn to smile, and Weils can see the person she must be when she's at home.

"Yeah," she says. "You."

Dulles Discovery Campus, they call it, a nice bit of government-speak for a campus that holds classes on money laundering and how to disarm a gunman. Diane's her de facto handler, and the person Weils talks to if she has a problem with one of her classes—ain't no degrees being handed out at Spook School, but the vast networks of information and activities opening up before her are a treasure trove, and it's all shit that she finds herself well suited for. Leaning toward. Her degree definitely helps, there's some crossover, but beyond that, the materials here—from combat classes to spyware installation and monitoring—just *fit* right, notch themselves just perfectly into the open spaces of her brain. If there's a problem, she goes to Diane and Diane walks her through it. She quits the tiki bar, puts her meager belongings in storage; Dulles has dorms and she moves in. She visits Diane sometimes, there on the ground floor of Building 1, where her office overlooks the campus. There's a picture on her desk of a young raven-haired woman in a wedding dress next to some clean-shaven kid in a powder-blue suit that she catches Weils looking at once.

"My daughter," she says, and Weils blushes with something, she isn't sure what. Intimacy, like she's rifled through Diane's things? Jealousy, maybe, Weils's own mother in the ground the way she is?

She's taking these classes with a bevy of other recruits; a lot of them are young like her, a lot of them wannabe field agents hoping to land in a million different intelligence agencies—NSA, NIA, DIA—and then here's Weils with her little UVA degree, courted by Diane from the civilian population; people are constantly trying to get a read on her. Weils just wanting to work, learn, grateful for it all, afraid of falling behind. Weils with her daddy doing his federal stretch and her trailer-park upbringing, and all of these other recruits looking like they fell out of an Ivy League Play-Doh factory. Everyone wholly competent too, if not downright adept and scary as hell for it. Competition is fierce and mean-hearted and Weils wants to win, wants to show all of them.

After five months, run ragged with the mental prowess needed to stay even remotely at the top of her shit, she is exhausted. She slips one night, talking to Aunt Joan back home in Charlottesville. She can hear the murmur of Joan's TV in the background, and it's clear that even if Weils is exhausted, her aunt's really only half listening.

"So *what* kind of classes are you taking again?" she says. Weils's eyelids are literally dropping; they talk maybe once a month, just real surface shit, but it's still a relationship she cherishes, after all the woman's done. She warily scans her textbooks—Bromwell's *The Analyzing of Intelligence,* Van der Beek's *Strategic Communications, Psychology of the Clandestine* by Camille MacPherson—and closes her eyes, feels the lurch of sleep. "It's just Spook School, Aunt Joan. We're just doing, you know, spy stuff."

"*What?*"

Weils's eyes open wide. She hears her aunt sit up, hears the creaking frame of her recliner as she rises. Weils winces, mouthing curses at herself. Her dorm-mate is out, thank God, some nice enough girl from Wyoming who is studying intelligence analytics and struggling with the physical stuff they did here.

"Sam, what do you mean, *spy* stuff? I thought you were doing computers over there."

"It's just all basic classes, Joan."

"Basic *spy* classes, though? What in the world do you mean?"

Poor Joan; she had taken Weils in at seventeen, after everything with her old man, and Weils's mother dying of cervical cancer two years before that. Weils had tried to make that last year before she moved out easy for her aunt. She'd be grateful forever for the space to sleep, the blessed quiet, the food.

"I just mean," Weils says, alarmed at how badly she's slipped, "we're working with computers, a little bit, information retrieval and stuff"—just digging herself a bigger hole here, her mouth going and going—"so I just call it spy stuff. Just, like, kinda sneaky shit, you know what I mean?"

"Sneaky shit," Joan parrots, clearly confused.

The next day she's in geography class: more notes, the lecturer up front, a presentation of geopolitical hotspots across the globe, the sixteen students all clattering away at their laptops with their heads down, when she feels a touch at her arm.

"Can I speak with you outside?" Diane whispers, and Weils's heart drops to the floor. She snaps her laptop shut, and they step out of the auditorium into the lobby of Building 2, Weils trying her hardest to will her heart calm.

"Follow me, please," Diane says, and they walk outside. It's a humid, balmy day, with an angry wash of gray clouds overhead that promise rain. Weils finding herself walking behind Diane, whose heels seem to stab the concrete as if making some declaration. Weils understanding explicitly that she's in deep shit.

Back to Building 1, and instead of heading to her office, they hit the elevators, Diane pushing the button for the fourth floor. The car's empty, Diane staring straight ahead, her jacket and skirt a smart black that matches her hair, and Weils can't stop herself from rushing ahead. "What's going on," she asks.

"You've got a meeting."

"Look, I know I fucked up, Diane."

A tight smile. "Oh, that's true."

Weils pauses then, a little stunned at the acknowledgment. Definitive proof that they surveil the dorms, that she is indeed being monitored. It makes all of this more real, the weapons training and jujitsu and money-tracing. She has it and she can lose it all. Is on this elevator right now specifically to lose it all, probably.

Fourth floor's for the high-end folks. Professors, visiting faculty. Chances are, you got that compartmented clearance, that Level 5 clearance, they put you up there. She is in, it seems, for a truly epic chewing-out.

"Just shitcan me," Weils whispers, but Diane's already swish-swishing ahead, her heels on carpet now. Weils cannot figure out why the big presentation. Some angry, red-faced senior agent chewing her ass out about operational security—what's the point? She's a first-year trainee—headhunted from civilian life, no less. This shit must happen constantly.

Down to an office at the far end of the hall, and Diane knocks twice, not waiting for an answer before heading in. Certainly not throwing Weils any kind of a lifeline, not even looking back at her.

The office itself—bookshelves, carpet, empty coatrack, single potted plant in the corner, window with fat accordion blinds—is functional enough as to be instantly forgettable. And Weils isn't really paying attention to any of it anyway—someone is already standing up, shaking Diane's hand over his own oak desk, then holding his hand out for her as well. Bald, white button-up, a smart blue tie he holds down with one hand.

"Samantha Weils," Diane says, "this is David Lundy."

A brisk handshake, the briefest tang of cologne in the air. Only the three of them in the room but suddenly it feels too close.

"Ms. Weils," Lundy says. "I appreciate you coming in."

Weils nods, waiting for the hammer to drop.

"Please," Lundy says, extending a hand, and she and Diane sit down in a pair of chairs that face the desk, Diane crossing one leg over the other, resting her hands on her knee. When she sits down, Weils can see a brief cut of gray sky through the wedges of the blinds behind Lundy. He leans back, his hands clasped over his belly, a knowing smile on his face.

"So," Lundy says. "Diane sent me your file."

Weils cuts a look at Diane, who sits motionless. Impossible to read. Wishing like hell she had debriefed her before they headed into . . . whatever this is. Handler my ass, Weils thinks.

"I thought it was interesting."

"My file?"

"You seem to be tackling things here well, showing a lot of progress. Assimilating, I guess. Holding your own. How you liking things so far?"

"Uh, it's fantastic," Weils says truthfully. "I feel very at home here. I feel very fortunate."

"Your instructors say you're taking to a lot of the active field material. You have the, uh, propensity for it, is what I'm hearing."

"I like it," she says.

"Good," Lundy says, nodding. "Can I ask you something, Samantha?"

"Yes, sir."

Here it comes, she thinks. But instead of asking about Aunt Joan, or operational security, or any of that, David Lundy stares at her with those ice-blue eyes, an arrogant lean to him, and he says, "Can you tell me what happened to Nathan?"

"I'm sorry? What?"

"Nathan Weils, please tell me what happened to him."

Diane still staring straight ahead. Weils turns back to Lundy, steadying herself. "He, um . . . He got handed four consecutive life sentences in USP Lee."

"There in Pennington Gap?"

"That's it."

"What for, you don't mind me asking?"

Of course I fucking do, she thinks. And it's not like you don't know. "He robbed a bank," she says.

Lundy frowns. "And got four life sentences for it? Seems a little severe."

"He killed a teller and three customers."

Lundy exhales, wincing. "He was on crank, wasn't he? Up for three days, something like that? Shot an eighty-seven-year-old woman who was cashing in rolls of quarters?"

"Sounds like you already know quite a bit about it," she says tightly, and Lundy smiles again.

"How old were you when it happened?"

Weils swallows, hears the click in her throat. Somehow the anger hasn't arrived yet, though she knows it will. "Seventeen."

"Seventeen," Lundy repeats slowly, as if it was some kind of equation he might decipher. "And your mom died two years before that. Breast cancer, right?"

"Cervical."

"Cervical. And your aunt Joan took you in that last year of high school. Got yourself a full ride to UVA. There was talk of rescinding your scholarship after the shooting, but you appealed. Offered quite a moving essay, it seems. Swayed a lot of folks."

"Yes."

"You must be proud."

"It's just what happened."

Lundy squints up at some unseen point at the ceiling and says, "Did you know, Samantha, that you failed your psych evaluation as it pertains to the National Security Adjudicative Guidelines? Like, hardcore fucking failed it, man. You flop-sweated through your poly, your written tests look like a series of cry-for-help Rorschachs, and if this was still the 1980s and we were doing MMPIs for our baseline psych evals, I'd be having Diane here put in the word with the state. You should be in a fucking rubber room, tell you the truth. Up to your eyeballs on a Thorazine scrip and far, far away from *anything* that might remotely affect national security."

Weils recognizes Diane's look now, sees it for what it is: rage. At her or Lundy she doesn't know, but it radiates from the woman like a crystalline fog.

Lundy went on. "So here's the deal, Samantha. You dropped the ball on that call with your aunt last night. That was stupid. And the thing is, while clearly strung wire-tight psychologically speaking, you are a *far* cry from stupid. I think that was young Samantha pulling the pin on the grenade, to tell you the truth. That was you probably feeling like you were getting in too deep with this whole thing. You're a long way from the tiki bar, you know what I'm saying? Long way from the trailer park."

"I'll go," Weils says, her voice small and clipped with fury, half rising from her seat before Lundy holds up a staying hand.

"Hold on. You can make a big production when I'm done if that's what you decide to do. But first, Samantha, tell me I'm wrong. Tell me that wasn't you flaming out."

"It wasn't."

"You want to do field work or no?"

"I do."

"Say it like you mean it. Jesus wept."

"I do."

"So here's the thing. You are categorically unfit to do field work for any reputable, above-ground intelligence-gathering agency on the globe. You are irreparably psychologically damaged—I'm betting your old man's four-person bloodbath at First National when you were seventeen is just the fucking tip of the iceberg, from a psychological standpoint—and this is coming from *me*," he says, "someone who understands pretty much better than anyone that a conscience can often be a liability in this work."

"The fuck do you want," Weils finally says through gritted teeth.

Lundy's face opens in delight. He actually claps once, then leans forward. "That's a good question," he says softly. "I'll tell you what I want. I want to send you to the Farm, Samantha. I want to send you to the Farm, I want to get you field-ready, I want to fucking *run you,* that's what I want."

"David operates his own program," Diane says, not even turning to look at her, her voice papery with contempt. "He's lucky enough to get to choose his people."

"Sometimes," Lundy says.

"Sometimes," Diane agrees.

"And Diane keeps her eyes peeled for me, don't you, Diane?"

A clipped nod.

"And you, Samantha," Lundy says, "you, I want."

"Why?"

"Why?" He looks to Diane and then back to Weils. "Why. Because if your evals are any indication, you, as the song says, got what I need. I need a finger on the trigger, I want to look to you and *know,* without a second's doubt, that you'll do it. And doing that, *every single time you're told,* no matter what? That's harder than you think. That's *worth more* than you think. You're my gun hand, Samantha. You're my bullet. That's what I want."

Weils's gaze jumping from Lundy to the wedge of sky behind him and back. "Do I get to think about it?"

"What is there to think about? I'm giving you a golden ticket. You finish up the rest of your courses here, do your six months at the Farm if you can manage it. You wrap it up there, I want you in my agency the second you graduate. Or you can say no thanks and go sling drinks, because no one else will have you. You tell me no, that's fine, but we'll need you to go back to your dorm and pack your shit."

"I don't understand," she said, hating herself for the smallness of her voice.

"Let me spell it out for you. Diane scouts for me. I got a specific parameter for the agents I need, and you, here, right now? You fit the parameter. Any other agency would run away screaming. I'm offering you the world here."

Weils stands up on legs that feel watery and disconnected. "I need to think about it."

"Cool," Lundy says, shooting Diane some indecipherable look. "I can give you a day. Tell Diane what you decide."

She walks to the door, burning with embarrassment. Rage. Tears blurring her vision, hot-faced with shame at the possibility that he's right. Had her evals been that fucked up? Is she honestly that broken? Instead of feeling reassured to be leaving, everything in front of her—the office, the building itself, the entire campus—seems flimsy, the world suddenly made of balsa wood and cheap glass.

"Oh, and Samantha?"

She turns, already dreading what he's going to say, but it is the first of many times he will surprise her.

He smiles and says, "I hope you say yes."

The next day she goes into Diane's office and says she'll do it.

Diane looks like she wants to say something, offer some advice, petition her to change her mind, but whatever it is on her face disappears and she just nods. Says she'll call Lundy right away, that he'll be in touch.

Nine months later, she's sitting on the bed of her dorm at the Farm. She did her six months of baseline training, watching the merciless attrition of the other trainees. She's one of eleven students to graduate basic courses. What it is exactly that made her run through it all, keep going every night, every day, she couldn't say. Still can't. Perhaps just the idea that it's either this—Lundy and his op—or it's nothing. It's back to pouring beers or struggling to pass the bar exam, wistfully telling everyone about that year she was headhunted for intelligence work.

She calls the number she's been given. She's on a burner phone and has taken precautions, swept the room for bugs—these are things she knows how to do now—but also, it doesn't matter. Let everyone at the Farm know. David Lundy's insulated, after all. Doesn't matter who knows where she's going.

"I'm done," she says when he picks up.

"I heard," he says.

Weils sits primly on her bed, looks down at a minute bit of hang-nail. Some part of her afraid that after all this, he'll tell her no. That he'll laugh at her. She swallows and says, "What next?"

"Now you come to DC, Samantha."

"Okay."

"Are you ready?"

"Yeah. Yes."

He takes the stunned relief in her voice for trepidation. "Listen to me," Lundy says softly. "I keep you safe, you keep me safe. That's how this works. Okay?"

"Okay."

"That's how we'll do this. You protect me, I protect you. You get me? You're the bullet, Samantha."

"I'm the bullet," Weils says, wanting to weep with gratitude.

And then she is standing in a concrete subbasement of the Harry S Truman Building in DC, watching through one-way glass as a pair of ARC agents use hacksaws to remove the wings off a man, a man-like thing, as he screams and bucks, his arms and legs lashed to a steel chair by a bevy of heavy chains. The hacksaws are something you'd buy at a hardware store, and the agents sweat and curse through the work.

This is Saint Michael. This, she soon comes to understand, is David Lundy's crown of power. Michael is the ladder that Lundy has used to crest the tide of the world. His spear and his shield. Lundy leans against the wall with his arms folded, watching. While the men still work, he walks over to a sobbing Michael and leans forward, holding his tie against his stomach as he slaps Michael's marbled face with his free hand. Demanding answers. Visions. It is these visions that are the blocks Lundy's used to build his castle in the air. To build ARC. The cords of Michael's neck are taut as he screams, as the men saw and saw at him, as he pulls at the chains lashing him to the floor. He begs Lundy to stop, Lundy gripping him around the throat, a kind of unleashed joy in it, and Weils is reminded of her own father and how he shambled continuous lengths of their trailer, filling it with his bold and endless proclamations, his grievances and hurts, holding court among the rooms.

She watches as Michael shrieks and whips his head back and forth, one wing finally giving way with a crack that she can actually hear through the glass. The wing breaks roughly, like cartilage or wood, the humerus with a jagged, unclean edge now, and a black, inklike material spills from the inside of it, pouring down the screaming man's back as he writhes and thrums, his feet drumming a mad tattoo on the floor, and she looks at Lundy with his hand around Michael's throat. With her heart a complicated maze of horror and a tremendous, aching sense of freedom, Weils thinks, *I'm home. I'm home, and I will be his bullet, and everything will be different this time.*

Weils on a rooftop in the Bronx. The tarpaper shingles warm beneath her, mica-flecked in the moonlight, the coo of pigeons in the darkness, the star-flung night above her. Sighting down a scope, the man beyond the curtains in the brownstone across the street becomes massive enough for her to note his pores. The tiny pellets of popcorn resting in his lap as he watches television. His face large enough to see the curve of TV light spread across his eyes, and she says, "Sighted," and her heart remains calm as a river. In her ear, David Lundy says, "Green," and Weils pulls the trigger, only the slightest recoil, a puff, so slight it might have been imagined. The man slumps to the left, onto the couch. A sudden spill of popcorn across the floor, the brief spatter of blood across the back of the couch, the wall.

"Green," Weils repeats, beginning to disassemble the rifle in a way that she has practiced in the dark, practiced after being up for four days, practiced with live fire going on around her.

Here is the first person she has ever killed.

She has no idea of his name, his intentions on the earth, certainly nothing like the sway or convictions of his heart. No idea who might lose or benefit from his death.

She is Lundy's gun. She is his bullet.

In her ear, his joy impossible to miss, Lundy says, "You saved me."

She becomes accustomed to the notion of home being a small thing. Attainable and compact. In this manner, Weils's home becomes an inch wide, becomes whatever she imagines it might be, whatever she might bring with her. A pillow is home, a book, the sound a car's wheels make when moving through rainwater. Small, intangible moments you might bring to yourself, might claim ownership over. Tel Aviv, Berlin, Lagos; they all have nights that are bejeweled with stars, they all have dust in the roadways, lights in the distance. All these things might be home for her. Weils carries her past with her, this belief that some vital, core part of her has been carved away, that David Lundy is right—he will have her and no one else. She is the gun he points in a specific direction and fires.

Always with Lundy keeping Michael near, like a lucky rabbit's foot he can't leave home without. A lucky rabbit's foot that screams and screams. A lucky rabbit's foot that occasionally offers visions that are wildly, incredibly accurate—people, places, events that will, if acted upon in a certain manner, truly change the world in this way or that. Lundy wringing Michael like a wet shirt, cracking those wings, threatening and cooing and cursing. If Lundy has to go some- where, it's Michael he brings along, his leashed oracle. "I used to be nice to him," Lundy says to her once, "but then he stopped being afraid of me," and isn't that the truth of it? Weils is afraid of Lundy, and profoundly grateful to him, and loves him in her own terrible way. Above all she worries about disappointing him.

She wishes he might someday see her as whole and unruined.

————

The two of them watching Michael through the one-way glass. He sits in his chair in his tiled room, elbows on his knees, the drain in the floor and the eyelet they run his chain through are the only adornments in the place. Weils is tired, punchy, biting a thumbnail. Lundy with his hands on his hips, thinking.

"You don't like him," he says to Weils.

"No."

"Why not?"

"He's not really anything to like."

Lundy looks at her. "The hell does that mean?"

"He's a utility," she says. "Something to be used."

Lundy laughs softly. "I see your point."

Michael's nubs are scorched, the pair of them erupting from his scapula, the stalks threaded with twining lines of color beneath the black. They've been removed as recently as, what, yesterday? The day before? Lundy had an agent take a blowtorch to them. She has been with him three years now, and she can tell that his wings don't grow as quickly as they used to. Where before they had been threaded with iridescence, the shimmering spectrum of a puddle of gasoline, the colors are muted now, quieter. He's changing. There is a growing silence within him too. Michael is often resistant now, turning that silence into a hard pit within himself that just makes Lundy more vicious and angry.

"If I told you to go in there and cut his wings off, would you?"

She considers it. She *has* considered it before, and is honestly surprised he hasn't ordered her to. It seems that every other agent has been tasked with it at some point.

"No," she says.

"You wouldn't do it, or you don't think you could?"

"If I went in there, I think I'd kill him."

Lundy laughs outright then, staring at the glass. Michael lifts his head quizzically, as if he might have heard them. "Jesus Christ," Lundy says.

"I'm serious."

"Oh, I believe you. I just wish you understood."

"Understood what?"

"That you and Michael aren't the same, Samantha. I never thought you were and I don't expect you to be. I certainly don't treat you as such. Your jealousy's going to trip you up someday if you don't keep a handle on it. Probably when it counts."

Weils's face burns as Lundy turns to her, offers his inscrutable half-smile. "Besides," he says, "killing Michael? You just might find that harder than you think."

"Maybe."

"Maybe," Lundy repeats, turning back to the glass.

He's a utility, she'd said. *Something to be used.*

But nothing like me.

Weils has been with ARC for five years when Michael finally leads them to the hand.

Lundy has some idea—some vague idea, run through the veiled gibberish that Michael offers—of its properties, its powers. Michael has been talking about the hand for years by then, and Lundy has become convinced of its worth, if only as a sort of talisman, a totem of belief. Michael directs the agency to Thailand.

Lundy has their strike team go into the warehouse where it's being held while he and Michael and the rest of the op set up an impromptu staging area in a rented office park nearby. Weils and two other agents hit the warehouse wearing hazmat suits and carrying HK MP5s. They dispatch the owner of the hand—"owner" only in the vaguest, most perverted sense of the word, she'll come to realize—and the rest of the warehouse's occupants, only to discover that the suits don't do shit. It's not biological, it's not chemical, whatever the hand does. However it works. Neurological, maybe? Minutes after the three agents leave the warehouse in a rented SUV, threading through Phuket's stop-and-start traffic, the hand begins its machinations. Weils suddenly feels like her frontal cortex is glowing coal-red. She's sweating like a fucking beast in her suit, hair pressed in wet whorls to her forehead, faceplate clouding with steam, and they're turning a corner, no one following, looks like they're going to make it, when the agent in the passenger seat, a cruel and wickedly smart Tongan named Bixby, suddenly screams and leans into the agent who's driving, grabbing at the wheel and biting his face. The SUV flips, glass and plastic and steel exploding on the crowded, sweating street. Weils, when the world settles, sees that the two agents in front are dead, in their hustle eschewing seat belts and now a mad jumble of broken limbs, bodies like poor origami, while she is curiously, incredibly uninjured. She grabs the hand in its heavy leather valise and crawls out of the SUV, her body gritting against the glass on the pavement. People have gathered around the vehicle, yelling at her in Thai, telling her to stay in the car, to get out, she's hurt, the vehicle will soon light on fire, authorities are on their way.

Weils stands up and runs. The hand snarls at her with every step. She feels the molten heat of it, sees the passing lines of faces as she runs here, there, down a dripping alleyway, finds an all-night market that sells cell phones, buys one and walks while she sets it up. Sends a code to a drop number. Uses more cash to pay for a hotel room. Second floor, with a wide balcony that looks out onto a busy street, enough room to jump if someone comes to the door. Two hours later—a lifetime with the gibbering hand shoved under the bed—a code is sent back to her. Coordinates for a pickup.

A twin prop plane gets her to Singapore, the hand stored in the rear of the aircraft, as far away from the pilot as possible. Then to San Francisco on a CIA charter, and Lundy comes through for her— some CIA lackey greets her there with a lead-lined box that instantly mutes much of the blood-song the thing throws at her. Worst of it is a headache, her sleep shot through with truly visceral, bloody dreams of her father over the fifteen-hour flight. When she asks how Lundy knew that lead would help, he tells her that Michael said so. She decides it doesn't change her opinion of him at all.

———

Back under the earth then. The Truman Building. Weils watching behind the one-way glass while Lundy sits on a metal folding chair in front of Michael, who lies curled on his little bed in the corner. She knows the hand is somewhere down there in the subbasement with them. Michael and the hand, a pair of poison seeds there in the State Department's belly.

Lundy sighs and says, "Michael, what the fuck is it."

Michael, curled like an apostrophe. Wings just long enough to start brushing against the wall now. Colorless, joyless things these days, the no-color of slate.

"Where does the hand come from, Michael?"

Michael clears his throat, keeps his eyes closed. "It comes from a devil."

"A devil," Lundy repeats, lifting his face to the ceiling lights in their mesh cages, rolling his head on his shoulders. "You know I don't really believe in that shit."

Weils marvels at this. The bravado. The grand irony of saying this to a thing like Michael.

Michael clears his throat again and sits up. For a moment, she swears that he looks right at her through the glass, that he speaks right to her when he says, "Sometimes, David Lundy, things are true whether you believe in them or not."

That, for a second, makes her almost like him.

Lundy, however, views it as impetuousness, and he walks over and thumbs the intercom, has Michael's wings clipped off with lawn shears.

Lundy is beloved and well-financed and insulated from both civilian and congressional interest. Lundy's programs are not on any Pentagon or State Department budget. The money is veiled, shuffled, invisible.

And then someone finds a hard drive in Finch's lab, in some closet somewhere, and on that hard drive is an audio file that no one can actually hear without being reduced to an animalistic rage. Like Michael, like the hand, Lundy is gathering his weapons about him.

But when Weils reads the transcript, she's unimpressed. There must be something there, but most of it, to her, reads like a high schooler wrote it. Bad poetry. No depth, lesser meaning. But Lundy feels otherwise, and takes to wearing the recording on a USB stick around his neck. The sole copy, he says.

Things are at play that he clearly does not understand. Weils worries about the moment slipping away from him. About him losing control. Finch's death unnerves her beyond words; how he was in the lab, the way he fell into that terrible dream-state with the song. There's something there, some key. She worries that Lundy's in over his head, and it's an odd feeling. Like seeing someone toe the abyss.

Lundy asks about Finch's suicide and Michael responds in half riddles. Lundy, enraged, spits in his face and has his wings burned off again. The stench is otherworldly and harsh, cloying, and then another agent is sent in to break off Michael's smoking wings in his gloved hands, tossing the blackened shards to the ground until Lundy thinks that Michael might use them to try to end his own life and has them swept from the floor.

In his office down there in the classified catacombs of the Truman Building, Lundy sits with his elbows resting on his knees, and looks up at her with watery blue eyes, the USB on its leather cord falling from the V of his shirt. For the first time she can remember, he looks lost, and seeing it is both thrilling and terrifying.

"So, this recording we found."

"Finch's recording?" Weils is sitting in her usual spot—in the chair facing his desk. But Lundy has pulled his own chair around so that the two are nearly touching knees. Lundy in palaver mode. There are no windows down here in the subbasement, and the clinical light overhead ignites the minutiae of burst blood vessels in Lundy's cheeks, his long, delicate eyelashes. He is not looking for advice, she knows—Lundy will never ask her what she thinks—he is simply looking to absolve himself to himself. Samantha Weils has long understood that she is Lundy's sounding board; she is the speaking mirror he gazes into when convincing himself he is innocent, simply a man harried by forces outside his control.

"You read the transcript?"

"Yes sir."

Lundy sighs, sits up, cradles the back of his head with his arms. Runs his hands over his head. "How's it feel to you?"

Wonder of wonders. Lundy actually asking her opinion. "I mean, I think it's nonsense. Someone trying their hand at being a bad guy. 'Dine in the bowl of their skull'? 'Make me a house of fever and wounds'? It's like bad poetry."

"Have I shown you footage of Finch's lab when that tech found the file? When she played it on her computer? We have video, Samantha. I promise you it's not bad poetry." He taps the USB stick there on his breastbone. "It's volatile. This woman, this lab tech? She weighed like ninety pounds. She just, I don't know, *changed*. A security guard had to put a round through her skull."

"Well, maybe it's not the words that matter."

"Maybe," Lundy says, clearly believing otherwise. "But we should be testing this thing, man. A lot more than we are. A lot more than State allows us to. Should be fielding the parameters of it. Of the hand. Like, what happens if you kill someone while they're listening to the recording? Or someone gets smoked in proximity to the hand? You know what I mean? There's so much we don't know. So much possibility."

That wild, searching look in his eyes. Lundy on the edge of the thing, Weils thinking again that he's in over his head with all this. Talking about killing people as experiments.

"You're getting in pretty deep," she says quietly.

He smiles and touches the talisman at his chest again. "I sometimes do think about playing it, Samantha. Not going to lie. Could I stand it, when it drives everyone else over the edge? What does it mean? Would it hurt? Would it feel good, falling over the edge like that? Would you feel relieved, like everything was finally over? Who knows. But I've considered it."

He stands up then, putting his hands on his hips and twisting. Wincing as his spine pops like bubble wrap. Coming back to some measure of himself. "That's the thing about shit like this: Once you own it, Samantha, you want to use it. I want a, what's it say, I want a king's house among the leaning world. Whatever the fuck that means."

"A fever house," Weils says, a little afraid of Lundy now.

"A fever house," he says, brushing past her as he leaves the room.

The months peeling away, a year, another year. Aunt Joan passes quietly in her recliner, her shows on, and Weils returns to Charlottesville to see to her affairs. It takes a week, a week and a half to get everything arranged, this last vestige of her old life severed—her old man in USP Lee does not count and hasn't and never will—and when she returns to ARC there in the Truman Building, it's hard to be surprised when Michael has become even more diminished. Falling into himself like some dark star. Lundy, hoarding his little treasures, panicked and nervous now that Finch is gone, busies himself with testing the parameters of the voice and the hand—until the end of that summer, when two things happen nearly simultaneously.

One, Michael begins talking endlessly of Portland, that events of some note will occur there, and Lundy, forever in thrall to Michael's abilities, moves the agency out to the shitty, dilapidated end of a military base on the outskirts of that city. Secondly, four months ago, Lundy sits Weils down—only days after their arrival in Portland—and informs her that she'll be babysitting an incoming agent, someone who's been passed off to them.

She's outside Lundy's new office in Camelot. It's all coldness and military utility, and flimsy compared to the depthless feeling of solidity that being underground in DC had felt. All that concrete above your head. Here, it's corkboards and dented cubicle walls, the screech of fax machines, the occasional gut-rattling thrum of a Chinook landing somewhere on the base.

Biting a thumbnail and leaning against the doorframe of his office, she says, "What do you mean, babysitting?"

Lundy sighs, motions her in. She shuts the door and reluctantly sits down, the fluorescents above their heads snapping audibly.

"I mean I got a call from State, and this guy Bonner will be joining us. John Bonner, guy's name is. A field analyst. He's in whether I like it or not. Which I don't, Samantha, believe me."

"Why can't another agent take him?"

Lundy frowns. "Because I want you to fucking take him, is why."

"Who is this guy?"

"I don't know. Some Ivy Leaguer who got in hot water back East."

"What kind of hot water?"

"That's on a need-to-know," he says, and watching the darkness cross her face, he smiles and holds up his hands. "Hey, I don't know either. They don't tell me shit."

"I thought you were David Lundy," she says, her voice deepening. Makes Lundy smile wider. "Big shot-caller."

"I think I'm in a little hot water too, Samantha, truth be told."

"Yeah?"

"Oh yeah. With Finch going out like he did . . ." Lundy sighs. "If Michael gave me another Century City bombing every, I don't know, five years? Even every ten, I get something significant from him? That saves lives? We'd be set. But he's not putting much out there these days, and funding is getting . . . a little restrictive. I'm hoping this change of locale will motivate him."

For a moment, she feels a pull of alarm. Restrictive funding? Without ARC, she's adrift. No one else will take her on. Her and her damages. "Do we need to worry about the op being dismantled?"

"No, no," Lundy says.

"Because I don't know what I'd do—"

"Look, everything is fine. Just take this guy on, let him do the driving, make him feel like he's doing something."

"You gonna brief him?"

"About what? The remnants?"

"The remnants, yeah, and Michael."

Lundy makes a face. "Let me worry about that." He pushes some paper around on his desk, squaring their edges. "He's dead weight, this guy, but he's connected. That's the only reason why he's here."

"Connected to who?"

"Terradyne," Lundy sighs.

"The *defense* firm?"

"Guy's uncle's a big shot there. Something Diane arranged."

Diane. Weils bristles. Diane was often on ARC's periphery, sometimes even down in the Truman Building, but she and Weils hadn't spoken more than a hundred words to each other since that day in Lundy's office.

Unable to help herself: "No disrespect, but is Diane the senior agent here or are you?"

Lundy levels a cool gaze at her. "Samantha. Believe it or not, Diane and I both have people we report to."

"I'm just saying, you don't find it alarming? This Terradyne mouthpiece moving in?"

"I don't think he's a mouthpiece," Lundy says. "Necessarily."

"Necessarily."

"I think he's lucky," Lundy says. "I think he fucked up and this uncle of his called in some chips for him."

"Yeah, but why?"

"I don't know, nepotism?"

"It's not a little cute to you, Terradyne landing an agent here, right after Finch opts out? And with Michael the way he is?"

"I think it's unfortunate, but that's life. One thing about this work, things are in constant flux."

"It just feels like we're exposed right now," Weils says.

"Look," says Lundy, "just keep your eye on him, okay? Everything is as good as it's ever been."

Bonner, she hates straightaway.

Clearly moneyed, blandly handsome, soft, he smacks to her of unearned righteousness and boundless privilege. How many men has she met like this throughout her life? Men who've been handed positions of power that she's either been passed over for or had to hang on to fiercely, resolutely, once she made it? He sits through briefings like he's drawn down to some interior part of himself, revealing nothing, sharing nothing, arrogance shot through every word when he does deign to speak. When they're out in the field he asks her endless questions, the answers either obvious or unknowable. Like he revels in the inanity of it. Weils would bet a year's salary that he's never pulled his weapon live, and certainly never used it. They settle quickly into their routine—Bonner the affable dipshit, driving with one arm out the window, tapping out rhythms on the door panel as they meander around trying to decipher Michael's idiotic clues, Weils fielding Bonner's endless comments. Fending off his questions about Michael, the agency; Weils can't help imagining that he's gathering intel. When they're not in the field, she has to drum up things at Camelot to keep him occupied, like a fucking nanny.

Then Seaver loses track of the hand, falls sway to it, takes it out of Camelot and leaves it on a *toilet* in a *dive* bar, and then everything—every last thing—falls apart.

Within hours, they have a fever house, something that Lundy in his wildest imaginings, it turns out, only ever touched the edge of. Only guessing at how bad it would get, and just how brutally fast.

So.

Weils in Camelot, the wet tarmac, Lundy gone, Bonner peering down at his vest and then back up, a second's worth of confusion on his face before she pulls the trigger.

Did she mean to shoot him in the head?

Hell yes, she did.

He's dead weight. At *best*, he's dead weight. Took her two seconds to run through the outcomes—if they stayed together, she'd be lugging him around the hell that was most likely waiting for them back in the city, or they'd be stuck at Camelot waiting for the State Department to roll in with whatever military response they'd inevitably have, realizing just how bad ARC has fucked up here. And who would be the last ones standing? Who would be the last agents sitting there, waiting to become the scapegoats? Lundy had left her, left both of them. Years of her life spent in service to him, and he leaves her, taking everything that matters to him.

Taking Michael, leaving her.

What is she without ARC? It's this or nothing, and Bonner, with his baby-fascist haircut and his knowing smirk, his millionaire-family connections, his boundless privilege, she meant to fucking drop him. It's a fever house, and if she's going to find David—and she wants to, if only to look him in the eye and ask him why he left her—she can't be hauling Bonner around.

And yet.

Did she also mean to pull the shot at the last second?

Yeah.

Probably.

Maybe.

She'd still felt some minute snag, some slight pull when shooting Bonner. A half-conscious remembrance of Lundy saying, years back, *You are irreparably psychologically damaged.* Just some tiny ember inside her. Some part of her bristling at it.

She doesn't know if it was mercy or patience, what stayed her hand at the last second. What made her bullet drift two inches to the left. And it *still* might have just been an unlucky shot. She'd missed Nick Coffin earlier, after all.

It doesn't matter, she tells herself. He's dead or he isn't.

If he's dead, no loss there.

If he's not, he can be the one the State Department collects when they roll up to Camelot. Let him take the heat.

Either way, she's got shit to do.

HUTCH HOLTZ

Some semblance of consciousness returns to him and he drives this circuitous route, keeps burning gas, hitting certain waypoints around town. Just driving. For one, it feels better when he sits, hurts less, but also there's something nattering at him, some answer to some question he hasn't even asked yet. Some grim insistence that he keep driving. How much has he turned by now, he wonders. Does it happen in an eyeblink? Some switch being flipped? Or is it gradual, a sea tide of change over a number of hours?

Like he'll even know when it happens, right?

Or give a shit.

So he hits these waypoints, too wounded to get out and actually explore any of them. But they ring his bell, don't they? All of them shot through with significance somehow. Is it that they truly contain some answer, or just that his brain's chemistry is already changing, random synapses hammering away in tandem with his memories. Altered in whatever fucking way Don was altered.

So he drives, considers briefly, each time he stops, getting out and exploring, but just the notion of stepping out of the car seems too painful an odyssey. There is the Regal Arms, that part of downtown a place of wilding now, people fighting in the streets, loose clusters here and there of cops in riot gear, cops who seem continually to be falling back toward some police cruiser. The Regal Arms, where the Coffin kid lives, the kid who should have given the hand to Peach and moved on, but somehow, it seems, fucked that up. Nick Coffin, who for some reason snags like a fishhook in his mind.

From the Regal Arms he heads across the river—the Burnside Bridge still open for now, but with enough flashing lights and emergency vehicles stationed at the foot of it that he imagines it'll be shut down soon—and over to Tim's apartment, a brick two-story deal with a nice, well-kept courtyard, only six units, his and Jessica's place there in the bottom left, a light on in the bedroom window. Hutch wondering what kind of shit Jessica's going through right now. If she even knows that Tim is dead, or if she's just glued to the TV or her phone, dread ripping through her as she sees what's happening on the screen, wondering where the hell her man is. If she's sending him text after text with no response. Wouldn't she have reached out to Hutch by now, if that was the case? Maybe she's out there too, already bitten and biting.

Hutch sighs, closes his eyes, almost drifts off. Comes to when someone behind him honks; he's double-parked, blocking the street.

From there it's Pie in the Sky, the place cordoned off with yellow police tape that's already been pulled down, hanks of tape fluttering like writhing snakes on the pavement. Hutch sees a man, naked save for a pair of bright orange tennis shoes, go jogging through the parking lot, a tremendous chunk taken out of his calf. Slapping through puddles, ass cheeks flexing, running to the end of the lot and smacking the chain-link fence and turning back. When he pivots, Hutch's headlights casting him in cold light, the man doesn't flinch, doesn't even seem aware. His face is chalk-white and full of a drawn horror, and there is something about this—how he runs to the sidewalk and turns, sprinting toward the far fence again, carved down to this singleness of purpose as the bite on his calf winds its way through him—that scares Hutch perhaps more than anything else he's seen tonight. As if the man has become some sort of automaton. Unable to stop himself. Hutch lets out a sob of recognition as the parallel between the two of them, he and the running man, affirms itself in his mind. He runs, I drive to these places and stop and drive and stop. It's happening to me too. My own brain-itch, brain-stutter. And even as Hutch understands it, he stuffs that understanding inside himself, buries it. Eager to move once again.

To Wesley's apartment next, this one taking a while, a number of streets blocked off by emergency vehicles. He traverses a side street off Burnside, maybe around Sixtieth, and finds a throng of people milling about in the middle of the road. They're watching a block of houses burn to the ground, and then someone runs through the crowd and everyone scatters like rats, people bouncing off Hutch's car, someone's face twisting against the windshield, close enough that he can see the gray threaded through the black swirl of the man's beard, and then Hutch is fucking gone, out of there, baby, mashing the pedal to the floor.

Making it finally to Wesley's apartment, the whole area a madhouse of wall-to-wall traffic. Exhaust and bass-throb, Hutch making the grand mistake of pulling onto the traffic of Eighty-second, getting himself stuck in that grinding, stop-start, bumper-to-bumper shit. He sits there a few minutes and then sees, not really surprised by it, a pair of tough boys walking down the rows of stalled traffic, the one on the driver's side with a comically large hunting knife in his hand. These kids can't be more than fifteen, sixteen years old, the one roving the passenger side with the price tag still hanging off his ball cap and fluttering in his eyes. He watches as they stop at each car and briefly converse with the driver through the glass. The driver's-side kid either accepts something handed through a wedge of window—money, usually, but also a phone and, a few car lengths up, a handful of candy bars—or he leans down and drives the knife into the sidewall of a wheel. The kid with the hat carries a red shopping bag in his hand, running over and scooping up anything they're offered. He marvels at it—a plot so brazen, even Tim wouldn't run something like it, Hutch is almost sure. Thinking about Tim seizes his heart.

Coming up on Hutch, the one with the blade backpedals, uncertainty clouding his face. Hutch on his best day would have garnered such a reaction, but now? He's surprised that the kids don't walk on to the car behind him. But Hutch's window is already open, too rich a temptation.

"Give me your money, motherfuck." It's like ventriloquism, this little kid shooting for a big man voice, trying so hard at being tough.

"Amazing someone hasn't just shot you in the cock yet," Hutch says, but he's not sure if the kid can hear him. Not sure if it's something he just thought. Everything sounds strange in his ears, ocean-like.

The kid with the shopping bag slaps the passenger window. The car ahead of him moves a half-length ahead. Hutch sees a group of people—maybe a dozen of them, a few muscly types threaded among the pack, everyone's stride bent with fury, arms swinging, one guy with his sunglasses perched on the back of his head. They're making their way down the sidewalk toward the kids.

"You got some fans," Hutch says, pointing, and the kid with the knife looks—Hutch, on a better day, might have brought the kid's arm into the car then, shattered the ulna bone over the sill, snapped all of his fingers. Goodbye knife, hello six months of physical therapy. But mostly he wants to not be here, wants to keep fording that river of memory, lose himself in that bittersweet fog. Drive aimlessly through the madness and ruminate on Tim and Jessica and his old man and Nick Coffin, something incessantly pulling at him.

The kid turns back to him. There's not much time before the pack arrives, catches up to them, and he says, eyes bulging, the knife making a quick, singular jab toward Hutch's face, "Money, bitch, now."

Hutch nods, lifts his leg up and pulls out the cop's pistol. Fires a round through the roof.

Everybody scatters. The car behind him smacks his bumper in an attempt to take off, heads onto the sidewalk. Hutch hissing, "Ah, fuck," as the kid with the shopping bag gets clipped in the hip by that car. The boy rolls, his bag scattering—cell phones and wallets fanning out on the tar-scribbled pavement—and then he gets up and keeps running with his knife-wielding buddy, now with a significant limp and a big line of road rash down one arm. The two groups collide and it's more madness. He sees the kid stick somebody in the gut once, twice, sees him slash at someone's face, then get dogpiled. He thinks of Tim in Rutherford, of him pressing that screwdriver against the man's belly earlier tonight, and then he puts the pistol in his lap and gently, as carefully as he can, turns the car around amid a chorus of honks, screams peppering the night, the scent of smoking plastic and weed in the air. Wincing at the way turning the steering wheel pulls at his guts. He drives on the sidewalk, almost scraping car against car, people angry or confused or not even paying attention to him as he threads his way along, coming to another side street. Even a block off Eighty-second, it's like an entirely different world.

Five minutes later, images playing behind his eyes now like some maddened calliope, Hutch makes it to Wesley's place. The L-shaped apartment building facing the parking lot, the dumpsters. It looks the same as it did only hours earlier.

Somehow, he is not surprised to see the woman, Shawna, stalking the sidewalk out front of the building. A phone pressed to her ear, a twist of oily hair being worried between her fingers, still in her sweatpants and her denim jacket.

Hutch leans out the window. "Hey."

She turns, takes in the car. Then sees his face, her eyes widening in sudden recognition.

"Get in," he says.

"Fuck you." She's poised on the tips of her toes, everything telegraphing that she's ready to take off.

"Come on, Shawna. Help me out."

"Where is he," she says, but even as she says it, she's walking toward the car. And her voice, the deflation in it. It's like she knows already.

She starts to get in, then pauses when she sees the gun in his lap. Hutch holds up his hands and carefully picks it up, gingerly setting it on the floorboards at his feet. Hoping she understands by looking at him that it'll pretty much take the will of God for him to reach it again.

She sits down and shuts the door, ragged and hard-faced and untrusting. "Where is he?" she asks again.

"Wesley?"

"No, the fucking president." She's grown brave in the interceding hours. Desperation or rage or just aware of Hutch's diminished state. All three, maybe. "Yeah, Wesley."

"He's out of the picture."

She goes still, her eyes looking at Hutch's chest, the blood in his lap, but it's like she's gone somewhere else. "He dead?"

"Yeah."

A nod. "Was it you that killed him?"

"I didn't, no."

"Who did?"

Why lie at this point? The world on fire the way it is? "An ex-cop. Wesley started biting him in the face, and that was it."

Agony ripples through her, there and gone so fast that Hutch is hardly aware that he saw it. Then another nod and a deep, deep inhale that lifts her shoulders. A breath that Shawna seems reluctant to release.

"We just wanted to ask him some questions, and he took it to the next level."

"Yeah, I'll bet," she says acidly. "You two looked like some good Samaritans to me. All pure-hearted and shit."

"Seriously. I didn't want it to play out like that."

"Did he do this to you?" A wave of the hand.

"No."

"That's too bad."

"Listen, Shawna—"

"Don't ask me nothing. You don't have the right to ask me shit."

"Shawna, listen, I'm sorry. Things got away from us."

She lifts her teeth into something wolfish, something meant to be a smile but isn't. "Yeah, well, you're paying the price, aren't you? Going through some shit yourself right now, aren't you?"

Hutch licks his lips, swallows. Blinks languidly, feeling like he's hardly there. "Listen, you still got that box cutter on you?"

"What?"

He closes his eyes, exhaustion rifling through him, opening every door. "That box cutter you took off the table, when you grabbed the dope. When we let you leave."

"I got it. Why, you want me to slit your throat?"

Hutch swallows, takes a slow breath. "I want you to trade me."

"What?"

"You seen what's happening out there? A box cutter won't do you no good."

"You want to trade me what?"

His eyes dip to the floorboards. "This pistol, for that."

She looks at him then, the cold assessing glint in her eyes. The frankness. "Why?"

"I just said."

"Yeah, but why?"

"I mean . . ." Hutch gestures vaguely out the window, meant to encompass everything. *Because of what's out there. Because of what we started.*

Because I owe you.

I owe other people a lot more than I owe you, he thinks, but I still owe you.

"You think that's gonna fix anything?" she says, and something in Hutch, wrecked as he is, bristles at it.

"Take it or don't," he says.

Looking at him, tucking a hank of dirty hair behind her ear, she leans over and digs into the pocket of her coat. He catches a whiff of meth-sweat. If she jabs him with the box cutter, tries to run it across him, he won't be able do anything about it. But she holds it out to him, handle first.

He gestures at the floorboards. "I can't get this. Come around."

"This a trick?"

Hutch lets out an exhausted laugh. "God, if it is, Shawna, just go ahead and stick me. I'm done, man."

She gets out, the knobs of her spine showing in the wedge between her sweatpants and her coat, the bones shadowed in stark relief. She walks around, opens his door. Crouching, her eyes on him, she reaches down at his feet and grabs the Glock from the floorboards.

He's about to ask her if she knows how to work it when a flat blankness falls across her face and she stands up and presses the barrel against his temple.

Hutch thinks of what he might say. All the things that might spill from his useless lips—*don't do it, it's not worth it, believe me, it will haunt you forever*—it all rattles hollow. He closes his eyes, waits for it.

"You're not worth it," she says some interminable time later. As if it's a revelation to her.

There's an explosion somewhere, a loud *whoomph!* in the night that ripples along the building and then seems to echo back at them in waves. A tanker truck, maybe a gas main.

"I am sorry," Hutch says, but when he looks over at his open door, she's already gone.

JOHN BONNER

The sky wheels about, the stars in a dizzying array.

A deep throb behind his skull like a giant has spent an hour thumping his head off the pavement. He rolls to the side and retches. Blinking hurts. He realizes after a time that he can only see out of one eye. He gags again, bile rising in his throat, and then he starts coughing. It hurts, sends him to some gray-lit place that's not quite conscious but not quite gone entirely.

He awakens with the sky still wheeling above him, star-spattered. Feels the cool asphalt beneath his fingertips. He tries to blink again and one side of his face is a tightened mask of dried blood. His head feels broken in some intrinsic, vital way.

Eventually Bonner sits up. A constellation of pain marches through his skull. Probing his face with shaking fingers, he feels a tremendous rise on the side of his head, there at the temple, a bloody, enflamed ridge that crawls back behind his ear. That eye swollen shut. Under the weak light, his fingers are tacky with blood. Weils shot him in the fucking head, but missed. *Mostly* missed. Grazed him. Left him breathing. What the hell could that mean? Clarity's impossible right now. It feels like someone's parked a car in his brain.

How long had Weils even had that silencer on her? Just waiting to use it.

Bonner stands up, leans over with his hands on his knees. Retches again.

The sedan's gone. His gun as well. Car keys, wallet. Gone.

It's a long, shambling walk from a darkened Camelot back to the active, populated part of the base. It's the middle of the night, but there are still little pockets of activity. The motor pool and its whir of pneumatic drills, ratchets in the work bays. Lights shining along the edges of administrative buildings. Bonner keeps to the shadows.

When he makes it within a hundred yards of the entrance, the guard's station with its fencing and its gate arm, he steps out into the light and walks. A few soldiers are hauling ass from one building to another some distance away. A Jeep passes him. Bonner dips his head and the driver goes on without slowing.

At the gate, the soldier takes in his appearance and his eyes widen. A different guard on shift now.

Bonner stands there like something brought unwillingly back to life. In a hoarse, raspy voice, he says, "Can you open the gate, please?"

The soldier has a phone in his hand. Bonner can see the barrel of his rifle where it's leaned up against his desk.

"Sir, you have identification?"

"I'm with the program in the back." Bonner hooks his thumb over his shoulder. Even this action pains him. "The one y'all aren't supposed to talk about."

"I'm still going to need some identification."

"Yeah, I don't have it." Bonner holds out his arms. "I got rolled."

"You got rolled *on the base?*"

"Yeah." He turns his head toward the light, lets the soldier take it in.

"Man, I gotta call my CO."

"Please don't do that."

The guy sets his phone down, picks up a handset. Bonner holds up a bloody hand. "Alright, look," he says. "You know how this is going to work, right? You're keeping a federal agent, with the State Department, with SCI clearance and on a dark project, you're keeping that guy *on* the fucking base? You won't let him leave? This goes up the chain, you think your CO's going to defend you to your division commander? To *anyone*? Come on. Write an incident report, take my photo, whatever. Open that gate, though, seriously." Bonner surprises himself with his righteousness. His anger. He realizes he's furious—perhaps lethally so. Whether it's at Weils or Lundy, he hasn't figured out yet. The speech makes his headache worse.

The soldier looks uncertain, but he still lifts that handset, he's still going to call it in. His gaze never breaking from Bonner's.

And then another grunt comes running up, one hand over his helmet, his rifle in the other. This guy doesn't even look Bonner's way.

"Got a green light from Sergeant Kent, Davis. We're heading into town."

"What?" The guard puts the handset down. "For real? We're drilling at zero-four-thirty? The hell is that?"

"It's not a drill, man. We're doing security, something's going on. All that crazy shit people are posting on YouTube. We gotta go, the whole unit's heading out. Who's taking over gate duty?"

The guard looks petrified by this question. "I don't know. Sanchez?"

"Well, don't fucking wait for him, let's go." The other soldier takes off, starts running for the barracks in the distance. Bonner looks back: there's new movement on the base, men running back and forth now, getting into formation, trucks stationing themselves on the tarmac.

Davis looks at him and hisses, "Fuck." He presses something and the gate arm begins to rise. He grabs his rifle, steps out the doorway and books it toward the barracks. Bonner's beneath the arm and through the cyclone fence before it's even opened up all the way.

He starts walking—God, even walking hurts—along the scrub-grass, the long stretch of weed-choked shoulder beside the road. Miles back to the city and whatever's happening there.

A long time to think about what he'll do next.

It's only then, running his hands along his pockets, that he realizes Weils has left him his phone. Intentionally or not.

He stops on the shoulder, just stares at it. Who is there to even call?

He could call Lundy.

Call Weils.

But what if she actually picked up?

What the hell would he even ask her at this point?

SAMANTHA WEILS

So where do you go when the world's been pulled out from under your feet? After someone who promised to protect you instead winds up doing the can-can on your shattered heart?

By the time she makes it downtown, downtown is a vestige of what it once was. Downtown is reduced to a word, an idea. It's a hothouse now—large swaths of the city ripple with flame while others are without power, the strange scatter of dark and brightly lit areas giving the world a carnival sideshow effect. Brief pops of gunfire can be heard amid the scatter of sirens and somewhere she can hear cops ordering people to disperse over an LRAD. Weils drives with her pistol in her lap.

She could gamify her rage, her heartbreak. Call it *What Would Lundy Do?*

Lundy would get Michael, his dying treasure, his cosmic poker chip, and get on a plane back to DC. That's what he'd do. Head away from ground zero, from this calamity that's ten times worse than any scenario he ever considered in briefings. She tries his phone one more time, gets nothing. Dials then, something tugging at her, Diane's number. It's been years since they talked—Lundy forever steering her, making a point of it, insisting that he solely ran Weils—and she surprises herself by getting the number right, Diane's voice coming through loud and clear, telling Weils that she's unavailable, to please leave a message. Diane constantly on ARC's periphery over the years but never directly involved. Where had she last been stationed? Lundy had mentioned it. Chicago, most recently? Or some small waypost off the coast of Iceland, a tiny island there, Weils hearing she was doing some weapons development thing. Rumors are like the tributaries of a river in this world. Winding, forked. Anyway, Diane is another person who helped shape her and seems wholly lost to her now, but here is Weils, still stirring the ashes of her past. Not knowing what else to do.

She drives. Bodies are scattered on the street here and there. She slows when she sees a woman in a puzzle of limbs on top of a parked car, like she'd been flung from the sky and landed there. Licks of flame burble from the windows of a high-rise a few blocks away.

She is looking at the fire when a man takes three running steps from around the corner of a building and swings a length of steel pipe into the passenger side of her windshield. He's wearing a white tank top that gleams in the dark and has beautiful, gym-sculpted muscles. That side of the windshield shatters into a white constellation. She brakes the sedan hard enough that her seatbelt tightens and Bonner's gear—pistol, wallet—falls to the floorboard.

"Let me in," he says calmly through the glass, leaning down and looking at her. His eyes are clear and full of death. He tries the locked door handle, still holding the pipe with his free hand, and Weils leans over and shoots him in the cheek through the passenger window, the gunshot like a sharp clap. Remembers telling Bonner not to do that exact thing earlier in the night, and here she is. She sets the pistol back in her lap, grips the steering wheel with both hands, and heads on down the street, her eyes drawn to the next lighted patch of city some blocks ahead. As if the light there actually signified some beacon, some oasis. A single bead of sweat treks from her temple to her jaw.

She approaches the Justice Center, thinks of going inside, flinging herself at the mercy of law enforcement, seeing what happens. Lundy's vanished, the hand's gone. *Here I am, Officer. What we did was sanctioned, as long as we kept quiet about it.*

She rolls her window down and even across the street can hear the faint rattle of the generator inside the Justice Center, mounted lights throwing a weak yellow glow along the perimeter of the place. Cops are erecting plywood barricades against the glass windows on the ground floor, a phalanx of them casually firing riot munitions when people get too close. It seems at this point most of the citizenry is made up of equal parts bitten folks, those just watchful, or people looting cars, running bricks through the windows of businesses, taking what there is to take. One of the cops—riot gear, helmet, tear gas gun with its wheel of ammunition hanging from a strap across his chest—seems to settle his gaze on her. He waves her on; she's blocking traffic. Weils looks at the man's faceplate, searching for his eyes in there, some recognition that they are, or were, on the same side. The cop shrugs at her refusal to move and lifts his gun. There's a distinct *pop!* and a tear gas canister arcs across the street and bounces off her door, clattering into the road. She marvels for a moment at the accuracy of the shot, and then catches a whiff of the acrid, chemical sting of the gas. Her eyes immediately start to well up and she takes off, turns right at the corner, those stoplights like dead sentinels up there on their wires. She'll find no quarter here.

Only a few blocks away, the city takes on a seeming normalcy: neon and streetlights and the patient red-yellow-green tattoo of stoplights. Commerce and structure. Weils surprises herself, leaning toward it.

It's in this island of calm that Weils sees a woman run around the corner. She is pale, gray-haired, wearing a thigh-length pink robe, its belt whipping like a tail. Beneath that, a pair of gray sweatpants and a navy blue T-shirt with a logo faded to illegibility. She is screaming and being chased by three men. Nearly clipping her knees against a newspaper stand that's been knocked over in her path, she veers past it at the last moment. Weils, in a fit of something—finally fearful, perhaps, of the vast depths of her ownership of all of this, of the fact that her fucking father sits forever like a ghoul on her shoulders, whispering recriminations, fearful that Lundy is right, that she is as damaged and psychologically dismantled and ruined as he always insisted she was—whatever it is, she screeches to a halt on the sidewalk, her right headlight exploding in a burst of plastic when she collides against the curved steel of a bike rack. She pushes open the passenger door, the bullet hole in the window like a single white eye, and then opens her own door and stands up.

"Hey," she barks, and to her relief, the woman turns. "Get in." Incredibly, in spite of the glassy, shell-shocked look on her face, she does. The men slow, begin trotting toward the sedan, reassessing. They look like they've been culled from an ad for a microbrewery. Bearded, fit, all probably in their mid-thirties. Nearly interchangeable with each other. The woman, in a kind of terrified hunch, scrabbles into the passenger seat. One of the men has a pair of gardening shears in his hand, so new that she can see the tag still dangling from the handle.

Weils sights and fires, puts a round in his arm, coming close to taking it off at the elbow. The shears go skittering along the sidewalk with a grating hiss. The men scatter, the one howling, clutching his dangling arm.

The woman slams the sedan door shut. Weils gets in on her side, reverses, then puts the car in motion. The woman's breathing is labored, almost vocal, and Weils realizes that Bonner's pistol still rests on the floorboard at the woman's feet. She's shaking. She wears plastic sandals that must have been terrible to run in, the sort you'd buy at the pharmacy for four or five dollars. And it's then Weils sees that the woman's ankle is caked with blood. She stops, peers down at the woman's legs.

"You're bit?"

It's like Weils hasn't spoken. The woman ignores her. Just that vocal, rabbit-fast breathing, an inch away from hyperventilating as she stares out the window. Knuckled hands, a loose gray ponytail hanging between her shoulder blades, the silver in it glinting against the thrown light. Her hands rest primly in her lap, but she breathes like the world is ice-blown and frozen.

"Hey," Weils says, snapping her fingers. "Are you bit?" She rests her pistol in that space between the seat and door, not wanting to scare the woman any more than she already is.

She turns to Weils then. Her wide eyes are a rich cocoa brown, with long, delicate lashes, and Weils watches as the white of one of the woman's eyes clouds with blood.

"I have a son," she says. Her voice is rapturous, as if what she's said is magnificent.

"Get out of the car," Weils says.

"I have my son with me," the woman says, almost dreamily now, "and we're on the beach." Sighing, she says, "We are holding hands, and his hand is *very* small, small as a bird," and Weils puts the pistol in her lap now, the barrel aimed at the woman's torso, her center mass, and still, killer that she is, she cannot shoot her. Cannot shoot this woman snared in her half-lit dream as she changes into something wholly different.

"He's afraid of the water," the woman says, as if begging Weils to understand.

"Please get out," Weils says softly.

"He steps on a shell. He has a cut *on his* foot," the woman gargles, as if her throat is suddenly filled with liquid, and she opens her jaws and leans forward, one hand latching onto Weils's knee, and the gun jumps in Weils's hand, shuddering once, twice, three times.

———

She drives on. The woman's body rests in the seat beside her, the car suffused with the rich, cloying stink of her spent life. Some kind of understanding coming to her at last, one door opening another.

The fever house is hell. Hell on earth. What else could they possibly have been courting? What did Lundy think would happen? A recording of a man talking and you listen to it and the words break your mind? A hand that made you want to die? And upon dying brought you back to some half-life, every ounce of you scrubbed out and replaced with a blank fury?

It's like they've spent years begging for this very thing to happen. Just staring in the mouth of the thing, daring it to bite down.

The night is a slow-moving ruin around her. She's up in the West Hills now, everything threaded with smoke. The horizon glows with fire. Burning trees, burning homes. She should turn around.

The scatter of the nightmare city spread out below her, she pulls onto the shoulder and gets out. Opening the passenger door, she gently takes the dead woman from her seat and lays her to rest on the side of the road, her poor face a cold ruin. Empty as a sky. Weils gets back in the car and spends a frenzied minute rubbing the woman's blood from her hands onto the thighs of her pants, reaching into the glove box for something to clean herself with and not finding it. She's doing this when her phone buzzes in her pocket.

She sits up, looks at the screen. Answers it.

"Samantha," Diane says.

Weils, for a moment, can't respond. It's been so long, those many years since her early, frenetic days on the Dulles campus, then her passing Weils off to Lundy.

"Diane."

"Samantha, oh God, you cannot—I am *so* happy to hear your voice. Are you okay?"

"I mean, that's . . . I don't know how to answer that."

"Listen to me, Samantha," Diane says, "things are happening here that you can't understand."

"I think I understand enough, Diane. If you could see what I'm seeing right now."

Diane sighs. "David got his wish, didn't he? A fever house."

"And it's worse than he ever thought." Weils laughs, the sound bitter and clipped in her own ears. "Didn't have a clue."

"Samantha, Lundy's dead."

"I know it," she says, and only after she's said it does she realize it's true. At some point after leaving Camelot, she came to believe it. Came to feel it in the stirrings of her bones.

"Michael's dead too."

"Good," Weils says.

"Hardly," Diane says, and then, "I need your help, Samantha."

"Mine?"

"Listen," Diane says, sounding distracted, a little breathless, like she's running, or walking very fast somewhere, "the fever house, it's not over, it's not stopping."

Weils laughs again, looks out at the strings of flame beginning to overtake the hills, the columns of smoke down in the city.

"That's because it's hell," she says flatly.

"No," Diane says. "No, Samantha, it's not. I want you to do something for me. Please. We can save ourselves."

"How?"

Weils hears a rustling, a murmur at the other end, Diane with her hand over the phone. When she comes back, she says, "You know he was full of shit, right? Samantha, right? All those years. I never should have let you go. Never should have let him take you. He just, he always ran through the world like that, ran right through people. Used them and threw them away."

"I went willingly enough," Weils says, looking out the window.

"He lied to you for years. All that bullshit about your psych evals. Please. It was just a way of keeping you under his thumb."

Weils knuckles a tear away. Angry at herself, at Diane, angry at the mad spill of fire out beyond the windshield.

"Is John Bonner with you?"

"No," Weils says. "What?"

"Is he dead?"

"No," she says, then, "I don't know."

"Do you know where he is?"

"I—Why? I left him at Camelot."

"Do you know where he went?"

"No. I mean, I thought someone from State would come in. I knew things were heading south, I thought maybe they'd take him—"

"Samantha, I've taken control of ARC. I'm brokering a deal. We can get out from behind this."

"You're what? A deal with who?"

"There's a way we can still insulate ourselves. Come out the other side. But there's not much time. I want you to come with us, but first I need you to do something."

"Diane, what are you talking about? What did you do?"

"Listen to me. Things are going to start happening very soon, and you can either get swept away, Samantha, or you can save yourself. But you have to do what I tell you."

She looks out at the fire-marred skyline, the whirling emergency lights, the great swaths of the city that have gone dark. Here is another person telling her that redemption might only happen this one way. Her father, David Lundy, now Diane. All of them with this fervent insistence that she's incapable of saving herself. Are they right?

Staring down at her loosely coiled fist—*You are my gun hand*—and the pistol next to her thigh, the scent of the old woman's blood still hanging in the car like some unyielding ghost, Weils says, "Tell me what you want me to do."

HUTCH HOLTZ

His thoughts weave and bend. Muddled, sorrowful things. A collection of splintered images all threaded with loss. His has been a small life. He has brought more pain into the world than he has lessened it. Hutch thinks of his father, how cancer had strode through him at the end, cocksure and malevolent. Those last cursed weeks in hospice care. His moans of delirium shot through with agony, his body brought to a place where the dope they gave him couldn't touch him anymore. The way he lay in his bed and tried to find Hutch with his eyes and sometimes could not; the pain simply too great. How he was winnowed down into a new man that ultimately leaned toward death, welcomed it.

His father had died six years back, before the thing with the bikers in Gresham, thank God. But six years into working with Peach too. His old man had had an idea of what he did for money. Not the details, but the idea of it. He could see it on the old man's face sometimes. But even on Dan Holtz's deathbed, tubes in his arms, his nose, caught in a moment of rare, stark lucidity, they'd never said a word about it.

He thinks also of Tim Reed, when they'd first met in Rutherford Youth Correctional as boys, mesh over the windows of the activity room, the absence of Hutch's mother clattering inside him like a stone in a cup. How Tim had showed him a Discman beneath his jacket and a burned CD copy of . . . *And Justice for All* that he'd somehow managed to smuggle in. The two of them each with an earbud listening to that album over and over again. Hutch released first and Tim calling him as soon as he got out. Neither one of them ever finishing high school. Hutch as Tim's best man when he'd married Jessica, Tim getting weepy at the end of the night, just the two of them and Jess, a few friends of hers. All of them drunk as hell at Tim's mom's place out in the sticks, stringed lights on the patio like a protective halo. *I would take a bullet for this man,* glassy-eyed Tim had said that night, pointing at Hutch—and God, hadn't that served as prophecy.

He understands what's happening. Sits with one leg inside the car, one on the asphalt. Knows with a grim finality that his body is being overtaken. Two bites on his arm? That's a page turning. That's a sure thing. Hutch, like Don, will become animated. His will be a body commandeered. He knows it.

It's like death, in its own way.

But also worse than death.

He scoots his ass around in the driver's seat, slowly puts both feet on the ground. His whole body a pulse of fire now, strange currents drifting in his blood. Memories continue to flood through him. Tidal things, red-threaded.

His father's watery blue eyes.

Tim, his head lolling on the back of a deck chair on his wedding night, cocking a finger Hutch's way. *I would take a bullet for this man.*

His mother holding Hutch to her chest when he'd shut his finger in the bathroom door. Five, six years old. The cooing sound she'd made before wrapping his finger in ice. The warm and perfect nest of her arms.

The first time Hutch took a fish bat to a man's mouth. Over fifteen hundred dollars, this was. How the man's teeth had fallen to the linoleum like thumbtacks, the blood spilling slowly from between his lips, and then faster, like someone tipping a bottle over. The odd thrill Hutch had gotten from it—that such a thing could be done to someone without the same pain being dealt back to him in equal measure. How that realization took root in him and grew.

Peach sitting Tim and Hutch down at Mercy's twelve years ago, Hutch at the time running the door there, continually broke, a rotten tooth in his head he couldn't afford to get pulled. Peach putting his ring-heavy hands on the table, smiling that fey, complicated smile. Asking the two of them if they'd like to start making some real money.

Hutch leaning into Wes's ear, telling him he was running out of running room.

Tim with his wheel gun up against Wes's head.

The way his body had floated in the river.

The hand as the catalyst to it all.

Hutch leans back now, his face purled in pain. He looks up at the sky and finds the cool grip of the box cutter on the seat behind him. Struggles to push the blade up.

Manages it, then lifts it to the soft underside of his chin, there at the throat. Tries to run it across the meat there. The windpipe, the carotid. Get it done.

But before he's able, some final neurological message is sent to the tortured nexus of his brain and he drops it.

Hutch Holtz—what had been Hutch Holtz, as he's now both more and vastly less than himself—rises from the car. Trips over the lip of the sidewalk, staggers and falls to his knees. He's still a creature of tissue and muscle, breath—his knees well with blood, though it's painless for him now.

He rises slowly, eyes like a pair of candles blown out.

He staggers down the street, searching, head swiveling. Dawn blues the trees and power lines above him. Perhaps there is some last distant desire that ripples its way through him, that animates him.

Some vestige of what could be considered his old life. A simple, stutter-quick intention that tattoos a single rhythm inside that new and ruinous brain. Like that man jogging in the parking lot, the same minute route over and over again. Some small flame of will left to him. A single notion that sends Hutch down a particular path, down this side of the street rather than the other. Toward this part of the city rather than that one.

Then again, perhaps not.

Who, really, could say.

NICK COFFIN

Something is happening back home.

Rachmann hands Nick his phone. He's pulled up a YouTube video that shows a man staggering down the street. He is in downtown Portland—Nick recognizes the bookstore, the pizza place, the record store—and the man's mouth froths with red foam. The camera zooms in on his face—his gaze is somehow both wild-eyed and entirely empty.

A young woman walks around the corner, oblivious, and the man falls upon her. The person filming screams, the phone crackling with the noise. The man's head, seen from the back, trembles and shivers— Nick understands implicitly, without seeing it, that her face and neck are being bitten. Another man runs up and tries to pull him off; the first man turns, snake-like, and bites him on the wrist. The video toggles up and down; people are running away. Off-screen someone yells "Another one! Over there!" and the video ends in a gray blur of pixels. Nick looks at the time stamp; it was uploaded two hours ago.

They are in Rachmann's room in Venice, where he has returned to his computer. He sits on the edge of his bed. Nick in a chair that faces the room's only window. The enormity of it all—being here, his mother, Herman Goud and David Lundy—it all feels now like he's seeing the mouth of some cave and trying to gauge by sight its circumference. The act of it is simply too enormous. It's all just guesswork.

"Alright," Rachmann says, and shuts his laptop. "We have a bus to catch."

He sees Nick's face.

"Don't flag on me now, Nick. This is us moving forward."

They're at LA's Union Station, waiting for the bus that will take them across the border.

Nick, unable to sit still, asks why they aren't flying instead.

"This is faster."

"It is?"

"Tickets, boarding, security checks, all that? If we want to get to Goud's place, this is faster."

Nick goes to a kiosk and buys a cup of coffee, a bad move for his jangly nerves, but what else is there to do? Sitting is its own punishment at this point.

His phone rings. It's his mother's number, and Nick feels a lurching mix of terror and relief when he sees it.

"Mom?"

"Hello, Nick," a man says. "I'm Special Agent in Charge Monahan. I'm with the State Department. We have your mother in custody here." Nick can't tell if it's the same man. The same voice. They all sound the fucking same, these guys. Everyone and their endless spy-play. There is a dangerously frayed quality to Nick's voice when he says, "The last person that called said she was being held by the State Police."

"Yeah, they were full of shit."

He's taken aback for a moment. "Oh, but you're telling me the truth?"

"I am."

"Ah, fantastic. Let me talk to her."

"You bet, Nick," the man says. He sounds conversational, some-one having a good time. "In a second. Her safety's paramount, be-lieve me. I'm just going to ask you—where's the hand?"

Nick takes a breath and then says, "That's not how this is going to work. Let me talk to her."

"Son, I'm afraid you don't get to dictate the terms here. We're far past that. Tell me where the hand is, right now."

Nick holds his breath.

"I'm not asking again."

"I put it under a dumpster in Southeast Portland."

Monahan seems to consider this. "Under a dumpster."

"It was somewhere near Hawthorne. Your guys—or someone's guys—had just shot someone in the face right in front of me. I had brains on me."

It's Monahan's turn to be quiet now.

"I panicked. I ditched it. Now let me talk to her."

"Nick?" his mother says, and her voice threatens to undo him. The plaintiveness. Katherine Moriarty, brought so far from everything that makes her safe, and she's done nothing to deserve it.

"Mom, are you okay?"

"Nick, they're blackmailing me."

"What?"

"They say they've got evidence that we're terrorists, that they're going to charge us—"

Monahan comes back on the line. "As you can see, all's well."

"Give me a fucking break, man." But he can't deny it—part of him floods with relief. If they plan on charging her, that means courts, litigation. *Time.* Boundless time, all things considered. She will stay alive.

"We need you to come in. Now. No excuses, no haggling."

"And you'll let her go?"

"Absolutely."

Rachmann's looking at him. "Mr. Monahan," Nick says, "can I ask you a question?"

Monahan laughs. "You don't really have time for questions, Nick."

"It's the devil, right? The hand, the recording you have. It's the devil."

Monahan inhales, and Nick thinks that he'll hang up. Instead, he names an address in downtown Portland not that far from Nick's own apartment, and *then* he hangs up.

When Nick looks up from his phone, a massive, slab-faced man in a dark suit and short, slicked-back hair is standing before him. Green tattoos crawl up his collar.

The man nods and says, "Gentlemen. Mr. Goud would like a word."

They follow the man a few blocks from the station where a sleek black limousine waits at a curb. He opens the door for them, Rachmann getting in first. Nick senses his unease, notes the most minute pause before getting in, and this goes a long way toward truly scaring the shit out of him. Rachmann has been unflappable up to this point. Almost enjoying himself through all of it. Nick peers around at the buildings and cars and streets surrounding him, as if it might be the last time he'll able to do such a thing. There is a substantial desire to run, and it takes a lot to tamp that desire down.

They sit beside each other, he and Rachmann, holding their bus tickets in their hands like children.

On the seat opposite is, presumably, Herman Goud.

Procurer of the devil's eye, he's a wizened, slumped old man who reminds Nick more than anything of a vampire in desperate need of a refill. Between his knees he clasps a glossed wooden cane with big-knuckled hands, the joints bulbed and twisted with arthritis. A thin stalk of neck and a wide, seamed face. Goud's eyes glitter with amusement. He shouldn't be frightening—the man is very small and physically unthreatening—but there is something about the way he peers at them, a twisting smile on his lips, that is utterly terrifying to Nick. Like he and Rachmann are bugs under glass. He gets it, when Beverly said he made her skin crawl. He could be sixty or eighty years old.

"Gentlemen," Goud says. "Good morning."

"Mr. Goud," Rachmann says. "It's nice to meet you. I appreciate your foresight. You've saved us a trip."

"Oh indeed," Goud says, grinning, and then whips a kerchief from his pocket like a magician about to reveal a dove. Instead, he leans forward, revealing strands of comb-over amid a gleaming, liver-spotted pate, and begins coughing so wetly it sounds like something that would make Nick, were he to experience it himself, begin drafting his will. The man who met them in the station gets in the driver's seat, his form hidden behind a panel of smoked glass that separates them.

Finally, Goud, with a trembling hand, wipes at the corners of his mouth. Puts his kerchief back in his pocket. Nick understands this: Sixty, eighty, or otherwise, death peeps through the keyhole at Herman Goud.

"My apologies," he says, his voice gravelly. "The world takes on a certain weight at this age." Without breaking their gaze, he reaches over his shoulder with the head of the cane and lightly taps twice on the glass. The limousine pulls out into traffic.

"Sir," Rachmann begins, "I'll make no claims as to how you found us, but it's clear you must know why we're here."

Their windows are tinted, but Nick can still make out the tinder-dry palm trees, their rough trunks, the sky clotted with streetlights and haze, the scattered jewels of lighted high-rises beyond.

"Of course," Goud says. He locks eyes with Nick and lets out one more pressed cough, his whole body going rigid for just a moment. "The eye. *Ojo del diablo.*" He winks.

"The eye," Rachmann repeats.

"I'm curious," Goud says, "how much it is you know about it. How did you find me?"

This is said without guile, as if Goud's man hadn't just stood before them in a terminal at Union Station. Their confusion must be clear, because Goud smiles and says, "How did you hear of me, then."

"It seems," Rachmann says, "that you're known among a certain sect of people."

"As a handsome fool, I hope."

"As the owner of the eye," Nick says.

"Ah," Goud says, and holds up a bent, trembling finger. "Not nearly as exciting. No one can own the eye, young man. Don't you know that?"

"We don't know anything," Nick says. "Beyond the fact that you supposedly have the eye, we're in the dark." The limo slows, turns. Another street—stoplights, commerce, hanging leaves of palm trees. "Can I ask—where are we going?"

Goud smiles. "This is a joyride, young man."

Rachmann asks how Goud found them at Union Station. "It seems a far cry from Colina Roja. That's where we were headed."

The old man flexes his hands and then slowly wraps them around the head of his cane again. He leans forward, his eyes merry, as if this is all great fun. "I saw you."

"You saw us."

"Through the eye."

Rachmann's composure has returned, Nick has to give him that much. Nick himself is slackjawed, leans back from Goud as if what he has might be catching. The man is unwell—of course he's unwell!—and Nick figures they're about five minutes from getting dumped in the desert somewhere.

"You can do that?" Rachmann says. "You can—"

Nick's had enough. He speaks over Rachmann, leaning forward. "My mother's been taken. Kidnapped. By people who want the remnants. I had the hand, and then I lost it."

Goud nods. "Oh, the hand's a troublesome thing, isn't it? Does you poorly." He makes a face, becomes even more crone-like, cragged. Holds up those hands bent into claws by arthritis. "Did you feel like this inside, young man? Did you scrabble against the walls of yourself? Bedeviled by terrible thoughts in your head?" His accent is slight. Like Rachmann's, indefinable.

"Yes," Nick says.

"I was the owner of the hand once. As a younger man." Again with the grimace. "I kept it in a box of a sort, a heavy one, which helped minutely, but still the thoughts crept in. The remnants, they travel the world. Never staying in one place for long. The hand, mostly—it's not so much a bullet as a cluster bomb. Take the time to peruse history, explore its dark corners, and you'll see the remnants doing their work."

Nick's mouth goes dry. "What do you mean?"

Grinning, Goud says, "Surely you didn't think you were the first to become inured to a devil's sway? Why, these sorts of things have been around for centuries. Forever, perhaps. London's Brinwall Academy Fire of, what was it? 1890? Something like that. A boys' school that lit up, ignited by a student, burned everyone inside? The Halsey Slayings in the small township of—ah, damn, my memory sometimes fails me. Some small town in what would be Montana, my own home. 1816, it was. A pastor named John Halsey holed up in his church and murdered nine of his parishioners as they came in for services before Halsey himself was gunned down by the law. Chopped them every one in the back of the skull with a kindling ax! All nine! Claimed to the tenth one, a deputy, even as he chocked that ax in the man's shoulder, that he was under the devil's instruction. And those are only two off the top of my head, young man. Surely you didn't think *your* hand was the only hand?" Goud smirks. "Have you seen Portland?" He turns to Nick. "That's where you're from, isn't it? Up north?"

Nick says nothing, but wonders how in God's name Goud knows that. How he knows any of it. "We've seen some videos."

"That's the work of the hand, or the voice. I'm not sure. One of them, surely."

Nick says, "The attacks, you mean?"

"I do. Remnants have done that. Believe it."

"These people," says Nick, "the ones who have my mother. We think they'll accept a trade. My mother's life for a remnant."

Goud nods again. "And is your mother's life worth a remnant?"

Nick stares at him for a moment, the heat and anger building in him.

"I'm fooling," Goud says, a dismissive wave of the hand. "Oh, I'm fooling, poor boy. Of *course* her life is worth more than any remnant. I'd have had Gunter throw you from the car if you'd said otherwise. They're worthless things, the remnants. Parts of a devil's corpse? Imbued with a little power? They're pain-makers, is all."

The driver gets off the freeway and they come to a residential area. Gated homes, cement walls with the tops of houses peeking over the lips like fallen giants. They glide through the darkness.

"Mr. Goud, we want to buy the eye from you," Nick says, and Rachmann shuts his eyes at the forwardness of it.

"Buy it?"

They pull into a driveway; a black gate slides open and the limousine creeps through.

A sweeping mansion, turreted and black. A fountain out front. The cherub in the fountain is a baby spiked on a pole, arms aloft, and water pours from the many wounds upon him.

They pull to a stop in front of an ornate, massive red door.

The driver steps outside, opens their doors. Nick smells eucalyptus, exhaust.

Goud begins the arduous process of unfolding himself from the limo. When he's done, he stands hunched and bent, looking at them with his glittering eyes.

"There's no need to buy it, young man. I've no need for money, clearly." He taps his cane on the driveway once, twice. "Why, I'm happy to give it to you."

JOHN BONNER

Weils had been right about one thing—Bonner had had an in. It was his uncle who got him free of the Pernicio thing. Uncle Jack, his mom's brother. He's the CFO of Terradyne Industries, which had been set last summer to receive a, what, eighty-billion-dollar contract with the Pentagon? Something like that. A new weapons guidance system being installed in the majority of all U.S. military aircraft, one that would link up to Callista, Terradyne's massive global comms system. Callista had already been integrated into vast swaths of military, commercial and civilian infrastructure throughout the globe over the past decade, hundreds of millions of users, and Jack was doing a great job at threading armaments and supplementary defensive packages onto Callista's back end for whatever nation was willing to pay. Terradyne—from cluster bombs to planetary satellite communications to quick-set hemostatic blood-clotters—they had their fingers in every pie. And there was Uncle Jack, his mother's older brother, in Bonner's mind forever looking like a plant-shriveled JFK in desperate need of watering. The old man with his chin tuck and his pastel boating sweater tied in a knot at his throat, grinning through life, the unrepentant death-dealer, untouchable forever. He hadn't talked to Uncle Jack in, what, two years, before the Pernicio thing? It'd been at some family get-together in Martha's Vineyard. He'd been both fatherly and casually condescending, grinning through a brutally joyless bout of small talk about Bonner's career before he'd gripped his biceps as a way of saying goodbye and then wandering back to the cluster of other old-timers gathered at the patio bar. Uncle Jack, distant and strange, if not a billionaire then markedly close enough to it, the quiet patriarch of the Bonner clan.

His mom had heard of the killing—Bonner still doesn't know who clued her in to what he was doing in Brooklyn, and it fills him with a bright, swampy shame whenever it crosses his mind, that his mother is the one that had ultimately gotten him out of a jam. A jam that should have, at the very least, ended his career, if not set him up for a years-long legal battle that might have actually landed him a prison sentence. His *mother*. She'd called Uncle Jack in tears, apparently, not knowing the specifics, just that Bonner had gotten himself jammed up, and Uncle Jack the string-puller, with major juice in the intelligence world, a man who knew the personal cell numbers of a great many powerful people, had done just that. Called someone. And that someone had called a congressman, who called someone else, who'd called Bonner's handler at the DoD and had him transferred to ARC rather than thrown to the dogs. It really was that simple, going up the chain like that.

The choice had been made clear to him in no uncertain terms: You've just been handed a life raft. Go into dark ops and disappear quietly, gratefully, keeping your head down in the land of no paper trails. Or jump dick-first into the whirling blades of public accountability. Killing a guy at a racial justice protest? Accidentally or otherwise? You fucking kidding?

Bonner should count himself lucky Brooklyn was still standing after Pernicio died.

He'd been undercover, appointed by Homeland Security, one of two dozen feds working the protests in tandem with NYPD. The previous summer had been one of massive unrest—police shootings rampant, nationwide protests against police brutality, right-wing extremists clashing with antifascists all over the country. A hot, bloody, dangerous summer, one where things had felt real close to unraveling. They'd wanted them doing intel, Bonner and these other guys. All in-person shit, no reports, no emails. No *record,* nothing that could potentially get traced back via some *Washington Post* or *New York Times* lid-blowing article six months down the line. Keep it quiet. Relay intel to your handler and shut the fuck up otherwise.

Homeland Security wanted demographics, basically.

Info on the protesters that marched nightly through Fort Greene and Williamsburg, throwing bricks and paint bombs. For weeks they'd been out there, three or four blocks deep around Williamsburg's Metropolitan Detention Center. There was a miasmic residue of graffiti and paint balloons and spent less-lethal rounds lying in the gutters from the night before, the week before. A summer where the peppery stink of tear gas lingered all day long, until the crowds inevitably came out the next night and the cops added to it all again. Same shit every night. There was an 8:00 P.M. curfew that everyone soundly ignored. Bonner, who had never once pulled his sidearm in the line of duty, even stationed in Kandahar, never fired it beyond practicing at the range, was a jumble of raw, screaming nerves and adrenaline. Lot of guys got off on that feeling, but he'd never been one of them, and sometimes he wondered what that meant, how well suited he was for all this.

The whole precinct had brimmed with testosterone. Bunch of Type-A personalities clomping around, trying to prove who had the bigger dick. Feds and cops both. This was, pretty much, Bonner's entire history of rubbing shoulders with law enforcement summated. Law enforcement, at least the guys that Bonner worked with, viewed the protests in general as a good thing. It meant endless overtime, and you got to suit up and use a bunch of the gear that the ballooned police budget had bought. Shit was fun. And who were you up against? Bunch of communists and radicals, most of them. Twenty-year-old socialists living in apartments bought and paid for by their lib parents. Most guys considered the whole thing a win-win. At the same time, everyone kept waiting for the shit to dissipate, for people to tire themselves out. Some kind of fatigue to settle in. These people were getting kettled, gassed, batoned and arrested every night.

But it didn't happen. Every night, hundreds, even thousands of folks kept marching around the detention center, the precinct. There were, for sure, the inevitable hardcore folks—shit-starters, provoca-teurs, plenty of black-bloc anarchists, folks intimately familiar with street tactics. Folks with gear, hand signals, formations. Sure. But there was also every other walk of life imaginable out there, citizens and moms and kids, and Bonner thinks now that the other cops knew that, it was just an uncomfortable thing to recognize. So much of policing—federal or otherwise—was based on this notion of *oth-ering*. It was ingrained in every echelon of training he'd ever gone through. This idea that there's cops, and then there's regular folks—soft-bellied, dumb, sheeplike—and then there's shitbags. A clearly delineated food chain.

Bonner kept his mouth shut about it in Brooklyn, but he still rankled people. Firstly, analysts, even IG guys doing undercover work, they weren't street cops. He was considered a low dog among the beat cops and homicide detectives of the precinct he was sta-tioned in. Not much further up the chain with the feds, either. He was, in essence, a scientist, and "science" was a dirty word in pretty much every briefing room and roll call he'd ever set foot in. Bonner was barely worth the Glock on his hip to most cops, the tac vest that lay over his skinny shoulders. Sometimes he wondered if it was all worth it, all this. But if he wasn't in intelligence, he'd be doing what? Prostrating himself before a bunch of Terradyne execs, glad-handing and ass-kissing, hoping his uncle would deign him worthy of a seat at the table. Either working at Terradyne or lobbying for them. Ei-ther one seemed like hell.

So Bonner's handler would fit him with a T-shirt from a local brewery, an N95 that covered the lower half of his face, and then they'd send him out. No gun, no ID. A RACIAL JUSTICE NOW button on his shirt that doubled as a body cam, which was just the most bitter, cynical irony he could imagine. They'd run the footage through facial recognition software later, and Bonner was urged to talk to as many fellow protesters as he could. The smart ones knew a little about operational security, but not everyone in a group of thousands was black-bloc antifa, right? And if he managed to catch someone on the software throwing a brick through a window or a paint balloon at a riot cop? Homeland Security would run with that shit, and if they got a match, that someone would be getting a knock on the door the next day, catching federal heat.

Nightly he'd march, catch the vibe of the crowd. Watching as protests against police brutality were met with expansive and joyous amounts of police brutality. One night he got kettled with a smaller group and pushed down by a cop who laughed in his face and called him an antifa cocksucker when Bonner complained that his cuffs were too tight. He was put into a transport van with a bunch of other arrestees, his palms bleeding, coughing and blind from the tear gas, snot everywhere. Handcuffed, fingerprinted, sent through processing as a John Doe. Refusing to blow his cover. Eight hours in a holding cell until some cop, red-faced and angry, came to the bars and told him to get out. "I don't know who the fuck you are, princess, but your Get Out of Jail Free card just appeared. Be sure to thank the State Department for that."

Bonner had waited until they were out of earshot of the cell and down the hall. The cop was beefy, older, had a mustache and a ring of fat around his neck. A tired-ass vice cop, probably, who'd gotten some nice OT to baton protesters. He was walking ahead of Bonner.

"Hey, motherfucker," Bonner had said to the cop's back. He stopped—a few other uniforms looking their way, eyebrows raised— and turned around.

Bonner walked up to him. The guy had a few inches on him, forty or fifty pounds.

"I'm UC with Homeland Security, you fucking brainiac."

A brief flash of panic in the cop's eyes, and then something else. Contempt. Guardedness.

"And you rat me out in a fucking holding cell? You out of your mind or just stupid?"

"Look, man, nobody told me nothin'—"

"They told you it came down from State, though? Right? Huh?"

"Listen," the cop said, and Bonner cut him off, jabbed a finger in his chest.

"No, *you* listen. You ever try that shit again, I'll have your pension pulled. I can do it. You'll be sixty years old, some mall cop earning minimum wage, armed with pepper spray and bad knees. Boring the Cinnabon girls to tears about how you used to work vice." All this so unlike him, and yet here he was, in the red heat of it.

"How about this," the cop had said, and licked his lips, his eyes pinballing around the room, his fellow cops watching the ass-chewing. "How about you touch me again, I break your finger off and shove it up your ass. Fed or not. How's that?"

That's when Bonner *had* shoved him and they were separated, Bonner kicking and writhing against the cops that held him. Guesses now that he was pretty lucky it didn't go any further. He'd been processed out, his ID-less wallet and RACIAL JUSTICE NOW button given back to him, no one supposedly the wiser.

He reported the incident to his handler—who already knew about it, of course. He was the one who'd gotten him out of holding. He told Bonner he'd done the right thing, that he was doing good work. They'd reviewed his footage and gotten some good material. He was told to show up the next night. Same time, same channel.

Nothing had felt any different the night he killed Sean Pernicio.

His throat still felt scorched from gas. His palms were still scabbed from where he'd been pushed to the ground. He was still angry. The energy was the same as it ever was—contained, expectant, combative, a simmering pot ready to bubble over. Chants rippled up and down the throng.

"Whose streets? Our streets!"

"Why you all in riot gear? We don't see no riot here!"

"Say his name! Say his name!"

Bonner marched along, raised his fist, chanted. Saw at his periphery people laying stencils down, spray-painting slogans slapdash and quick on walls, on streets. There and gone, fast and coordinated.

Night fell and they kept at it. Speeches over bullhorns, the occasional squeal of static. Standing around and marching and standing around some more. Bonner chatting up the people in his cluster, trying to stick with people whose faces were unobscured. A few CS rounds were fired here and there, mostly as redirection, to keep the crowd from getting too close to any bridges or overpasses. Also because, and he'd heard the cops say as much, they wanted to get the shit over with and get home. Overtime was nice, but so was sleep. Guys missed drinking in bars after their shifts, and a lot of times these protests wouldn't end until way after closing time. Every once in a while, one of them would fire a round into the crowd just to see if they could kick-start a confrontation, get the spark lit. Go home early. It pissed Bonner off—people out here protesting, and cops throwing what amounted to giant firecrackers at them, trying to rile them up. But he'd made a career, such as it was, out of keeping his mouth shut, and this night would be no different.

By ten o'clock they'd wound up at the detention center again. The crowd was still pretty serious in size. Maybe seven, eight hundred people. Some of the normies had gone home, but there was a lot of black-bloc out, balaclavas and black hoodies, homemade shields meant to deflect less-lethals and pepper balls.

Bonner was in the middle of the crowd when he heard the reverberating sound of the cops over the LRAD speakers, telling everyone to move north, that this street had been closed. Moments earlier, they'd been told to move *south* by another group of cops, and it was in this mix of confusion and anger that a new salvo of less-lethals were launched into the crowd. Just right in the middle. Indiscriminate. Flash-bangs that sounded like God slamming his fists into the buildings around them. Rubber bullets and pepper balls. Bonner caught a beanbag round in the shoulder. It came in arcing low over people's heads and hit him in the collarbone. Fucking hurt. He spun, fell to the ground.

Beside him, a man was crouched down on one knee. Bonner, in a daze of pain, watched as he began pulling a gun out of his backpack.

"Don't," he said, and for a brief moment the man had looked at him. The edges of his balaclava were frayed; Bonner could see his eyes, see that he was unworried, patient. Filled with a willingness. Bonner pushed himself to his knees—his collarbone was fractured for sure, if not broken—but the man was already raising the pistol.

Chaos, CS gas clouding the street, Bonner retching, his vision swimming. The LRAD distorted all sound, bounced against the press of buildings around them, everything indecipherable. This press of bodies. Someone helped a young woman from the pavement a foot away, blood running in red threads down her arm, a bandanna covering the lower half of her face. The deep, menacing *poom* of the flash-bangs going off all around them. People screaming, cursing, jeering at the cops. Someone staggered by, blinded by mace, and a person gently touched their arm, led them somewhere. Bonner rose, his shoulder entirely numb, vision blurred, and ran at the man who was raising the pistol. It was a black, sleek thing at the end of his fist. *Why you dressed in riot gear, we don't see no riot here.* The man was rising, shouting something, the words lost, the balaclava muffling them. *Poom poom poom.*

Bonner kicked the back of the man's legs and hooked an arm around his throat. Got him in a choke hold, felt the close heat and press of him. Bonner grabbed his wrist, bent it inward until the gun clattered to the pavement. He held him, that arm around his neck, the man tapping at his arm, trying to scratch at Bonner's face. He had *felt* the will leak out of the guy, actually felt the life leak out, and still he'd held on. Even with a broken collarbone. Sean Pernicio's last breaths eking out of him amid all that writhing chaos, the smoke and rage and noise.

And then the inevitable: someone pulling Bonner away, Pernicio lying lifeless on the ground, the mounting fury and dawning recognition from the surrounding crowd. Someone kicked the gun away. Bonner read the faces in front of him and hauled ass, still nearly blind. Pressing through the crowd, a group running after him. He'd run all around the detention center in a veering, circuitous route, throwing his mask away in a garbage can on Thirty-third Street, tears spilling from his eyes. Doubling back and running—fucking *running*, seriously now, his heart pounding in his chest, busted arm curled up—into the Seventy-second Precinct, a building that looked like the saddest office park in the world. Running into it like a little kid running home, calling for his mother.

It didn't take long before Pernicio was on the front page of every paper in New York. Sean Pernicio: half a dozen arrests for unlawful assembly, disorderly conduct. All protest-related shit over the past few years. Twenty-six years old. An *activist*, they said. College student, taking history classes way the hell out at Coney Island, at Kingsborough. Mom was a professor, Dad a linguist. His parents didn't bankroll his rent, but it sucked, other than that, how close he fit the trope, the same party line the cops always hammered about leftists. Pernicio: Mommy's little socialist.

Except for one very important thing.

It had been an airsoft gun.

Shot BBs. Pernicio's big plan, apparently, was to ping a couple BBs off some helmets. Insane. And more, he'd painted over the orange tip of the pistol. Stupid, man. And Bonner, in the dark, amid the gas and the madness of it all, had killed the guy over it.

Bonner was *hot* on social media. Leftists wanted blood. A lot of people did. They combed whatever scant imagery was available from cell phone footage of the protest, trying to ID Bonner. Tried to correlate, triangulate imagery to get a confirmation. Online opinions were still mixed as to whether he was UC or not, and if he was, if he was with the NYPD, State Police, or a fed. Blurred images of him in his T-shirt and mask populated doxing websites and hundreds of Twitter accounts. So far, no one had named him. He wasn't a street cop, and being that he was a fed that worked short stints with a bunch of satellite agencies, he was relatively cushioned. But it was only a matter of time. There were too many people invested in finding him.

The Pernicio family wanted blood. Or so he heard; Uncle Jack had already made his calls and Bonner by then was being shuffled away from New York. The NYPD was told, in no subtle terms by the Department of Justice, that they would be taking over the investigation of Sean Pernicio's killing. The NYPD did not argue. The NYPD, truthfully, gave zero shits; the unspoken sentiment among law enforcement there was that if a left-leaning commie asshole got made dead during a protest for bringing a gun with the tip painted black and aiming it at cops, he'd earned his funeral. DoJ, meanwhile, made sure their investigation flagged. Forever. No clues, sorry, Mom and Dad. We're working on it. We'll definitely keep you posted, you bet.

And Bonner got thrown a life raft, almost against his will. Had he gone to trial, maybe he'd have won, maybe not. At the very least he would've been shit-canned, never working anything beyond a night security gig at a water treatment plant or something. But he was from royalty—defense contractor royalty—and so he got an out. Got sent to ARC. Rewarded with an agency-wide cold shoulder and a partner who looked at him like a particularly virulent strain of the plague, and a collarbone that snarled at him when he lifted his arm the wrong way. Spending endless nights replaying the chaos of that protest, wondering if he was remembering it right or adding elements to give himself a pass.

Wondering for the life of him why he hadn't just fucking let go of the kid. Why he'd kept the pressure on. Kept squeezing.

Now Bonner sits in the backseat of a Portland Police Bureau cruiser as they thread their way toward some kind of apocalypse. They edge closer to the city's heart, and the unease he feels, and senses from the cop up front, is palpable. What had started at the medical examiner's office only a few hours ago has apparently taken root. Bloomed like a metastasizing cancer.

The cop had picked him up on the highway a mile outside the base. A short blip of his siren, the trouble lights on his roof casting a few red and blue revolutions through the dark. The cop had stepped out of his cruiser with his hand on his pistol. He was a florid young man with a linebacker's build and close-cropped red hair. He asked Bonner how he'd been injured.

"Car accident."

"Where's your car?"

Bonner had gestured vaguely toward the base, then held his hands high while the officer searched him. No wallet, no gun, no ID. Pointless to tell him that he was a fed. Under the best of circumstances, he was a ghost. With Lundy abandoning Camelot, he was someone's loose end.

He'd expected more questions, but the officer was distracted, the handset on his shoulder constantly riffing a barrage of call numbers and emergencies. The cop handed him a bandage from a medical kit in the cruiser's trunk and put him in the backseat, informing him he'd be dropped off downtown. "All the medical crews are swamped right now. Ambulances are backlogged. I gotta head back to my precinct."

Within minutes they pass a burning car beneath an overpass, an actual burning car, something from a film. The flames and oily smoke rippling against the cement underside and up into the night sky. Bodies lurch and stumble near the flames. The officer curses under his breath and keeps going.

A half mile later, a semi has left a trail of debris a hundred yards long where it's flipped and gouged its chassis into the hillside. Incredibly, the semi's emergency lights still flare in the dark.

"Man," is all the cop manages.

They stop in Old Town. Scattered glass, the blat of car alarms. Another police cruiser goes screaming past in the opposite direction.

Halfway up the block, Bonner sees a foot, a leg, lying between the shadows of two parked cars, and wonders if there's a body attached to it, then takes a moment to realize that that's a thought he just had.

The cop gazes at him through the mesh screen and points north, tells him where the hospital is, and what he can expect when he gets there. None of it is good. Emergency rooms are flooded with the injured. Bonner's head has retreated to a dull ache that pulses in time with his heartbeat.

"Be careful," the cop says, and Bonner wants to laugh. Stepping rudderless into a night that smells of smoke, the cruiser speeding away, trouble lights rippling along the faces of the darkened buildings. Taking the bandage from his head—it's dried now, tacky with blood—he tosses it into a garbage can. Gunfire some distance away. A block? More? Who can say. He passes the leg that was between the two cars, and there's a body attached, but oh look, the body is missing an arm. An entire arm, just gone somewhere. The man's eyes are filled with the pooled glass of reflected streetlight. The world has taken on the surreal, hammer-strike cadence of a nightmare.

Down Third Avenue he goes—away from the hospital, just walking to walk, to feel some kind of movement—and a man sitting on the curb with the dejected posture of a drunk slowly turns his head, affixing a pair of glittering eyes on Bonner. Blood is smeared across one side of his face and darkens the collar of his shirt. He's wearing a suit. He staggers and pivots, begins galloping toward Bonner on legs that seem strangely suited for it. A thought rips crazily through Bonner's mind—the man looks like a child pretending to ride a pony. It's only when he staggers around the garbage can and comes fully into view that Bonner sees that his ankle is broken. He is running on the bone itself, the ankle bone, his shoed foot flopping uselessly to the side. The man is heavyset, balding, slow. Horror seizes Bonner's throat. He sidesteps, tries to keep the garbage can between them. The man hisses, cocks his head. Through the blood, Bonner can see that the side of his face is a galaxy of bite marks.

He turns and runs.

Back toward the heart of downtown, where the courthouse lies, the police station, the Justice Center, those vestiges of a supposed normalcy. His footsteps echo like gunshots in his own ears. The wretched thud of his heart. The dimmed world still spied through that one good eye of his, the way his head shrieks as he runs. The police station, yes. That's where he'll go.

A cop running toward the safety of other cops, a cop who believes he hates cops, doubts them, considers himself above them, above their cruelty, and that's what he will do next: Run there, seek solace there. Again.

Bonner, never as strong as he thinks he is.

Weils was right. She's always been right.

The city's lost.

It's a fever house now.

KATHERINE MORIARTY

Monahan and Willis are gone. First ARC, now these men. With the State Department, if they're to be believed.

Just her and the desk now. Her and the chair. She tries grinding the zip ties against the lip of the desk but it doesn't work. Doesn't even dent them.

Hunger mutters through her. Thirst. How the body just keeps rattling along.

Eventually the door opens, and a woman is standing there. She's in street clothes, a T-shirt and jeans, her auburn hair done up in a messy bun. There's a sidearm on her hip and she holds a stack of magazines to her chest. She's Nick's age, if not younger.

"Hey," she says. She gives Katherine an awkward little wave and sets the magazines in a spill on the table. "I can't let you have your phone back or anything, but here's some stuff to look at. Best I could do. Sorry."

She pulls something from her back pocket and gestures Katherine over. Katherine pauses, and sees that she holds a pair of shears.

"For your ties," the woman says.

Katherine walks over, slowly. The woman is careful, and the zip ties fall from her wrists, a bloodless line around each. Katherine steps back, flexing feeling back into her hands.

The woman begins thumbing through the magazines, listing the titles. Fashion magazines, news. "*Tattoo Monthly*, that's kind of cool. I don't know. Anyway, it's pretty much doctor's office shit, but better than nothing, right?"

"Why are you here?"

The woman looks up from the magazines.

"Listen, I know you're stuck here, and I know that it—"

"No," Katherine says, "I know why *I'm* here. Why are *you* here?" She gestures at the woman. "No fatigues. No paperwork, no threats. You're the Good Cop, right?"

The woman sits down and blows her bangs away with a breath. "I guess so, yeah."

"And they're watching from some camera. And after we talk for a while, you'll tell me to sign the confession. Admit to the charges."

"There's no camera," the woman says.

"Okay, sure."

The woman sits there, her chin cupped in one hand. She scratches at an eyebrow and leans back. "I mean, there's a camera, but no one's watching you. I don't know how to tell you this. I'm not trying to hurt you. We're kind of low-priority at this point." She exhales, stares at the dented table as if it might offer some answer. "We're waiting for your son, and trying to line some other things up, but beyond that, there's not much we can do. All the players involved have kind of . . . vanished right now. We're just in a holding pattern."

Acidly, Katherine says, "And it sure would help you if I told you where he was, wouldn't it?"

The woman shrugs. "Ms. Moriarty, at this point? Honestly? I don't think it matters too much."

Katherine walks over and sits in the chair across from her. She gazes at the smear of magazines across the table, the frozen gloss of them. The beautiful, rigid faces. "And why's that?"

"You don't know what's happening out there."

Katherine spreads her feet beneath the table. "Why? What's happening out there?"

The woman says, "Well, for starters, it looks like the entire Pacific Northwest's—" and Katherine pushes the table into her with as much force as she can manage. The edge of the table catches the woman in the chest and she falls back, her chair toppling. She sees the soles of the woman's shoes—waffle treads, shoelaces flying—and then hears the deep *thunk* of her head connecting with the cement floor. Then Katherine's around the table and on her, grasping at the holster on her hip, a hand around her throat. The woman offers little resistance; her eyes are dazed and glassy.

Katherine unholsters the pistol and presses it hard into the woman's ear; even now, with terror flooding through her, sure that men will burst through the door, she cannot put her finger anywhere near the trigger. Thankfully, the woman doesn't know that.

Katherine leans close and says, "How many are outside?"

"Many," she says in a husky whisper. Her eyes flutter dreamily.

"*How* many, goddamnit."

She puts her hand softly on Katherine's wrist. "Manny. Manny is outside." She licks her lips. "You don't have to leave. You're safe here."

Katherine nearly laughs. They have done all this, and now—*you don't have to leave?*

She wiggles the gun in the woman's ear. "You stand up and I'll shoot you dead."

Rising, there's the desire to press her ear against the door, to wait forever for some sign that it's okay. The Katherine of hours ago would've done it. Her hair would be snow-white and down to her decrepit, arthritic ass before she'd ever open that flimsy door. Content to wait forever, the old Katherine.

But this one?

She steps through, pistol trembling before her like some lethal divining rod. Another high-ceilinged room. Cement floors. Boxes and leaning pallets and garage bay doors, their little windows clouded with black paint. A few interior doors here and there. The stifling air of industry about it. She's in another warehouse.

Manny—someone—steps through one of the doorways, and he's tucking in his shirt and there's a gun on his hip as well. Katherine lets out a little shriek and he looks up at her, big-eyed. Reaching for his own gun.

"Stop," she says, aiming at him.

He puts both hands out. Holds them up.

She doesn't pull the trigger.

No words between them. Katherine weeping now, tears blurring her vision, the gun wobbling in her hands.

"I didn't *do* anything," she says.

Manny lifts his chin at the world beyond her.

"The door's open," he says. "But there's nothing out there for you."

She glances back, fast as she can, and next to the bay doors there's a metal door with a push bar. She walks backward and leans against it with her hip. It opens.

Katherine steps out, expecting gunfire and helicopters. Men in a perimeter around the door, screaming at her with their weapons drawn.

Instead, the night smells of rain. A city street, a boxy white moving van parked at the curb. A street of featureless office parks and garages. More warehouses. Alleyways dark with tangles of blackberry bushes. Lights shining from windows like squares cut out of dark paper.

The door clicks shut behind her. Katherine breathes for a single moment and then runs out into the world with her gun.

THE BLANK LETTERS

"I Won't Forget It"
from *All Your Wasted Days*
Geffen Records

All the politicians and martyrs
The bosses and the cops
Never taught me shit, they just told me to drop
My eyes to the pavement instead of looking up
To realize these hours are mine, not theirs

I won't forget it
I won't sit down
I won't beg for air
Even if I drown
I won't forget it, no

All the gods bent down
Down on a wing

And offered me a choice, to either choke or sing
And I spit in their eye and said, "It's the same goddamned thing"

I won't forget it
I won't sit down
I won't beg for air
Even if I drown
I won't forget it, no

Oh, how heaven grew smoke-filled
And every devil grew weak-willed
And you know, it was sorrow that I killed
Yeah, it was sorrow that I killed

I won't forget it
I won't sit down
I won't beg for air
Even if I drown
I won't forget it, no
I won't forget it, no
I won't forget it, no

NICK COFFIN

The unrelenting gaudiness of the place. Peach is a small-time hood next to Herman Goud. He's a man trying desperately to flash you his watch, whispering incessantly of his riches, Peach is, while Goud clearly has gold flowing through his sluggish blood. His house is a joyous travesty against good taste, filled with gilded banisters and chandeliers that seem destined to tumble earthward under their own glittering weight. The thick-necked driver, Gunter, escorts Nick and Rachmann through the foyer and down a marbled hall to a sitting room that's bigger than Nick's entire apartment. High-backed chairs flank a wall, a gleaming oaken bar running the length of the wall opposite. Gunter, in a gravel-laced baritone, invites them to help themselves, then leaves the room.

They don't drink, but Nick does sit. The pair of them are silent. The window looks out onto an emerald lawn lit up beneath lights, a searing blue rectangle of a swimming pool, its surface minutely shimmering. He imagines Herman Goud's wizened body in swim trunks, cutting through the azure coolness, sinking to the bottom like some kind of ancient grub.

Rachmann forever looking at his phone, leaning against the wall with his ankles crossed.

They hear the thud of Goud's cane along the floor. Nick stands up, his hands in his pockets.

Goud ambles through the doorway. He seems in good spirits, having changed into a button-up shirt and silk, plum-colored lounge pants. The nubs of slippers poke out beneath the cuffs.

"No drinks?"

"No, thank you," Nick manages. Rachmann, finally, puts his phone away.

"Industriousness it is then," Goud says cheerfully. He waves a gnarled hand for them to follow.

They walk behind his hobbling form, Gunter appearing once more and trailing behind the three of them like smoke. Nick tries to stay calm. Tells himself if there was trouble to be had, they'd have squarely arrived at it by now.

They pass rooms and doorways and other staircases. Glass curios on glossed tables punctuate the hallways here and there, filled with any manner of strange and halting things. Nick cranes his head at some as they pass.

Here is an ebony skull, lacquered and striated with gold, and resting on a velvet pillow.

Here is a small gray hand, desiccated and brittle, so different than the one that sang to him, that started this whole wretched mess, but similar enough to give him pause. A withered hand that's been chewed on by something; it too rests on a pillow.

Here is a snakeskin pinned and spread with what looks like a woman's screaming face on the back of it.

Here, a single bullet resting on cotton batting, the round flattened, mushroomed out.

Without turning, Goud lifts a finger over his shoulder and says, "The bullet that killed Igor Krishukov."

"Who's Igor Krishukov?"

Goud turns at this, smirking. "The nineteenth-century Russian nobleman? Claimed to be a werewolf? Ate forty of his own peasants before being shot through the heart by his mistress. Killed his ass dead. And no," Goud says, smiling wryly over his shoulder, "if you were wondering, the bullet is not silver."

They enter, finally, an antechamber. A carpet of black with gold diamonds. Maroon walls, heavy draperies. Dracula's showroom, Nick thinks wearily. Tired beyond words with the theatrics of it all. Now that he's here, this man seems less the evil mastermind that the woman in Venice had claimed he might be.

And yet they'd been found at the bus terminal, hadn't they? Somehow.

A trio of chairs have been set up in the middle of the room. Two facing one. Gunter, hands clasped, places himself at the doorway— Nick is not so distracted that he doesn't notice this—while Goud slowly sits down. Nick and Rachmann sit as well. This trinity.

"I'm not trying to be rude," Nick says, "but having my back to your, uh, assistant makes me a little nervous."

Goud seems so happy to have them here. He grins again. "Would you like to switch places?"

"No," Nick says after a moment of consideration. "I guess not. Thank you. Do you mind if I ask, Mr. Goud, but we thought you lived in Mexico."

"I maintain a vacation home there," Goud says, "but this, as they say, this is where the heart beats."

Nick once again marvels at their grand luck. If that's what it is.

"So," Goud says, pounding his cane once into the dark floor. "We're here to talk of the eye and its attendant mysteries." He lifts his cane and points the handle at Rachmann. "You, I imagine, are the mover and the shaker." He laughs, a wet chuckle that threatens once again to get away from him. "The hired gun, perhaps. And you," he says, laying those rheumy eyes upon Nick, "are the *invested* one. The one with something to lose. Am I correct?"

"Yes," Nick says.

"And you said, young man, that you had possession of the hand at one point, correct? One of them, at least."

"One of them?"

"Oh yes, there have been a number of hands out there. A number of eyes. Hearts, cocks, tongues, what have you. It's a removal process, you see. Part of a ritual."

"A ritual," Nick says flatly.

"Oh, a gruesome one, from what I gather."

"I did have a hand, yes," he says.

"And you gave it away?"

"I hid it. I wanted to get rid of it."

"Of course," Goud says, nodding. "Of course. I once had a hand as well—forty years ago, this was. A lifetime for you boys. And I felt befouled of it as well, and also filled with a strange lust. A madness. That's part of its power, you know? It's a cheap trinket, the hand, but a dark one. You understand?"

Nick, remembering the way it muttered at him, pulled at him, nods. "And it's a devil's hand? How?"

Goud makes a face, a flicking, dismissive motion with his own hand. "It's *of* a devil, yes. A lesser one. A weak one. Minor enough in the grand scheme, but one certainly significant enough to leave its anguish rippling through the world. From what I gather, this ritual is performed and then the hand might be imbued with . . . certain properties. Rituals performed by men who might petition certain forces. Might attempt to barter with them. Does that make sense? Yes? Now then, a question for you. Your name is Nicholas, correct?"

Nick nods. Had he said his name before?

"Do you understand how the eye works, Nicholas?"

"I just, I heard about it yesterday. This is all very new to me, Mr. Goud."

"The eye," Goud says, shifting in his seat and lifting a crooked finger, "offers itself as a portent. A window." Nick has come by now to understand that Goud considers himself an instructor. Enjoys the telling, the showing.

Movement behind them, and Nick whirls around in his chair. Gunter has walked over to a hutch and opened it. He removes a wooden box and brings it to the old man, who places it in his lap, his fingers curling loosely around the wood. The box is ornate, a golden scrollwork of details on each side, clasped shut with bejeweled hinges. The wood is oiled, gleaming. Like everything else here, it is gaudy, showy.

Yet there is no sense of darkness about any of it. The box, Goud himself. Nick senses none of the maddened swamp that the hand brought about, the blood-red howl behind his eyes.

"Here," says Goud, "rests the eye."

He turns the box to them, opens the lid.

Shriveled and dry but whole, locust-yellow, the iris a rich umber. It is simply what it appears to be: a single eye resting on a velvet bed. The optic nerve lies coiled and brittle, a pale little snake.

"Don't look too long," Goud warns.

"Why?" Rachmann asks.

Goud closes the box, smiles at them. "I was a young man when I first heard of the devil's remnants. My family has long been in textiles, generationally so, and with my father's passing, I was left to run our various businesses. I had a charmed life, to be honest with you. Rich. Young. Well-heeled. Engaged to a lovely woman. But I found myself greatly interested in the hand upon hearing of it. I had dabbled in the occult up to then, in occultish things, séances, mysticism, like that, the way one might dabble in painting. Might collect rare books." Nick, for a moment, felt a stirring, some memory—his father and his tarot cards, a cigarette hanging from his mouth, squinting against the smoke as he flipped the cards. Gold-spined books on witchcraft among his dog-eared copies of *Rolling Stone*. Goud went on: "It was a weekend hobby at first, a thing done under the belief that such things might be owned. Possessed. Controlled. Certainly not things to be *influenced by,* you understand? Krishukov's bullet, for example. *That* is an object, imbued with nothing now. Its purpose has been spent. It is a spent shard of history. Nothing more. The eye, though. That was different. The eye and the hand were less things to be owned and more to be . . . in proximity of." He winks. "And yet, I thought, were they actually in my possession, I would be the only one who had them, yes? They would be *mine.* So I pined for the hand, *a* hand, because I had heard of what it could do, and this was me as a young man trying to own an unownable thing. Which, as I'm sure you know, is like trying to snare the wind with your hand. Foolish beyond words."

Here Goud shifts his shoulders, peers at both of them. Gunter has retreated once more to the doorway. "After some significant expenditures, financial but not *solely* financial, I came in possession of one of the hands traversing its way around the world. Its power was clear immediately; within moments of holding it—it was in an ornate wooden box much like this one—I felt its effects. That kind of . . . reaching. The way it slithers in. Afloat on a dark wave. The thing is, fellows, I did not shy from it. I was, after all, young and wealthy and unaccustomed to being afraid. I enveloped the hand's darkness, even as it enveloped me. It was not an incremental thing, but immediate and bracing. I fell into madness willfully. Fell into the hand's accompanying violence. Within hours. You do understand that the hand's violence is the key, yes? Violence is its only wish. Its only *capability.*" His eyebrows raised, he looks at both of them as if gauging their comprehension. A teacher waiting for the correct answer. "I held the hand, walked the rooms of my home in thrall of it. The next thing I knew, my fiancée, my beloved Patricia, lay dead on the floor. Strangled by my own hands. I had become unrecognizable to myself! I called out to my assistant and he did what was necessary to protect me; he hid the hand in a guest house on the property, and only with some distancing from it did anything like remorse come to me. And the remorse, fellows, was a terrible thing. I found myself going out to the guest house the next morning, loss and fear and sorrow wracking through me like tremors. I tried to find it, you see. I searched for it, choosing the embrace of the hand over my own guilt and shame. Madness, I'd decided, was better than grief. I discovered the hand where it had been hidden, loose under a floorboard, my assistant himself unable to procure a spot more lasting, harried by its voice as he himself was.

"That day, he and I were to discover, terribly, *something happened* to those that were killed near the hand, who died at the hand's urging. My family's home—this was back in godforsaken *Montana*, of all places, desolate and culturally bereft as it was," Goud rolling his eyes here, "and we had our own cemetery, a graveyard tucked back in the rear of the estate. My assistant had placed Patricia in the family's mausoleum."

Nick and Rachmann are still, frozen, carvings placed in their chairs. Nick is chilled at the old man's candidness. At his willingness to admit—even years after the fact—to murdering someone, under the influence of the hand or not. Perhaps it's his wealth that insulates him from concern. Nick wonders if it's something else. Proximity to these objects, maybe. How that might burn out some integral, core part of a man over time.

"He'd put her there until such time as he could bury her. It was winter, you see, and the ground was hard as stone. Imagine his surprise—and mine!—when not even a day later, Patricia could be heard howling and clattering about inside the mausoleum. Slapping at the walls, crying out. I had by then retrieved the hand from the guest house and killed again—a staff member, a cook, a man I'd known since childhood and brained with a wine bottle, savaging his skull in such a way that there would be no returning for him. Destroy the brain, you see, and there is no coming back for them." Goud taps his own liver-spotted temple. "Not that I was thinking of such things. I was simply blood-mad, gentlemen, full of murder. My thoughts were dismal, churning things.

"My assistant—normally subservient, a man of his word—upon seeing the cook, grappled with me, wrested the hand away. It sounds pedestrian and silly, telling you now, four decades after the fact, but we stood locked in mortal combat. I wanted to kill him. Savage his body, his face. Devour his heart. But as he took the hand from me, I felt again that release, that dark cloud scuttling away. He took it from me and ran from the house, hiding it somewhere on the property this time, the intent being that I never find it again. Later that day he entered the mausoleum with a shotgun and ended Patricia's wretched half-life in there, shot her through the head. He was paid handsomely for his allegiance and then left, freighted with my secrets. Within the year, business interests brought me away from Montana. An heir, and still young, I busied myself once again with the acquisition of things. Successes. Competition. Keeping all that business with my mourning and sorrowful heart at arm's reach. My memories of the hand took on the countenance of a dream. I ached for Patricia, of course, and even as I rose in prominence and financial successes, I fell deeper still into my studies of the occult. I felt if I could *understand* the hand and its power, I might be able to deflect its impacts. Become impervious to them. I called my assistant sometimes, musingly, and asked him where he had buried the hand, but he would never tell me. Thank God. I knew if I ever found it, I would never part with it again, unto death itself. This is what devils do, you see—they make you a miser, clutching your scant, bloody riches to your chest.

"My studies brought me closer to various rumors. Rumors that the hand was but one of many elements, many parts of a whole. As if, through this ritual I had heard of, one might be hacked apart, body parts scattered and imbued with these terrible powers. Why? I don't know. But I heard tales of an eye, a foot, a penis. A heart that bent others toward your will. A head with a tongue that cackled and spoke backward and brought the brains leaking from the listener's ears. Tell me, did your hand have a tattoo of a crescent moon here, on the middle finger?"

"No."

"Was it a man's hand, or a woman's?"

"A man's."

"Ah, see," said Goud, shrugging. "Different hands. I dreamt for years of mine. Of Alfonse the cook. Patricia's cries in the mausoleum, poor girl.

"I had done well in business, and eventually devoted my life to searching for the remnants once more. They haunted me. There was no place I was unwilling to go. After Patricia, I'd never had a family, no one to tether me to the world. No interest in it, honestly. My closest friends were my assistants, and they were little more, truth be told, than manservants. With all respect, Gunter! I scoured dusty shops in the world's corners. Traversed war-torn swaths of nations, slept through gunfire, saw men die before me. Heard whispers on the wind. *Here rests a piece of the devil himself.* But again, why? Does the why of it matter? Wanting forever to find proof of this ritual one might perform, evidence, be it a book or a written set of incantations, something. And never finding it. But perhaps the rumors are true. Your hand is different than mine; perhaps there are other eyes too. Perhaps the remnants of devils abound across the earth, all doing their dirty business.

"It was in a church in the small town of Forenza, Italy, that I first saw my eye, this one here. This was only, what? Seven years ago? Eight? Gunter?"

"Eight, sir."

"Traveling internationally wasn't quite as arduous for this body then. The eye was being held there by an Italian priest who was furious at the Popehood and the Church, for they had recently rebuffed the thing as a falsehood. The priest wanted vengeance, a salve against his bruised ego and humiliation. It turned out a satchel of cash soothed him just fine. I promised him that I would keep the eye safe and he waved me away. 'There's no keeping such a thing safe,' he said. 'Safety is the least of your concern.'

"'Why? What does it do?' I asked the priest.

"'Look at it and find out for yourself,' was all he would say.

"Upon return to my home here in the States—Los Angeles be-

came my home years ago—I felt that with possession of the eye, finally, I could resolve to destroy the devil's hand. As if owning one
might cancel out the other's pull, its glamour. I was weak, you see,
still resolutely a fool. I flew back to Montana, to the family estate,
with the eye in my possession. The homestead was as I'd left it—
abandoned and cold. I hadn't been back in years. I was an old man
now. The caretaker I kept on salary—one in a long number of them—
had done fine work with the property. I thanked him and sent him
away. I hired a team of a dozen men and they ravaged the place, digging and destroying, looking for the hand my assistant had buried all
those years ago. For six months I dismantled that place and never
found it. The grounds, the house itself. Screw by screw, panel by
panel. Every pile of dirt sifted through. My original assistant, the one
who had dispatched Patricia, was long dead by then, my secret buried with him. I never found the hand.

"Did someone else find it, there on the property? Ferry it away? Is
it out there now, performing its wickedness upon the world? I know
it wants to. Or is it still buried in all my acres, hidden in some un-
turned pile of rubble? I don't know. I've told myself I have no desire
to see it again. That I'm glad it's lost to me. But I still remember how
it *felt*, you understand? That sense of glorious drowning. Tumbling
willfully into darkness and blood. To be captive to it was like willfully
drowning in blood. Compared to *that*, the eye is relatively useless."

A moment of silence then, taking in all that Goud has said. And
then, from Nick, "How so?"

"Well, the eye only works once, young man. For each that uses it,
one time."

Nick swallows. "And what does it do?"

Goud smiles and taps a bent finger to his temple again, where the
hair is thin and white. "Why, it tells you the manner of your death."
He points that finger at Nick. "And do you know what I saw, boys?
When I used it?"

"No."

"I looked in the eye and saw," he says, "the world's end. Streets overrun with the dead. Great buildings falling. Saw my own terrible complicity in it." He leans forward then, with some effort, and with trembling hands, holds out the box. He is grinning terribly, full of a dark mirth. "And I saw you two, my little harbingers of the world's end, waiting for me."

Goud motions to his assistant then, who steps forth and wordlessly hands Herman Goud a stiletto with a black handle, the blade already sprung. Nick starts to rise until Gunter puts a stilling hand on his shoulder. Goud gazes down at the blade for a moment, considering, some unknowable smile on his lips, and Nick understands the good cheer the old man has carried with him has actually been a kind of rage. Sustained perhaps for years. Goud glances at him and Rachmann for a moment, and then the old man drives the blade into his own throat, left to right, giving a savage twist at the end. Nick feels the warm spatter of blood across his outstretched hands, his knees, and then Goud falls to the floor with a gasp, his legs kicking weakly. The hand on Nick's shoulder lets go.

For a terrible moment, Goud's eyes pass over him again, and there's something there that Nick doesn't want—is utterly afraid—to see: a grim satisfaction. He reaches toward the old man, and this time Gunter doesn't stop him. But Goud is already gone.

He is allowed to wash the blood from his hands, and then they are marched through the cavernous house once more.

The night, when Nick steps outside with Gunter and a glass-eyed Rachmann, is warm and comforting and soft, and thusly so strange, like finding flowers on the moon.

They are escorted down the driveway and through the gate. Onto the sidewalk where light traffic passes by.

The gate is closed behind them; the eye in its box is held in Nick's trembling hands. He leans against the fence before he falls down.

KATHERINE MORIARTY

"**W**here are we?" Katherine, the pistol snug in the back of her jeans, asks the first person she sees—a woman walking to her car after stepping out of the bland, worn facade of what looks like a machine shop. It's night, and the woman eyes her suspiciously.

"What do you mean?" She takes Katherine in—the dishevelment, the exhaustion—and takes a step back.

"I'm sorry, what city are we in?"

"I can't help you, lady." She waves a hand and begins veering around Katherine, walking into the street to do so.

"Please. Just, what city are we in? What part of town?"

Something in the woman softens. Some understanding. If not the details, a general sense. She is hard-faced, young, grim lines already etched on each side of her mouth, but she says, almost kindly, "You're in Chicago." She points a lacquered fingernail over Katherine's shoulder. "Expressway's right over there. You hear it?"

Chicago.

Chicago?

Some industrial swath in some unknown quadrant of a strange

city; she hasn't been to Chicago in years. It was a secret acoustic tour, just her and Matthew. Well, less a tour and more an attempt at feeding oxygen to their starving marriage. A year before his death, maybe? Nick had stayed with friends back home, and she and Matthew had played a dozen select cities over two weeks, staying in Chicago long enough to play the record store, Arthur playing stand-up bass the last half of the set, then all of them heading back sweat-wrung and exultant to Arthur's town house, where three-fourths of the Blank Letters had listened to records and drunk too much wine. A reunion of sorts, lamenting Doogy's move to Europe a decade before, that he couldn't be there with them. God, it had been good to see Arthur. Then she and Matthew had gotten back into the rental car the next morning, hungover and mostly happy. Happy enough, anyway. But that was Chicago for her—the record store, Arthur's town house next to Lowens Park. She remembers the name of the park, at least.

In Portland—even without the ring around her—she has a sense of the place, an innate knowledge of where she is. She's moored to the ground there.

Chicago, though? Katherine is lost.

She thanks the woman, who nods and seems poised to say something more. To offer some help or guidance. But she thinks better of it and walks away.

The scent of rain is gone; the air now smells of plastic, diesel. Katherine runs along another block of nondescript industrial buildings behind hurricane fencing, then slows to a walk. To run is to draw attention, and that's the last thing she needs. A few panel trucks trundle past.

It's perhaps a mile when she comes to a small pocket of businesses. A taco place. A bodega with sun-faded signs for cigarettes in the windows. A cell phone store, closed at this hour. Katherine tucks her hair behind her ears and walks into the taco place, smiling at the cashier as she heads to the bathroom in the back. It is unlocked, small, clean. Worn linoleum and indecipherable tags on the mirror and the steel paper-towel dispenser.

Katherine is careful to lock the door. She sits on the toilet, pulls the pistol out. It hangs limply in her fist. She breathes, tries to calm the impossible maelstrom.

Sometime later she steps out. Stands in line, the gun in her waistband again. A woman ahead of her orders in Spanish and takes her number and sits down at a booth at the far end of the room. The place is half full. It's late. The cashier is young, with a wispy caterpillar of a mustache.

"What can I get for you?" he says.

"I'm so sorry," Katherine says, and takes out the gun. She keeps it at her waist, against the counter, so that he can see it. The boy—he's younger than Nick, a teenager—looks crestfallen. Disappointed, somehow.

He says, "Fuck, man. For real?"

"I need the money in the register."

"Fuck," the kid says again. He opens up the till and starts scooping up the bills. Hands them to her.

"Thank you," she says, taking the money. "I'm sorry."

"Man, fuck off," he says wearily, and Katherine is out the door, the bell ringing above her.

She walks quickly, still heading toward the expressway, through a neighborhood of small, single-story homes tucked behind chain-link fences. Flower boxes and brushed cement stoops and twenty-year-old cars in the driveways. Caliente music or jazz seeping softly from the occasional window, night music. Eventually Katherine reaches another stretch of commerce. In a dimly lit bodega that smells of incense and dope, she buys a bottle of water, a plastic-wrapped sandwich and a burner phone. Devours the food and water, spends a few precious minutes setting the phone up outside. She has eighty-nine dollars left, and here comes another tidal wave of resignation. There's no fucking point to any of it. Where is there to go? What is she supposed to do?

She remembers her son's phone number, and calls it, and some part of her is oddly relieved when she gets his voicemail.

"I'm in Chicago," she says. "They took me to Chicago. I don't know how to get back. But I'm trying. Call me. I love you." A shaky breath, a half-truth: "I'm safe."

She goes back into the bodega, and with obvious reluctance—Katherine has an unstable air about her, like a jittering wire sparking on the pavement—the cashier calls her a cab. When the cab arrives, she tells the driver to take her to Lowens Park.

The driver is doubtful. "That's a ways, dude. You got money?"

Katherine shows him her cash, holds it in a wad so that he can't see how many ones are in there. The idea of pulling the gun is easier now, and that ease is terrifying in its own right.

She gives him everything she has when he pulls up next to the park. She sees the town house and memories flood through her. That show at Roundhouse Records, she and Matthew actually holding hands on the way there. Thirty or forty people in the audience, taking videos with their cell phones. It wasn't financially viable, of course, but they could afford it. Playing, being enveloped in the safety of the old songs; there were times when they truly had brought out the best in each other. The acoustic tour had reminded her of that. Matthew had seemed happy. Less locked in the arms of his own shortcomings, less strange, less fear masquerading as bluster. Matthew was perpetually riding that line between arrogance and self-loathing; it was instilled in the very bedrock of his personality. But playing, man, when he played music all that vanished. Playing—even those tiny acoustic shows—he was like a conduit for unbridled rage and joy again, a man who would never need anything else.

As Nick grew older, she and Matthew had found themselves alone with each other more often, and it had felt like an anvil at times, their marriage like a weight they dragged around on a chain. Matthew and his eventual inability—his unwillingness—to be swayed by her needs. When it came to it, when it was Matthew Coffin's desire or that of his wife and kid, the motions of love that being with them dictated, necessitated, he eventually ran in his own direction. And the way it *had* been, their good years with the band, hustling for shows, struggling together, all that sat there like a ghost. Like an afterimage. Were they just bandmates who had convinced themselves they were in love with each other? Sometimes she thought so.

Up the stairs of the town house, her footsteps are hollow, quiet things. She rings the doorbell, hears it echo through the house.

A form behind the curtain. The door opens, and there is Arthur. Holding, look, a glass of wine. Undeniably older, skinny as ever, and that sense of forlorn amusement at the world is, for once, replaced with true shock. He's stunned to see her standing on his porch.

"Katherine?" He leans over and sets the wine down on an end table inside and she can't help it, she starts crying. She covers her mouth and says, in a high, pained voice, "Hi, Arthur."

"Jesus. Katherine. What are you—Here, come in. Come in, hon." He opens the door wider, and she steps through the doorway, all of her dismal past trailing and rattling along behind her.

OPERATION: HEAVY LIGHT

S/NF/CL-INTEL A-02/12—SECRET TRANSCRIPT—EXCERPT

DATE: XX/XX/XXXX

Q: Hello, Michael. How are you feeling this morning?
A: I'm fine, David Lundy.
Q: The specialists mentioned that your head was hurting.
A: It's fine now, David Lundy. I feel better.
Q: Michael, I've told you, you can just call me David. It's fine.
I'm your friend.
A: David.
Q: There we go. Listen, Michael, I was hoping, well, I was
hoping to ask you some questions. Would that be okay? I
know you've only been with us a short time, less than a year,
and we're still so grateful to you for that bomb in the televi-
sion studio last month, over there in California. I'm so grateful
for that. Honestly, Michael, I was on my way to an early re-
tirement before they put you in my care. I hope you under-

stand how important that was, the studio thing, what you've done there. The lives you've saved. I hope you understand that what you've done is so meaningful to so many people.

A: I understand.

Q: Good, good. Have you had any—Michael, I was wondering, have you had any new visions? I wanted to ask you. I know you haven't had a viewing session yet today.

A: I haven't seen anything, David.

Q: So you haven't seen anything related to the hand you talked about?

A: No.

Q: But you'll keep trying.

A: Yes.

Q: Okay. Okay, thank you.

A: David, may I ask you a question?

Q: Of course.

A: Why do you cut my wings off? It hurts me.

Q: No one wants to hurt you, Michael.

A: Why do you do that, then?

Q: Sometimes . . . well, my friend, sometimes you need motivation.

A: I don't understand.

Q: Your work is important, Michael. We need your help. But sometimes you're reluctant.

A: I believe it's wrong to hurt me.

Q: I understand. And that's something we can talk about at a later time. My question, Michael—you're saying a man will die, will "take himself apart." This is something you told another specialist in an earlier session. That he, that this man, will "petition the dark." What does that mean?

A: . . .

Q: Michael, when does this happen? When does this man die?

A: I don't know.

Q: Is it a week from now? A year? Ten years?

A: I don't know time. I don't understand it like you understand it, David.

Q: Okay. Okay, we'll work on that. We'll get people to help you with that. But what do you mean, this man will "petition the dark"?

A: He's not a man.

Q: I hear you. Okay. It's just, as scientists, we like to label things. Calling him a man simplifies things.

A: But it's untrue. He'll be a man, and then he will become something else after he dies.

Q: How does he die, Michael?

A: He dies, but he is also killed.

Q: See, you paused there. That's surprising to me. I wouldn't think you capable of deceit, Michael, but I suppose it's possible. What do you mean?

A: He will be killed, David, and he will die. But he'll become deathless too. He makes a promise.

Q: Okay.

A: . . .

Q: Michael, I don't . . .

A: . . .

Q: Does he kill himself, or does someone kill him?

A: Both.

Q: Both. Okay, great.

A: Lesser devils can be made. He makes a promise.

Q: Do you always speak in goddamn riddles, Michael? Jesus Christ.

A: . . .

Q: Oh, don't clam up on me now. How so? What does he promise?

A: When the remnants are used together, a lesser devil is brought forth. He makes a promise, and becomes deathless. He walks again.

Q: Lesser devil? I don't even fucking . . . I don't understand what you're saying.

A: . . .

Q: See, it frustrates me, Michael, when you do this. It's so frustrating to me, to my superiors. You know when some cocksucking terrorist cell has a bomb planted under a desk in a television studio three thousand miles away. You know *that* down to the floor plan. But when it comes to actually answering questions I ask you, you're suddenly mute? That I don't get. You understand why that's frustrating to me?

A: Yes.

Q: Yes what?

A: Yes, I understand.

Q: So who is this man that will die? And what do you mean, "he makes a promise and becomes deathless"?

A: . . .

Q: Jesus Christ. Who does he promise, Michael?

A: . . .

Q: Michael, who does he promise?

JOHN BONNER

Word is, they'll hit the streets with search and rescue missions soon. There are plenty of cops still stranded out there in the dark.

At some point, is the word from above. Once enough resources are assembled.

But for now . . .

For now they fire from scaffolding, from slit-windows on the second floor.

With live ammunition.

Bonner sees the chaos outside. Smoke and flame. Hears screams ripple through the dark. Figures limned against fire.

Chaos inside too, endless gunfire, the clatter and ping of spent rounds falling all the way down to the ground floor.

He sees fevered ones running through the darkness, falling on people unlucky or desperate enough to still be outside. Writhing, biting.

Bonner sights down the end of his rifle. Sees one limping along, its head cocked at that telltale inquisitive angle.

He puts the head in his crosshairs.

Readies himself. Breathes. Lives for a moment in that under-standing—at some point they have made the transition, if only in his own head, from human to monster. *It.*

Portland, perhaps even more than Brooklyn, had reeled the summer previous from the protests. Bonner remembers reading about it, had even felt a vague, stirring kinship with the Portland cops. Portland had been wracked with nightly scuffles around the Justice Center and courthouse, all of it so serious and unceasing that eventually, feds and Portland cops had begun firing rubber bullets and beanbag rounds from a latticework of scaffolding they'd erected around the interior of the Justice Center, firing from second-story windows they'd cov-ered with plywood. Protesters had called them "murder slits."

Tonight, it's become literal.

He has a perfect vantage of the street below. The fevered man in Bonner's scope, his head still tilted, staggers behind a building across the street and with something like gratitude he loses the shot. Gun-fire echoes through the building as officers beneath the scaffolding yell into phones, pass gear around, everyone still desperately trying to figure out what the fuck is going on. One thing is clear: Someone's greenlighted the use of lethal force. And if there's been any hesita-tion in using it, Bonner hasn't spotted it here. They've all seen what happens when the fevered get ahold of a person. All these guys are firing willingly.

He scans the street again, sees the chaos, the writhing shapes, fevered snapping at faces and upturned hands. Across the street he sees a woman push a guy in bike shorts up against a car. She bites two of his fingers off, and Bonner exhales shakily and fires. Most of her leg comes off in a red spray of meat and blood. She tumbles si-lently to the cement, the man falling with her, his screams cutting briefly through the sound of gunfire.

The man, Bonner knows, will rise, weeping, blood pouring down his face, and eventually some shift will happen inside him, and he'll begin seeking out someone to bite. How in Christ's name Lundy ever thought he could contain something like this is beyond reasoning.

The cop next to him—the insane, idiotic intimacy of sharing a *murder slit* with someone—nods his approval. "Was that you? Nice shot, man." He's a patrol cop in short sleeves, no riot gear. Huge, young, muscled. A gym rat with some kind of tribal sleeve on one bicep. His jaw works metronomically at a piece of chewing gum.

The woman crawls over to the man in bike shorts, shattered leg dragging behind her, and begins savaging him again. Pieces of him hanging in elastic strings from her mouth, her face gore-slicked and expressionless.

Dear God, Bonner thinks.

"Check it," the cop says, and sights down. Fires. Her head explodes.

This mad collusion between insanity and everyday life. A dozen fevered ones scramble toward a city bus, beating at the windows with bloodied hands. Faces of the living pressed and screaming behind the glass. The bus clips a parked car with a crunch of plastic and the calliope-tinkle of shattered glass. It grinds to a stop, the engine screaming.

"This is insane," Bonner says.

"Hell yeah," says the cop. "Craziest shit I have ever seen in my life." His voice is parked in that nexus between joy and madness.

The fevered find the accordion doors of the bus and push their way in. Muddied shapes rove and tumble inside. Screams, jets of blood, hands now slapping against the inside of the windows. The cop next to Bonner fires rounds into the bus indiscriminately, the windows starring with bullet holes.

The man in bike shorts pushes the woman off of him and slowly clambers to his feet. He lifts his chin and tests the air as if for a scent. For some darker knowledge of where to go. He trips over the woman's body and falls to the ground.

Bonner is one of maybe thirty people on the planet, he realizes, who has some inkling as to what's actually happening. And even as all of this is unfolding before him, there's some part of him that's still wondering if Weils meant to drop him, if she meant to pull the shot.

His head throbs. That one eye mostly swollen shut. A fevered falls out of the bus, taking a small, wiry man with him. The man has a jacket wrapped around his hand—smart—and is so far fending him off.

Bonner shoots this one in the arm. The shoulder explodes in a red mist, the arm hanging useless. The fevered man is flung against the bus for a moment, and then rights himself.

"Head shots," the cop says, casting a glance his way, as if he's growing suspicious of Bonner's reticence. That gum working, working. Cops killing people all around them.

Bonner says, "What if they're just sick?"

The cop fires again. "What?"

"What if they're just sick? What if they can get better?"

The cop doesn't answer, fires again.

Bonner says, "Who ordered this?"

The cop adjusts the rifle stock, settles, and shoots a woman in the back as she staggers down the sidewalk directly below them, amid a growing crowd of fevered that are beginning to press themselves against the doors. "I don't know, man. My sergeant just put me up here." He casts another glance at Bonner, takes in the street clothes, the blood on his shirt. The ruined roadmap of his face. "The fuck happened to you?" And then, "You a fed?"

"Homeland Protection," Bonner lies.

The cop nods, goes back to it. Sights down. "End of the fucking world right here, dude," he says, and fires again. Then looks over at Bonner, grinning.

Bonner's had enough. He puts the safety on his rifle and walks away, begins making his way down the ladder that will take him to the ground floor. Another uniformed cop sees him coming down and yells up, asks if he can take his spot. Bonner hands over the rifle, puts the extra clips into the man's upturned palms. Sweating, he staggers out of the nerve center of the building. Up on the scaffolding he hears someone laugh and yell out, "Right in the cock!"

Down the hall, his vision swimming. Cops on radios, cops thumbing away madly at their cell phones, cops layering themselves up in riot gear, preparing to venture outside. He wants to beg them to view the fevered as sick people. Which is exactly, he thinks bitterly, what an eternal desk man would think.

They hammer it into you, how there's you and them and a mile of difference between.

I just blew a woman's leg off.

Pernicio's suddenly right there, right in front of him, Bonner could reach out and feel the weave of the balaclava he wore, touch the frayed edges of the eyeholes. The way his neck lay notched in the crook of Bonner's arm just so.

He bangs into a bathroom stall and leans over the toilet and heaves, bile tumbling into the bowl like someone's gleefully yanking it out of him. Again that mad juxtaposition: the smell of disinfectant and the hollow, overlapping *poom pa-poom* of men firing guns into people on the street.

Bonner would not be surprised to discover that no one's authorized this at all—that someone merely climbed the scaffolding and started shooting, and other men, angry and afraid, followed suit.

Back out in the hallway the lights flicker and dim. Men hoot and call out to each other. When the lights return, it's excitement drawn tightly across all their faces, excitement and fear.

Have we all been waiting for this, he thinks. Some part of us always expecting it, or something like it? A clear, *easy*, blood-hewn delineation of us versus them?

A pair of double doors lead to the main lobby, the entrance of the Justice Center, manned by a trio of cops in riot gear and bristling with rifles. The men he'd convinced to let him in after telling them he was a fed doing UC work. Desk man or not, Bonner knows the language, is versed in the world these men tread in. They'd let him in, handed him a rifle. Now, Bonner stands before them and asks for a sidearm. "I gave the rifle to someone on the scaffolding."

"Cool." The cop with the clipboard nods. "Let me radio someone, we'll get you into the armory. You just have to sign out on it."

"Okay," Bonner says. "I've got to get out of here."

The cop looks up from his clipboard. "Wait, what? You want to *leave?*"

They've barricaded the doors, the windows on the ground floor covered in plywood as well. The overhead lights flicker again, with only the glow of the men's cell phones cutting through the darkness. Bonner hears the whir of a generator start up somewhere, and the lights return. The cop's face is implacable behind the visor of his helmet. "Nah, man, I can't. Sorry. There's not a chance my sergeant would let me hand out weapons to go off-site." The fevered slap against the front doors, loud and insistent. Bonner swears he can see the plywood sheets trembling. A gathering of them—a *horde* is the word that reluctantly skitters through his mind—behind that thin veneer, slapping it with their hands, ramming against it. The cop licks his lips, his eyes jittering to the doors and back.

"Okay," Bonner says. "But I need to get out."

"Dude, *why?*"

He tells the truth, or most of it: "My partner's still out there."

The inevitable change falls across the cop's face. The understanding. Bonner milking it. He's grown better at the necessary deceits. The cop hands his clipboard over to another officer and motions for Bonner to follow.

Led through a hallway and down a set of stairs. At its end lies a single door. Metal, gray, innocuous. The noise dissipating a lot here. There's a cop stationed in riot gear, finger resting on the trigger guard of his rifle, and Bonner's escort talks to him for a second before the man walks back the way they came, back toward the nerve center.

"That's the parking garage," Bonner's cop says, pointing at the door. "Street entrance is to the left."

"Thank you."

"Goddamnit," the cop hisses, "hold on." He pulls his own Glock from his hip and holds it out. "Take this."

"You sure?"

"I'm sure."

Half-jokingly, he says, "Can you give me a cruiser too?"

"Just get going as fast as you can. I don't want a lot of attention on this door, you know what I'm saying?"

"Okay."

He takes a breath, holds it, pushes the door open. The garage is dim. Cop cars, SUVs, a few civilian rides scattered here and there in the gloom. He exhales and steps out. The door clicks shut behind him.

And then he walks.

He passes up dozens of chances to intervene in attacks. Sees everywhere a litter of stilled bodies cast about on the ground. Large groups of fevered wander, snarling, snapping when they bump into each other, scrambling after the few living people they come across.

And somehow, the hand is responsible for it all. David Lundy and his grand ambitions. His insistence that he might tame something untamable.

Bonner's phone pings. He freezes, as if that sound might somehow reach out through all the other sounds in the night and alert the fevered around him. He turns and trots into a walled-in parking lot. Sliding down the side of a car away from the street, he takes out his phone, a drop of sweat falling on the screen. It trembles there like a drop of mercury.

A text. He's gotten a text. Amid all this.

A text from Uncle Jack.

Two words:

CALL ME.

SIMON OSTERBERG

Describe your possessions, Simon thinks, the words like a pounding, a very particular snaking sort of *pounding* in his skull, this rhythm in the red meat, in the meat of his brain, this one sentence over and over again, and the severed hand—the key, the very important *thing*, the beautiful *key*—bounces gray and stinking and bloodless at his chest, wrapped around the wrist and fingers with a hank of yellow nylon rope Simon has found and tied like some gruesome talisman around his throat as he strides down the avenue, snarling, a piece of rebar he's found that fits perfectly in his fist, perfect as if God made it for him, *describe* your possessions, *describe* the sleeping bag, *describe* the red meat of your mind, the blood caked at the edge of the rebar, how much damage he has done already since touching the hand, since finding it beneath the dumpster and making it his own, making it safe, since a man fell upon him sometime back and bit him in the fat, soft part of his upper arm, how his arm burns, his body burns, how he strides toward a group of people that are fighting now and flings himself into the group, blood-maddened, joyous, the sleeping bag in the mud, *describe* your possessions, and someone grabs at him as he raises the piece of rebar, his arm no longer hurting, and they latch onto the rope around his neck and *pull,* someone's fingernails graze his cheek, and the rope *snaps,* is the thing, oh, the hand tumbles to the ground, Simon stricken with panic, Simon's mouth making an O, his foam-flecked mouth, the hand falling to the ground, the rebar falling, Simon scuttling, everyone reaching, grasping, everyone falling on top of each other, Simon screaming and hitting anything he can, biting at the red river of the world, the people beneath him, the hand somewhere near, but no longer around his neck, no longer safe with him, the loss of it, the vast and unfair loss of it, the ache, Simon gnashing his teeth, having everything and losing it, *describe* your possessions, oh, describe them.

JOHN BONNER

A man is being devoured by two fevered in matching sweatsuits. Lime green outfits, a husband and wife presumably, and elderly. The old man's baseball hat has been knocked to a rakish tilt as he dines on the young man's thigh. There's a desire, yes, to lay the Glock against their skulls, end the obscenity of it, the terror, and then he remembers Pernicio grabbing at his arm, scrabbling beneath him.

CALL ME.

Nothing his uncle has to tell him will be good. Bonner imagines he knows what it is—Jack calling in his chip. Payment for getting Bonner out of a jam. Such is the transactional nature of the world, and nothing Bonner's ever experienced with his uncle leads him to believe this will be different. He owes, and now he'll pay. Somehow.

He gives the couple a wide berth, his finger tapping madly at the trigger guard of the Glock. Pushes down the urge to retch. To weep.

Smoke thumbs the sky, fires turning the skyline strange and glowing. The West Hills appear to be on fire.

Crossing the overpass at Fourteenth and West Burnside, Bonner sees that the 405 beneath him is at a standstill. Traffic in a mad scatter. A cacophony of alarms, screams popcorning from below. A straggler can be seen here and there, drifting among the vehicles. Looter or fevered or simply someone swept along by the highway's great tide of ruin, who could say. Almost directly below him, he sees a Subaru hatchback with all four doors open, and notes a pair of legs hanging from the rear right door—little legs with a missing shoe, a pink sock dark with grime. Even as he looks at it, the foot twitches, spasms, and a child pushes herself up from the seat and out into the night. Blinking and black-eyed, she flexes her little hands, the front of her yellow sundress awash in blood, her arms festooned in bites. She walks around the front of the vehicle and beneath the overpass.

Bonner understands then. All is lost.

The world has ended.

He realizes then that the hand should never have been contained—such a thing can't be, won't be—but instead destroyed. It is an abomination. And they kept it in a *box*, poking and prodding it, wondering what would happen.

Here's what would happen, Lundy.

There's the urge to sit down. Or just hook his legs over the railing and dive onto the pavement. Let gravity and the curve of his skull resolve the matter. He leans against the ledge and retches. The chemical stench of burnt plastic hangs on the wind. The cop's pistol is a small dark thing in his hand. He considers simply putting it in his mouth. But he can no more do it to himself than he could someone else, there's that same reluctance.

He keeps walking.

A car passes; the people inside scream something indecipherable, filled with mirth, lunacy. He flinches, walks on.

Bonner walks along the streets of Northwest now, the hills above him wreathed in flame. He walks among century-old Victorians nestled up against blank-faced box condos, the streets tightly packed with vehicles, the growing chaos of people running. The hospital, he realizes, is five or six blocks over. The one the cop told him was close to being overrun. He can see it, even—red brick and glass—and spends a precious, dangerous moment imagining himself going to the hospital and throwing himself at their mercy. *Let me help you! Let me bandage and stitch! Let me heal, instead of destroy!*

He hears the slap of footfalls behind him and steps off the sidewalk, pressing himself up against a building. He turns to see a kid in a hoodie just hauling ass, and behind him, a pair of fevered moving along at a decent clip. One of them settles her eyes on Bonner.

He turns and runs as well.

Running at an angle across the street, a car honking at him and jerking to a halt, nearly clipping his ankle, he makes it onto the sidewalk opposite and then realizes that he's still, goddamnit, running toward the hospital. Then comes the notion: Where *is* safe at this point? Where *is* there to go?

Up, he realizes.

One of the most basic rules of reconnaissance. Go up high. Get a vantage point.

His phone pings again, and Bonner hisses in panic, speed-walking throughout the neighborhood, eyes pinballing from threat to threat until he finds what he's looking for: a grated alcove, an apartment building's open-air stairwell.

He opens it, the accordion gate rasping on its hinges. Closing it, he latches it shut from the inside. Peering up the half-set of stairs, trotting up to the landing and craning his head to see if anyone's hiding in the rest of the stairwell, Bonner finally takes out his phone. Another text from his uncle:

JOHN, CALL ME. URGENT.

A man runs by on the sidewalk, fever-stricken, fingers grazing the gate and making Bonner jump back. He drops his phone, searching for it in the lightless alcove, and when he finds it and stands up, the fevered man has come back. He stands there, staring at Bonner through the grating.

The man wears a black T-shirt and a pair of khaki shorts that hang below his knees. Balding, a beard, Bonner puts him in his late twenties. He wears a braided bracelet on one wrist, and one of the lenses of his glasses is stippled with blood. He has a bite, teeth marks that form a near-perfect pair of crescent moons, directly between his eyes. Gently, as if afraid of being burned, he reaches out and touches the grate, recoils. Reaches out and touches it again.

They spend some time staring at each other. Bonner stands frozen, hoping the fevered man might lose interest and drift away. Instead he tries to jam a hand through the diamonds of the stairwell's grating to get at Bonner. Will he push until his fingers break? Until the skin splits? How singular is his intention? His eyes rove Bonner's face as if seeking some answer, his lips slightly parted. Bonner takes a step back and raises the pistol and the man's clouded, confused gaze never changes. Bonner takes a step forward and pushes the pistol barrel through the grating, pressing it against the fevered man's head, right inside that bite mark. And still the eyes rove about, the mouth hangs open as if shell-shocked with wonderment.

"Who's in there," Bonner murmurs.

The moment unfolds, draws itself out.

"Ah—" the man says, and then Bonner's phone rings, shrill and bright in the cement alcove, the two of them jumping minutely, each surprised, and Bonner's finger touches—hardly, *slightly*—the trigger. The handclap of the gunshot and the fevered man drops, legs splayed out, arms wide. Truly dead as anything now.

There is no mad dash toward him in his little cement stairwell. No heads swivel hungrily at the noise. No horde swarms him. No one cares. He turns, hot-faced, his throat constricting, and runs up the stairs toward the roof, toward some imagined safety.

Up on the roof, the city is a scatter of fire. Beautiful in its way. Flames sculpt the night, hang tendrils of smoke into the sky. A number of high-rises downtown seem to be fully ignited now, their lengths sputtering like candle flame. A calm but insistent rain has begun to fall.

Bonner finds that he is vastly different than Weils when it comes to killing someone, fevered or not: His hands are shaking so badly that he has to hold his phone with both hands. He sits cross-legged with his back against the half-wall of the roof's edge, his pistol beside him. Just the lightest feather-touch had done it. The man was vocalizing something—possibly *saying* something—when Bonner pulled the trigger. An hour ago, he'd petitioned that cop with the notion that they were simply sick. And now this.

Reception on the roof, it turns out, is excellent.

His uncle answers on the first ring.

"John," Jack says. "Hold on a second."

Even as hell unfolds, the man tells Bonner to wait.

Perhaps a minute later, Bonner half listening to the sounds of the world unraveling five or six stories down, trying to calm his galloping heart, his uncle says, "I'm back. Sorry about that."

"Hey, Uncle Jack. What's, uh, what's going on?" Bonner says. Only through sheer will does his voice not crack with terror.

"Well, John, things are afoot, as I'm sure you're aware."

The mundanity of this conversation. Two people talking on the phone while the world breaks itself open. "Yeah," Bonner manages, "I've got a vague idea."

"Please tell me, John, that you're not on the tarmac at O'Hare."

"What?"

"With ARC. Are you with the rest of the agency right now?"

"They're in *Chicago*?" A moment later, there's an explosion somewhere on the street below him.

"Jesus Christ," Jack says, "I heard that. You're deep in it, aren't you? You're in Portland?"

"Yes."

"Okay," Jack says. "Okay. Listen to me."

"Wait—"

"John, listen to me—"

"Why is ARC in Chicago?" Bonner says.

"John, *listen*. It was an emergency landing. They landed at the military airstrip there at O'Hare. After your director was killed."

"Lundy?"

"Lundy, yes. And this Saint Michael, he's dead too."

Cold sweeps through him when he hears this. His uncle, reciting to him top secret, SCI-clearance shit, things very few people on the planet are aware of. "How do you know this?"

"Christ, I've had my finger on this thing for a while, John. There are a lot of moving parts here."

"The hell does *that* mean?"

But of course he knows. It means Bonner's a chess piece. Has been a chess piece since Brooklyn, since Pernicio. Uncle Jack and Terradyne working with ARC. Deals being made, allegiances crafted, Sean Pernicio's death like a picked lock, a way for Terradyne to finally get their foot in the door of state-sanctioned black ops, and all the shit that comes with it. The hand? The recording? Michael? All of that—any of that—run by a *defense firm*? Christ.

"So you've just been running me this whole time," he says distantly.

"No," Jack says slowly, like speaking to a child. "You killed a man, John. *I* believe it was justified, but in this climate, this culture, the way things are, well, you'd have been fed to the wolves. We both know it. I saved you."

"You used me," Bonner says. "For what? What are you getting out of it?"

Uncle Jack says, "John, this thing with your artifact or whatever you call it, this hand, it's gone beyond anything containable. The Pentagon—well, you don't even want to hear what the Pentagon's considering right now. I am trying to put a tourniquet on this damn thing. To keep American bloodshed to a minimum, because if we don't do something? This is just the start."

"Jack, Christ, *specifics*, please."

Jack clears his throat. "There comes a point, John, where you can try to contain a spill, and if that doesn't work, you just have to accept it. Okay? You just have to kick the whole damn pail over and start again."

"What the fuck are you talking about?" Bonner says, his voice shaking.

Jack says, "There may be collateral concerns, but you know the saying. Eggs being broken and all that."

"Is this—are you talking about a nuclear event?"

"No! God, no. Again, the Pentagon, there's chatter leaning in that direction—"

"What—"

"—but I swear to you, *I* want to mitigate that. Terradyne wants to mitigate that. And there's a way to do it."

Bonner, on a roof, rain beading his hands, darkening the legs of his pants. The gun next to him, that small, boundlessly lethal thing. Hearing all this from a man he's known his entire life.

"We're in a moment of profound weakness right now," Jack says. "As a nation. What's happening there in Portland, it can spread. It *will* spread. We have to isolate it—"

"Jack, I don't know what you're—"

"We have to isolate the problem, and we have to send a distinct message to those who would be *tempted by our weakness* in this moment. Our great vulnerability in this moment. If we don't do something to level the field a bit, John, we might not be able to come back from this. And the Pentagon will move forward. Thankfully, we now have the means to do it."

"Uncle Jack, what are you—please don't do anything. A distinct message? Please, man, don't do anything."

"I want to thank you, John. It'll be alright. I'm proud of you. Your dad would be proud of you. I know your mother is. You made something of yourself. You've done your part to protect this country. You've waded through it."

Bonner, wanting to vomit at the veering, upside-down falsehood, with the pure dread shirring through his guts now. "What are you doing, Jack?"

"I'm leveling the field, son. Callista's leveling the field."

"Callista? What? Terradyne's—the comms system? You mean your comms system?"

"I think we'll be fine. And morally, I am steadfast in the rightness of this thing. But for caution's sake, John, don't answer your phone for the next few hours. Just in case."

His voice cracking, Bonner says, "Jack, what do you mean 'we'?" but the line is dead.

Ten minutes later he stands before the Regal Arms. Ten minutes is all it takes to get there; he's come full circle, back to the place that, in his mind, started it all. If only they'd taken Coffin here, when he came out holding the bag. All of this could have been avoided.

He pushes the front door of the building open. The lobby remains brightly lit. He takes the stairs, his hands cupping his pistol, the building so quiet and yet so heavy with the sense of occupation that it feels as if he's walking inside a beating heart. His call with his uncle makes him want to plow through the place, slap the walls and bellow out his name. Just damn it all. But training, it's a hard thing to slough off.

On the fourth floor, he stands at the landing and listens. For the tread of feet, the groans of the fevered. But there's nothing. He walks down the hall.

The door to the Coffins' apartment is open. The last door at the end. He thinks of Weils shooting that old man dead here in the hall-way. This spot here. Only hours ago. Bullet holes still in the wall.

He steps through the entrance and into the living room, its crates of LPs flanking the record player, the bright orange couch. Blown-up posters framed on the walls.

Bonner coming here because he doesn't know where else to go. All roads seem to lead here. Katherine Moriarty and her dead husband write this song years ago, and then Finch inlays an oddly lethal recording into it. And then Moriarty's *son* gets involved. This family irrevocably entwined with the remnants somehow, in some way he can't yet discern. He sees the threads but not the tapestry.

In Nick Coffin's bedroom he sees a laptop shut smartly on a desk, a single shoe and a Ramones T-shirt poking out from under the bed. Bonner goes to the closet, careful to slide it open as quietly as possible. Hanging clothes, a hamper. A suitcase covered with a few peeling stickers. He runs his free hand over the top shelf, again, his training drilled into him, the thoroughness, even as his mind clamors with questions. He flinches when a cardboard box falls to the ground, the scatter of papers. He stops, listens, tries to quiet his beating heart. He picks up the box, puts it on the bed. Some of the papers seem like forms, copies of paperwork—he sees a Geffen Records logo on one page—but there are others as well. Notebooks with meticulous dark ink crowding the pages. The text is small, at times veers off the paper. He squints and bends down, trying to decipher it.

I will make him a house of fever and wounds and he will let me come back—

"Bonner."

He backpedals, heart hammering, pistol flying up.

Weils stands there in the doorway to the bedroom, her arms folded. As ever, quiet as smoke. "I figured if you didn't get grabbed at Camelot, you'd wind up here at some point." Her face is soot-smeared, tears at some point having tracked their way down her cheeks. A scratch zippers across her forehead.

"There must be some reason," Bonner says, his pistol still aimed at her, "why I don't shoot you in the goddamn head right now."

"We should talk."

Bonner laughs, incredulous. "The gall, Weils. Jesus Christ. You're amazing."

"I mean it," she says. "Get that gun out of my face. You're acting like there's all this time."

Bonner drops the Glock to his side.

She says, "Lundy's dead."

He shrugs. *So what?* "As if I give a shit."

"There's a vacuum in the agency," Weils says. "Diane Rodriguez is running the show now."

"I don't even know who that is," Bonner says.

"It doesn't matter. She's peripheral. But she's got a plan, and it involves getting you out of the picture. You and Nicholas Coffin and anyone else involved in this."

"Me?"

She nods.

"Why me?"

"Standard shit, Bonner. You're a loose end. The world's landscape is going to shift here significantly, radically, and Diane wants to offer up a singular explanation once the smoke clears. We don't want alternating viewpoints out there."

Bonner laughs. "And that's what I am? An alternating viewpoint?" Thinking, *Drop her. Right now. Do it.* "Weils, listen. Terradyne's planning something."

"I know," she says.

"You know?"

"Diane gave Terradyne the recording after Lundy died."

The depth of it moving through him then. The vastness of what that means. Doors unlocking as Bonner deciphers it. His uncle saying, *We have to send a distinct message. I'm leveling the field.*

"Weils," he says. "Why?"

She smiles at him. It's a sad smile, a pitying one. She still thinks he's a fool, after all this. "For one, money. She sold it to them. To your *uncle*," Weils says acidly. "But beyond that, there's no *reason*, Bonner. You keep looking for a reason when there is none. The recording's a powerful thing, and people want to use powerful things. They'll find reasons to. They'll make up reasons to. What's the point of having a thing if you don't get to use it?"

"That's not a good enough answer."

"It's the only answer I have for you. It's the only answer there is." She shrugs. "The world—there's no coming back from this. Nothing will be the same. But Diane thinks we'll be safe."

"We?"

She shrugs. "People from ARC. The people that are left, anyway. Not you. Trustworthy people."

"Man, fuck you, Weils. I didn't ask for any of this."

"None of us did. But it's still happening."

"There's got to be a way around it," he says. He gestures at the kid's bed, its mad scatter of papers. "There's something *here*, Weils. This family, they're all connected to the remnants somehow. This kid gets ahold of the hand. His parents write a song, what? Fifteen years ago? And Finch suddenly hears it and wants to layer the recording into it? But he winds up going mad, running a bullet through his brain? The hell is that? These people, it's all connected somehow."

"It doesn't matter."

"It's *all* that matters," Bonner says.

"Diane doesn't want anything traced back to us. All of this stuff has to go."

"So you're just taking it?"

"I'm torching it. Torching the building. It's another loose end, all this shit."

"Man, all these people just pressing your buttons, Weils. You don't get sick of it? How they just run you down the line? Why don't you just shake that hand off your fucking leash for once."

Weils's hand drifts toward the holster on her hip. "And why don't you shut your mouth."

"Just *look* at this stuff with me, Weils. Work *with* me. I think there's something here."

She shakes her head, gives him that grandly pitying smile once more. "It's the end of the world, Bonner. That's as complicated as the math needs to get. It's over. Whatever's in this apartment doesn't matter. Now we just go hide in our holes for a while and wait for the blood to dry. Come out of it rich and safe."

"Do you know what they're going to do," Bonner says. "Terradyne? It's something with the comms system. Callista. I think they're going to pl—"

Someone careens into Weils from behind, a bloodied hand latching onto the pale stalk of her neck. A huge man who spends a moment—just a second, not long at all—looking at Bonner over Weils's shoulder, and perhaps there's some flicker of humanness there, some veiled and buried awareness of what he has become. So much like the man on the street, the moon-shaped bite, the steel grating between them. Then that second's gone and the man sinks his teeth into the side of Weils's neck, his arms locking around her torso. He's massive, wearing a windbreaker and what looks like the soiled remnants of a hospital gown. It's the passenger from the parking lot shootout, Bonner realizes. Weils screams, and the pair of them stagger out of the doorway in a mad pirouette. Bonner steps forward and presses the barrel of the Glock above the man's eyebrow, there near the tremendous dent in his skull, and pulls the trigger.

The man's second death is unceremonious, immediate. He falls, and Weils falls with him.

Bonner helps her to her feet. Her breathing sounds like a series of small screams. Her hand is cold. Bonner can see the blue workings of her neck, the blood pouring from the bite.

"Fuck," she screams. Her hands flex. "Fuck."

"Weils," Bonner says weakly.

"Fuck you," she screams at him. "You weak—You fucking—" Her rage and sorrow dissolve into a wordless shriek. She bends over, touching her neck with trembling fingers. Her hand scrabbles madly at her holster.

"Weils, don't."

She takes out her pistol, her hand rising.

She sneers at him. Weeping, her face opened wide with rage and sorrow, she wipes her hand under her nose and says, "I should fucking bite *you*, you coward. You fucking waste."

"Weils," Bonner says. "Weils, listen—"

She puts the pistol to her temple. A single diamond on her cheek—one more tear making that slow and inevitable trek through the grime on her face.

She pulls the trigger.

NICK COFFIN

There is a question that won't stop bothering him. He is exhausted, punch-drunk, the corners of his vision flickering with strange shapes. Numbed after the nightmare of the ending of Herman Goud. Waiting still for some other shoe to drop, some new catastrophe, even as he and Rachmann bounce along the tarmac in a private plane in a private airport outside of Portland, even as the steward solemnly informs them that they are quite lucky—the airport is now moments away from being shut down, all flights grounded, after what appears to be some kind of terrorist event downtown. A kind of mass-gassing, perhaps. The steward seems fazed not at all, though, and Nick wants that. Wants that grand luxury of distance.

The question that won't let him go: Why hasn't any of this happened before? Why only these minor events—relatively speaking—throughout history? Horrors, undoubtedly, but nine people murdered in a church is a far cry from the madness that they're seeing right now. Is it just a matter of population density? The hand doing its work in rural settings versus a city? How is this only happening now?

The eye, if Goud is to be believed, holds little sway over the owner. More an oracle, offering some vision of what's to come. And this eye at least has been held by Goud for a number of years. Contained.

The hand is different.

He looks over at Rachmann, who no longer grips his armrests now that they're on the ground. They've spoken little of Goud's death in the hours since it happened. To speak of him would be to invite the old man aboard the juddering plane, and Nick's world is already weighted to the brim with death. He cannot get the image out of his mind—the light-kissed stiletto, the jet of blood, that brutal twist at the end. The way Gunter had simply walked them outside.

"Do you believe him?" he says. "Goud?"

Rachmann eyes him. "About what, Nicholas?"

"That there's been more than one hand? What did he say? That it's part of a ritual?"

Rachmann frowns. "I don't know. I wish I could say. I don't see why he would lie about it."

"And why is all this happening now, if the hand only does small-time shit? You know what I mean? Murders and fires are bad, but this . . . this is something else."

"Yes."

"Like, what ritual? And how," Nick says, laughing again at the incredulousness of it, "is my mom involved in all of this? How is this all somehow about a song my parents wrote when I was a kid?"

"Beyond the notion that a devil might be a prankster? Like watching bugs burning under a magnifying glass? I couldn't say. I wish I knew."

The plane slowly taxis to a stop, stars salting the sky through tattered clouds, lights burning along the runway.

Their section of the airport seems abandoned. Few customers, staff that seem terse and on edge. Nick swears, in the walk from the plane to the terminal, that he can smell smoke in the air. The eye sits in its box inside his bag. Inside the terminal, he and Rachmann speak to the woman at the front desk. Rachmann, who saw a man slit his own throat only hours ago, now says something that makes the woman laugh and cover her mouth as she calls them a cab.

Nick refreshes Twitter on his phone. Portland is trending—an unending stream of chaos unspooling. Law enforcement is trying unsuccessfully to form some cordon around the city. A curfew has been called, though it's obvious no one is adhering to it. The event's bloomed from downtown—if that's where it actually started—and moved beyond.

They stand at the windows, their own sallow ghosts reflected back at them.

"Cab will be here in a moment. Though if I'm to be honest with you, Nick, I don't know where to go. I feel as if we're jumping into the lion's mouth."

"Rachmann, man. If you want to bail? There's no obligation."

Rachmann surprises him—he looks shocked. "What? No, Nick. That's not what I meant. I am invested."

"I can't give you the eye."

Rachmann with his hand to his chest. Maybe he actually is offended. Nick's too tired to even guess anymore. "I wasn't asking."

"It's the only thing I have of any worth. If it comes to that. You know?"

"Of course. Please understand me—I don't want it."

The bright red and blue lights of some emergency vehicle out there, cutting through the night's ink and then gone again. Moments later, a pair of headlights appear, and a yellow taxi rolls up in front of the terminal doors. A man dips his face down and peers at them through the passenger window.

They slide into the backseat, and Rachmann casts him only the briefest glance when Nick gives the driver an address.

The driver is reluctant. "That's, like, right downtown, man. That's right in the middle of it."

"Okay," Nick says. "How close can you get?"

"The cops are getting roadblocks and shit set up."

Nick waits him out. He's a young kid, a gold bracelet on his wrist;

the car smells of something fruity, a tinge of cinnamon—he's doused himself, or the car, in body spray. Finally, the driver sighs. "I think I can get you in past a checkpoint, but I'm wanting the money up front. Triple rate."

Rachmann hands him some bills.

It is a quiet ride through the mouth of hell.

As they come closer to the city, Nick finally sees what it is that has thrown him so badly—vast sections of Portland's skyline have gone dark. Sections of city light just absent, like missing teeth in a jawline. The highway is an origami of cars deadlocked or abandoned. At one point the driver eases the taxi onto the shoulder and in the weak light someone slaps the trunk in passing. Nick nearly pisses himself. Has no idea if it's a furious pedestrian or a blood-maddened one.

Through a stretch of tunnel—the lights above mercifully still on—the taxi slows, easing its way through the maelstrom of stalled vehicles. Nick sees a woman lurch right in front of them, bending over the hood accordion-like. The driver doesn't stop. She folds and claws at the glass. Raven-haired, a horrible road-rash peeling the right half of her face down to yellow bone, she drools and snarls against the window, smearing it with blood and sputum. With a kind of horrified hyper-awareness, Nick sees that she is missing finger-nails, the bones of her fingers clearly broken, bending backward against the glass as she slaps and scrabbles at them. Nick feels his gorge rise, looks away. The driver curses and honks his horn, still creeping along.

"Any of y'all got a gun? Goddamn."

Neither he nor Rachmann says anything.

"Wish someone would shoot this motherfucker," the driver mutters. It's the same thing that Nick has witnessed on the viral videos he's watched on Twitter and YouTube—how quickly the horror turns to annoyance. Perhaps, he tells himself, it's shock. The fear buried underneath it all. Perhaps not. Perhaps this ferocity, this casual cruelty, has always been there.

By the time they make it out of the tunnel, the woman is still hanging on the hood. She grasps a windshield wiper and pries it off.

"That's it," the driver hisses. He stops the taxi.

"Don't do it," Rachmann says.

The driver ignores him, jumps out and begins punching the woman. She makes no attempt at blocking the strikes and instead begins grabbing at his arm, snapping at it with her teeth. Nick knows what's going to happen. It's telegraphed. The stupid inevitability of it is written in the stars. Within seconds, she's latched onto the man's wrist and clamped down on it. The driver yowls and rips his arm away. He pushes the woman off the hood and the two of them fall to the asphalt. It's only then that Nick becomes aware of the night's sounds—gunfire and screams, the rib-cage-heavy thud of what sounds like dance music being played somewhere. Sirens, always.

He looks at Rachmann. "We can't take his car."

"He's dead. He's a dead man. You know what happens."

"I can't do it."

Rachmann closes his eyes and folds his hands together for a moment. "Fine. But Nick, please understand, the rules are not the same right now. Perhaps never again."

"I know."

"I hope you do."

They step out, Nick with his bag cinched tight around him, legs thrumming with fear. They make their way through the city as it shivers and howls through its transformation. Behind them, they hear the driver scream and call out for his mother. He sighs, then, or perhaps it's the woman sighing. Or maybe, Nick thinks, it's just the sound of the wind sloughing through the spaces between buildings, the spaces of the world. The city itself turning into something else.

It's a half-mile journey or so from the taxi—gauging distance is tough with everything like this—and yet they see only furtive movements, hear only the random blat of car alarms and emergency vehicles, the distant echo of gunfire. A fire truck grinds slowly down the street past them, at times gently clipping abandoned cars, the men hanging from its sides still and solemn as ghosts. The air is full of smoke.

They walk gingerly over bodies flung like trash in the street. The humped shape of a man half in the road, knuckles grazing the pavement, mouth open. Eyes half lidded, lips pulled back, as if bracing for the impact of death's arrival. And the stunned manner in which he and Rachmann become inured to it, or at least mute. How they see the hunched, furtive shape of a man—or a group of people—coming down the street and they calmly backtrack, or turn a corner, slide down an alley.

Once, a single bullet ricochets off the pavement somewhere near them, a *zing!* that fills Nick's inner ear with its insectile whine, and they both pivot on a heel without even looking at each other, running back the way they came. A sniper of some sort, stationed in some upper floor, firing down at people. Or an errant shot from someone blocks away firing at something else entirely. Who could say.

They come upon a man with filthy matted hair and a green peacoat who dips his fingers into a tube of potato chips in front of a convenience store, its window a blue spill of pebbled glass behind him. A six-pack sits at his feet. He chews, holds out the cylinder as they pass.

"No thank you," Nick says, a moment later wanting to cackle madly at the ingrained response. The societal niceness of it, even as the world upends itself.

They walk to the Regal Arms.

In the lobby, they stand there listening. There is no sound save for the distant pneumatics of something—riot-control munitions, explosions—that comes through the glass.

"I'm on the top floor," Nick whispers.

"I'll follow you."

They take the stairwell. The press of the paint-lacquered walls, the faint, closed-in smell of the carpet. He pushes through the doorway that takes them to the top floor landing. The hall splits in a T. Nick looks both ways, listens. They could be the only people in the world. No television sounds bleeding through a door. No radios, no murmur of conversation.

The police tape is a yellow snarl on the hallway carpet.

His apartment door is open.

Nick hears something inside—the unmistakable rattle and snap of papers being shuffled. He looks over his shoulder—Rachmann's heard it too.

What to do. Step inside or keep running.

It might be Katherine, he thinks. It's not impossible.

And isn't the whole point to come back here? To see what there is to see? Why else thread this maelstrom?

Nick steps inside and in the living room, sees the body of Hutch Holtz splayed out on his back, the top of his skull a wet pulp, a halo of blood leaching into the rug. He takes another step, cold flushing all through him, and sees the body of a woman he doesn't know, flung in a similar pose.

There's a man standing in Nick's bedroom. He's holding a sheaf of papers in his hand.

Matthew Coffin's archives are spread out over the bed.

The man looks up and lets out a shaky breath when he sees them. He has a pistol in a holster at his hip, and another gun in his waistband. His head is bloodied, one eye nearly swollen shut.

"Nick," the man says. He runs a hand savagely down his filth-caked face, wiping tears away. "Nick, tell me, how did Matthew Coffin die?"

KATHERINE MORIARTY

Arthur has grown wealthy in the years since the band split. Wealthy enough to own outright the town house she's currently sitting in, no easy feat in Chicago these days. Katherine sits primly on the couch while Arthur is upstairs, seemingly unconcerned about her "dropping by," though it's the middle of the night and they've hardly spoken since the record store show years back and she's *clearly* fucked up right now, obviously in some kind of distress. But their relationship has always been like that—a switch flipped, and it's like no time has passed at all. And fucked up is nothing new for either of them, is it? Katherine's always cherished Arthur's easy grace.

The band's platinum records hang framed on the wall and she walks over to them. Like Katherine, Arthur has landed regular work scoring films and television series. Unlike her, his jobs are varied and successful. It's afforded him a strange kind of continued celebrity. He is famous enough—his fame *varied* enough—that he's invited as the half-ironic judge on cooking and quiz shows. A guest on popular music history podcasts. Where Matthew is revered, Arthur has become uniquely beloved. While Katherine's moored herself to one place, chained herself to time and its bevy of old and immovable ghosts, Arthur has breathed, stretched, shirred his hands along the grasses of the world.

He comes down in a Replacements T-shirt with a hole at the collar and a pair of jeans, slippers. Freshly showered. His thinning hair combed, a spot of water on his glasses.

"I'm so sorry to bother you, man," Katherine says. Even with all that has happened, it's true.

He scowls. "What? No. Jesus, Katherine. Not a big deal. I'm happy to see you. You want something to drink?"

The kitchen holds a stone-topped island, chrome everywhere. Arthur opens a shelf above the sink and pulls out a bottle of whiskey, turns and holds it up. She nods, and he pours them each a generous amount in a pair of tumblers.

"Ice?"

"Sure. Please."

They stand there for a moment, each with their drink held to their chest, their shared history strung between them like an acrobat on a line.

She wants to tell him something—all of it? the bare minimum?—but can't quite get there yet. Instead, she makes a show of looking around the kitchen. "You have done *very* well for yourself, Arthur, damn. You're a man with marble countertops, good lord." Katherine making small talk with a pistol in the back of her jeans. A dead man's blood on the soles of her shoes. Jesus Christ.

Arthur grins. "Remember when we stayed at that guy's house in Murfreesboro? Probably the second tour? And he had that coffee table with all those human teeth lacquered onto it? Shit was nuts."

She grins. "And now you're all, 'Buy a new sink, you say? Why, I'll take the chrome fittings, please.'"

Arthur rattles the ice in his glass. "It's the horror movies that did it."

"What's that?"

He gestures expansively at the kitchen, the house. "I do a lot of scoring—intro pieces, set music—for some horror franchises, a couple of 'em, and it seems like there's a new movie every month. I'm busy, dude."

"And there was that alien movie," she says, surprising herself with the fact that she's remembered it, "with Brad Pitt. The alien abduction one."

"*The Long Way Home,* yeah, I lucked into that one. And you do *Bad Luck Gun,* right? What is it now, the fifth season?" And this is Arthur—excited, excitable, but never gutting with his own accomplishments. Never using them as a bludgeon. It's a shame that she's dropped off the face of the world like this. It's good to be among the people that know you. My God, she thinks, the bitterness suddenly threatening to overtake her. The years I've wasted. The endless, pointless morass of it. Ah, Arthur. Goddamn, I missed you.

"Something like that," she manages. "Yeah."

He gestures toward her, a kind of *Look at this!* gesture, and says, "Katherine! I do have to ask, what the hell, what brings you to town? What brings you by?" He is gracious enough, she understands, to give her this. To give her an opportunity to offer him her own story, now that she's arrived unannounced, disheveled, with a clear panic in her eyes.

"Honestly?"

"Well, yeah."

"Arthur, I'm in some deep shit," she admits. She laughs a little, looks away.

He nods at the floor, sips his drink. "You never had much of a poker face, Katherine. You want to talk about it?" He puts out a hand like a traffic cop. "Let me rephrase that—*can* you talk about it?"

"I don't think you'd believe me," she says, the whiskey suddenly catching up with her. The whole mad circus of the preceding days. She realizes that she's putting him in danger by being here.

"Maybe not," Arthur concedes. "But we've been through some weird shit together, Katherine."

"This is true."

Arthur clears his throat and says, "I still dream of him, you know."

For a moment, Katherine isn't sure who he means. But then she understands. Of course. "Me too," she says.

He looks up and away and the light catches the lenses of his glasses, a gesture she is so familiar with. It turns him into the kid she knew—twenty-three years old and just beating the living hell out of his bass. Strutting around, leaping. Just an animal. "The guy," Arthur says now, speaking of Matthew Coffin, the father of her only child, the man she pledged a lifelong allegiance to, bound the twined strings of her heart to, "could be a real fucking asshole. Could be great sometimes, but also just a monumental asshole."

Katherine smiles. "Agreed."

"But there was something about him, wasn't there? You know better than anyone. Just this, I don't know. Magnetism. Charisma. Right?" He looks at her, gestures past his own foolishness with a wave of his hand. "Of course you know."

And she does. Matthew Coffin drew people to him. *Magnetism* was the right word. His mercurial mood swings, his insecurities, his callousness and bottomless self-concern—it all evaporated against the spotlight glare of his boundless charm. And he had loved her once, loved Nick. She believes it. Matthew Coffin's death had been a surprise to everyone, if only because it seemed that a man who loved himself that much would never willingly die.

"I know," Katherine says. "I'll find myself thinking about him, and then I'm like, 'Goddamn, he was so good to me sometimes, so good to us,' and then that starts a whole cycle of thinking about him all over again. It's just this . . . it's a loop."

Another moment of standing silently, the pair of them moored in the past, strangely peaceable enough, sipping their drinks. Arthur steps into the living room and puts something on; Archers of Loaf's *Icky Mettle* begins punching its way out of speakers tucked away somewhere in the kitchen. He comes back and refills her tumbler.

"He went to some dark places after the band split," Arthur says, and Katherine finds herself nodding.

"Hell yes, he did," she says, her voice loud in her ears. She puts her hand out, steadies herself on the island. "You don't even know, man. The shit I saw those last few months."

Things she's never told anyone.

Arthur looks up at the ceiling, as if some answer might be etched there. She sees the old-man lines in the meat of his throat and feels a vast tenderness toward him. He says, "I thought he'd turn inward, you know? When he got down like that. Thought he'd go all alt-country and shit. Write a singer-songwriter album, leave us all in the dust. But just going dark, not making anything? Not writing music? Depression's a hell of a thing, man. I called him, did I ever tell you that?"

"You called him? When was this?"

Arthur frowns, thinking. "Maybe . . . a couple weeks before the accident? Before he, you know." He gestures loosely with his tumbler, signifying everything.

"What did he say?"

"I mean, I was kind of drunk. Really drunk, honestly. Going through my own divorce with Michelle and all that, and just feeling, you know, down. Wanting to hang on to something that had felt right, you know? Just wanting to bask in the good stuff a bit. So I called him, and it turned out to be kind of a shitshow. He said you'd kicked him out."

"I did," she says, unflinchingly. Daring him to say something about it, to place any sort of blame at her feet. But that wasn't Arthur's way, never had been.

"Yeah, he was . . . he was not terribly lucid, honestly. Not drunk, just . . . dreaming, almost. Sleepy. Like he was on downers. He said he was living in a loft in the Pearl District, and that was pretty much all that I got out of him that made any sense."

Coldly, with a strange sense of detachment, as if staring down at herself from the ceiling, Katherine says, "What else did he say?"

Arthur looks up at her with his watery eyes. "He said he was getting into some crazy shit. Those were his exact words. He laughed, but it didn't sound happy, and he was like, 'I'm into some crazy shit right now, Arthur. I got the pull after me.'"

Katherine's mouth goes dry. A dread stir of recognition running through her. "The pull?"

"Hell, you remember the pull, dude. Remember how he talked about wanting to record *Knife Wounds* in New Orleans when everything started to fall apart for us? When we just couldn't get anything down, demo-wise? Matthew wanted all of us to move there for a few months, just throw ourselves into the songs? 'New Orleans has good pull,' he'd say."

"He loved New Orleans," she said, panic starting to rise up in her, uncoil itself. "We talked about moving there for good after Nick graduated."

"And remember how we were on tour there when that *Rolling Stone* interview came out? And Matthew was just *pissed,* thought it made him look like a dumbass, and he got wasted and paid that witch we met on Decatur Street to hex the writer? Remember that? How she didn't want to at first—she kept saying he was running down a dark road or something—but then he just kept dropping bills on her table until she said yes?"

"Vaguely," Katherine says, remembering every last moment of it.

"And he always talked about the *pull* that places had. Not even cities, just places. Venues and shit too. Bars. How New Orleans had pull, or this hotel room had pull, just this idea of possibility inside him. Like, to him, it was the quality of a place's energy or whatever, right? Its luck. The sense of, I don't know, lightness about the place. He'd always been into his occult shit, even back when we were in LA." Arthur swirls his drink around, his face brightening, the clink of ice against the glass. Oblivious to the horror mounting inside of her. "Remember, like, six months after we got together, when we all went to that party in Glendale and that woman who'd died for seven minutes or whatever was doing séances in the living room? And the ghost they were talking to levitated that ashtray and everyone got too freaked out except for him? And then it was just the lady and coked-up Matthew doing the Ouija board with everyone else watching from the kitchen and the fucking, the thing was just moving so fast and going *Yes, No, Yes, No* to all their questions. And then Matthew, because of course he would, he asked the ghost, 'Am I destined for great things?' and the little piece, the planchette or whatever, went right to *No* and Matthew threw his arms up and said—"

"Fuck you, chickenshit," Katherine says softly.

Arthur beams. "Fuck you, chickenshit, exactly, and then the sliding glass door just exploded, and all that glass went all over that one dude, how he got all cut up? You remember what Matthew said when we left?"

"Good pull," Katherine answers.

Arthur smiles. "Hell yeah. 'That party had good pull.' And then you guys had finally reached this impasse and he'd moved into his buddy's loft for a while—"

"Yeah," Katherine manages, cold again.

"—and he said that the *pull* had followed him this time. That feeling, but it had flipped. Become this dark thing, rather than a good one. How it was, like, I don't know, *pressing* on him sometimes. How it had been beautiful, this sense of widened possibilities, but now it was turned on its head."

"Was it—did it come from the loft? This feeling?"

"That's what I asked him! But he said it was a feeling that had started back when he was at the house. Your apartment. Had been with him for a while. He said it was like a cloud that followed him around. Said it was getting worse. He was having terrible dreams. Hearing shit." Arthur blinks, a little stunned, and runs a hand slowly over the crown of his head. "Goddamn, it sounds terrible when I say it like that. Pretty much a textbook cry for help, right? He just seemed exhausted, though, you know? And I was just like, 'Cool, talk to you later, man. Go make up with your wife. Go break some guitars and write some country songs, you'll be fine.'"

"He wasn't depressed, Arthur." She says it plaintively, the alcohol singing through her blood now.

"No?" He looks up at her almost hopefully, wanting, perhaps, to slough off such obvious ownership of Matthew's death. One of the last people to speak to him, and he had missed the signs, or ignored them outright.

"No," she says. She lifts the tumbler to her lips, clacks her front teeth against the glass. She hasn't eaten or slept since when? It all wants to come flooding through her, all of Matthew's dark history, the rage, his seething silences. The darkness he flung himself into at the end. All that he saddled her with.

"I mean, he was depressed. He was on that bridge, yeah. But there was something else going on," she says.

Arthur gives her a look.

"I'm serious," she says. "This *pull* you talk about. You don't . . . you don't know the whole story."

He nods at the floor. "People do unthinkable things when they're that despondent, Katherine. It's heartbreaking."

It's the same argument she's always heard—Doogy had said the same, her mother, even Nick, convincing himself of it with that righteous surety that teenagers armor themselves in. Matthew was depressed, they said. But Katherine knows. What had happened to him, it was something else.

Something toothed and insistent.

Something bloody.

And this notion of a *pull*; she understands now.

Lightness, turned on its head.

Lightness, turned upside down.

Something drawing itself toward him.

The day before Matthew died, she had said goodbye to Nick when he left for school and then gone to see her estranged husband. Seeing what the split was doing to her son, she felt obligated to try. If not reconcile entirely with him, at least talk. She remembers Nick that morning with his backpack hanging off one shoulder, a fifteen-year-old boy quiet and withdrawn, skinny and bezitted, lonely as hell.

His parents in the midst of a terrible, acrimonious separation. She had finally told Matthew to leave the apartment three months before, had told him that he was no longer welcome, that she no longer felt safe with him. His erratic behavior. His anger. The way he was withdrawing into himself.

"I don't know who I am anymore," Matthew had admitted to her in a brief moment of clarity.

"I don't either," said Katherine, and he'd left. Agreed with her and left.

She went down to the Pearl that morning, that final look Nick had given her when he'd left the house still sending acid down her throat. Another reason to scorn Matthew—that the boy blamed *her* for his absence.

At first, she'd thought Matthew wasn't home. The loft was in an industrial section of the neighborhood, everything repurposed and modernized, and she could hear her knocks reverberate through the steel door. A part of her was grateful—there were things to do today, errands to run. Laundry, a trip to the pharmacy. The Dustbins, a local band she'd taken a liking to, were playing the Ash Street Saloon that night, and she wanted to go. Maybe Mr. Contrallo could pop in, make sure Nick wasn't huffing glue or setting the furniture on fire. Knocking on the door again, she felt like this might be a good thing in the long run. How long had she petitioned him for his love back? For him to become the man he'd been years before? Hadn't she exhausted herself with it? If he was unwilling to change, wasn't it better this way?

Perhaps she could be free. Perhaps such a thing was possible.

And then Matthew Coffin, her husband, the father of her child, her bandmate and lifelong but woefully mercurial friend, had opened the door wearing dark sunglasses. Shirtless, his chest stippled in blood. Everything had changed in an instant.

His hand had latched onto her forearm. He pulled her inside— not violently, but insistently—and shut the door behind them.

"Matthew, what the fuck—"

"Katherine," he said. "I'm so glad you're here." The loft—all cement and repurposed wood and soft, pastel-painted walls—smelled fetid and closed in, and in the dim light of the lamps scattered throughout the place, she understood why: There was a pool of blood in the middle of the floor. Larger than a body, its edges smoothed and unblemished. As if it had just been poured there. The rich animal scent of it filled the place, in strident combat with Matthew's own unwashed press of body odor and filth. She felt her gorge rise, found herself looking around for the cause of the blood. Its owner. Katherine saw her own horrified face in the lenses of his sunglasses.

He said, "Katherine, I need you. You and me, listen, I'm working on it, I'm close, it's not too late—" He put his hand over hers again and his skin was hot, hot.

She took a step back and shook him off. He wore a pair of ragged boxers, the waistband soaked in blood. Always a thin man, the three months he'd been gone had turned him emaciated, skeletal.

"Matthew, what the fuck is going on? Why is there—Whose blood is that?" Her voice was shrill, taking on a knife-edge of panic.

He waved her away, as if she were asking the wrong questions. "It's not mine, don't worry, it's a *key*, Katherine. It's just a *key*, and if I do this right, if I do this, everything can be better."

The acrid stink of chemicals on him. Dope, exhaustion, paranoia. Probably all three.

The disgust on her face, she could feel it. The confusion and fear. He held up a hand to stop her and turned, and that's when she saw the runes carved into his back. (It was not until months later that she would wonder *who* had marked him that way. Matthew certainly couldn't have done it to himself.) She saw an eye carved there, and what seemed a cloven hoof. A cross inverted. Illegible words, or perhaps crafted in some more archaic tongue. His narrow back a transmission station. She retched, brought a fist to her mouth.

"Listen," Matthew had said, sounding almost like his old self then, and he walked away from her, directly through the pooled blood on the floor, leaving long, smearing footprints. He went to a dented aluminum pot that rested on a nightstand next to his bed and reached in, coming back to her holding something cupped in his hands, hands that were gloved in blood now, and Katherine for a singular, flare-bright moment was reminded of his eternal boyishness and charm, his excitement. The way those long fingers could play a guitar, could touch her.

"Katherine," he said, "I have done so much shit wrong in my life, gone down so many wrong paths, and I know that you and I, we're done, I've fucked it up, I know it. My, my distancing, my rages, my ego, looking at Nick as a, as an anchor, how I'd just leave sometimes, leave the house and not come back for a few days, not answer my phone, I know it—"

"Matthew—"

"—my infidelities and running around, my, just my fucking *boundless* resentments toward you and the kid, all this shit, Katherine, it's insurmountable, you know—"

"Matthew, stop it," she hissed, weeping.

"—there's no coming back from it, the hate in me, the two of you just dragging me down endlessly—"

A single black rill of blood trekked slowly down the drawn valley of his cheek, beneath the lens of his sunglasses down to his cracked lips. Katherine still, frozen, rooted to the ground. Her voice had broken with a single sob of terror. She'd whispered his name, almost like a question.

Matthew kept on.

"But listen, I can do this right, is the thing, I can do it *better* this time—" and he had opened finally the cupped bowl of his hands, and an eye had rested there. Her husband gingerly cupping an eyeball in his blood-slicked hands, and Katherine had screamed her loudest scream, her shrillest scream, a scream that might empty that moment of its meaning, that might walk her back from what she had just seen. Matthew, still holding the eye with one hand, had taken the sunglasses from his face with the other, and of course it was *his* eye he held, his own eye that he—or someone—had taken from his head.

The red-rimmed socket still weeping that single line of blood. He had looked at her with his little-boy smile, and said with an earnestness that promised to haunt her life forever, to decimate her, "The hand, the tongue, the eye, Katherine. The hand, the tongue, the eye, all these things used at once, brought forth at once, and we might do this *again,* you and me and Nick, and *better* next time, do it *right,* He's promised me, He's promised I can come back, and I'll be *different* and *changed* and *better* than I am now," the words coming faster, and the eye in his hand had *moved,* had *moved* there in the cup of his hands, the eye casting its sight upon her, animated now with its own dark and terrible life.

She had run screaming from the building, the dreary gray street outside like a baptism, like a door shutting forever.

The eye had moved in his hand.

Had gazed upon her.

Matthew had leapt from the bridge the next day. Witnesses had seen him step calmly over the railing and leap. His body had been dredged up three days after that. It had been gnawed at by things beneath the water. She had been allowed to see the medical examiner's report. The body was greatly damaged, chopped up by a motor at some point, presumably. His back still carved in those markings. Toxicology reports were made more difficult for the body being in the water.

One of his eyes was missing entirely, the optic nerve cleanly cut. A hand removed at the wrist. Tongue severed. None of those pieces were found at the loft. Found anywhere.

The police considered Matthew Coffin's death a murder investigation until they reviewed footage of him stepping over the railing of the bridge. Alone. Until they spoke to witnesses about his mental and emotional decline. Until they investigated the loft, found the blood, the tools of his ruination—hacksaws and scalpels. It was ruled a suicide, made even more terrible for the fact that in the footage on the bridge he walked like a man in a dream, holding the railing gingerly with his remaining hand. Stiff and awkward, lurching, but not pausing at all before leaping. An automaton performing a final, singular function.

Katherine's world grew pinhole-small after his death. Apartment-small. She became convinced the eye might follow her wherever she went. Would find her and cast some dark judgment upon her unless she was still and quiet enough. Unless she made herself small.

Thusly, the ring. Her diminished world. And never, ever, did the ring she walked include that loft. The closer she got to it, the more her throat tightened, the more her body became wracked with chills and sweat, her heart like an endless fist against her ribs.

And every time she did manage to step outside, even years later, every single time, she thought of that eye that had moved in the bloody bowl of her husband's hands, madness and death caroming about the room.

I'll be different, he had said, *and changed, and better than I am now.*

She had gotten the police report—a few pages at least, certainly nothing as gruesome as autopsy photos—and some of his notebooks in the mail a month afterward, anonymously, and been made ill with it. She still doesn't know if it was a gesture of sympathy or malevolence by someone in the police department, sending her those things. Inside was information about the state of Matthew's body after being dredged from the river, the missing parts of him, the loft's appearance. The blood on the floor, the report said, had not been his. She'd skimmed the paperwork, afraid to read it more thoroughly, and thrown it in his "archives," that gathering of notebooks and lyrics and contracts that had been left when he'd moved out. Sometime later Nick had brought the box into his room and she'd always wondered when it would be that he would find it. Find the evidence that his father had mutilated himself in that way. Had gone mad like that. But Nick never did. Like her, he never looked through the papers. Some dim part of her realizes she's been waiting all these years for him to do that. For the light in his eyes to change.

Both of them having some inkling of the danger there and turning away from it.

And now here is Arthur, here is Katherine, here is Chicago. Here is a gun warming the small of her back. Here she is, forever seeing the eye and the way it had moved in his hands. Matthew with this ridiculous, self-centered notion that he was making things right somehow, after confessing that she and Nick were anchors about his throat. Only he could be that arrogant.

She puts her glass down on Arthur's stone-topped island. Her hand trembles, telegraphs her terror. It's all too much. She asks him where the bathroom is, and he leads her down the hall. It is, of course, massive, with a shower large enough to lie down in, the whole thing again lacquered in marble and chrome. Two sinks. Rugs that she could wrap herself in, fold herself up and disappear.

She shuts the door on a concerned, confused Arthur, smiling wanly at him, offering some bland, half-murmured apology.

She locks the door. Turns on the hot water and scrubs at her face. The eye.

The words upon Matthew's back. Who had done that to him? Who, or what, had provided the blood on the floor?

Did Katherine really, truly want to know the answers to any of this?

Something had finally taken notice of Matthew, after a lifetime of petitioning ghosts, messing with his half-assed witchcraft, his spells and incantations.

Lightness turned on its head.

Something had seen Matthew's profound weakness—that arrogance, that belief that fixing something later is better than fixing it now—and capitalized on it.

She pulls the pistol from her waistband and lays it on the countertop. She takes out her phone and dials Nick again. She doesn't expect him to pick up, and he doesn't. But she hears his outgoing message, the distracted way Nick tells the caller to leave a name and number, and it is a salve on her heart, those few words he speaks. A bridge between the two of them.

"I will see you again," she says. She wants steel in her voice, as if the sound of conviction might translate to her own heart, but her voice is a small, cracked thing. "I will be home soon, Nick, and I will see you again. I love you."

She hangs up as steam begins clouding the mirror.

The way Matthew had said, *He's promised me I can come back.*

She thinks, Who promised you?

Oh Matthew, who promised you such a thing?

NICK COFFIN

His name, he says, is John Bonner. Tasked with the job of finding the remnants. A fed, he tells them.

Bonner stands there, weeping, thumbing through Matthew Coffin's papers. He seems to Nick a man balancing on the point of a knife blade. He spends a moment considering what might happen were he to try and wrestle the pistol from this man who looks simultaneously enraged and heartbroken and maddened beyond words. A man with two corpses at his feet and tears streaming openly down his face.

A man, Nick thinks, surely looking for any excuse.

Bonner asks him in a choked voice if he's looked through his father's papers. He's ordered Nick and Rachmann to sit on the bed.

"Not really," Nick admits.

"Why not?"

What's the answer to that? Matthew Coffin had died when Nick was fifteen years old. Nick had loved him and sometimes feared him. But a decade after his death, Katherine Moriarty was where Nick's allegiance lay. He knew there were Blank Letters archives in the closet—handwritten lyrics, recording notes, contracts, riders, note-books, tour itineraries and faded handbills—shit that Katherine mentioned might be worth some money someday. But ultimately, it felt better to let it all rest.

Because there was also something about that box full of papers, wasn't there? Some gritty, bad feeling. Something that emanated from them, almost tangible. A toothache of the soul. A notion that there were things in there he might wish he could take back, once he saw them. He had considered more than once bringing the entire box down and throwing it in the dumpster outside the building.

"Because I don't give a shit," Nick finally says. A lie, he decides, is better than giving this cop a single thing that actually belongs to his heart. His phone vibrates, an incoming call. Everyone ignores it.

"That's too bad," Bonner says, tossing a few pages into the box. "Because there's a lot to learn in here. A lot of terrible things. He killed himself, didn't he?"

"Yeah," Nick says, the word like a stone lodged in his throat.

"You know what else he did?" Bonner holds out a folder, POLICE stamped on the front. "Look at this."

"No."

"Do it," Bonner hisses.

"No."

"You know he cut out his tongue? His eye? You know he cut off his own fucking *hand* before he jumped off that bridge? That ringing any bells with you?"

When Nick swallows, it makes a clicking sound. He looks away. "Bullshit."

"And they were never found. Those parts of him. Read the report. It's been in the box all this fucking time. You've had the answer all this time. No wonder it all comes back to you, your family."

Rachmann pushes off the bed, slams into Bonner low like a spindly-ass linebacker. The two of them fall against Nick's desk, the computer crashing to the floor, then Bonner falls, Rachmann on top of him, a knee on Bonner's chest, grasping at the pistol in its holster.

A thought flits through Nick's mind like a bird flailing against an updraft—*help him help him*—and Nick stands to do that, but then, in a notebook on the bed, he sees his father's handwriting.

Black ink on a yellow legal pad, the top corner darkened with something that's either a coffee ring or a sigil stamped in dried blood. There is a single stanza, immediately decipherable, in his father's blocky, cramped handwriting:

The house of the tongue the eye the hand
House where i shall live again. House of fever, house of wounds,
house of the worm. The pact I made.
The house of second chances and the devoured world

Bonner reaches up and digs a thumb in Rachmann's eye socket. Rachmann shrieks like a child, rolling off of him. Bonner grunts and pulls his pistol, Nick finally moving, holding a hand out as if he might stop him, but Bonner doesn't shoot, instead bringing the butt of the gun down onto the bridge of Rachmann's nose, twice. Rachmann shrieks again, cupping his face and bowing to the floor as if in supplication. He drips blood on some of Matthew Coffin's papers still spilled on the floor, and Nick, his mind looping and crazed, imagines some dark figure rising from it, some deathly genie freed from its constraints.

His father with a missing hand? A missing eye?

House of fever, house of wounds, house of the worm. The pact I made.

"You want to do something too?" Bonner asks, breathing heavily. The pistol is pointed at Nick's face, that round, dark eye of the barrel.

"No," Nick says. Even now, terrified like this, he finds that he has to drag his eyes away from his father's papers. From those words. "Please."

"Get him up. Go into the living room."

Nick hoists a sagging Rachmann up by his arms. Together they step over the bodies in the doorway and walk to the living room, toward the merry orange couch. Bonner follows behind. There is an angry red scratch around Rachmann's left eye. His nose is split along the bridge and freely frothing blood. Nick sets him on the couch and then sits down beside him, his bag on his lap.

Bonner stands before them, the pistol still aimed at Nick's face. He looks down at his phone, as if unsure who he might call. He puts it away, lets out a single heaving sob, and then his eyes settle on Nick's bag.

"It's your father's voice, isn't it? On the recording. He made some . . . made some *deal* before he died. With something."

From far away, Nick says, "I don't know what you're talking about."

Bonner searches his face, almost shocked. A baleful look, equal parts sorrow and disgust. "Where's the hand?"

"I left it underneath a dumpster."

"So it's gone."

"I guess."

"Give me that," Bonner says, nodding at the bag.

So stupid, Nick thinks. So goddamn stupid. Should've left it in the bedroom. Left it in the lobby. Stupid.

Rachmann curses under his breath.

Nick hands Bonner the bag. Bonner reaches in, takes out the box, lets the bag fall to the floor. He spends a moment gazing at the scrollwork on the side. The dark wood, the golden hinges.

He sets it on the coffee table and crouches down, still gazing at it. Without looking away from the box, he says, "I know you're thinking it, man. I just broke your nose. Don't fuck around. I've about had my fill today."

Rachmann holds up a hand in a gesture of defeat, still cupping his nose with the other.

What will he see, Nick wonders, when he looks into it? And what will he do after he sees it?

Bonner cracks the lid of the box.

All three of their phones go off at once. An arrhythmic chorus of stilted notes and vibrations.

Bonner says distractedly, "Don't answer that," and opens the lid all the way.

He stares down at the box.

He says, as if dreaming, as if underwater, "Is this what I think it is?"

"Take a look," Rachmann sneers, pulling his own phone out of his pocket. "Take a good look, motherfucker. Tell me what you see in there."

Bonner stares down at the eye.

Rachmann puts his phone to his ear, answers his call.

Nick sits and readies himself. He waits for the next thing to happen.

Tinny and quiet over Rachmann's phone, he hears the song. His mother's song, his father's music. And he sees the eyes of both men, Rachmann and Bonner, go wide and uncomprehending.

And then Nick doesn't have to wait anymore, because the next thing is happening.

KATHERINE MORIARTY

At some point there would be a discussion regarding Callista's capabilities, and where the error was made. If, truly, it was an error. How those at Terradyne presumably meant to play the recording of "I Won't Forget It" by the Blank Letters—threaded as it was with its lethal message—*only* through the comms systems of nations viewed as a threat to the United States. Terradyne's way of leveling the field as Portland, and presumably elsewhere soon enough, shuddered to its knees.

How it didn't work that way.

How the message was relayed instead throughout the *entirety* of Callista's network, hundreds of millions of waypoints. Every telephone and computer and *fax machine* throughout Callista's vast military command structures; throughout civilian cell phones via massive commercial networks that piggybacked off Callista's comms capabilities; rich nations, poor countries, hundreds of millions of avenues for this information to trundle down, this song, the words beneath the song, the message beneath the words, the blood-maddened physical and physiological response that inundated the listener upon hearing it.

At some point there would be a discussion among certain parties about Callista's failings, intentional or not.

That discussion would not happen for a long time, though.

By the time it did take place, Katherine would have zero interest in hearing it.

She would have a number of other concerns by then.

For now, however, the moment that the recording is sent out via Callista's vastly latticed systems, Katherine is in Arthur's bathroom in Chicago, gazing into the steam-clouded mirror.

And in the mirror she sees a shape move behind the frosted glass of the shower door behind her.

She reaches for the pistol on the counter as she watches in the mirror a gray hand slowly pull back the shower door. One finger is missing a nail. The flesh on the back of the hand is wormed with veins, scored in tiny bite-marks. This is a hand, she knows, that spent days underwater all those years ago. Days in the river below a bridge.

A hand that belongs to a body that is now animated with some sort of second, abysmal life.

She turns, faces the shower door.

He's promised me I can come back.

Steam clouds the room.

The door, slowly pulling back.

Her phone begins to vibrate, making its way slowly toward the lip of the counter. She reaches behind her, her hand blindly searching. She finds it, and now both of her hands are full—pistol, cell phone.

The glass door, finally, is pulled back entirely.

Matthew Coffin stands revealed.

Blue-veined, skin mottled gray, bloated as the day they dredged his corpse from the Willamette River those years back.

A clot of dark green weeds lies tangled in his hair. The runes he carved upon himself—or someone carved upon him—are puffed and white, bloodless things now. They cover his entire body. His cock dangles amid a thatch of pubic hair that writhes with small pale worms.

He tilts his head inquisitively. One eye is white and blind. Where the other should be is a dark crater.

He steps from the shower. She hears the wet, squelching footstep on the marble floor and sees he has only one hand. A gray-black stump where the other had once been.

Her husband holds out his free hand, beckons her with it.

He opens his mouth and a great spill of bile and river water rolls down his chin. It falls to the bathroom floor, and dark things wriggle in the mess.

Matthew is tongueless.

Katherine screams and fires her pistol. The round goes above his shoulder, a hammered explosion of ceramic tile. He doesn't flinch, just stays there with dark water still pouring from between the grayed nubs of his teeth.

After so many chances in life, *this* is what he chose? This abomination of love? Love skewered through the devil's prism, made a mockery. Some flailing second chance, with hell trailing along behind him.

A million chances in life, and this is the road he chooses.

Dead, deathless, alive, he holds out his hand toward her.

Her phone vibrates and she hears Arthur's phone ring in the hallway, hears him answer it in a panic, and a moment later he cries out, followed by the sound of his phone clattering to the floor. Her own phone still vibrating in her hand, insistent.

And then Arthur slams himself against the bathroom door and Katherine screams again. He rattles the knob, pounds on the door. He makes animal sounds, these strangled, keening noises, something snared in a trap, and the door judders under his weight. Faintly, she thinks she hears a song she wrote a long time ago. Coming from Arthur's phone, perhaps, or the mad, shunted, broken parts of her own mind.

He screams and slams against the door again. Something vital in the hinges cracks, nearly gives way.

Resurrected, Matthew takes a step forward, hand forever held out, as if she might join him in this new darkness he's created.

Tinny and small, she hears herself snarl in the hallway, *"All the gods bent down / Down on a wing / And offered me a choice, to either choke or sing."*

Katherine tightens the grip on her pistol. Slowly puts her phone in her pocket. Runs a hand quickly beneath her eyes. Breathes.

She readies herself.

Arthur beyond the door is silent, the world hung in that pause between horrors. She unlocks the door and in a fluid movement, the best she can manage, she pushes it open, clipping him in the shoulder, surprising him. He staggers, mouth frothing, utterly changed, face twisted into some mask of rage, and then she is running down the length of his town house, slipping comically on the runner in the hall. Nearly firing the pistol into the ceiling as she rights herself, Arthur barking something nonsensical at her, a word but not quite a word. She risks a look back and there he is, running toward her, hands splayed into claws, a lifelong friend turned suddenly into some enraged movie monster. Ridiculous were it not for the fact that terror strides through her, makes her want to curl up. But she can't. As ever, there is Nick to consider.

She fires blindly down the hall, something tinkling musically in the kitchen, Arthur not fazed at all. Katherine opens the front door and slams it shut, just as he collides with it full-tilt, his face limned against the curtain inside and then breaking the glass windowpane. She thinks about shooting him through the curtain and does not, turns instead, nearly falling down the half dozen steps that lead to his stoop.

Back down on the street, she hears a scream farther down the block, and then another in the opposite direction. As if in response, a gunshot.

Matthew is somewhere. Perhaps still in the bathroom, perhaps treading his way down the hall. It would be foolish to think that he is simply a relic of a dream. No, she'd heard his footsteps on the floor, seen the door draw back. He is real, as much as a nightmare might be made real. He has summoned himself through untold darknesses to be here. To do this.

Katherine runs then, her footfalls on the cement. She begins running toward her son, toward his life, toward whatever remains of their lives together.

Nick, she thinks—his name her mantra, her love flung out mercifully into the world—I meant what I said.

I'll come to you.

I'll find you, wherever you are.

Katherine runs through the night, toward her son.

ACKNOWLEDGMENTS

Writing a book is such a solitary endeavor, you know? Fun, yeah, but damnably lonesome sometimes. And then, if you get really, really lucky, maybe a bunch of people step in and help you craft something larger, better, meaner, funnier, darker, and more moving than what you could have crafted on your own. I'm positive I'm forgetting folks, but I am profoundly indebted and grateful to the people mentioned here for helping me make this novel *more*.

A huge thank you to my literary agent, Chad Luibl of Janklow & Nesbit, who changed the trajectory of my life in a phone call, straight up and no joke. Here's hoping we get to navigate all this stuff again with *so many more books*. Best agent.

To Caitlin McKenna, my editor at Random House, who took on this wild fever dream of a novel and said, "Let's put this out into the world," and then proceeded to give me both the space and a series of clear-eyed edits to make the book even more expansive than it was. Another person who changed my life. Your guidance—and the steadfast belief that I can do this—has proved immeasurable. Thank you.

To Kristina Moore at UTA, who has patiently helped me navigate the weird and thrilling world of film and television. I'm very lucky to have you advocating in my corner, and for kindly answering my endless series of dumb questions.

To Tricia Reeks, who put out my first four books via Meerkat Press and has never wavered in trying to get my work out there. Thanks for everything.

To Richard Price, writer of literature, master of dialogue, and another endlessly patient professional. Who knows what the future holds, but I count myself lucky as hell to have been able to work with you.

To the rest of the Janklow & Nesbit, Random House, and UTA teams that helped, in a bevy of ways, to make this wild-ass book better than it was, and to get it out into the world: Roma Panganiban, Noa Shapiro, Celia Albers, Maria Braeckel, Windy Dorrestyn, Rebecca Berlant, Cindy Berman, Michael Steger, Lianna Blakeman, Stefanie Lieberman, Molly Steinblatt, Adam Hobbins, Lawrence Krauser, Elizabeth Eno, and Ella Laytham.

To all the librarians and booksellers out there, for fighting the best and most meaningful of fights. I don't know where I'd be without you.

Soliciting blurbs is such a painful process. "Hey, Writer I Profoundly Admire, might I bother you for a comment about my book to put on its back cover, and thusly rob you of some of your own precious hours?" That said, I'm profoundly grateful to those authors who took the time to read *FH* and say nice things about it.

To the friends and writers and writer friends who dragged me out of the house and into the world, in spite of my best efforts: James Mapes, Jeffrey Arnsdorf, Shawn Porter, Ryan Sotomayor, and Nathan and Brandi Cornelius.

To Lyndsay Hogland, who saved my ass not once but twice in Douglas County. I owe you and your family big-time.

To EV and Rosie, of course. I'm tremendously proud of the people you are, and the people you're becoming. You are both hilarious and kind and curious, you rule, and please wait until you're older to read this book.

To Robin, who never wavered in her belief that this was the right path, and who is always there whether it's a good writing day or a bad one. Me and you.

Lastly, to the readers. I hope this one worked for you. Let's do it again soon.

Can you resist the hand? Read on for an excerpt from the next Fever House novel, *The Devil by Name,* coming in 2024.

Five years after a powerful broadcast turned a sizable portion of the world's population bloodthirsty and mad, communities have begun the slow steps of righting themselves. John Bonner monitors activity in the walled "fever house" of Portland, Oregon, while Katherine Moriarty has fled to the East Coast in an attempt to build a new life for herself. Meanwhile, in France, a young girl appears to have gained an unimaginable ability . . .

NAOMI LAURENT

Nevers, Bourgogne-Franche-Comté region, France

Always, always, there is the barter to be considered.

Denis loves the barter.

The table where they're seated, a large and rustic wooden thing, the top of it glossed smooth and dark by years of use, sits in the middle of the kitchen. Naomi wonders if the rest of the house is like this: old, well worn but beautifully curated. She wouldn't know—she, Denis, and Emilie were ferried from a side door straight to the kitchen, their sense of being interlopers confirmed by the way the rest of the house is closed off to them. The woman who'd greeted them at the door—mid-thirties, dour, wispy auburn hair shot through with gray—has retreated elsewhere after asking them to wait. Naomi wonders how old the table is, how many thousands of meals must have been taken here. As ever, Denis tells Naomi nothing, offers no information about who these people are, how they've contacted him. She's not an equal; she is a tool. The table stands in stark contrast to the brushed-steel appliances on the counters, the oak-topped island. It's a massive kitchen, clean, with a picture window that overlooks the road and the idyllic green field and its cows. You'd never know, looking out there, what sort of world it's become on the other side of the glass.

The woman comes back with a man in tow. They walk through the door that leads to the rest of the house, the woman gently shutting it behind her. There's a lean and hunted look about the man, and Naomi recognizes it immediately for what it is: He's desperate.

"Thank you for coming," he says. His eyes bounce between Denis and Emilie, as if afraid of what might happen should he stare at Naomi too long.

Denis pushes off the wall and offers a hand. The man takes it, and when Denis asks him to tell them what happened, the man's face floods with a mixture of emotions. She sees fear, confusion, guilt, sorrow. All in a span of seconds.

"Does it matter?" the woman asks, and then dips her head after the man turns and gives her a sharp look. She walks past Naomi to a carafe on the kitchen counter, pours herself some water. Naomi's stomach gurgles, but she says nothing; propriety is as much a part of the barter as anything else. She'll get her food and water after.

The man is thin and haggard. He might be handsome, but the depth of those feelings inside him have turned him into something else. He needs a haircut, Naomi thinks. They all need haircuts.

Denis quietly assures the woman that everything matters.

The man tucks a hank of hair behind his ear and then shoves his hands in the pockets of his jeans, stares at the floor. "We lived in Nice," he says. "His mother and me." Naomi's eyes cut to the woman, who in turn looks to the floor. She's not the mother then; she and the man come together after. "When the Message came, Antoine—that's his name—was just an infant. Ten months old. I was outside, readying the garden." He shakes his head. "Just, you know, messing around. It was a thing that calmed me, gardening."

"Sure," Denis says softly.

"Amanda—my wife—she was the one who got the call." He looks out the window and then steels himself to finish. "She answered it. She was affected, of course." Naomi feels a thudding sense of inevitability to this. The mirroring of her own horrors.

"I'm sorry," Denis says. He does this sometimes—surprises Naomi with his diplomacy. Denis is a killer, but he is political with his kindnesses.

"I, we—Amanda didn't survive. So it was just me and Antoine. Just me and this baby."

Naomi thinks of her mother in their living room, all of it sun-shot and bright, Naomi dizzy with the flu as she'd trod down the stairway of their little house. Seeing her brother Hugo's twitching fingers on the floor. Remembering the inhuman sounds her mother had made. The pool of blood on the floor slowly widening.

"We survived in Nice as long as we could, but the city just got too dangerous. Me with a baby? Trying to find formula? Raiders and murderers everywhere? There were so many fevered there, and Antoine, he was always crying."

Naomi's throat clicks. She shuts her eyes. No one pays any attention to her.

"Outside of Planfoy—God, I was so fucking tired by then, so frightened—I left him to go wash myself. It was just a moment. There was a little creek bed there, just a moment to myself; he was sleeping, bundled up, and I heard him cry out." His voice is cracking now. "I was so fast, it wasn't more than a moment, but a woman was leaning over him, biting him, biting at his arms—" His voice has a rushed, brittle cadence to it, like each word is a splintered thing being forced from his throat.

"He changed," the man says, still staring at the floor. "He's so small, it was only minutes later."

"I'm so sorry," Emilie says, and she sounds sincere.

"I came here," he says, gesturing toward the woman, "to Lisette's home, and here we've been."

Denis says, "You brought your baby from Planfoy to Nevers?"

"On foot, yes."

"That must be two hundred fifty kilometers. And he was turned?"

"I put him in my pack." The man scrubs at his mouth. "I put a bandana over his face." He cracks a single, unlovely laugh so close to a sob as to be interchangeable. "He has six teeth. They're very small." He fixes them with a smile that's as close to madness as any she's seen in all her years with Denis. "And so," he says brightly, "we have heard of you," gesturing to Denis, "and we've heard of her, and what she can do."

"You know our prices?"

"You told me a working gun, a week's worth of food for three, or a thousand euros."

He nods. "Which do you prefer?"

"But can she do it? Can she—"

"She can do it. Which do you prefer?"

The man spares a glance at Lisette—his sister? An old lover, one taken before his poor dead wife?—and then walks through the doorway, comes back with a stack of currency. He hands it to Denis, who counts it and puts it in one of the pockets of his pants. The hotel last night had cost them twelve euros for two rooms and the breakfast.

"Where's the baby?"

The man shuts his eyes for a moment and then motions them toward the doorway, farther into the house. Denis holds up a hand to Emilie, who sits back down, hurt. Perhaps he doesn't want Naomi to be too crowded down there. God only knows what rattles around in Denis's brain.

They're led through the living room, all dark wood and a shotgun scatter of framed photos on the walls, faces passing by too fast to see.

He brings them to a stairwell. The stairs creak beneath their feet, and Naomi is enveloped in the press of mold, of damp walls. The sound of the generator grows louder as they descend. They step into a large, sunken basement with a few naked bulbs throwing out yellow light. Support beams carve up the open space. Yes, this woman, Lisette, this man, they certainly do have resources, don't they? Cows. Propane. A thousand euros ready to give away. Naomi sees a pair of wine racks, each filled with dozens of bottles.

Somewhere down here, the baby lets out a screech, and Naomi's heart floods with ice.

The man leads them to a small alcove where Denis's head brushes one of the overhead bulbs; the room is lit in a mad swing of illumination, shadows that bend and twist all around them.

Naomi has seen people come up with countless entrapments meant to contain the fevered. They don't seem to feel any pain. She's seen a fevered man turn his hands into a red, boneless mess in an attempt to free himself from a pair of handcuffs. You put a fevered in a room with a living person and a thousand blades between them, the fevered will cut herself to ribbons trying to get through. They're automatons. Trying to contain them is like trying to capture the wind. They're elemental in that way. They can be held captive, they can be dismembered, but short of beheading or some kind of vital brain interruption, they will not be stopped. Naomi's seen any number of terrible, unforgettable things over the past five years.

But she's never seen a fevered baby.

There's no need to lash this one down or lock it up.

It's too small for such things.

The man has simply stacked some cardboard boxes in front of the doorway to block any escape. The alcove is roughly four by four feet. Size of a closet. There's a blanket on the floor. Naomi sees toys on the ground too—a stuffed elephant, a plastic baby book, a rattle—and feels some vital part of her heart come unmoored. She thinks of Hugo and wants to vomit, wants to scream, wants to rip her hair out.

The baby is gray. He wears a matted onesie black with filth and lays on his back, kicking and gurgling. When he sees them, his eyes widen and he begins rocking until he manages to turn himself over. He crawls to the stack of boxes and pulls himself up. Blood vessels have bloomed red in the whites of his eyes. His mouth opens, little nubs in the gray gums. His jaw snaps shut.

She turns and presses her hand to her lips. Swallows the nausea down. The generator chugs and kicks over, the lights flickering for an instant.

"He hasn't grown," the man says. "Not for five years. He doesn't cry, he doesn't sleep. Just lays there, and when he sees me, he tries to bite." He's weeping now. "Six teeth. You wear your gloves, you wear your heavy shirt." He scrubs at his eyes. "I try to hold him sometimes and he just pushes and bites."

Denis puts a stilling hand on his shoulder, and it might look like a gesture of comfort, but Naomi knows that it isn't. He's gently steering the man back away from the alcove.

"She needs to be alone with the child," Denis says, and this is new, new and decidedly untrue, and some part of her *knows,* even as she catalogs the quiet horrors of the situation, what Denis is doing. The part of her that saw the wine bottles, the cows, the generator, the money, some part of her *knows,* and still she reaches down for the child, reaches to touch him, to change him back, a larger part of her insisting *Denis won't do it, not with the woman upstairs; he's not that crazy.*

And *still* she screams at the sound of the gunshot, bright in the closed-in space of the basement.

She is still screaming, in fact, as the child's little jaws snap at her, as her fingers graze the cold crown of his head. Denis pulls her back from the alcove.

"Don't bother," he says.

Naomi is babbling. "Please, Denis, please, it's a *baby,* let me help the baby, I can change him back," but he pulls her over the man's body and up the stairs. He drags her by one arm as she screams. He pushes through the door upstairs and through the living room and to the kitchen, where Emilie looks at the two of them wild-eyed, the butcher knife still dripping in her hand. Blood stippling her face. The woman—Lisette, was it?—splayed in a red pool on the tile at her feet. Slash marks on those pale hands.

"I heard the shots," Emilie says, sounding stunned, pulled from some dream. "I thought this was right."

"Well done," Denis says. This is as close to praise as he's ever come with either of them, and Naomi decides to just keep screaming forever.

Sign up here to be alerted when *The Devil by Name* goes on sale.

https://www.penguinrandomhouse.com/authors/2278613/keith-rosson/

ABOUT THE AUTHOR

KEITH ROSSON is the author of the novels *Smoke City, Road Seven*, and *The Mercy of the Tide*, as well as the Shirley Jackson Award–winning story collection *Folk Songs for Trauma Surgeons*. His short stories have appeared in *Southwest Review, PANK, Cream City Review, Outlook Springs, December, Phantom Drift*, and others. He lives in Portland, Oregon, with his partner and two children. He can be visited online at keithrosson.com.

ABOUT THE TYPE

This book was set in Caslon, a typeface first designed in 1722 by William Caslon (1692–1766). Its widespread use by most English printers in the early eighteenth century soon supplanted the Dutch typefaces that had formerly prevailed. The roman is considered a "workhorse" typeface due to its pleasant, open appearance, while the italic is exceedingly decorative.